Dirty Rich

OBSESSION

D1616741

NEW YORK TIMES BESTSELLING AUTHOR

LISA RENEE JONES

CHAPTER ONE

Reid

"You're a true-blue prick, Reid Maxwell."

"Finally, something we agree on," I say, leaning back in my leather chair, the phone at my ear. A real estate investor who just lost his ass on the line. "And my client likes that I'm a prick. It works for him, not you. The thirty-day notice stands. We're taking over that complex September first." I hang up, my gaze lifting to the doorway to find my pain in the ass sister standing in the doorway, holding a garment bag.

"Forget it, Cat," I say, tossing the pen in my hand onto the desk and leaning forward. "I'm not going to the party."

"You have to go to the party," she says, hanging the bag behind my door. "You're being auctioned off for charity." She stops in front of my desk, her dress a sparkling mix of pink and purple, while her blonde hair is draped over her shoulders. My sister is a beautiful pain in the ass. "Tonight," she adds, stopping in front of me. "It happens tonight, and you've known about it for two months."

"I said no about ten times."

"This is me doing PR for the firm. It's a big deal with lots of press. And you *need* good PR since our dear uncle and father got in all that legal trouble, because in case you didn't know Maxwell, Maxwell, and Maxwell is a law firm."

"That dear uncle, wasn't our uncle, but a 'friend' of dad's, he made us call him uncle as kids. And I use the term friend

1

lightly, considering he committed crimes while working for us which is why he's long gone and so is the scandal he created. And thankfully, since he recovered from his stroke, the only thing our father's guilty of is being an ass."

"Like you?"

"Yes," I agree without hesitation. "I'm an ass, but not like him."

"Your own very special version of asshole," she says. "Right. Check."

I ignore that remark that. Where Cat is concerned, I deserve it and with growing regret. "Cat."

"Yes?"

"You write true crime novels and your 'Cat Does Crime' column. Exactly why are you heading this PR operation for a problem two-years old? You don't work here. I tried to get you to work here, but you refused."

"You tried to bully me into doing what you wanted, yes," she agrees. "And I'm heading your PR efforts because obviously, you cannot. Asshole and PR are not two terms that fit together."

"Well then, how does having me auctioned off help?"

"Women foolishly love arrogant asses," she says. "You'll get big bids and attention for the firm. Bids for charity which means good press. That means, we hope, good press about you and the firm. And since I know what motivates you, good press means more money for the firm and you. The biggest names in New York City will be present. I've already said all of this. If Reese wasn't married, he'd do it for his firm, too. It's the most eligible bachelor thing, and as you know, at thirty-eight, you're still a bachelor."

"I prefer most ineligible bastard, and as for Reese, I couldn't give a shit what your asshole husband would do."

"Is that right?"

I glance beyond Cat to find Reese standing in the door in a damn tuxedo that looks like a James Bond costume. Shoot me the fuck now. "If you don't see asshole as the compliment I do," I say, "you aren't half the attorney I thought you were."

"I'm a criminal law attorney," Reese says, "not a corporate raider like you."

"I don't raid," I correct. "I help those who do, and in the end, the companies become bigger and better thanks to my efforts."

"Put your tuxedo on," Cat says. "We leave in fifteen minutes."

My brother, Gabe, appears in the doorway next to Reese, and of course, he's wearing a tux. "Aren't you pretty?"

"Prettier than you," he says. "How about a wager to prove it? If I auction off for higher than you, I get that bottle of whiskey you've been hoarding. The Dalmore 50 Crystal Decanter."

"That's a twenty-thousand-dollar bottle," I say.

"And?" Gabe presses.

"And bring it on," I say, standing up and looking at Cat. "This is my last PR event ever."

"It's your first PR event."

"Exactly," I say. "Now all of you. Leave. I'll meet you in the lobby in fifteen minutes."

Everyone leaves but Cat. "The good press has already started." She sets her phone in front of me, and I read the headline: *The blond, thirty-something hunks of Maxwell, Maxwell, and Maxwell give it all for charity.* I stop reading and look up at her. "Is this supposed to convince me to go or stay here?"

She laughs. "Oh, you blond hunk you. We both know you're going." She sobers abruptly. "Too bad dad won't come."

"If the idea is to keep the attention on us and off his misdeeds," I say dryly, just as damn sober as her now, "then I think that's smart. He's not a dumb person. He had to suspect what his best friend, who was like his brother, was up to. I damn sure know what Gabe is into at all times."

"Right," she says, swallowing hard, and when I see the way our father affects her, I hate him more than I already do, but then, I'm just like him in her eyes. "You're right, of course." She waves a hand in the air as if wiping away her emotions. "See you in fifteen minutes," she murmurs, turning on her high heels, gone in a blink, and pulling the door shut behind her.

My phone buzzes on my desk, which means it's my secretary, who too often and too like my sister, doesn't understand the word no. "Yes, Connie?"

"Carrie West is back on the line."

That name grinds down my spine in a way few could. "Get rid of her," I say, "but tell her she gets an A for effort. What is this now—the tenth call?"

"Eleventh," she says. "She asked me to tell you that one way or another you will talk to her. Should I give you the rundown on her since she's clearly not going away?"

"She *is* going away," I say. "Make it happen."

"She said to tell you that if you don't take this call, she'll be seeing you sooner than later. And I know. Make her go away." And then in a tart final statement, she says, "Yes, master," and disconnects.

Like that woman would let any man be her master, I think, rubbing the back of my neck and stepping to the window, overlooking a city now shrouded in darkness, while city lights mark the inky night. Carrie West is a potential problem, namely because I've promised to stay away from her. Not an easy task considering she's the daughter of a man I've ruined, and while my reasons were not of my choosing, they were, in fact, necessary. The bottom line here is that a debt exists, and nothing Ms. West can say to me will change the fact that it has to be paid.

The event is in one of the many five-star Manhattan hotels, in a ballroom with diamond-drop chandeliers, ice sculptures, and waiters serving finger foods and booze. I'm in the middle of a good three hundred people, and yes, I'm in the damn tuxedo. For two hours now, I've been standing next to, or near, my brother and sister, all of us "mingling" as Cat calls it, while women fawn over me and Gabe, assessing us as bid-worthy. I endure. Gabe soaks in the attention, laughing and joking with every pretty little thing, and everyone in between, that we encounter. He gives off this façade of being one of them. He's not. He's just as fucked up as I am for some of the same, but many different reasons. He simply chooses to convince people he's not. I don't see the point. Why pretend to be what you are not? I am who I am and no one but me needs to have intimate knowledge of what that means or how it came to be.

I'm two whiskeys into the night, which is one more than I'd allow myself during a negotiation, but I already lost this negotiation or I wouldn't be here. Cat won. And hell. It's a children's cancer foundation. I'm not such as an asshole that I can't be softened for kids in need. I just prefer to do it in my own private way that involves my checkbook. An announcement sounds over the intercom, and it's time for the "bachelors" to come to the stage at the front of the room.

I down the last of my drink and hand the glass to a well-timed waiter. A lady that must be about eighty slings her arm through Gabe's and he lets her guide him toward the necessary direction. Cat steps in front of me and surprises me by kissing my cheek. "Thanks for being a good asshole tonight."

I chuck her under the chin. "Just tonight."

"Of that, I have no doubt," she says, and while she's smiling it doesn't quite reach her eyes. We have a lot of damage between us and it's starting to cut a little too deep.

She steps away from me and Reese wraps his arm around her shoulders. I work my way through the crowd, bodies parting as I close the distance between me and the front of the stage. One of the announcers, a pretty brunette in her thirties spies me, and she points. "There he is. Our second Maxwell, Reid Maxwell himself." Clapping ensues because all of these people have had a great deal of wine and can't wait to bid on a date with someone they do not even know.

I walk up the stairs and take my place with another half-dozen men, next to Gabe who leans close and says, "That bottle of whiskey is going to be oh so good."

My lips quirk. "How many women did you promise an orgasm to drive up your bids?"

"Only the one I want to win," he assures me with a laugh.

The bidding starts, and fuck me, I'm going to be last, which leaves me on this stage forever. "Opening bids are five thousand dollars," the announcer explains. "This is for the children. And so, let the bidding begin."

Bachelor number one goes for ten thousand. Number two for five. Lucky bastard number seven goes to the same eighty-year-old grandma that helped Gabe to the stage, and for a whopping forty-five thousand. "You should have promised her an orgasm," I murmur to Gabe.

"Obviously," he chuckles. "But if my woman of choice wins, I'll let you keep the whiskey, with no complaint."

"And now," the announcer says, "the Maxwell brothers. Hunk number one, Gabe Maxwell. Do I have a five-thousand-dollar bid?"

"Twenty thousand," comes a soft female voice, and my gaze lands on a pretty redhead in the front row.

"And there she is," Gabe says. "Sold for twenty thousand."

"Twenty-five!" comes another bid.

The redhead shakes her head. She can't do it. Gabe looks at her and nods, telling her he'll pay. She smiles and says, "Twenty-six!"

And that wins. Gabe is sold for twenty-six.

"You got your woman and it only cost you twenty-six thousand dollars," I say.

"All to help the children," he says, heading down the stage to claim his woman.

"And finally, our last man of the night," the announcer says. "Reid Maxwell." She runs down my stats. "Thirty-eight, six-foot-two, and two hundred pounds of pure hotness."

I need another whiskey, and to throttle my sister, I think, as the woman adds, "A corporate attorney known as a killer in and out of the courtroom. Do we have a five-thousand-dollar bid?"

"Right here," a woman proclaims, stepping directly in front of me, and holy hell, she's stunning. I soak her in, her knee-length emerald green dress hugging every one of her perfect, slender curves, while her ample cleavage offers me one of her many distractions.

"Ten thousand!" someone shouts.

The woman in emerald steps closer and her eyes hold mine. "Twenty," she says, speaking to me, not the announcer.

"Twenty-five," someone else says.

"Fifty," my little temptress retorts, and she is a temptress up to no good. I see it in her eyes. She *wants* me to see it, dares me to do something about it.

"Do we have a bid for fifty-five?" the announcer calls out.

There is a silent moment or two, or it could be ten. I don't know. I'm too focused on this woman still standing directly in front of me, contemplating how many ways I can fuck her to figure her out, when I hear, "Sold to the woman in green for fifty thousand dollars, and the highest bid of the night."

I don't move, and neither does my new date. I have this sense I know her. She's familiar and yet, she is not. This isn't a simple auction and a donation to charity. This is a game of some sorts, and she's confident enough in her ability to win to bid fifty thousand dollars.

She's wrong.

I'll win, but I'll make sure she enjoys every second.

CHAPTER TWO

Reid

I'm still stuck on the stage, listening to the auctioneer, Evelyn I believe she said was her name, ramble off donation data, among various other topics that no one wants to hear when they are laden with drinks, food, and fun. I watch my new date step to the sidelines and accept a glass of champagne from a waiter, resting her elbow on a standing table. She sips from the beverage, her eyes on me as mine are on her, and even with me up here and her down there, the edge of mystery and sexual tension between us is palpable.

Finally, Evelyn declares it is "time to fill the dance floor" and soft piano music begins to play. Ready to let this little game with my emerald princess take flight, those primal, hunter urges that ignite me both in work and play crank up to full force, and I turn to exit the stage, only to have Evelyn call out, "Mr. Maxwell!"

I grit my teeth, forcing myself to stop and face her. "Yes, Evelyn?"

"Stay, please. We're going to have all the bachelors and their dates in several photos." She motions to my new date to join us.

My date shakes her head, declining decisively. I like this woman already. Evelyn grimaces and looks at me. "Can you please go convince her to join us?"

"The lady paid fifty thousand dollars," I say. "Do we really want to make her uncomfortable enough to decline to do so on another occasion?"

Evelyn's lips clamp shut for all of two seconds. "Point well taken, but please ask her again, Mr. Maxwell. Obviously, you have some sort of influence with her."

Indeed, I do, I think, and I want to know what and why. "What's her name?"

"I have no idea. You can ask her while we take photos."

"I think she's made her point. No pictures." I don't wait for Evelyn's reply. I head toward the end of the stage and waste no time walking down the stairs.

I approach my emerald princess where she stands, stepping close enough to smell her rose-scented perfume, and confirm she's stunning up close and personal while her eyes match her emerald dress perfectly. Eyes filled with challenge as she says, "We can either call this date over," she downs her champagne and sets it on the table, a droplet of the liquid pearling on her pink painted lips, that begs to be licked away, "or," she says, "we can go to my room. Choose now."

"Is that really a question?"

"I thought you might be afraid to go to a stranger's room," she replies.

"We both know you didn't think I was afraid to go to your room, but it certainly makes for amusing verbal fodder."

A flicker of admiration stirs in the depths of her beautiful eyes, which she quickly banks as if she doesn't want me to know it's there. Interesting, considering she paid fifty thousand dollars for a date with me. I'm about to tell her to lead the way to her room when she turns and starts walking away. She's forcing me to follow, a challenge that for most wouldn't work. I'd turn and leave, and pick another, but she's stirred my curiosity in a way few do these days. I want to know what she's about. I want to know what is under that dress. I want a lot of things where she's concerned, and all before I even know her name.

I give her a small lead, letting her wonder if I will actually follow. When I finally start walking, I'm back in hunter mode, on the prowl for this woman, and looking for far more than answers. I catch up with her just as she steps into the elevator, but not before I've confirmed her ass in that dress is just as perfect as every other part of her. I join her in the car, stepping into the center, my big body consuming the small space, and effectively claiming the control she just tried to claim by walking away from me. She punches in a button and uses a key card that says she paid well for the room. The doors shut, and she leans on the wall, facing me. I turn to face her, close, but not close enough considering how damn much I'm looking forward to stripping that dress off of her and kissing her pink painted lips.

But first, answers. "Why am I worth fifty thousand dollars to you?"

"The *charity* is worth fifty thousand dollars to me."

"You could have just written a check."

"Yes. I could have."

I close the space between us, my hand pressing on the wall. "Why am I here?"

"Because you want to be."

"Why am I here?" I repeat.

"Because I want you to be."

"Why am I—"

"Because you're my bonus for doing a good deed, and I really need a bonus tonight."

"Why?"

"That's my business. I don't need a bartender or a counselor," she says. "I just need—*you*."

"You mean you need to fuck."

The elevator dings and the doors open. "Yes. Exactly. Are you going to let me off this wall before the doors close?"

I stand there, studying her, looking for the truth, and what I find is a hint of anger in those green eyes. The kind of anger that says you're burned, and you want a different kind of burn. The kind a good fuck can give you, at least until it's over. I can believe that's what she wants and needs, but my gut is telling me there's more to this woman than a need to escape. And yet, I'm not turning away from her. I'm in this far. I'm going all the way.

I step back, giving her space to exit and waving her toward the door. "Ladies first."

Her eyes linger on mine just a moment, a probing push in their depths before she cuts her gaze and exits the elevator.

I join her in the hallway, and this time she waits, standing toe to toe with me, that sweet rose scent of her heating my blood. "Last chance to back out," she says, but I'd be willing to bet my right hand that she simply didn't want me at her back, stalking her down a narrow hallway.

"I always finish what I start," I say, "and in this case, what you've started. Unless *you* want to back out?"

"I don't want to back out, Reid Maxwell. Not even a little bit." She turns and starts walking and something about the way she says my name sounds really damn personal. It might be directed at me, for some sin I might or might not remember, but as far as I'm concerned, the best way to fight a war with a woman like this one is naked. I pursue her, stepping to her side in the narrow hallway, the charge between us crackling with a mix of lust, her anger, and unanswered questions. I focus on the lust. That's how I get my answers. With her legs over my shoulders.

She stops at a door and swipes her key, reaching for the door handle, and this is where this game becomes mine. She enters the room, and I'm right behind her, letting the door shut behind us, and locking it, ensuring there won't be any surprise visitors. I scan the open concept room with one bed and a sitting area, and once I ensure we're alone, I snag her hand and pull her around to face me. That first touch is pure fire, and we both react. One minute, our eyes collide with a punch, the next, my fingers are in her hair, and my mouth is slanting over hers. I lick into her mouth, the taste of her pure anger mixed with a shearing lust, hot enough to make me fuck her right here and now, but the anger, that anger, just can't be ignored.

I back her into the room, toward the living area, pressing her against the window next to the wall between a desk and an oversized chair, her purse crashing to the floor. "You know my name," I say. "You know *me*. We both know you do. Now it's time to tell me who you are. What's your name?"

"Pick one. I'll be her tonight."

"Oh no, baby. That's not how this works."

Her hands plant on my chest, her grip firm. "No name. Take it or leave it. Take *me* or leave me."

My lips quirk. "We both know you don't want me to leave." I reach for the skirt of her dress and pull it up her legs, my hands settling over the lace of her thigh highs, a choice I approve of one hundred percent. "We both know why I'm here."

"It's not about names."

"Isn't it?" I challenge. "You hate me, but you want to fuck me."

"I hate all men right now."

"And yet you want to fuck me." My thumb strokes up her inner thigh, back and forth, goosebumps lifting beneath my touch, her body softening with submission, while mine just keeps getting harder and harder.

"For me. Not you."

"Oh, I assure you, sweetheart," I say, "that every place I lick you, touch you, and the many ways I plan to fuck you, is very much for us both, or I wouldn't be here. You know I can get your name from the charity."

"I bid anonymously."

I arch a brow at that telling statement. "Is that right?"

"I don't need credit for the donation. I just need what it makes me feel."

I turn her to face the wall, forcing her to catch herself with her hands, and I yank her dress all the way up to her hips, my legs shackling her legs, my gaze doing a sweeping inspection of the black lace thong before I yank it away. She yelps and I lean in close, holding up the panties. "Something to remember you by," I say, shoving them into my pocket, my lips at her ear. "Now. Let's get to what's important. Your name on your lips and then *you* on mine. *What* is your *name*?"

"Samantha."

I smack that perfect backside of hers, not hard, but enough to sting. She gasps, and arches forward, right as I slide my hand between her legs and cup her sex. "What are you doing?"

"Punishing your beautiful backside every time you lie to me." I press my lips to her ear and caress the wet heat of her body. "And apparently making you really fucking wet. What's your name?"

She laughs this bitter, raspy, aroused laugh, and says, "You're such an asshole."

14

"Name," I bite out.

"Samantha."

I smack her backside again and she pants out a breath, her back arching against the sting of her cheek, even as I tease her clit and stroke the seam of her body. "Oh," she breathes out. "I hate—"

"Name," I say, "and I'm growing impatient. And you know what happens if you say Samantha."

"Samantha *is* my name."

I smack her cheek, this time hard, and then I turn her to face me, my thighs gripping hers. "I have all night," I say. "I'll get your name from you."

CHAPTER THREE

Reid

"What's your name?" I repeat, holding my emerald princess against the hotel wall.

"Why does my name matter? You aren't marrying me or taking me home to your family. That's not what this is."

My family. No mom and dad, like the saying goes, which could mean nothing, or it could mean that she has intimate knowledge of my life and the fact that my mother is gone. I cup her backside and pull her to me. "What do you know of my family?"

"Just that I don't want to meet them."

I lower my lips just above hers. "There's more to your story and you're going to tell me," I say, my mouth closing down on her mouth, my tongue stroking against her tongue in a deep, possessive, hungry kiss that is all demand, and a promise of what is to come. I want her, and I want answers, and I'm going to have both.

For the briefest of moments, she is stiff, unyielding, but her resistance fades into a moan, the tense lines of her body melting into every hard part of me. "Now I know how you taste here," I say, brushing my lips over hers again. "What about here?" I press my fingers between her thighs, into the wet heat of her sex. "Should I find out?"

"Do I actually have a say in the matter?"

"You can tell me no anytime you want." I release her and press my hands to the wall. "Do you want me to lick you, *Samantha*?"

"You're such an asshole."

"So I've been told, but you aren't going to make it seem as if I started this. You started this. So I ask again. Do you want me to lick you," I reach down and slide two fingers along the seam of her slick body, "*here*?"

She curls her fingers on my chest and cuts her gaze. I lean in, my lips by her ear. "I don't know if you're pissed off that you want a man that you hate, or you just went from bold to shy on me. Either way," I tangle fingers in her hair and drag her gaze to mine, "it's sexy as fuck." I kiss her again, a long stroke of my tongue against hers, and I caress her breasts and pull the top of her dress down to expose her nipples, my fingers stroking over one, and then tugging roughly.

A soft, sexy sound escapes her lips and lands on my tongue, and I smile against her mouth. "Now for that taste." I brush my lips over hers once more and allow my hands to settle at the sides of her breasts, and I lean in and drag my tongue around her nipple before settling on one knee.

"You haven't answered my question," I say, shackling her hips and glancing up at her. "Do you want me to lick you?"

"Is that really even a question?" she says, her voice a raspy, sexy affected whisper.

"I thought you might have a problem with a stranger licking certain, extremely intimate parts of your body. Do you want me to lick you?"

Her eyes burn hot. "Yes."

"Where?"

"If you don't know where," she challenges, "I picked the wrong guy."

I laugh, which is not something I do often, but she gets an "A" for creatively getting out of that answer and I reward her with my tongue, a quick lick over her clit. She sucks in air and I glance up at her. "There?" I ask.

"Yes," she dares this time. "*There.*"

I could make her tell me exactly where *there* is, to name her spot, to say please, but I really want to hear this woman moan, not beg. I lick her again and this time I suckle her swollen nub, stroking fingers along her sensitive seam and delving inside her. Just as I could make her beg, I could tease her now, force her to trade an orgasm for her name, but you don't strip everything from a person at once unless you mean to destroy them. And I want to know her story, not destroy her. She interests me. I haven't been interested beyond a fast fuck in a long damn time, but I am now.

I drag her leg to my shoulder, cup her backside, and I lick, suckle, and stroke her sex until she is arching into me, her fingers tangling in my hair, wrapping around the strands with a fierce grip, which confirms what I already know: she doesn't want this to feel good. She doesn't want time to feel good. That she can't help herself, pleases me. Drives me onward, and when she tenses and moans, it's only seconds afterward when her sex clenches around my fingers and she jerks with the intensity of her orgasm. I soften my touch, my mouth, my tongue, and when her knee buckles, I catch her waist, ease her leg to the ground; sliding up her body to bring my mouth to her mouth.

"This is how you taste on my lips," I say, closing my lips over hers, and kissing her, "and now you have something other than how much you hate me to think about." I reach around her and unzip her dress.

"I *do* hate you," she confesses, catching my hands when I would ease the front of her dress down. "Passionately. With all that I am."

"Then you have two choices." I shrug out of my jacket and sit down on the couch. "Undress or talk."

She doesn't do either. She comes down on top of me, her legs straddling my hips, her hand settling on my face. "I will not undress because you order me to undress. I will not do *anything* because you order me to do it."

I cup her head and tangle my fingers in her hair. "Is that a challenge or a promise?" I drag her mouth to mine, and she doesn't pull back. She sinks into the kiss, leaning into me, and when I'm about to flip her to her back, suddenly a cuff is on my wrist. The shock loosens my grip on her hair, and she scrambles off of me. I jerk at my arm to find it attached to a steel bar that runs the length of the couch.

"What the fuck is this?" I demand, sitting up, even as she pulls her dress down and up in the appropriate places.

"*Me* fucking *you*," she says. "That's why I came here today. To fuck you."

"Yeah well, sweetheart, bring it on. Here I am. Now what?"

"Now I leave. You have a phone. You can call for help. I only wish I could be around when you explain how it happened."

"You didn't kiss me like a woman who wants to leave."

"I kissed you like a woman who wants to fuck you, which I do."

"Only we didn't fuck. Come *here*."

"We didn't fuck, but I fucked you." She grabs her purse from the bed. "And this is me leaving you to enjoy the glow of the aftermath."

"Are you going to tell me what this is about?"

"No."

"Then what does this achieve?"

"It reminds you that you're human, and I don't think that's something you remember often. And maybe, just *maybe,* that saves someone from your wrath, though I'm certain it won't save your soul." She starts for the door.

"Do I at least get to know your name now?"

She turns to face me. "Carrie West, the one whose phone calls you've refused to take over and over again. And just so you know, I still run West Industries, the company that was my father's company until you stole it from him. That makes me your employee, with check-writing authority. I'm writing a company check for the donation as I leave here tonight. I expect to be fired. I don't care."

She starts for the door again and flips the lock. "Just remember this, sweetheart," I say. "You *will* see me again. I know where to find you and I will, and when I do, both of us will still remember what you tasted like on my tongue. And among your many debts you owe me after tonight, one will be that orgasm you moaned your way through with my mouth on you."

She rotates and laughs bitterly. "We both know that you won't find me," she says. "You'll have security escort me out of the building Monday morning, out of the company my father built from the ground up and that's good. The staff will see the real you, not the man handing out cash to keep everyone on board. And as for that orgasm, you owed me that and a whole lot more." And with that bold statement, she exits the room, the door slamming shut with a heavy thud behind her.

I yank at the cuff and then stare at it in disbelief. "Fuck." I scrub my jaw and laugh. What else can I do at this point? She got me. Not many people can outsmart me, but she did; really damn well, and holy fuck, *I want* that woman. I'm going to have her, too, and the next time, she'll be the one cuffed. Only I won't walk away like she just did. I'll make her pay for every second I'm stuck in this room, which might make staying a while worth it.

I tug at the cuff. It's not coming off, but I had to try. My hand goes to my pocket, searching for my phone, only to realize that it's in my jacket pocket, which is, of course, has somehow landed several feet away. I reach for it, stretching long and wide with no luck. I take the damn couch with me, lugging the huge piece of furniture until my fingers snag the jacket. Sitting back down on the couch, I dig out my phone and dial the only person I can dial. Royce Walker, the owner of Walker Security, a firm my brother-in-law hooked me up with, who I pay, and pay well, to basically find out shit for me.

"Aren't you being auctioned off tonight?" Royce asks when he picks up.

"Yes, which is how I got where I'm at now. How much is it going to cost me to have you get me out of a personal mess and keep it quiet?"

"Nothing we do ever goes beyond us and you."

"Good to hear," I say, glancing at the cuff. "Because this one requires discretion in a whole new way."

"I can have Rick Savage come talk to you tomorrow."

"I'm going to need help tonight."

"Tonight," he repeats. "What can't wait until morning?"

"I'd rather not explain on the phone. I'm in a hotel room and I won't be able to answer the door when your man gets here."

"In other words, bring pliers," he says.

"This isn't your first rodeo," I reply dryly, hating being a part of a pool of fools.

"I've seen it all," he says. "Are you at the event hotel?"

"Yes."

"What room number?"

"1182, but again, I can't get to the door."

"We can get in," he says. "Expect one of my men in a half hour." He disconnects.

I set the phone down and consider the family debt between my father and Carrie's father, and the fucking burden it's now become to bear. One I'm legally obligated to protect with my silence. Carrie can never know, and most certainly if she did, I wouldn't be cuffed to this damn couch. But every action has a reaction, and my emerald princess now has mine. Carrie West just rewrote her story and did so my way. I lift my cuffed hand and my lips curve. I'll keep these and return them to Ms. West personally.

CHAPTER FOUR

Carrie

I wake Monday morning to sunlight and the memory of Reid Maxwell between my legs that has me throwing aside the blanket and pressing my hands to my face. I hate that man. He took everything from me, even the damn orgasm I didn't want him to have. I let out a very unladylike growl and climb out of bed, resolved to survive this day. Today will be my last day at West Enterprises, the company my father founded and took public. He's already gone, in a Reid Maxwell driven hostile takeover. It's all Reid. He did this, but in truth, this was coming anyway. I already knew from my father that I was going to be phased out and quickly. I already knew we were going to fumble the ball before we did. My father took risks that were out of character, and dangerous.

After my date with Reid Maxwell, I might be on a job hunt sooner than I might have been, but at least I leave on my terms, and after showing that man he was human. I will not go down a slave to Reid Maxwell and his investors.

I shower and dress in my lucky pale pink dress with a perfect pencil skirt, right along with the black Jimmy Choos my father bought me when I graduated Yale law school and then claimed my own office in his company. I was to be legal counsel for the company, overseeing the brokering of some of the biggest real estate investments our company booked. In the past ten years, I became so much more; he checked out on day-to-day operations. I ran this place, I brokered deals. I became, I am, the face of the company, when my father often was not.

I leave my apartment, which is mine, all mine, thanks to a huge real estate deal I brokered for a downtown Denver complex halfway across the country. It's not big, only two thousand square feet, but it has a gorgeous city view, and the right payments for me on my own. Now, nothing is certain, and the payment feels large, so very large. I step onto the street, only a few blocks from the office, which was another reason I chose my apartment. There was never going to be a time that I wasn't living my work at West Enterprises. Until today.

Overtaken by emotions I rarely allow myself to feel, I stop at a coffee shop just to slow down the day. I order two of my favorite hazelnut lattes and skip any food. I don't know if I can even drink the coffee, let alone eat. The second latte is for my assistant, Sallie, who not only loves this drink as well, but who I adore. We aren't really friends—work and friends don't work—but maybe we will be now. I won't be her boss.

I enter the offices and wave to the receptionist before walking down a long hallway to cut left and then right to the executive offices. Once I'm on the other side of the glass doors, Sallie, who is a beautiful blonde with an equally beautiful personality, gives me a beaming smile. "Good morning."

"Good morning," I say, setting her cup on her desk. "Thank you for everything you do."

"I love what I do," she assures me. "Thank you."

I head to my office door, but I pause just before entering to stare at my father's dark office and the empty desk in front of it. Jessie, his assistant, is on a two-week vacation he granted her. I'm going to have to call her tonight. I enter my office and scan the photos on my desk; me with my father, me with the staff, me at Yale graduation when I felt this journey started. Me with Kiki, my dog, my best friend, who is gone now, and that's still really raw. I want to scoop them all into the box next to my desk, but as I round it and set the box on top, I resist. I don't want to scare the staff, but what is going to happen when I leave?

I need to do something, so I stuff my stapler into the box on my desk, preparing to be walked out any minute, and yeah, it's a stapler, but Reid Maxwell doesn't get my office supplies. He's getting everything else and then some. I have a flashback of my dress hiked to my waist, that man on his knee, his hands on my hips, and his mouth—well, everywhere. I swallow hard with the memory as I've had too many times in the last few days. I never planned to actually have sex with the man, which technically I didn't, but Lord help me, I might as well have. And the truth is, had he not given me the opportunity to cuff him when I did, I would have. I don't know how I could want a man the way I wanted him when I hate him the way I do. He's just so—

That thought is cut off by a commotion in the hallway. "Sir!" I hear my assistant Sallie shout. "Sir!"

I stand up, certain this is where I get escorted out. I thought I was ready. I thought I could handle this, but my hands are shaking and my heart is in my throat and—Reid walks into my office, and I can barely breathe. He's here, not some random person he sent to get rid of me. That's how pissed off he is about those cuffs. He stops just inside the door and scans the space, taking in my conference table and sitting area before refocusing those ice blue eyes on me, and just that easily he consumes the room, power radiating off him. Tall, broad, and devastatingly, arrogantly male in a perfectly fitted gray pinstripe suit, his long legs eat up the space between the doorway and my desk, those damn eyes of his pinning me in a stare.

"Hello, *Samantha*," he says.

I lift my chin, not about to cower. "I'm surprised you came," I say, "but then that's the point, right? To take me off guard?"

"Actually, *you* came," he points out. "I didn't have that pleasure."

Heat rushes over me and before I can form a reply, Sallie appears at the endcap of my desk between us. "I'm sorry, Carrie. He just charged in and—"

Reid looks at her. "You need to leave myself and Ms. West alone now."

She gives me a desperate look. I nod. "It's okay, Sallie. Mr. Maxwell and I have company business."

She doesn't look convinced, but she slowly backs up and heads for the door. "Shut it behind you," Reid orders, his eyes focused on me, sharp, hard, and somehow intimate, like he's thinking about where his mouth has been and wants me to do the same.

I am.

Lord help me, I am.

The door shuts, and he flicks a look at the box on my desk. "Going somewhere?"

"Isn't that why you're here? To personally fire me, maybe even walk me out of the door?"

He leans forward, his hands on my desk, his eyes, those ice blue eyes, fierce, while his woodsy male scent reminds me of how much I smelled like him when I left that hotel room. "I'm not the kind of man that sends someone else to do a job I can do better. And I can do this one better."

Anger flares in my belly. "Bring it on," I say, leaning on the desk toward him, my intent to square off with him, but it's a mistake I can't back away from. He's close, so damn close. "Whatever you have planned," I add fiercely, "no matter how bad it is, will be worth leaving you in that room in those cuffs."

"And every second I was in that hotel room, I tasted you on my lips, *Samantha*. You left a lasting impression."

We stare at each other and Lord help me yet again, my nipples are tight and I'm wet. Ridiculously wet by way of a man that has destroyed my life. "Do what you're going to do," I breathe out.

His lips twitch again. "Oh, I will and I am." He pushes off the desk and only then do I even realize he's brought a briefcase that he apparently sat in the chair next to him. I quickly straighten while he grabs a folder and tosses it on the desk. "You have six months to buy back the business. The conditions are outlined in that contract. I'll summarize. You will produce a certain level of revenue in that timeframe which allows my family and the panel of investors I used for this transaction to leave feeling adequately compensated. They've all agreed, for one reason and one reason only. I've agreed to take control. I'll be here on-site."

"Why would you even take your time to do this?"

"I have my reasons that I don't intend to share. Study the document. You have one hour to decide. If you don't sign the deal, it's over and you're done here."

I flip open the folder and start reading. He's made it to the door when I read the ridiculously large figure I have to earn in six months. "This is just a game to you," I say. "A way to taunt me or fuck over one of the investors, or whatever it is. I'm not playing."

He turns to face me. "You based that assessment on what?"

"The profit you want me to produce. I can't do this. It can't be done."

He walks back to me and leans on the desk again. "The woman that not only seduced me into following her to her room, who managed to get me to give her an orgasm, and then cuffed me and left me to think about her, wouldn't say can't. You even paid for that orgasm with a company check." He straightens again. "Be Samantha or fail. She doesn't think the number is too much. Your father made you feel that number was impossible. It's not. If it were, I wouldn't have put my name on this deal with my investors. You have one hour to get from 'can't' to 'can'. I'll be in your father's office, which is now mine." He turns and walks to the door again, and this time he doesn't stop. He leaves.

CHAPTER FIVE

Carrie

I stare at the doorway where Reid has just exited, in disbelief. His office? My *father's* office. Furious, I grab the folder and stand up, rounding my desk with the intent of telling him where to stick this contract, but right when I'm about to exit my office, Sallie appears in front of me. "He just went into your father's office. Am I supposed to let him?"

I open my mouth to say about ten things I can't say. Reid Maxwell is her new boss and it cuts so damn deep I might bleed out right here and now. "Yes," I say. "You are. I'll explain later. I need a few minutes." I present those words as calmly as I delivered the news that the Waterbrook project had crashed and burned only three weeks ago, but just like then, I'm melting down inside. "I'll get with you in a bit."

"Okay." She backs up and I charge forward, toward my *father's* office, where that man is now sitting with the door shut, which he clearly did to push my buttons. I pass the empty secretarial desk, and when I reach the office, I don't bother knocking. I open the door and enter, shutting it behind me and sure enough, Reid's sitting behind my father's massive mahogany desk, in the office where I'd played with Barbies as a child, when all I wanted was to grow up to be just like my father. Worse, he looks good behind it, which only pisses me off more.

He arches a brow in that arrogant way he does everything and then leans back in his chair. I move toward him, and he, of course, watches my every step with apt attention. I stop directly in front of him, between the visitor's chair, and repeat his earlier actions. I toss the folder on the desk, and then lean on it, hands flat on the wood. "I'm not going to play your games with you and your loads of money and time to kill taunting me."

He leans forward, and now we're close, damn—*really* close, those blue eyes so ridiculously blue. "People with loads of money," he says, "don't have it because they waste time playing games."

"And yet, here you are."

"I don't do anything that wastes my time," he repeats. "And I'm going to say this one more time and never again. If the numbers weren't doable, I wouldn't be here."

"You won't say it again?" I demand incredulously. "Like I'm a child you're reprimanding?"

"You do like to play with toys," he comments dryly. "And not very nicely. You reeled me in and left me in that room wholly unsatisfied."

"You have a hand," I snap, shoving off the desk.

"But I'd rather use yours," he says, never so much as blinking, his voice now a warm, silky taunt, "but that won't happen. I don't fuck where I work. I don't mix business with pleasure. This is business."

I laugh in disbelief. "Because you won't let it happen? Like I would."

"Do you really want to challenge me on that?"

"Apparently I couldn't if I wanted to."

His lips twitch but he changes the topic. "The investors behind this stock leverage want a return. I promised them that this," he lifts the contract, "doubles what I predicted previously." He drops the contract again. "Can or can't," he says. "Sign or don't sign, but decide now."

"You gave me an hour."

"I changed my mind. Now or never."

"I need to read it."

"Read it now, here, with me. You're an attorney and a good one from what I've studied. You'll find it simple, precise, and clear. It guarantees your salary for six months which isn't a small salary. Losing that would hurt."

"You're such an asshole."

"One who hands out orgasms and paychecks."

My lips purse but I grab the folder and walk to the black leather couch to my left and sit down, setting the folder in my lap to begin reading. Reid thankfully stays where he's at, opening his MacBook to actually do his own work. I'm a few pages into the document, and I reluctantly admit that he's right. I need my paycheck. I gave my savings to my father to start a new firm he's off chasing. And everything in the contract is as Reid claimed; simple, precise, and clear, at least to someone used to reading the language, which I am. I buy back my father's stock by way of that profit figure. That *huge* profit that sets me off again.

I shut the folder and walk back to the desk, setting it back in front of him. "Lower the number."

"No," he says simply. "Sign or don't sign. Time's up." He sharpens his stare. "Your salary remains the same. Your bonuses remain the same, and we both know you cleaned out your savings to help your father leverage one of his side deals. You need this deal."

I don't blink despite the fact that he jolts me with his knowledge of my personal business that he shouldn't know, but he's right. I did write a check to my father. I was all in, even when my gut said to pull back.

"Knowing this," he adds, "makes your move Friday night all the more gutsy. You were walking away from a paycheck."

"I'd already heard I was one foot out the door."

"The only two people that can walk you out of the door are me and you. Can or can't," he repeats.

My lips tighten, and I lean in to reach for a pen on the desk and suddenly his hand is on mine, the spark of electricity up my arm rocketing my eyes to his. "Can or can't?" he demands softly, his eyes somehow hot and cold at the same time.

"Can," I bite out.

"What changed your mind?"

"You."

"Explain."

"I have let this become emotional, which is always a mistake," I admit, the truth of those words cutting like so many things right now. "I let myself believe that meant you had as well, but that's not you. This is about money to you, not me and a pair of handcuffs."

He studies me a few beats, and then releases me, sliding the folder closer to me. I sign the document. "Now what?"

"Sit."

"I don't want to sit."

"Sit, Carrie," he orders and while his voice is soft, it's absolute.

"Carrie?" I challenge. "Not Samantha?"

"I'll save Samantha for when we're alone."

"I'll save asshole for you when we're alone."

"I can live with that," he says. "Sit."

I sit and he gets right to the point. "Tomorrow morning, the board will name me the new acting CEO. I don't want or need this job, but it's mine for now. I'll name you second in charge with the understanding that I'm evaluating you to replace me when I step aside."

Evaluating me to take the job that was always supposed to be mine, but I don't say that. "Which will be when?" I ask instead.

"As far as the board is concerned, I represent the majority stockholders. When I decide it's safe to step aside and hand you the keys, they'll accept that decision."

"They have to agree."

"They'll push back tomorrow because you're your father's daughter. They'll stop pushing back when the numbers say they should."

"They'll think it's all you."

"If I let them, but I won't. I have a company to run and it's not this one."

"In other words, I have to trust you, a man I cuffed and left in a hotel room for being a bastard." I don't give him time to reply. "Will I attend this meeting?"

"No," he says. "They want a closed-door management discussion, but it'll be recorded. You can listen to it, but so can others. In other words, we have to deal with this here, in this office, today."

I cut my gaze and swallow the knot in my throat before looking at him. "What are you going to say?"

"I'm going to tell them your father retired and I stepped in to help take the company to a new level, something you support and endorse. My role is temporary."

"They will figure out what really happened."

"That is what really happened. Ultimately, your father voluntarily retired. You are the future of the company."

"Why would your investors accept this option?"

"I told you—"

"You promised them double returns."

"Yes." He studies me. "I need to know you see the real picture. Where did it all go wrong?"

I want to shout at him that he's what went wrong, but that's me getting emotional again. "The Summerton and Waterbrook projects," I say. "But Waterbrook sealed our death."

"What was your role in those projects?"

"Advisor to my father."

"Then you told him to go on them?" he challenges.

My lips thin. "He made the calls."

"*Did you* tell him they were good moves?"

"I told him to walk away from both."

"Why?"

"As you know, I'm sure, Summerton was a resort project in another country. The financial instability of the group investing, legal ramifications to a variety of terms, and location challenges were among my list of concerns. There were others."

"And it ended up half-built without funding."

"Yes."

"And Waterbrook. Tell me about Waterbrook."

"Waterbrook was an early development project in Casper, Wyoming, where an oil and gas boom has started, and the city is just taking shape. On paper it made sense."

"But?"

"I disliked Max Waterbrook, the key investor in the project. It was a gut feeling. I couldn't find the facts to support it, but I knew he was trouble. And now our project is dirt, quite literally, and he's disappeared with the money."

"If there's a snake in the grass, you make sure he's your snake."

"Like you?" I dare.

"If you believe that, you shouldn't have signed the papers. I don't lie or cheat, Carrie. I'm here because there were people on that board losing big money over your father's decisions. They sold off stock to allow the takeover. They wanted him out. They want the money he lost back, and if I were them, I'd damn sure want the same. My investors, however, just want money as fast as they can get it. None of them sought out West Enterprises on a personal mission."

I'm angry with this assessment for about ten reasons, but he's moved on about a second before I unleash on him. "I need to see every project you've touched in the time you've been here and your recommendations on each, along with the outcome," he says. "How fast can I have it?"

"As fast as it takes me to email it to you. I record that data and have from the day I started to work."

"Good. We'll go over it together, later. After we deal with the staff. When can we hold a meeting?"

"It has to be after hours."

"After hours it is then," he replies. "Make it happen, and then we'll review your track record."

My track record.

We will review my track record.

Anger is starting to burn in my belly all over again. I stand but I can't let him off, I can't let him pretend this is anything but what it is. I press my hands on the desk again and look him in those baby blues. "You aren't a hero. You're the reason I didn't get the chance to save the company and I would have had you not swept the stock. You're the reason my father was pushed out."

"Your father needed to be pushed out and you couldn't save it until he was. Deep down, I know you already know that."

"You really are an asshole."

"There she is," he says. "Samantha live and in person. Keep her here because we both need her, and you were wrong earlier. This *is* about you, me and the handcuffs. I wouldn't be here if it wasn't."

"What does that even mean?"

"You came at me. You weren't afraid. You even got something out of it. That was impressive. That earned you a chance you can use that killer instinct here, but don't underestimate me. I'm not here to be your friend, but I'm not here to fuck you either."

"Because you already did. You fucked me. You fucked my family. You don't need to do it again and yet I know, *I know*, that in the end, I will claw and fight to save this company because I have to, because this place is all I have, and yet, you will. You will fuck me, and I just signed the contract that says I approve." I straighten and head for the door, but the minute I reach for the knob, his big body is behind me, his hand on the knob. I'm now caged between the door and Reid Maxwell.

CHAPTER SIX

Reid

"Let me out of this office," Carrie demands without turning to face me, my hand still planted on the door above her head; her pink dress hugging her perfect ass that's a lean away from being pressed against me.

"If you walk out of this office with an attitude," I warn, "you fuck me and you," her damn floral perfume scents the air like I know it does her skin. "If you divide us," I add, "I'll be forced to let you pack that box and leave. Is that what you want?"

She rotates to face me, lifting that perpetually defiant chin, those perfect, pink lips tilted upward, begging me to kiss them. "If I wanted this to end that way," she says. "I wouldn't have signed that contract."

"Then stop thinking of me between your legs, because obviously only one of us can do that and still get our jobs done."

"Are you trying to be crass or is that just natural for you?"

"Does it make you hate me more?"

"Yes."

"Then hate me, Carrie, but do it behind closed doors, with or without me. In fact, if you want me to yank your skirt up and help you fuck it out of your system, we can do that too, but you will not do it in front of the staff."

"What happened to you not fucking where you work?" she fires back.

"Seems like breaking that rule might be a public service."

"Stop being an ass. It doesn't help me help you, and don't tell me that I'm not helping you. You've made it clear that you wouldn't be here if I wasn't."

"I'll make no apologies for who and what I am. Support me or move on. Can or can't."

"Can," she bites out. "I already said 'can,' so you're the one who needs to *move on.*"

"You said 'can' and then you insulted me and charged for the door."

"As you said. I'll save the hate for more *intimate moments,* the ones spent *without you.*"

In other words, my reminder of our encounter won't intimidate her. My lips quirk. She's got balls and I fucking love it. "You're with me. We are one. *Say it.*"

"I'm with you," she bites out, anger vibrating off of her. "We are one."

She's defiantly submissive, which on her is both sexy as hell and the best I can hope for just minutes after I've stripped her of the control she believes should be hers. "Don't make me regret this," I say, pushing off the door and heading back to my new desk.

She stands there at my back, watching me, and when I round the desk, she's still looking at me. "I will make you regret this. Not now. Now you'll get your payday, but one day." She turns and leaves, shutting the door behind her.

She hates me and I've barely gotten started. I've yet to force her to make hard decisions, like seeing her father in his true light. The path to getting there will surely be filled with more hate, but at least if we do end up naked, there's no risk of her actually confusing me with that hero she already assured me I am not. And I'm damn sure not the guy any woman, most especially this one, takes home to their father. My cellphone rings on the desk where I set it and I glance at the caller ID. How well-timed. I decline the call. My father is toxic. He needs to stay away from this, and everything for that matter, and so does Carrie's father. It can be no other way.

Just like us fucking has to happen and so does her hating me. Our families are enemies and she doesn't even realize just how deep that runs. Which actually makes her perfect for me. I can want her all fucking day and night, but she's safe. There will never be more than hate. And so, we'll hate fuck when this is over—or hell, maybe before it's over. It won't make it all better, but I will. I'm going to make all of this bigger, better, and then I'll be gone, which is just the way Carrie West will want it.

Carrie

Don't think of him with his head between my legs? *Asshole.* He *really* is an asshole. He said that to make me think about his head between my legs and his mouth, too. And that damn cologne of his, woodsy and earthy, I couldn't stop smelling it when I left him in that room.

I walk past Sallie, and just as I'd feared, she follows me into my office. By the time I'm on the other side of the desk, she's shutting the door and crossing to stand in front of me. I sit. I would rather not be eye level. She sits. Wonderful. "What is happening?" she asks. "And why is that man still in your father's office?"

The words I have to speak hang in my throat, but I have to say them to everyone tonight. I need to practice now. "My father's retiring. Reid Maxwell's firm is now the majority stockholder. And Reid Maxwell is the man sitting in my father's office."

"Oh my God," she whispers. "A hostile takeover." Panic lifts in her voice. "We're under siege. My God." She stands up.

"Sit," I say, feeling like I'm repeating what just happened between me and Reid.

"I can't sit."

"You can. Sit. I need you to listen to me."

She sits. "Are you being fired?"

"No. I'm working with Reid to make some positive moves forward and the plan is for me to reclaim the role of CEO."

"And controlling stock?"

"I'll have the opportunity to be majority stockholder, not controlling. Not now."

"That's not good."

"A successful CEO of a monster company like this one is not bad." It's true, I remind myself. "We are going to be bigger and stronger."

"Without your father?"

"This kind of thing happens often, and if we do what Reid Maxwell wants us to do, we'll all have bright futures."

"So you *will be* CEO, right?"

"I don't know. We'll see." I want to comfort her and tell her everything will be okay, but I've never made promises I can't keep. I don't lie. I hate lies. They've burned me. They've hurt me. I don't want them to hurt anyone else.

"That doesn't make me feel better."

"We made mistakes, Sallie. You know that."

She nods. "Yes. The two big projects that went bottom-up in six months."

"Yes. Stockholders don't take kindly to those kinds of losses."

"You were against those deals," she says. "We did report after report to convince your father to walk away."

"It's done. We can't look back."

"You need to make sure the board knows you said no to those deals."

"Reid knows."

"Which is why you're still here and your father is not. Will you get your father's seat on the board?"

"That's up in the air," I say, and I hope it really is at this point. "For now, there will be a mandatory staff meeting at six. No one can miss it. Please arrange it."

"I will." She starts to get up.

"Sallie."

"Yes?" she asks, settling back into her seat.

"Please don't bail. If I make it to the other side of this, I'll take care of you. I promise. I'll make it worth your while."

"And if you don't make it to the other side?"

"Do a good job, and you might survive even if I don't. I'll make sure Reid knows how good you are, and you do the same."

"He's a hot piece of arrogant man. That means demanding and difficult."

"Yes to all. Is that a problem?"

"Just one of my random observations."

Which I normally like, but at this moment, I've had enough arrogant, demanding man for one day, and the day has only started. "An accurate one," I say, and with that, she stands and heads for the door while my phone buzzes with my father's extension. I pick up the receiver. "Yes, Reid?"

"*Yes*," he says, as Sallie shuts me inside my office, in what could represent peace, if not for this man on my phone. "I like that word," he says. "My secretary, Connie, is joining us tomorrow, after the announcements. I need her cleared to get past security."

I wonder if he's been between Connie's legs and before I stop myself, I say it. "Have you been between Connie's legs, too?"

"No. I have not. I told you—"

"You don't fuck where you work unless it's a public service, and who knows how easily you decide it's a public service."

"Never," he says. "As in *never*, Carrie, but you changed our dynamic, not me."

"For the record," I say. "I never planned to actually—"

"Have an orgasm?" he supplies. "Those are the best kind. The unexpected ones."

"I didn't say it was good," I say.

"You didn't have to," he says. "I was there, remember?"

All too well, I think. "I'll have my assistant Sallie handle Connie's security clearance," I say tightly.

"I'll have her call Sallie. When can I expect you and those reports to be back in my office?"

"Soon," I say, which translates to *too soon*.

"In other words, you haven't had time to call your father and talk about me."

That comment pisses me off. He's trying to find out if I function without my father. I don't say a word. I hang up, grab my MacBook, round my desk, marching out of my office and toward *his* office. This man will not make me cower, and *damn it*, I think, when I reach the door about to open it, *he will not make me quiver, quake, or moan either. Period. The end. I won't let it happen.*

44

With that vow, and once again, without knocking, I open the door and walk into Reid Maxwell's new office, ready to prove I mean it.

CHAPTER SEVEN

Carrie

I enter Reid's office and pull the door shut to find him, once again, sitting behind the heavy wide desk that somehow fits him, like this entire office fits him a little too well. This isn't his place and yet it is, and I still haven't had time to digest this, to accept it. He arches a brow and looks too damn good doing it. He's so damn good looking that it makes every arrogant action ten times more arrogant. "Did I hear a knock?" he asks.

"You did not," I say, and I offer no apology. I walk toward the small round conference table to the left and just in front of the sitting area, and claim one of the four seats, choosing the one that allows a view of Reid and the door. "Which email do you want the reports sent to?"

He stands up, towering over the desk. He is just as big as he is good looking. Tall and broad with the kind of body that comes from hard work and good genetics. His brother looks just like him. He's probably just as arrogant.

Reid grabs his own MacBook and crosses to claim the seat immediately to my left, no doubt to allow him a view of the door as well. Close. So damn close that his knee brushes mine and I quickly yank it away. Heat radiates up my leg, and my God, my sex clenches. Those full, harsh, beautiful lips of his quirk with my reaction. He now knows that outside of me intentionally seducing him, he affects me, and I hate him and me for it, too.

47

I want to get up and change seats, but I can't without handing him power that I won't give him. Not when he already has too much. "You can't reach your father," he says, "but you rushed in here to prove to me that you don't need to speak to your father to do your job."

"I didn't try to reach my father," I say, leaving out the part where I've tried plenty and failed. "Which email do you want these reports to go to?"

"Reid underscore Maxwell at Maxwell dot com. Tell me exactly what your father told you about the takeover."

"That's irrelevant," I say, keying in his address and attaching my document before hitting send. "The file's in your inbox."

"What did your father tell you?" he repeats.

My lips tighten. He won't let this go. "On a professional level, he told me nothing we haven't talked about."

"I want more than that."

"I've gathered that to be your way in all things."

His lips quirk. "Have you now?"

"Yes," I say, and of course, we're once again talking about him between my legs. "I noticed."

"That was the idea," he replies, his voice now a silky taunt. "I do want more. Are you going to give it to me?"

I'm spared this verbal sparring when his phone rings and he pulls it from his pocket, grimacing as he does. "I said no," he says, without preamble. "No means no." He hangs up and sets his phone down next to him.

"Was that a client?"

"That was my pain-in-the-ass brother, who you'd probably like a whole lot more than me, and perhaps more than your own brother. He's in Japan, correct?"

"You had me investigated," I say flatly.

"Weeks ago," he says. "When I was being asked my opinion on the next CEO of this company. I even had a photo, but you were blonde, and—different. I like you better brunette."

"I'm brunette because I like me better brunette and that photo is ten years old. Back to you investigating me. Obviously, something in that investigation led you to believe that I need you as a babysitter."

"No," he says. "I'd decided to leave you in place without me taking over, right up until the night I met you at that charity event. And no. That has nothing to do with you cuffing me and forgetting to fuck me properly."

"I thought I did it quite properly. I assume that's the problem."

"Fucked properly would have been a) me naked, you naked, lots of moans and pleasure, or b) what I was about to do to you before that night. I'd all but finalized a deal to have Smith Mitchell Investments swallow you whole."

I blanch. "You what? Is that what this is? You're selling us off?"

"Not anymore," he says. "I told you. I convinced those I had to convince that we could come out ahead, going another direction. We get a big payout, you get your father's stock back and my position on the board, while everyone ends up with a winning investment."

"You changed your mind because I cuffed you to a bed? I'm expected to believe that?"

"Because all this company is missing is a good driver."

"And that's you."

"That's *you*," he says, "but thanks to your father, you need assistance to get back up the hill or perhaps to the top on your own for the first time. *Back to your brother.*"

"What about Anthony?"

"When was the last time you spoke to him?"

My brow furrows. "Why does my brother *in Japan* matter? What game is this?"

He stands up and walks to his desk, grabbing a folder and then returning before he sits down, and slides it in my direction. "The week your father made that final kiss-of-death deal that put us in this room together, he spoke to your brother every day, at least three times. How many times did he talk to you?"

He didn't, I think. He shut me out. I open the folder, finding proof of the conversations between my father and brother. My call logs are included. I spoke to my father twice, and they were each sixty seconds. Of course, my call logs mean nothing. I was right here with my father, and he was behind a closed door, with me on the other side. I shut the folder and glance up at him. "My brother must have needed advice," I say, but deep down I know that's not what happened.

Reid fixes me in an ice blue stare. "Make sure your brother doesn't need advice from you."

"I like you slightly better than I like him," I say. "We don't speak. Since you know everything there is to know about me, I'm certain you know that, too."

"Why don't you speak?"

"There's really nothing complex about this," I say. "We don't like each other."

"Why?" he presses. "Answer, Carrie."

"You already know the answer."

"Tell me yourself."

"He wanted us to invest in a shopping development in Japan. I was against it, and he said I thought I knew it all because I was an Ivy League attorney fresh out of school and he's not an attorney at all."

"Why isn't he Ivy League?"

"He didn't do the work. I did, but it didn't matter in this case. In the end, I convinced my father to pull out."

"And?"

50

"And it turned into a great investment," I admit. "I was *wrong*."

"No," he says. "The only wrong move is one where you lose money."

"We could have made a lot of money. We lost money."

"If you beat yourself up for every time you missed out on money," he says, "then you will be afraid to say no to anything. Were you afraid after that? Are you still?"

"That was seven years ago," I say. "I was twenty-five, fresh out of law school."

"How hard did you push your father to say no to the duet of failures that got us here?"

He's hit ten nerves and I swallow hard. "Not hard enough, obviously."

"Is that what you believe?"

Anger comes at me from a deep, overflowing pit that has nothing to do with Reid. "I pushed. He shut me out."

"Because your brother convinced him he was right again and you were wrong."

"My brother works for a tech giant in Japan. He's been out of this for years. I don't know why he'd be advising my father about anything."

"But he is. He's still at your father's ear."

"Maybe."

"*He is*. And for the record, your distance from your brother was one of the only reasons I said yes to you staying on board. *Keep* that distance."

"That won't be a problem," I say, my words acid on my tongue. "I told you—"

"You like me better than him. I heard you. I have to be in court at two. What time is our staff meeting?"

"Six."

"I'll be back by five. Go through the data with me between now and then."

"How can you run this place and still manage a caseload?"

"I have me and you. We're an army. Go through the data with me."

"You've already been through it. That's obvious."

His eyes meet mine, his penetrating in a way that is wholly personal, and yet, his words are seemingly all business. "I've seen the reports, but they only tell me the end result, not how you got there. Tell me your story."

This place is my story, it's all I've ever let be my story, which means this man already owns all of me, he controls my future, my life, my everything, but I won't say that to him. I don't trust him not to use it against me. I cut my gaze and plan to start reading the data. His phone rings again and he glances at the number. His jaw sets hard and he answers. "A call from the district attorney himself," he answers. "To what do I owe this pleasure?"

The district attorney, I think. Of course. This man is all about power.

"Let me be clear," he says, his tone harder than steel. "People not only died, but you let it happen. You went after an innocent man, and then let his conviction stand in the public eye. Not only was another woman killed while the real killer ran loose, the brother of one of the victims attacked one of my clients."

My eyes go wide. *My God.*

"I'm aware that this is not my normal territory," Reid says, "but I made an exception and we both know that's not to your benefit." He laughs. "You're kidding, right? Try three times that much. And for the record, my fee is being donated to the families of the victims, right along with my client's settlement. It would look pretty low for you to be cheap since you already look like scum." He gives a brutal laugh this time. "You'd better make this worth my time." He disconnects and looks at me. "We'll continue later." He stands up and shuts his computer. "I'll be back in time for the meeting."

With that, he walks to his desk and grabs his briefcase. I stand and pick up my things. Right when I would exit, his hand is back on the door, his big body behind mine. "Turn around."

I do it. I don't know why, but I just do it, and suddenly I'm suffocating in this man, in the scent of him, the size of him. The power of him. "I know your story better than you do and that's a problem," he says. "You weren't wrong. The Japan deal wasn't, and isn't, something you want on your books. Figure out why and you might be ready to run this place."

"What does that mean?"

"Open the door, go to your office, and figure it out, because you're only as good as that answer."

"Or the private eye you hired."

"I hired," he says. "*I hired*. Think about that. I got answers."

"Then you want me to hire yet another private eye?"

"The answers you need aren't hard to find. Find it. While I'm gone, what are you going to say to the staff?"

"Nothing until the meeting."

"That won't work. What are you going to say? What will you say if someone asks why I'm in your father's office?"

"I'll tell them we'll explain in the meeting." He stares at me, waiting for another answer. "My father retired," I say. "You're here to offer valuable counsel in his absence that will be discussed in the meeting tonight."

"Good. What else?"

"You're the new CEO."

"*Acting* CEO and don't say that until we talk to them together."

"Why? Isn't that what you want? Power?"

"I have it," he says. "I don't need to flaunt a title that will ultimately be yours."

"They'll know. You said that."

"And we'll handle that tonight, in the meeting, in an appropriate way. What else are you going to say when I'm gone?"

This man is confusing. So very confusing. "Nothing. I will say nothing. I'll talk around everything else."

"Wrong answer. What else?" he demands, his gaze lowering to my mouth and lifting. "What do I want to hear?"

I'm not sure where or how our conversations slid between personal and professional, but I say what I know he wants me to say. "I'm with you, *Reid.*"

"That's right, *Carrie.* You're with me. Don't forget it. And in case that conversation you heard with the DA makes you think that I'm a good guy deep down inside, I'm not. *Do not* let me find out that you're plotting against me. You will fail and force me to hurt you and hurt you badly. Now turn and leave before I don't let you." And with that loaded comment, he pushes off the door.

I don't even think about leaving. I fight back. "It never crossed my mind that you were a good guy, Reid. You're the kind of man a woman gets naked with and then if she's smart, she walks away before she gets burned. I can't walk away, and just to be clear, as you like to *be clear*, professionally, I'm *with you*, but I don't intend to fuck you or get fucked, in any sense of the word."

I turn away from him, and his hand comes back down on the door. He leans close, and this time, his hand settles on my waist, branding me, flooding my body and mind with memories of all the places he's touched me and kissed me. "But you'll want to," he says, his breath a warm fan on my neck, "and that could become a problem for both of us. And we both know where that leads." With that double entendre, he releases me and this time, I exit his office, walking rapidly toward my own with him watching my every step. I feel like a prey and he's the hunter, and it's eternal hours that are mere seconds before I am finally over the threshold of my own personal space, and shutting the door. I fall against the wooden surface, trying to catch my breath, and damn Reid Maxwell, I'm wet and hot, and I can still feel his hands on my body. Which is exactly what he wanted.

If I'm not careful I'm going to end up naked with that man and this time, I have no doubt, I'm the one who'll end up at his mercy. Who am I kidding? I'm already at his mercy.

CHAPTER EIGHT

Reid

With a text confirmation that my client will meet me at the DA's office, I slide into the back seat of my hired car, and I swear the scent of Carrie's damn perfume follows me. Holy hell, that woman is under my skin or I wouldn't be thinking about her perfume and her perfect backside rather than her role in the company where I need to turn a massive profit. The problem is that there are a lot of people busy fucking her right now that *aren't* me; namely her own father, and I wish like hell I could just tell her, but there is that damn debt and a contract that's silencing me. For now, I've settled for making it clear where her loyalty needs to lie: with me. If she gets fucked, I now get fucked, which means a lot of wealthy people get fucked.

I dial my secretary, Connie, who is a ten-year veteran of dealing with my shit and thus far the woman just won't quit. "Your humble servant at your service," she answers.

I ignore her smart remark, as I do all her many smart remarks. "I need you to coordinate with Carrie West's secretary, Sallie, to get clearance for you and Gabe," I say. "Gabe needs clearance in time for a six o'clock meeting. I need you with me by tomorrow morning."

"Got it," she says. "I can't go another day without being ordered around by you in person anyway. I feel lost. How hostile is the hostile takeover?"

"They aren't as hostile as me," I say. "You'll be fine."

"I was talking about you. How hostile are you to them?"

"I'm only half as nice to them as I am to you," I reply dryly. "Anything I need to know before I hang up?"

"You know it's my birthday. Of course, you know. I'm forty today, and single because I have no life but servicing you, and it's depressing. Thank you for the gift."

"What did I buy you?"

"Tickets to see Jason Aldean because you know how much I love him."

"Well," I say dryly, "that was thoughtful of me."

"It was, and everyone who thinks you're an asshole clearly doesn't have access to your black AmEx."

"You're the only woman that ever has," I assure her.

"You know what they say about women who never marry?"

"What?"

"They never found the right man. Do you know what they say about any man over thirty-five, say thirty-eight, like yourself, who hasn't married? He has something wrong with him."

"Do you have a point?"

"No point. I have fifteen messages for you. Only three matter, therefore I've emailed those to you with notes."

"I'll be in the DA's office and then headed to court. Text me anything else important but make it real damn important."

"Got it. Don't text you. Wait. Don't hang up. Why did I just get a note that Carrie West is holding for me?"

"Good question," I say. "Put me on hold and take the call."

She does as I say and quickly comes back to the line. "She wants your cellphone number."

And she hunted it down. I do like this woman. "Give it to her."

"Will do. See you tomorrow." She disconnects before I can because it's Connie. She knows when I'm done.

I wait for my line to ring with a call from Carrie, but it doesn't. She doesn't call. Interesting. She went out of her way to get my number but does nothing with it. This woman keeps me guessing. The car pulls up to my destination and I exit to meet Cole Brooks, my client, and a top criminal attorney in the city, at the door. He's also the man who with his wife, and co-counselor, got an innocent man charged in a serial murder case off, only to have the DA refuse to look for the real killer. Not only did someone else end up dead, but the brother of one of the murder victims attacked Cole's wife in a public bathroom.

"What's this meeting about?" he asks.

"I hope it's the money meeting," I say, "but feel no pressure to settle. Your wife was attacked. We'll settle when you feel like she's safe and not a second sooner."

"Attacked because the DA let the attacker believe that we got his sister's killer off when the real killer ran free," he says as if he just needs to make sure I know this. "I might punch the man if I go upstairs. You need to handle this."

"Oh come on, man," I say. "You're a hell of a criminal defense attorney. If you punch him, you can defend yourself and we'll call it mental distress and get those victim's families more money. I'm in for the beating if you are."

"You handle it," he repeats. "But the man who attacked my wife is under psych evaluation. Make sure I get word if he's set free *before* he's set free. I trust you to handle this."

"And I will," I assure him.

He offers me his hand and we shake. "Thanks, Reid." He gives me a weak smile. "Everything your sister said about you wasn't true." He intends this to be a joke but I'm damn glad when he turns and walks away before seeing my flinch.

I forcefully shove aside my history with my sister and focus on Cole's need to protect his woman, and I get it. He's tormented by the idea that he was the indirect cause of her attack. He fell in love and then found out how easy it is to have someone close to you come under fire, which is just one of the reasons I took this case. I know what that feels like. I know, and I will never know again. *Ever.* I don't do relationships or anything that resembles a relationship. I do, however, apparently do obsession, since I can't stop thinking about Carrie, but then I half fucked her, and I never do anything halfway. I clearly need to be inside that woman to get her out of my head.

Carrie

It takes me all of fifteen minutes to find out what Reid meant about my decision on the Japan property being the right one. The company we would have been in bed with is now being investigated for a long list of international crimes. I didn't know and should have known, but I didn't follow the deal once it became ammunition for a war with my brother. No. I didn't follow it because my father blamed me for losing the deal, and that cut and cut deeply.

I stare down at Reid's number now in my phone thanks to his assistant, *not him*, and all because I wanted to call him and tell him I figured out Japan. And why? *Why* do I want to call him? I have nothing to prove to him, only it feels more like he proved something to me. He proved I was right about Japan. He's such an asshole, and yet, he's the one who told me I got it right. He's the one who says he's behind me, but he's also the one who took down my company, even if he would claim it was my father. Deep down, though, I know it was my father. Not even deep down. My father let this happen. Reid just happens to be the kind of man that takes advantage of poor decisions.

Meanwhile, he's off helping the families of murder victims. He's a confusing person and his words replay in my mind: *In case that conversation you heard with the DA makes you think that I'm a good guy deep down inside, I'm not.* Okay he's not, but he's also the man holding the key to my future. If he doesn't believe I'm with him, really with him, I might as well leave now. The way I handle him could influence how he handles the meeting with our staff.

I start to call him and decide he could be in his meeting with the DA. The one where he's helping families of murder victims free of charge. Good guy. Bad guy. I don't know. It can't matter. I type a text: *I found out about Japan. I should have known. I know you think I'm going to call my father and my brother, but I'm not. And for the record, you might not be a good guy, but you're doing a good thing for those victims' families. I'm sure it must come with some personal gain, but I'll pretend it does not. It helps me to know the man I'm in business with has now helped them. Because I have a moral compass, even if you do not.*

I read the very long message and decide not to send it. Instead, I return messages, answer emails and deal with a number of "problems" Sallie sends my way. Not for one second is my mind fully off Reid and my family, or some combination. The truth is, I'm mostly replaying every word I spoke with Reid. He doesn't trust my family, and my father knows what I'm dealing with, and he hasn't called me.

It's a full hour later when I look at that message again and it pretty much sums up everything I need to say to Reid, and a text message with that man is safer than a conversation that gets too close and too personal. I hit send and set my phone aside without expecting a reply, and yet I am waiting for one. A full sixty seconds pass before he does indeed reply: *And your moral compass allowed you to cuff me and leave me to suffer? Don't say I had my hand. It wasn't you.*

I stare at that message and I don't like the warm heat pooling low in my belly or the memories of me on top of him before I cuffed him. I'd almost convinced myself I could finish what we started and cuff him later. I hesitated. I am supposed to be trying to build a bridge before the staff meeting, but this man pushes my buttons and I just can't help myself. I reply with: *I liked cuffing you. In fact, it was one of the most memorable moments of my life.*

His reply is instant: And here I thought that was the orgasm I gave you.

I grimace and type: Really it was getting you to give me the orgasm before I cuffed you.

He calls me. Of course, he calls me. He has to be in control. I answer the line. "Nice of you to give me your number in case I needed you," I answer, going on the attack.

"You proved resourceful in your needs, all of them."

Of course, that's a reference to my remark about getting him to give me an orgasm, and I actually can't say I regret that orgasm. I decide that's better unsaid and move onward. "Don't you have a meeting?" I ask.

"It's over. I walked out. I'm on my way to court."

"The DA didn't give you what you wanted?"

"No. He did not, but he will."

In that moment, I envy his confidence, even his arrogance. He knows who he is, what he can do, and where he's going. "I hope you win."

"What happened to all the punches you were throwing me in the text message?"

"At present, you aren't taunting me," I reply.

"Is that what you think I was doing?"

"Isn't it?" I challenge.

"Because I told you I want you more than my hand?"

I scowl. "Do you just say what comes to your mind or are you intentionally crass to me?"

"If I said what was on my mind, you'd hear a whole lot more than that. Is that what you want? It can be arranged."

"Yes, please," I say. "I prefer everything be on the table."

"Do you now?"

"Yes. *I do.*"

He's silent for several beats that feel loaded for reasons that I am certain I do not understand any more than I understand my father's recent decisions or even Reid himself. "I'll be there in time for the meeting." He disconnects, and I have no idea what just happened, but I know one thing. Reid knows more about me than I know about him and I already know that I can't do that without help. I tried before the auction. He's shielded himself and well, but I'm here. I am up close and personal, and I want to know who he is and what he really wants because it's not what it seems. He said to trust my gut and that's what my gut says.

CHAPTER NINE

Carrie

I spend the rest of my afternoon preparing a report on the two projects I've been chasing and why. I feel like Reid might need this for the stockholder meeting tomorrow. For the staff, I prepare a speech that Reid may throw right out the door, but I practice delivering it with a positive presentation. I'm actually pacing my office, memorizing it when my door suddenly opens and Reid appears.

"Did I hear a knock?" I ask, trying to cover up the way my damn heart races with his presence. He's just so overwhelmingly male and so damn good looking.

"No," he says, stalking toward me. "You did not."

I resist the urge to take a step backward, standing my ground with Reid, knowing that I can't allow myself to be his prey and survive this man. He stops in front of me, so close that anyone watching us would think we were intimate. We *are* intimate in ways I can't escape and I'm not sure I want to when I should. He is not my friend. "You really want to hear what I think of you?" he asks, his voice a hard line that I cannot read.

"Professionally," I clarify. "Yes. If I knew you would really tell me the truth. I don't like hidden agendas. I don't like back-stabbing. It's not who I am."

"And yet you want to be CEO of a company that thrives on back-stabbing and hidden agendas." It's not a question, but a statement.

"You don't have to win that way. You just have to be smarter and faster, and I would have been."

"When your father was not," he supplies.

I force myself to be direct. "When my father was not," I concede. "And for the record, you were right. I should have known about Japan. I should have followed my own decision to see where it led."

"Why didn't you?"

"Does it matter?" I challenge.

"Yes," he says, those blue eyes of his piercing. "It does."

"It was a book I thought was closed," I say offering him the most unemotional answer possible.

"It was painful," he says his voice soft, but he doesn't give me time to reject his assessment when I really can't anyway. He sees the truth. "To be clear, I've told you what I think of you, but I get it. You don't trust me."

"How can I? You took over my family business and now you control my entire life."

"You could walk away," he points out.

"But I don't want to, and you know that which means you can use me and when this is over, I have nothing."

"I gave you a contract for a reason," he counters. "So you don't walk away with nothing."

"I get nothing if I fail."

"You won't fail, but you want to feel my confidence in that statement. I'll double your salary in back pay if this ends with you leaving, and yes, I'll put that in writing. And as for trusting me. Use the instincts that made you see Japan for what it was. Wrong. Japan was a wrong move. I am not."

"I didn't trust my instincts about Japan, remember?"

"You should have. Your instincts were right, but if you need facts to back up why I'm the right move for you, you have them. The stockholder meeting is public record. You'll know what I say in that meeting, and in the end, you'll see that it comes down to one thing. In all things, we want the same thing."

In all things, we want the same thing.

Those words land between us and hang in the thickening air, heat rushing over me that I don't want to feel. "Do we?" I challenge, fighting this incredible urge to sway toward a man who is probably my enemy, a wolf who doesn't bother with sheep's clothing. "Because I want to trust you."

"As I do you, Carrie, but you need to understand that I put my neck on the line for this deal. I cannot let you burn me. Don't think about trying."

I give a bitter laugh. "I tell you that I *need* to be able to trust you, and you react by threatening me again? You're such an asshole and you do it so well that you must have been perfecting this skill your entire life. Congratulations. You are the ultimate superior ass." I try to walk around him but he catches my arm, and heat rocks through me, over my shoulder to do a slow spread across my chest. I can't breathe with the impact, with the realization that this wicked hot connection between me and this man defies the hate and distrust between us.

He pulls me in front of him, and he doesn't let go of me, his long fingers wrapping around my arm, his gaze raking over my face. "If you burn me," he says, his voice low, hard, "it burns you. I'm the best asset you have."

"And I'm the best you have, or I wouldn't be here," I counter. "You kept me for a reason. To make money."

His lips twitch ever-so-slightly. God, I hate how easily I remember those lips on my lips. "I kept you for many reasons, Carrie," he says, his voice low, seductive, "but yes. Money was one of them. Did you call your father and your brother?"

"No. I did not."

"Why?"

"My father hasn't returned my calls in twenty-four hours and I haven't spoken to my brother in two years."

"Why two years?" he demands.

"Not that it's your business, but if you must know, even a sister can only take so much. I hit a wall."

His expression doesn't change but there is a sharp punch of tension that radiates off of him. "If you lie to me, I'll know."

I snap and grab his lapel. "Stop threatening me, and let me be clear, I'm working with you, Reid, and I'm doing so when you burned my family. I might not be cutthroat. I might not be devious, but I am smart. *I am* the woman who cuffed you and left you in a hotel room. In other words, I need to trust you, damn it. Be honest with me, Reid, even if it's not what I want to hear. If you lie to me, I promise, I *will* fight back."

His hands come down on my arms. "What will you do to me, Carrie?"

"It depends on what you to do me," I say, and the air shifts, a whip of heat flaming around us and I'm suddenly not sure we're talking about work anymore.

"A sin for a sin," he says softly. "I can live with that if you can." His gaze lowers to my mouth, lingering, and I know he's thinking about kissing me and Lord help me I want him to. I hate this man, and yet I want his mouth and his hands on my body.

"What do you want from me, Carrie?" he asks softly.

"I told you what I want. Honesty."

"Then you want to know what I'm thinking right this minute?"

"Yes," I dare. "I do."

"I'm thinking, that until I'm finally—"

My phone buzzes and Sallie announces, "Your father is on the line. He says you aren't answering your cellphone."

My body wants to scream at the timing and Reid's jaw hardens a second before he sets me away from him. "Come to my office when you're done and tell your father it's really fucking cozy." He turns and walks out.

I blink, shocked at his reaction that I need to understand. That I can only assume he believes my father will make me understand and this does not please him. "Carrie?" Sallie asks.

"Put him through," I say, rushing around my desk to grab the receiver, aware the call is likely being recorded. "Hello," I say, preparing to manage this call with extreme caution.

"Hey, honey. I—" The line crackles. "Horrible service." There is more static. "Working the Montana land deal I told you about," More static. He curses. "You okay?"

"Yes. Yes, but—"

"Good. Did you—" The line crackles. "Oh hell," he murmurs. "I'll try later, honey. I'll call back soon. In case you can hear this, I'm in Montana. The land deal looks good. Our new future. Poor service. More soon."

Frustrated and uncertain about a new firm that starts with a land deal in Montana, I set down the receiver in the cradle, and decide I'll get my answers from Reid. Just not now. Not when I have half an hour until I talk to the staff. I glance at my cellphone, which shows no call from my father. I don't think he even tried to call before now. Frustrated, I snatch the folder I've prepared for Reid and round my desk, wasting no time exiting my office and making my way to his. I start to open the file again, but I can't fight with him right before the meeting.

I knock. He actually opens the door and before I know his intent, he drags me into the office, shuts us inside, and presses me against the door, his big body once again crowding mine. His hands are on either side of me.

"Stop shoving me against doors and walls. I'm not your property."

"And yet you are."

"Don't go there, Reid," I warn.

"I already did. And you are *mine*. I own you. I know it and you know it. The question becomes, do you accept it or did your father convince you to run?"

"As I remember it, you're the one who got owned. That's what's going on. I owned you and now you have to own me."

"You're pushing me, Carrie. Are you sure you really want to go where that leads?"

"I'm pushing back and you aren't used to it because you live to intimidate."

"What did your father say to you?"

"We were disconnected. He's in Montana trying to get in on some land development project. And what do you think he's going to say when I do talk to him? He'll say Reid Maxwell's an asshole who's stealing his company. He'll want me out, but I'm not getting out because I need the money, love the company, and apparently, I'm also a glutton for your punishment." I shove the folder at him. "I did up a speech for you to approve."

"My approval?" he asks, but he doesn't reach for the folder. "Now you want my approval?"

"Yes, Reid." I yank the folder back. "I did. I do. I want the company back. That means I win with you. I get that. I spent all day thinking about that. It's why I almost called you today. To tell you that I really am with you. Either give me a real chance or let me go to start fresh. It's your turn. Can or can't with me?"

"That's a loaded question right now," he says. "One we don't have time for me to answer properly, but I will and soon." His gaze lowers to my mouth and lifts. "You can count on it." And in that moment, his stare is hot simmering coals and pure unbridled lust, a cage of heat erupting around me that I cannot escape. I'm suffocating in the connection I have with this man until finally, he grabs the folder. "Come sit down." He walks toward the desk, and the air is instantly thinner, my lungs filling easily.

Reid claims his seat behind his desk and motions to the visitor's chair.

"I can't sit," I say, crossing to stand behind the chair he's indicated, my hands settling at the back. "And it's not a power play thing. I'm not looking forward to this meeting. Can you please just read the speech and tell me if it works, at least in premise, as a launching pad to start the conversation with the staff? If not, I need to know ideas."

He studies me several beats, his expression unreadable, before he opens the folder, reads a full minute by my estimate, and looks up at me. "You listed every reason us working together works and it's spot on."

"I told you. I thought a lot about this today. I'm in, so can you please not be such an ass to me until after this meeting? I know this is just a conquest to you, and I'm the woman who cuffed you and left you in a hotel room, but this is my life, and this is not easy for me."

He's staring at me again with that unreadable look, seconds passing like hours in which we both know that since I entered this office, I allowed myself to be vulnerable with him. I admitted that I need and want to be here, because that's what I want to hear from those who work with me. I feel it's what he needed to hear.

He stands and walks around the desk to join me, and when I turn to face him, I find him close again. He is always so damn close. Power and arrogance radiate from this man, pieces of a puzzle that he is, and I can't begin to understand. "If you're with me," he says, "I'm with you, Carrie. That's how this works. I have every reason to make that clear in this meeting. Let's go get it behind us."

It's not the pushback I expect, and I don't even know how to respond. I simply nod and when I would turn away, he catches my waist, more heat radiating up my arm. He pulls me a little closer, so near that I could lean into his hard body. "There's nothing wrong with being a conquest if it feels good, and you *did* feel good." He releases me and motions me forward.

Stunned, I grab his lapels again. "Did you just suggest that I was your conquest in that hotel room?"

"Right up until the moment you cuffed me and left."

"Which made you my conquest."

"And yet," he says, "not only do I still remember how you taste, you're standing in front of me now. I'm not sure how that makes me the loser." He grabs my shoulders and turns me, placing me in front of him, his hands on my shoulders, and his lips at my ear. "We are not enemies, Carrie West," he says softly. "Go into this meeting knowing that in *all things*, we want the same things."

There is a seductive gentleness to his words that I do not know as this man. I want to turn and search his face, to know I've not imagined it, but I have this sense that he's turned me away from him for that very reason, to ensure that I cannot see him and read him. I am now certain that there is so much more to this man than meets the eye. I am also certain that he's right again. He does own me, and you do not want to be owned by a man like Reid Maxwell anywhere but in bed.

CHAPTER TEN

Reid

Carrie walks toward the door, and holy hell, I'm obsessed with this woman's ass in that pink dress. I'm obsessed with everything about her; the sweet way she smells, those emerald green eyes, and my absolute fucking need to be inside her. All acceptable and expected after our half fuck that needs to be finished, because the obsession will end once we finally do fuck. What isn't acceptable is the way I'd actually wanted to pull her to me and promise her everything was going to work out. I don't comfort people. I don't do tender and gentle, nor do those things help Carrie. She has to swim with the sharks, and that means people like me, to claim this company and the job she otherwise deserves.

I follow her to the door and I'm just behind her when she exits, stepping to her side in time for my brother—impeccably dressed in a blue pinstriped suit, to saunter in our direction. "We need to tighten security," I say, and not quietly.

Gabe laughs. "True. They let you in." He stops in front of us and gives Carrie a warm stare. "You must be Carrie West. I remember you from the auction. You looked stunning then and now."

"Thank you," she says.

"I'm Gabe, Reid's brother. I'm only here to show added support in the meeting, without any planned participation, but if you need anything, I'm at your service." He winks. "Reid and I do the good cop, bad cop routine well. I'm always the bad cop, as I'm sure you can tell."

She laughs, a soft sweet laugh that has my cock twitching and my anger at Gabe for being so damn charming, spiking. "Obviously," she replies, casting me a teasing look. "I can't imagine why anyone would see Reid as the bad cop." She scrapes her teeth on her lips, amusement dancing in her eyes, and I know she's thinking about those damn cuffs. And so am I.

Sallie rushes toward us. "Everyone is accounted for. We're ready when you are."

Carrie sucks in air, a nervous reaction that wipes away her smile and I answer for her. "We're on our way," I say, lifting a hand.

Carrie turns to me. "You didn't tell me what you're going to say."

I glance at Gabe, who nods and walks away. I step closer to Carrie and lower my voice. "I'll follow your lead."

"You'll follow my lead? We both know that isn't how this goes." She grabs my arm and closes one of the two steps left between us, the unexpected contact, along with those fierce green eyes locked on mine, tightening every muscle in my body. "Do *not* embarrass me in there. I'm sorry about the cuffs, okay? But that was private. Punish me in private. This is—"

"If I want to punish you," I say, wrapping my fingers around her arm and maneuvering us so that my back is to the door, blocking Carrie from prying eyes, "it will be in private and that pretty little backside of yours will be mine."

Her beautiful green eyes flash with defiance. "You will *never* own my backside, whatever that even means."

"Words that would mean so much more if I hadn't already licked your—"

She points at me. "Don't even say what you were going to say," she hisses, and it's all I can do to not tangle my fingers in her hair and drag her mouth to mine before I demand, "What are you thinking right now?"

"That *you're* making me crazy."

"Then maybe I should amend my prior statement. Maybe you *do* need to think about me between your legs, instead of creating a problem that doesn't exist. Yes, you left me in that hotel room, Carrie, and by doing so, you denied us both what we wanted in the name of misplaced revenge, but right now isn't about that. Right now, we're walking into that meeting and it's about making money together. I'm not going to hurt your ability to make that money. We are not enemies."

"You're just an asshole?"

"Yes. It works for me. And since you cuffed me and brought me here, you need to make it work for you. Let's go do this." I step back and to the side. She inhales and steps forward and I fall into step with her.

We arrive at the glass doors that separate the executive offices from the rest and I reach for the door but pause to glance over at Carrie. "Your father's failure will be seen as yours. Standing with me outside your father's circle to better your financial resources means job security to your staff. That's what we want to give them tonight before the stockholders' meeting goes public."

"I know. I put all of that in the copy I gave you."

"You included everything but a direct statement about your father's failure. That will be discussed in the stockholders' meeting. If you don't address that elephant in the room, they'll whisper about it later."

"Right," she says again cutting her gaze but immediately meeting my stare again. "He did fail. I don't understand why he made those decisions. I don't know how to explain that to the staff."

"Don't. Keep it simple. Mistakes were made. We're going to make up the hit for those mistakes delivered in triplicate."

"Right. I understand."

I study her a moment, and I find steel in her jaw that settles in her eyes. Satisfied, I open the door and allow her to exit first because I might be an ass by design, but my mother taught me to open a damn door for a woman. It was *another* woman that taught me never to get close to anyone. It's not a lesson Carrie West is going to make me forget.

Carrie

Reid walks beside me toward the meeting room, radiating confidence, power, and sex. He's an animal, a wolf on the hunt, willing to kill, no hesitation in him. These things and this man affect me. I can't pretend it's not true and survive. I am aware of Reid Maxwell in every fiber of my being, this man I hate and also crave.

This man who could walk in front of my staff and destroy me and yet, I never even considered that option until right before we were entering the meeting. He's the man that orchestrated a hostile takeover of my family business. I should have considered that. I'm crazy to want him. I'm crazy to trust him. I don't trust him. I can't, and the closer we get to the meeting room doors, the more I doubt his promise that he isn't working against me. Actually, he didn't promise at all.

Lifting my hand, I indicate our destination to Reid without looking at him, not about to risk him reading me. I want this over with one way or the other, and when I would just enter the room, Reid catches my arm, heat radiating over my body with the contact. He leans close, his mouth near my ear. "I am not your enemy," he says softly as if he's read my thoughts, as if he knows I expect the worst of him.

I glance up at him, my eyes daring to meet his piercing blue stare. "We'll see inside, won't we?"

"Yes," he says. "We will." His hold on my arm loosens but I have this feeling that he doesn't want to let me go, and it's a feeling that I don't understand. That stirs a funny feeling in my chest, that I don't want to feel with this man.

I shake off the sensation and enter the room, where fifty-seven people in rows of chairs wait. A room where Reid and I either stand together or apart. We reach the front of the room and I begin to talk. I introduce Reid and he nods. He takes the microphone from me after that introduction. "I just want to be clear," he says, which I'm coming to know as one of his signature statements. "I'm behind the scenes helping Carrie navigate a ship with a hole. She's captain. Everything goes through her."

One of the tech guys says, "But you're CEO?"

Reid gives him a deadpan stare and then says, "That is what we said," and hands me back the microphone.

It's not long after that when I send everyone home and Reid huddles up with me. "I'm not your enemy. I'll be in my office with Gabe when you get done here."

"Not tonight," I say.

His lips twitch but he says nothing more. He just turns and leaves.

Sallie steps to my side. "He's such an arrogant piece of perfection." She glances over at me. "How's that working for you?"

Too well and very badly, I think. I'm about as naked as a girl can get with a man.

It's a good forty-five minutes before I clear the building and make my way back to the executive offices. My father's office door—no, *Reid's* office door, is open. I walk that direction and I've just reached the edge of the door when I hear Gabe say, "Let's talk about Carrie."

I freeze in my footsteps and suck in a breath. "Let's not talk about Carrie," Reid replies.

"Then we won't talk about her, but in the interest of full disclosure, I'm going to show her some extra moral support."

"Stay away from her," Reid says brusquely. "And I mean, stay *the fuck* away from her."

I'm stunned by how intense his reaction is while Gabe simply laughs. "Easy, brother. I'm not going to distract her. I know how much money is on the line."

Right, I think. I'm money to Reid. Just money. And of course, he wants to sleep with me, but that's a conquest thing. An unfinished thing.

"Hear me and hear me well, Gabe," Reid states tightly. "You will not offer her anything but your professional services, which will come through me. Now, either move on to the next case we need to review or leave."

Leave?

Crap. If he leaves, I'm busted listening in and about me of all things, though one could argue I have a right. I inhale and decide I can't even consider rushing away. I could get busted. I have to charge forward. I straighten my spine and march toward the office, appearing in the doorway, and I am instantly blasted by the force of Reid's stare. As if he expected me. As if he knew I was there all along.

"Carrie," he greets, and I'm aware of Gabe turning his attention on me but I only see Reid.

"Everyone's gone," I say. "The coast is clear when you decide to leave. You won't be accosted."

He arches a brow, and I can feel my cheeks heat. He's thinking about the cuffs. Or I'm thinking about the cuffs.

"And where will you be when I leave?" he asks.

"Most likely in my office working." I glance at Gabe to find him watching me with a cunning stare and intelligent eyes, certainly sensing this push and pull between me and Reid.

"You did good in there tonight."

"Thank you," I say, "but we'll see how true that is based on how they all handle tomorrow." I glance between them but damn it, I'm pulled into Reid's magnetic stare again. "I'll leave you two to work."

"I'll walk with you," Gabe offers.

"No, you won't," Reid states, giving Gabe a hard look before his eyes find mine. "Go back to your office, Carrie." It's an order and in his stare there is possessiveness, intense, fierce possessiveness. It overwhelms me. It consumes me.

And this time I take his command for two reasons: a) I'm suffocating in all that is this man, and b) I have no desire to start trouble between him and Gabe, which is where I believe this could lead. Someone else might see that as an opportunity, but I do not. I don't wish that sibling divide I have with my brother on them. I, in fact, envy that they work together and obviously well.

I nod at him and then at Gabe and exit the office. They are silent in my departure, no doubt by intent, and I cross the lobby quickly entering my office to sit down. Reid was possessive, and Lord help me, on a pure female level I know what it's like to be touched by that man like he owns me. My body says, oh yes, more, but my mind warns me to tread cautiously, to set boundaries.

I grab my phone and send Reid a text message: In case you think me taking that order means you now own me, you do not. It means I have more manners than you.

His reply is instant and yet another command: Don't leave without me. I have something for you.

Damn him, I could assume that means about ten things, including his mouth on my body, and he knows it. He means to make me squirm and it worked.

CHAPTER ELEVEN

Carrie

An hour after Reid's text telling me he has something for me, I'm sitting at my desk when Gabe appears in the doorway, looking as devastatingly handsome as his brother, with one variance: he actually smiles. No, two differences. I don't think Gabe hates me. I should want *him*, not Reid, but that's just now how I work, apparently. Instead I want the man who tortures me, taunts me, and in general, infuriates me. "You really were amazing in that meeting tonight," he says.

"Thank you," I say. "I appreciate that. I was—am, actually—concerned about how the staff will handle all of this."

"You'll get them through it," he assures me. "And I also meant it when I said you can come to me if you need anything. However," he pauses for impact, "it's clear that would not please my brother."

"That was pretty evident," I say and cringe even as his eyes light.

"Then you did hear our conversation," he concludes.

"Does he know?"

"Not unless you tell him like you just did me and from what I can tell, you hold your own with him." He winks. "Goodnight." He disappears around the corner, leaving me smiling with that comment over any other. I *do* hold my own. I cuffed the man and left him.

Reid appears in my doorway and he all but scowls at my smile. "I take it you like my brother."

"He doesn't seem quite as obnoxious as you," I comment. "I do, however, prefer you over him at this point."

"Do you now?"

"Yes, I do, because while I'd never let my guard down with either of you," I say, despite being a little guilty of that with Gabe just now, "I prefer the brother that is what he is, without taking any prisoners."

"You think Gabe's a wolf in sheep's clothing," he states.

"I know he is," I assure him.

"And that makes me what?"

"A wolf in handcuffs."

He gives me a deadpan stare. I laugh. "That was funny," I say. "You know it was. You opened yourself up for it. You wouldn't even respect me if I didn't take the opening."

His lips quirk with a hint of what might be a smile. "Let's leave for the night. I'll walk down with you."

That gets my attention and my rejection. I do not want to be in an elevator with this man simply because I want to be in an elevator with this man. "I'm going to stay."

"No," he says. "You're going to walk down with me."

"Back to bossing me around?"

His eyes burn into mine. "I'm not leaving without you, Carrie." He says my name in a low, seductive way, a hint of the same burn in his eyes as in his tone.

"You're ridiculously overbearing," I comment dryly.

"Don't you want to know what I have for you?"

"I feel quite certain that question is a trap."

"It's an invitation. To leave with me now."

To leave with him now.

And go where?

And do what?

My gaze meets his and the air around us thickens, the charge between us palpable. I want this man and he wants me. I don't know how I do that and work with him, which means I can't sleep with him. I am, however, not getting out of the elevator ride, nor am I going to try. I'm not going to sleep with him and this is my chance to show us both that my willpower is steel. I grab my MacBook and several folders, sliding them into my briefcase before sliding it and my purse over my shoulder. "I'm ready," I announce, and I swear I feel like I just said something naughty. I can't put it back in my mouth and I don't even try to talk over it.

I round the desk and walk toward him, but he doesn't back out of my doorway and I can't just back-up or stop without seeming scared or intimidated. I keep walking and end up stopping a foot in front of him. "I thought we were leaving?"

He just stands there, big, beautiful, and all power and control; a man who I am certain in this moment wants to control me, to own me. Oddly though, I'm not sure this pleases him. I search his face and...no. No, I do not believe it does and yet, it's there. His need to do just that. It radiates off him, a hard push that all but demands I submit, and I am suddenly warm all over. I want to be owned by this man, but in that wholly female, while we are naked kind of way, that ends when I put my clothes back on. Only it won't with Reid. I know this. That will be the price for my pleasure. He'll own all of me.

That's not going to happen.

I lift my chin, letting him see this decision in my eyes, and he must. He abruptly steps backward as if he senses or reads my limits, as if he actually cares what I feel. I would like to think that he does. I want to believe he has that capacity in him. Or maybe his need to reject me wins over his need for a conquest. I dislike this thought too much and shove it aside. I join him in the lobby, falling into step with him as we walk toward the door. He holds it for me, and I pass through, aware of him watching my every move.

We start walking again, and the silence between us is not comfortable. It's heavy, it's filled with the push and pull between us, with his charged energy doing both right now. All I can think of is the tiny elevator car, and that moment arrives when I step into the compartment with just him, and my heart is thundering in my ears. Reid punches the lobby level and we stand side by side, his energy filling the tiny space, while his earthy male scent teases my nostrils.

"Gabe was right," he says.

Surprised by this comment I do not expect, I dare to look at him. "About what?"

"You handled the room well tonight."

When Gabe had complimented me, it had felt nice, but from Reid, it's unexpected. It's different. It stirs a funny feeling in my belly that I want to reject but instead hold onto, pull close. "And you," I say, considering him, "gave me room to do it."

"I told you, Carrie." He turns to face me, compelling me to do the same, as he adds, "I'm not your enemy."

"I'm trying to believe that."

"As I am of you," he says.

"Why would you think that I'm your enemy?"

"Our first meeting wasn't exactly friendly once we got past the orgasm."

"No," I say, hating the memory of his tongue on my clit now in my mind. "I suppose it wasn't."

"Then you know why I might be concerned that you're an enemy. We need to learn to trust each other."

"How?" I dare to ask, when he may well deliver one of his crass comments in reply.

"How indeed," he says, but the elevator dings before I can object to that non-answer, and he's already holding the door for me. I walk past him and he is immediately on my heels, the two of us walking toward the exit with him doing nothing to make good on his claim to have something to show me. We step outside and he motions to the right, my normal evening path toward Battery Park.

"I'll walk you home," he says.

"I'm fine," I say. "I walk home every night by myself and," I frown, "how do you know where I live?" I hold up a hand. "Never mind. We already determined that you had me investigated."

"That, and I too live in Battery Park."

I blanch. "How is that even possible?"

"Exactly what I said when you left me in that hotel room."

My eyes go wide. "Did you, Reid Maxwell, actually just make a joke and at your own expense?"

"Never. I don't tell jokes." He motions me forward. "Let's walk."

But he did. This hard-as-stone man made a joke with himself as the punchline. This tiny glimpse of the man beneath all the hardness has me curious enough to happily comply. I turn and start walking and Reid is easily by my side, keeping pace. "Not that I'm trying to get rid of you or anything like that," I say after a few steps, "but isn't it hard on your firm for you to be away like this?"

"Gabe runs the firm day-to-day," he says. "And I make a hell of a lot more money doing what I do instead of managing a regular caseload."

"How did you even start doing this kind of thing? It's not exactly standard corporate lawyering."

"When I was still fresh out of law school my father managed corporate takeovers for Jean Claude Laurette."

"The billionaire behind some of the biggest hostile takeovers ever done, and who is also a real estate developer?"

"Exactly, and no, he's not involved with your company."

My company. I like that he says this.

"I handled a great deal of the legal filings for my father in relation to his affairs, and it slowly morphed into more."

"So, you're more corporate raider than attorney?"

"My father's the corporate raider, or he was until he had a stroke last year and finally decided to slow down."

"He's okay now?"

"As okay as a bastard like my father can ever be," he says dryly.

I decide to leave that alone for fear he'll stop talking, and I focus on him. "If you're not a corporate raider, what are you?"

"Where my father would look for the big win at all costs, as would Jean Claude, I'm in the position now to pick or choose my moves. I work with a group of investors that home in on companies where everyone is losing, and we then ensure everyone wins."

"Except my father."

He glances over at me as we step on the sidewalk that leads to my building. "I can't save your father from his mistakes. I can only save everyone else."

Despite the truth of his words, they cut, and I look away, thankful that we are now in front of my building. I turn to face him. "Good luck with the stockholders' meeting," I say, the wind lifting off the nearby ocean, the Statue of Liberty alight in the near distance.

"I don't need luck. I need to be good on my word." He changes the subject. "You heard the conversation between myself and my brother."

It's not a question and I don't play coy. "Yes."

"Then you heard me tell him to stay away from you."

"Loud and clear," I assure him.

He arches a brow. "You aren't going to ask why?"

"You want to own me," I say. "Which means I know why."

His hand snakes out and snags my hip, jolting me with the unexpected impact as he drags me to him. "I do own you," he says. "Until the profit I've promised the board is delivered, I don't want you distracted."

My hand is somehow now firmly planted on his even firmer chest; my legs pressed intimately to his. "And you don't think touching me like this a distraction?" I challenge.

"It is a distraction. One we can fuck right out of our systems and then it's over."

"Or you decide you really do own me and I'm not taking that risk."

"Better safe than sorry, right?"

"Better stop while you're ahead."

"And yet neither of us are ahead now." He surprises me by allowing his hands to fall away, a silent invitation to stay pressed intimately to his hard, perfect body, or move away.

It takes all that I am, but I step backward. I've barely recovered from his touch and the chill I now feel blasting off the water, which didn't seem to be there moments ago, when he offers me an envelope. "What is this?" I ask, reaching for his offering, but he holds onto it, those blue eyes burning into mine.

"I never make a promise I don't keep, good or bad." He releases his grip. "Remember that," he adds, and then he just walks away.

CHAPTER TWELVE

Carrie

The envelope in my hand scorches me the way the man who handed it to me does as well.

I watch Reid disappear around the corner, the path between my apartment and his, a well-frequented community area that runs along the beach, lined with buildings, most of which have outdoor restaurants, and all of which offer ocean views. I will not open this envelope where I might be seen. Therefore, only when Reid is out of sight do I rush into the building and make my way to the elevator, punching my floor. Once the doors shut, I stare down at the envelope, but I don't open it. I dread opening it and while I'm not one to avoid or hide from trouble, the biggest, cruelest way, Reid could punish me for those cuffs would be to build me up and then push me right back down. To give what he'd taken and then take it away. I don't want to believe that's who he is, but he learned from Jean Claude Laurette a man nicknamed "The Beast of Wall Street."

And so, I watch the floors tick by, which is quick since I live on the third floor and for a reason. It was cheaper. It's what my first three bonus checks with the company allowed me to buy and three seemed a lucky combination. I thought it was and yet I've now put my place up for sale. Just the thought knots my belly, but it's the right move. It's what I need to do before I get in over my head.

The elevator dings and it's only seconds later when I exit the car, walking left and sticking my key into the lock of my first home purchase, wondering if I will ever feel secure enough to buy in a building in Battery Park ever again. Shoving aside that negativity, I enter my little place, its dark hardwoods beneath my feet, and toss my keys on the table to my right. I walk down the hallway and through my living room without dwelling on the three oval windows that line the front wall that I completely adore, and the realtor assures me will help the place sell quickly, even despite the fact that my view is of the walkway, rather than the water, and the apartment is small with a rather compact kitchen to my left. It's a beautiful space and location.

I head up the stairs and into my bedroom, the only other room in the apartment, and set my purse on the teal-covered bed. I then walk to the lounge chair in the same color, which is by a drape-covered window, kick off my shoes, and stare at the envelope with dread in my belly. It's possible that Reid wanted me to say good things about him to the staff before he gave me my walking papers. I know this, though I don't think that's something Reid would do in such a cowardly way. He's hard, arrogant, and impossible, but not a coward. I seem to be, though, since I haven't opened the stupid thing.

I rip the seal and quickly scan the document inside. It's a promise to double my pay at the six-month mark from the date of the takeover, in a lump sum. Part of me revels in this promise he has kept. The other part fears that he knows my demise will eventually be confirmed. Of course, this idea assumes he has a heart. Does he? I go back to the case he took for free, for the families of murder victims and the word "save." He chooses takeovers that save everyone involved. If he does have a beating heart in his chest, is this payment his way of ensuring I leave with more, not less, but I still leave?

My stomach knots all over. I need to know. Straight up. Head on. Tell me how it is. I stand up and walk to the bed, grab my phone and return to the chair where I snuggle back down, ready to take whatever is thrown my way. I don't hesitate. I dial Reid. "Decide you want to be owned tonight?" he asks, answering on the first ring.

"Reid," I say softly, skipping all the games.

He knows what I want immediately. "It's a testament to my confidence in you," he promises. "Don't read more into it. I say what I mean. I do what I say."

"But the board doesn't believe in me."

"They will," he says.

"That's a no. They do not."

"Did you find the card inside the envelope?"

"I didn't see it. Hold on." I dig for it and find his business card. I flip it over to find the words: *Call-in number, stockholders' meeting, nine am.* "You're letting me listen in on the meeting in real time?"

"Yes. I am. It won't be easy to hear what is said about your father."

"I'm not in denial over my father," I say. "I can handle it." I soften my voice. "Thank you, Reid."

He's silent several beats and I almost think he's hung up when he speaks. "The case I'm managing, with the murder victims' families. The brother of one of the victims attacked my client's wife. He was under mental evaluation. We were supposed to be told before he was released. We weren't, and he went after her again."

"Oh God. Is she okay?"

"Yes, but I'm going to need to deal with this after the stockholders' meeting tomorrow."

"What are you going to do?"

"Take a piece of the DA's ass. I think he did this on purpose, just to show us who has control, and it backfired when the guy came back at my client."

"But you're not a good guy taking care of people who need you for free, right?" I tease.

His response is hard and fast. "No, *Carrie*. I am *not* a good guy. Don't forget that either." He hangs up. It's a real Reid move. I get it. He doesn't want a thank you and me looking beneath his skin. He doesn't even care about me and his brother. He just doesn't want me distracted. In fact, his need to own me and my focus is probably why he gave me that money. Now I don't have to worry about finding another job, in case this one ends. In other words, this is his way of reminding me that he might want to fuck me, he might need me for financial reasons, but he doesn't really like me, and he doesn't even want me to like him.

I wake up the next morning in a ball of nerves over the stockholders' meeting. I run five miles in the park and still manage to be at work an hour before the rest of the staff and dressed in a red power statement suit dress. I even have time to pick up scones and set one on Sallie's desk with a note on the bag that reads: *Now you have to make me some of your butterscotch cookies,* because I love those cookies and because she loves that I love them. By eight-forty, I'm well caffeinated and nervous about the stockholders' meeting.

Sallie buzzes my office. "Connie is on the line. She's Reid's secretary. And FYI, she is setup with security clearance."

"Great, thanks."

The line buzzes and I answer. "Hi, Connie."

"Hi, Carrie. Looking forward to meeting you soon."

"I thought you were coming here today?"

"Reid meant after the stockholders' meeting, which we're hosting, which I know because I have learned to decode his meanings over the past ten years. So that most likely means tomorrow. Aside from that, I just wanted to tell you that if you have any trouble dialing into the meeting, call me. Sallie has all my contact numbers."

"Oh. Great. Thank you."

"Thank you. There is a novel combination of words. Perhaps together we can teach them to Reid. No. Never mind. We'll just get drunk together at some point." Reid's voice sounds in the background. "Speaking of the beast. Gotta go. Bye, Carrie." She hangs up.

I like her. I like her a lot. Sallie pokes her head in the door, giving me a thumbs-up that means she likes her, too. And she's been with cranky, mean Reid for ten years? I shove aside that thought for later reference and ten minutes later I dial into the meeting, though no one in the room knows who is on the closed line.

Reid calls the meeting to order and he cuts right to the chase. "As you all know at this point, I'm now partnering with Carrie West to reach our profit projections."

Partnering.

It's not a word I expect him to use.

There are several questions about me that follow and Reid shuts them down. "I don't waste my time or money, or yours. Carrie is not her father. She was against the bad decisions that were made, which are documented in each case. She's CEO material: smart, sharp, embraced by the staff and the backbone of the profits for the corporation. I expect to recommend a power shift from me to her in the next thirty days."

There's debate and talk of that timeline being too fast, but Reid is strong in each turn that is taken. Once they get past talking about me, the talks turn to financials, future projects, strategies, overhead, and the list goes on. I take detailed notes on my open computer. During lags in the meat of the meeting, I type out my rebuttals to each question, comment and statement I feel deserves them.

It's a full two hours later when the meeting ends and I resist the urge to text a thank you to Reid. He made it clear last night that he doesn't want that from me. Instead, I quickly finish typing my notes and email them to Reid, when my cellphone rings with Reid's number.

"Hello," I answer quickly.

"Get me answers to every question in that meeting," he says without preamble. "I need your point-of-view to compare to mine before I head into a lunch meeting."

"Already in your mail."

"I need *details*, Carrie."

"I typed as I listened and perfected when I was done. You *have* what you need."

He's silent two beats. "I'll be into the office by five. Plan for a later night." He hangs up in full asshole mode again, which worries me.

Just how much pressure is he getting outside the boardroom and on what? Me? Is that why he wants my notes? Are the board members rejecting me even as I sit here and push Reid to the point of no return? I think of exactly what that man wants me to think about; him between my legs. And from there, I can almost feel his big body crowding me against his door or some wall. He keeps touching me. He keeps pushing every female button I possess. And maybe that's the point. It's not the board that's the real issue. It's Reid who wants to push me to the point of no return, but to what end?

CHAPTER THIRTEEN

Carrie

I don't hear from Reid for the rest of the day, but right before I expect him to arrive, Sallie pokes her head into my office. "I'm about to leave, but your father is on the line."

"Put him through and I'll see you tomorrow."

"I'm bringing cookies," she says with a smile, then disappears, and I hope she brings a ton because I'm a really good stress eater.

The line buzzes, and dread fills my belly, which I shouldn't feel over my father's call, of all people, but I do. "Hey, dad," I answer.

"I just read the transcript from the stockholders' meeting," he says, without his normal preamble. "They're never going to accept you."

His words punch me in the chest. "Thanks for the confidence, dad."

"This isn't about you. That's the point. You don't deserve to get punched in the teeth because of me. I thought you were simply transitioning out."

"I thought I'd be walked out," I say. "Reid Maxwell decided otherwise, and he made it worth my while to stay."

"How worth your while?"

"Worth it," I say, hating that I don't want him to know the figure. "Enough to keep me from selling my apartment."

"Since when are you selling your apartment?"

"Since I don't know where I'm headed. At least this gives me more time to find out."

"Carrie, honey, this isn't going to go as you expect it to. Come here. Help me close this land deal."

No, I think, and it's the first time I've reacted this way to my father, which is a weakness. Maybe if I'd said no sooner, we wouldn't be in this mess. "Unless you have six figures to help me exit the company, I'm staying."

"You'll leave humiliated."

Those words punch me in the chest once more. "Did you really just say that? Do you really have that little confidence in me?"

"I told you, this isn't about you. I believe you can hold the world up, but it won't matter. You're a West."

"I'm my own person."

He's silent for several beats. "You don't understand what you're dealing with," he finally says.

"*Make* me understand."

"It's not something I want you involved with. That's the point." He makes a frustrated sound. "This isn't a conversation for the phone. Come here."

"I have a job."

"I love you, daughter, but this is not a good choice for you."

"It's the right choice. It's my only choice."

He's silent for several more heavy beats. "I hate that you feel this is your only choice. Call me if you need me." He hangs up and I have this sense that there is something he isn't telling me. Is that something that will lead to my humiliation? I dismiss that idea. My father would not leave me hanging out to dry. He wouldn't do it.

Reid

After a day of being hammered on by stockholders, the DA, and a laundry list of others, I'm still in my office, my *real* office, trying to pack up to leave for West Enterprises. I reach up and fight the urge to loosen the blue tie that matches the blue three-piece suit I chose for the stockholders' meeting. There's too much on the line for me to even begin to look anything but fresh and ready at all times. I'm about to stand up when my cellphone rings with the call I've been expecting all day: Carrie's father. "What happened to the debt between us?" he blasts through the line. "My daughter is to be left out of all of this."

"The contract states that your daughter was to be kept in the dark about the specifics of that debt."

"You're going to punish her, aren't you?"

I have a momentary fantasy of Carrie across my lap and that perfect ass naked beneath my palm. Yes, I'll punish her, but not in the way he's talking about. "I have no intention of making your daughter pay for your sins. Just you."

"If she finds out—"

"She won't find out. I don't break legally binding contracts. I won't tell her your secrets. Your poor decisions with West Enterprises are another thing."

"And there it is. The reason you kept her there. It's not enough to finally push me out of my company."

"That's not how this happened and we both know it, but if that's the narrative you need to deliver to look yourself in the mirror, so be it. You made your daughter believe it and that's the real problem, isn't it? You're afraid I don't have to tell her the truth. You're afraid she'll figure it out herself and she will." I think of the recent revelations I've made about my own father, and I bite out, "Don't make her find out herself."

I disconnect, aware that he'll encourage Carrie to leave, but I don't believe she will. She'll stay. She'll see her father for what he is and while that won't expose his true betrayal, maybe it will protect her from a future betrayal. Not that she's mine to protect. I scrub my jaw. So why the fuck am I?

My cellphone rings with a call from Royce Walker, the owner of Walker Security, and the company managing all things West Enterprises for me. By the time I hang up with him, I'm furious for about ten reasons. Number one, I was just provided critical security information that Carrie should have known and damn sure better know in the future. Number two, I can't stop thinking about her. The list goes on from there. I can't stop wanting her. I keep fucking defending her. I want to protect her. The best way to protect her is to push her. To make her protect herself, and the board, better than she is now.

It's after six when I enter the West offices, fully committed to pushing Carrie. She needs to be pushed. She needs to feel this pain, and I will make sure she damn sure learns from this. Sallie's desk is empty, giving me a clear path. I walk to Carrie's door, open it, and enter to find her on the phone, her perfect ivory skin flushing at the sight of me. "Yes, Joe," she says quickly on the phone. "It all sounds interesting, but I'll need to call you back. Yes. Thanks. Bye."

By the time she hangs up, I'm in front of her, my hands on her desk, and I'm staring into her stunned, emerald green eyes. "Joe Michaels, Rick Smith, and Kent Moore," I state. "They will not return tomorrow. Fire them." I push off the desk and walk toward the door.

"What's going on?" she demands.

I turn to look at her. "For once, prove you can do something I want without making me fight you on it." I turn and leave.

I exit her office and cross the expanse of the lobby before entering my temporary office and it *is* temporary. I've barely made it in the door before Carrie is behind me and I snap. I shut the door before she can, lock it, and shackle her wrist, pulling her to me. "Do not chase me down after I tell you to do something. Just fucking do what I say for once."

She grabs my tie and not gently, her voice a low rasp of anger. "I'm not calling three employees in here while you're in a temper tantrum without knowing why."

"If I wanted you to know it in advance," I bite out, "I'd tell you."

"Why am I firing them?" she demands. "They're all long-term employees."

"Who've been stealing from the company?"

She pales. "What does that mean?"

"It means prospect lists, proposals, and everything in between. You should have known. Your job—"

"I suggested cybersecurity and my father rejected it as an unnecessary expense. I didn't have control and you know it."

"Now you're just making excuses." I release her before I fuck her the way I want to fuck her, and walk away, taking up a spot at the window, giving her my back, telling her to leave. Telling her to get her ass to her office and do what I've told her to do, but I should know by now that's not Carrie.

"Now you're just going to extra efforts to be an ass," she says, her voice right behind me.

I rotate to find her close, so damn close that I could pull her right back to me and inhale that floral scent of hers perpetually scenting the air around her.

"Why, Reid?" she presses. "Because you think I see you a little too clearly? Because you think I saw something about you last night that you don't want me to know?"

"You see nothing I don't let you see."

"Liar," she accuses, the word a taunt on her tongue.

Worse, she's right, and I'm pissed all over again, more pissed than I've ever been, and it's all aimed at this woman. My hand snakes out and I catch her hip, dragging her to me, my fingers tangling into her hair.

"What are you doing, Reid?"

"What you wanted when you dared to charge over here and get in my face."

"I don't want—"

"Liar," I say, and I don't wait for her denial that will be another lie. "You know what I want?"

"To fuck me so you can try to control me? It won't work."

"I was thinking I'd like to shut you up for once and I know exactly how." My mouth closes down on hers.

CHAPTER FOURTEEN

Reid

I want this woman.

I want her in a bad way, and my tongue licks hungrily into her mouth even as I tighten my grip on her hair. Her hand is warm on my chest, but her elbow is stiff, her entire body is stiff, and I don't accept this from her. I want her submission. I want her to admit she wants like I want, so I deepen the kiss, my hand settling between her shoulder blades, molding her close.

She moans into my mouth, a sexy, aroused sound, but she still fights me. She still shoves weakly at my chest, and her eyes meet mine. "This is just—"

"Hate sex," I supply. "Works for me." My mouth slants over hers again, and this time, she doesn't hold back. She kisses me like she did in that hotel room, her hands sliding under my jacket, over my shirt, and I am hot and hard and ready to be inside her.

I reach up and skim her jacket off her shoulders, my mouth barely leaving hers. I cannot get enough of how she tastes, I damn sure can't get enough of how she feels, and my hands are all over her, caressing her breasts, my finger ripping away a button of her silk blouse.

"You owe me a button and alterations," she hisses, tugging at the buttons of my vest. "And I hate this thing."

I walk her backward and press her against the desk. "And I hate these damn buttons," I say, yanking two more off.

"Reid!"

I snap the front clasp of her bra free.

Her hands go to my arms and I pant out, "I'll buy you another."

"What are we doing, Reid? We work together. You're my—"

"Boss," I supply, cupping her backside and molding her closer. "*Yes*. I am. Start remembering it."

"I remember, and hate that fact, quite well."

"Like you hate me?" I challenge.

"Right now?" she says. "Yes."

I tangle my fingers in her hair again, dragging her mouth to mine, "Exactly why we need to fuck," I say, cupping her breast and pinching her nipple. "So we can both stop thinking about how much we want to be naked together." I kiss her again, swallowing another of her soft, sexy moans while yanking her skirt up her hips, over the lace of her black thigh-highs to her hips.

With that sweet little ass of hers finally bare to my touch, I palm it and squeeze. She yanks hard on my tie, and I have no idea how that makes me hotter and harder, but it does. She does. Every taste of her. Every sound she makes. Everything she does. "Can you just be inside me already?" she demands.

I could, I think. I should want to, but that question, that need in her to just do this and be beyond it and me, grates down my spine in an unexpected way. I don't like it. I turn her and press her to the desk, forcing her to catch herself on the smooth surface. Her ass is perfect, and that too should please me, but it pisses me off. I smack her backside and she yelps, looking over her shoulder.

"Did you really just—"

I yank the red silk of her panties, and the tiny strings rip under my tug. She gasps, and I step into her, smacking her backside again. "Yes," I say, my hand sliding around her, fingers cupping her sex, my lips by her ear. "I did, and," I stroke through the slick wet heat of her sex, "you liked it."

"I didn't—"

I turn her, and kiss her, my tongue doing a quick, deep slide before I demand, "What happened to trust? I can't trust you if you lie to me."

"I don't lie," she says, yanking at my tie again. "Maybe you just think I lie because that's all you know."

"And yet, I never deny anything that feels good the way you just did." I lift her and set her on the desk, spreading her legs and settling on my knees in front of her.

She tries to squeeze her legs together but it's too late. My hands catch her knees, opening her wide. Her eyes meet mine. "You want to pay me back, don't you? That's what this is?"

"You mean lick you until you almost come and then cuff you to the chair and leave you? I could. You wouldn't even stop me." I drag one of her legs over my shoulder, her hips shifting forward, and I lick her clit. "But I'm not going to pay you back," I say, the taste of her on my lips rocketing through my senses. "I want you to come on my tongue again."

"I don't believe you," she whispers, swallowing hard. "I want—"

"Finally, you say it. You want. *I want.*" I lick her again, and she tilts her head back, moaning softly, and that easily she's giving me that submission I want from her. Pushing her to give me more, I suckle her, stroking two fingers along the seam of her sex and then sliding them inside her. She arches her hips, lifting into my mouth, into the pump of my fingers and I love this about her. She's not shy about wanting. She might resist, but once she commits, she's all the way.

"Oh God," she cries out, and then her body is tensing, only seconds before she spasms around my fingers, her legs quaking, and I do own her in this moment. Fuck. I want to own this woman more and that pisses me off. This is a fuck. This is one fuck. I don't ease her into completion. I strip away my fingers and mouth and while she gasps, I shrug out of my jacket, remove my wallet, yank out a condom, and stand up.

Her eyes meet mine with a punch between us that I tell myself is just how badly we both need me to be inside her. That it could be anything else is why I grip her hair, and not gently, reminding her of who is in control. "Now I taste like you again," I say, "but I never forgot how you taste." I close my mouth over hers, a wicked hot kiss, that equals an explosion of lust between us.

I'm kissing her. She's kissing me. My hands are all over her, but hers are on me, too. Stroking my cock through my pants, her fingers driving me crazy. At some point, I rip open the condom and she isn't shy. She's the one that unzips me. She's the one who pulls my erection free, her soft hands stroking along my ridiculously hard length. It's her who puts on the condom and me that cups her backside, pulls her to the edge of the desk and then, when I should just drive into her, fuck her finally, here and now, I tease us both. I stroke my cock along her sex until she hisses, "Enough already. Or not enough. Reid, damn it, I—"

My mouth comes down on hers, my tongue wanting to taste my name on her lips while I press my cock inside her and drive deep, burying myself to the hilt. Our lips part and our foreheads press together, and suddenly we're breathing together, not moving. Why the hell am I not moving? And yet, I'm not. I'm savoring rather than devouring, and that's not what this is. This is sex, hard, ready now sex, and I pull back and thrust into her. She moans, and I drive again, pressing her backward, forcing her to hold onto the desk behind her, not me. But I don't let that become an escape. I'm right here, I'm kissing her. I'm licking her nipple. I'm pumping into her, and yet, it's not enough. I slide my hand between her shoulder blades and lift her off of the desk, holding all of her weight. Somehow we're just there, melded close, and breathing together again, and then kissing again, our bodies more grinding than pumping us into that sweet spot of release.

Carrie gasps and stiffens again, and the minute she begins to orgasm I'm right there with her, my body clenching with the force of my release. I hold her tighter and at some point, I set her back on the desk, gripping it on one side while my other palm remains between her shoulder blades. My face is buried in her neck, and I come back to reality to the feel of her fingers flexing on my shoulders. I want to kiss her again and that is not normal for me. I should pull out. I should end this as fast and hard as we just fucked, and move on, but I don't. What the hell is this woman doing to me? I linger there with her, her body soft and yielding next to mine. I inhale the floral scent of her, and I know, I *know* that I am not done with this woman.

That's a problem.

Fuck.

I pull out of her, lifting her off the desk and then I walk to the trashcan, dump the condom, and right my pants, pressing my hands on the desk when I'm done, letting my chin touch my chest. Pulling myself the hell together while she dresses. She isn't my enemy, but neither can we ever be more than sex. There are reasons, *too many* reasons, personal reasons of my own, that damn debt between our families, and I can't forget those reasons, ever. I won't now.

I lift my head to find her back to me as she finishes dressing. The minute she turns, I push off the desk and straighten. "Fire them. Don't let them back in the building and then go home."

Her eyes meet mine, emotions glistening in their depths that I can't read, and I want to read them when I should not. "Right," she says. "Fire them without proof. That makes me an excellent CEO candidate."

I could leave space between us, but I won't let my need for this woman, or this woman herself, hold me captive. I round the desk to stand in front of her. She doesn't move. She doesn't back away She won't let me intimidate her. "I'm always thorough," I say, "as I'm sure you've now figured out. Proof is already in your inbox."

She studies me and then says nothing before heading to the door, which for her feels like a problem. I catch her hand. "Don't even think about not coming back tomorrow."

She whirls to face me. "Right. Because you hold me captive. You hold my company captive, so yes, I'll be here, but consider that my last duty fuck."

My lips quirk and I know this reaction will piss her off, but I can't stop myself from pushing her, and for a reason. She's pushing me. She doesn't get to push me. She doesn't get to break my rules. "Right," I say dryly. "Duty *fuck*."

"You're such an asshole and I don't know why I—"

"—already want me inside you again? Or is it my tongue you already want again?"

"You're about two seconds from a knee in the part of you that was just inside me, and the irony of that placement would really amuse me right now. Let me go, Reid."

Her eyes gleam with anger on that command and just that easily, I'm hot and hard again. Exactly why I release her, but she doesn't run like another woman would. She stands her ground. She looks me in the eyes and claims her space and mine, and it's sexy as hell. I want her again, and in the seconds that tick by, a band of lust and anger hums around us, about to snap. She knows, too. Her chin lifts slightly, a silent "fuck you" before she turns and leaves.

The minute she's gone, I walk to the window, but I don't see the skyline before me. I think of that moment when I was on my knees between her legs. I *could* have denied her. I could have teased her and *then* denied her, but I didn't. I wanted her to remember how good I can make her feel. I wanted her to remember me making her come, not me fucking her in an office. I wanted her to want more when the idea of fucking her, was to end my damn obsession with being inside her. With everything about her.

I failed.

CHAPTER FIFTEEN

Carrie

I hate him.

I want him.

I *hate him* and the fact that as I walk into my office, my blouse gapes with my missing buttons. And I smell like him, all earthy and raw. I don't let myself think beyond hate because there is more, so much more, beneath my surface that I don't want to exist. I grab the sewing kit Sallie keeps in my drawer, which I would not have without her because she's everything I am not, which makes us a perfect pair. Reid and I are not perfect at anything but hate. Not even close. Nor is the repair work I do on my blouse with a safety pin, but at least, my breasts are no longer on display.

I pack my things and I head for the door. I'll deal with the terminations from home. I'm walking out of my office toward the lobby in two minutes. I want space between me and Reid, who I just had sex with. I'm a crazy person. I'm not fit to be CEO. I can't even keep my clothing in place. I step into the elevator, relieved when it shuts and Reid doesn't show up, but Lord help me, I'm disappointed, too. I don't want him to be an asshole. I'll analyze that later, much later. Once I'm in the lobby, I talk with security about the terminations and then I am gone.

I exit to the street, and I am incredulous at what an ass Reid really is. And I didn't like it when he smacked my ass. Not really. Not that much. Never again! I cross the street and enter the park area where Reid also lives. How is that even possible? How many times have we passed each other and not cared? I continue this line of thinking all the way to the front of the building where I notice the restaurant that I love has been shut down by the fire marshal. I don't even want to know what that means since it's almost directly under my apartment.

I step onto the elevator, deciding I should call and ask what happened, but then why? No matter what I told my father, I have to be smart. I'm not going to feel secure again anytime soon. I have to sell my place. I'm going to be gone soon. The ride is forever, and I manage to conjure an image of Reid between my legs. I know why he let me come. His ego is too damn big to risk me thinking he couldn't get the job done. I think I'll tell him that. I grab my phone to call him and thankfully the elevator dings me back to my senses. I stick my phone back in my purse.

Ten minutes later, I'm in my kitchen with my files spread over the top of the navy granite countertop with my computer open. I open my email and download the report Reid sent me and start reading. It's bad. I kick off my shoes and drag my fingers through my hair. I can't just fire these men. It's not enough. I glance at the name and number on the report: Royce Walker. I dial him.

"Royce Walker," he answers.

"Hi Royce," I say. "This is Carrie—"

"West, you got the report."

"Yes. Thank you so much for catching this. I need to go to the police. I need permission to use your data."

"I can handle it all for you. Reid said it was your call."

"You mean Reid was testing me to find out how I'd handle this? He's such an ass."

Royce chuckles. "Well perhaps, but he predicted you'd want to go to the police. I'm a former FBI agent and our team is a mix of law enforcement and special ops military. We're connected. We can deal with this so you don't have to. I can even fire them."

"Oh no. I want that pleasure. I just wish I would have found out in time to do it at the office today in person, but my question is this: Should I fire them? Or should I talk to the police first? Do we have enough to ensure they go down?"

"We have plenty to take them down. Let's just get rid of them."

"Okay." I'm silent for a few beats. "You investigated me."

"Yes. Something you want to know?"

"I know everything about me, so that's not necessary. Did you investigate my father?"

"Yes."

"Why did he take those deals?"

He's silent for a long moment. "You don't think it was bad judgment?"

"He's never had that kind of bad judgment. A few bad calls, yes, but this wasn't that. Why?"

"Even if I had an answer," he says, "and I don't, it would be a conflict of interest for me to tell you. I work for Reid."

"Can I hire you? I need to know why." *I need to know what's in Montana that made him rush there the minute he had my money*, I think, because this land deal feels off. "He didn't even stay and fight," I add.

"If Reid—"

"Never mind. I get it. You work for him. Thank you anyway. I have three men to fire. I'll text you when it's done. Goodnight."

"Carrie."

"Yes?"

"Talk to Reid."

"Talking is what we don't do together."

LISA RENEE JONES

"I'll talk to him. Text me." He hangs up.

I dial the first of the three thieves, and it's all quite easy. "You're fired. You know why." Those three words work all three times. Lucky threes. I text Royce: *It's done.* And with that, I'm a ball of nerves that has me changing into leggings and sneakers for a run, my way of calming my mind. I pop in my headphones, turn on a music mix, and head downstairs. Once I step out into the now inky night, the touristy crowd has thinned out and I make my way to the sidewalk, running along the ocean and all the buildings. I skip my stretches, which will give my mind time to get the best of me.

I take off running, cranking up my music, and still, I'm in my head. I'm back in Reid's office. I'm reliving every moment with him. I thought—God, what did I think? It was hate sex and nothing more, and yet when it was over, he didn't want to let me go. I felt it. I didn't want to let him go. And then he did, and I still don't know why I want him at all. I think more of myself than to sleep with a man that—

I run into someone and gasp as Reid catches my arms, and he too is in running clothes, sweats, and a T-shirt. "Are you stalking me now?" I demand. "Was investigating and fucking me not enough?"

"No," he says. "That's the problem. It's not." He's barely spoken the words and his hand is cupping my head, his mouth closing down on mine, his tongue licking against my tongue and I want to resist. No. I try to resist, but there is something about Reid. Something that calls to me even as he punishes me, tries to control me and generally treats me like shit. I want this man, and I can't stop the want. I sink into the kiss, and *he* moans, like he needs this as much as I do, his hand flattening between my shoulder blades, molding my chest to his.

112

I am lost in this man, how he feels, how he smells, every lick of his tongue and then suddenly, he's lacing his fingers with my fingers. "Come on," he says, stroking a hand over my hair and caressing my cheek.

I'm dazed by the gentle touch to the point that when he starts walking I follow, but a blast of ocean air has me blinking into reality, digging my heels in, and tugging against his hand. "Wait," I say, pulling him around to face me. "Where are we going?"

"My place."

His place.

Yes.

No.

"No," I say, rejecting how close I am to letting this man own me in all ways. "No. I'm not going to your place."

"Then we'll go to yours." He starts walking.

"No," I say, trying to dig in my heels again, but he keeps walking. "No!"

He rotates to face me and before I know his intent, he's kissing me again, and damn it, I want him to kiss me again. I don't resist. I melt into him. I kiss him back. And when he pulls back and strokes my hair again, he says, "We need to be alone."

My hand firms on his chest. "Alone is the last thing we need to be. I can't do this, Reid. I *won't* do this."

"It doesn't seem to me that either of us has a choice."

"You," I say, "have *many* choices, many of which involve me. I have two. Stay or go. And right now, I'm going."

"Let's go talk," he says. "Just talk."

"We won't talk. We'll fight or fuck, and neither of those things work in my favor. Let me go, Reid, or I swear to you I'll start screaming."

"We both know you won't do that." His eyes harden. "But if that's what you want, I'll let you go." He does. He lets me go and I should be pleased, but I'm not. I hate that he let go. I hate he didn't fight me on this as much as he fights me on everything else, but why would he? It's a fuck. He, no doubt, has a proverbial black book of women. He's Reid-fucking-Maxwell.

I step around him and start walking, steady and controlled though I don't feel controlled at all. I feel the weight of his attention, of him watching my every step, and when I reach the corner, I tell myself not to turn, but I do. I turn, and I find him at the railing dividing us from the ocean, his hands on the steel bars, his head lowered. As if I've affected him. As if the unbreakable Reid Maxwell has a crack in his steel. I don't know why I want to believe it matters, or that I matter. The truth is, he isn't a man that knows rejection. I'm a rejection to him and rejection has to be conquered. I can't forget that. I am nothing but a conquest to this man in all ways. I admire that in him, but I hate it, too. I turn away and start walking. I hate him and yet, I don't.

I don't hate him.

And that's a problem, a weakness. And a weakness is not something I can allow myself to have with a man like Reid Maxwell. All he can see is me meeting him head to head, conquering him as he tries to conquer me. And I will, just not tonight, and not with his mouth all over me.

CHAPTER SIXTEEN

Carrie

Instead of sleeping, I spend the night alternating between thinking about Reid and thinking about Reid. By the time I finally try to sleep, I'm back to Reid—there's a surprise—wondering what it would have been like to go home with him. Wondering what the apartment of a man like Reid looks like. Wondering too much about a man, who—oh God. He has my panties! He doesn't get to keep my panties. Not him. Not after ordering me to go home after fucking me on his desk.

I grab my phone and I'm about to hit Reid's number when I come to my senses. What am I doing? I can't call him about my panties. Why would I even consider such a thing? In fact, he can keep my panties. That's as close to owning me he gets to come. Except maybe when he kissed me by the water tonight. He'd felt different like he had during that few minutes in his office when he'd held me and didn't seem to want to let me go. It wasn't just him though. I'd been different. *We'd* been different. In those moments, we'd felt connected beyond handcuffs and some unspoken mutual conquest between us. In those moments, I'd felt myself falling for Reid, which was, and is, insanity. He's the man who stole my father's company.

I'm not falling for Reid Maxwell. I'm not that stupid. I ran from him tonight to make sure I'm not that stupid. I punch my pillow and roll over. "Sleep," I order, myself. "Sleep."

I sit straight up. Oh God. I ran. He's going to see that as a weakness. I can't afford to have that man think I'm weak, which is exactly why I can't be getting personal with him. He'll judge what he sees outside the office. I reach for my phone again and set it right back down. Calling him would also seem weak. Tomorrow I will own my decision to walk away tonight. Because that's all Reid will respect.

I don't remember falling asleep, but suddenly the alarm is going off and I sit up, exhausted to the bone, but I'm out of the bed in seconds, hurrying to the shower. I need to do something. I need to take action and win back my company. Nothing else can matter. Reid will not distract me ever again. Exactly why I dress in a simple black dress with no buttons. I'm keeping my top on and my panties, too. In fact, I wear my favorite black lace panties that I'd never allow to be torn.

I arrive at the office early on a mission to own the CEO job. I'm barely behind my desk when it feels like a reasonable time to call Royce Walker again. I've wanted to call him for an hour.

"Problem?" he asks.

"No," I say. "Well, except for the fact that I had to fire three people for stealing company secrets. I need to keep this from happening again. Can you help me with security and how much will that cost?"

"We're already working for you, which is why you found out about those three men."

"Right. Of course. Did you come to terms with Reid to provide security long term?"

"Yes. We did."

"Thank you, Royce. We need you. We should have had security in place before now."

"Why didn't you?" he asks.

I have no idea how well he knows Reid, but well enough, I decide. "I wasn't in charge or we would have," I answer honestly and then push for answers, even indirectly. "To cut costs by way of leaving ourselves exposed is just another of my father's decisions I don't understand."

He's quiet for several beats and I hold my breath, hoping he tells me what he knows about my father's decisions if he knows anything at all, but he does not. "If you have concerns, call me," he says simply.

"I think I've proven I will."

"You have," he agrees, "but just so you know, I'm available twenty-four-seven. More soon on our now ex-employees and criminal charges."

"Excellent."

We say a brief goodbye and disconnect. Sallie chooses that moment to appear in my doorway, holding a sealable baggie in her hands. "I made cookies. It just seemed like a cookie kind of day."

"As much as I love your cookies," I say. "I think I might need a cake, too."

Her eyes go wide and she hurries forward, sitting down in front of me and handing me the bag. "Comfort food."

I open the bag. "Three employees were stealing company secrets and selling them to the competition. They've been fired and we'll be pressing charges."

"Who?"

I slide a piece of paper with the names listed in her direction. She reads it while I devour a scrumptious cookie. "Delicious," I murmur, thinking she should open a bakery, and if I still had my money I gave to my father, I'd finance it.

"I'm speechless," she says, shaking her head and scooting the paper in my direction. "They're long-term employees. And my God, I had the hots for one of them and don't ask who. I'm not saying after this. Do you want to say anything to the staff about the terminations?"

"Not yet," I say. "I want to talk to Reid first."

"Understood," she says. "What can I do for you in the meantime?"

"Just keep doing what you're doing."

"I could take cookies to Reid. Maybe that will make him a little less cranky?"

"No," I say. "Reid does not get any of your cookies." I brush crumbs from my hands, right as Reid buzzes in my office and says, "In here. Now."

"Take him a cookie," Sallie suggests. "It's better than nothing. His assistant called. She will be here soon. I'll give her cookies. Getting her on our side has to be smart." She disappears and I almost snort.

Considering last night, I'm pretty sure a cookie won't satisfy Reid. I have a brief moment where I consider ignoring his command, but then he'll just come to me. Not only will that lead to one of our many fights, he'd then think that I ran last night and plan to hide today. I stand up and hurry across the offices, and of course, his door is shut.

As has become our norm, I don't knock, but as my hand comes down on the knob, I mentally steel myself for the impact of this man after he kissed me the way he did last night. *Oh God, don't think about it, Carrie.* I open the door and step inside, the force of this man's presence washing over me even before I confirm that he's behind his desk, a safe distance away, he's as good looking as always, in a dark gray pinstriped suit that draws attention to his piercing blue eyes.

I shut the door. "I'm here," I say, and I don't linger by the door. I walk toward him, and he watches my every step. I stop between his visitors' chairs and I don't speak or sit.

"Sit," he orders.

I suck in air, but I do as he says. I sit down.

His eyes narrow on me. "And she did it without fighting me," he says. "I thought for sure I'd get yet another no from you." The glint in his eyes tell me that he's not talking about work, at least not in full, before he says, "Royce told me you called him."

"I did, and I'll spare you my reasons. He obviously told you. I'd like a copy of the Walker Security contract."

"As you should."

"What do you want to tell the staff about the firings? How do you want to handle this?"

"You tell me," he says.

"I want to send out a memo that defines the breach of security and assures the staff that new security is in place. That way if someone else is betraying us, they'll bolt."

"Works for me. Let's get this behind us and get to the money-making."

"Right. The money-making." Because that's what this is to him. It's why he does everything.

"And for the record, you did the right thing by calling Royce. It's what I expected you to do."

This statement hits me ten shades of wrong. "So it was a test."

"An expectation."

"A test," I bite out. "Then I guess when you ask me to go home with you, that was part of the test, too. Had I been there with you, I wouldn't have been focused on my job."

He leans forward. "Or you could have asked me those questions instead of Royce."

"The implication being that we would have talked. I don't believe that for a moment. I'll go take care of business so we can make that money we both want to make. Oh, and Sallie made cookies. She wanted to bring you one but I was afraid she'd end up on top of your desk so I didn't let her." I stand and head for the door.

"Stop," he all but growls.

I do. I stop and I whirl around to face him, to find him already on this side of the desk, moving toward me with a predatory grace that makes me want him almost as much as I want to punch him. He halts in front of me, that earthy scent of him tantalizing, even when I don't want it to be. "No one but you will end up on my desk."

"I'm not playing your games."

He presses his hands on the door, beside me. This is becoming a habit of ours apparently. I want to tell him to back away, to stop doing this to me, but I can't seem to make the words come out this time. "I would not fuck Sallie, or anyone else, on my desk."

"You fucked me."

"Except you and I had a history when I walked into the office. We are not a game. Last night was not a test. What we are is a distraction that we can't afford, not with the powerful people counting on us turning this company around."

"You're the one who wanted me to go home with you last night."

"I did. And I wanted you to go home with me when I shouldn't have. But maybe had you just said yes, we'd be past this. I know that I for one hoped like hell that a night of fucking you would get you the hell out of my head." He pushes off the door and walks away.

I feel punched in the chest and I don't even worry about looking like I'm running. I'm suffocating in this man and I need air. I open the door and I leave, thankful that his assistant isn't yet at her desk, nor is Sallie at hers, which allows me a clear path into my office. Once there, I shut the door, and fall against the surface. Reid just told me that he can't stop thinking about me, but he's angry over it, too. The part that stands out to me is the part where he told me. He let me know I have that power over him. Why? Why would he give me that power? Well, of course, it's not really power, since I feel the same way. Maybe that's the point. We're in this together.

Or, he's playing me, and I cannot let myself forget that he has everything to gain, and I have everything to lose.

CHAPTER SEVENTEEN

Carrie

I draft the staff memo and give Sallie a heads up that it's going out. I then send a copy to Reid's email and, in turn, find an email from him in my inbox labeled: *Walker contract.*

I open the email and there are no words. *Nothing.* He didn't type anything at all. It bothers me. I think he knows it will bother me. At that moment, my email pings with a response from Reid on my staff memo that reads: *Brutal perfection.*

Two words. Good words. I inhale with the compliment, which I find myself far too pleased over. He affects me. What he says, and what he doesn't say, affects me. He also challenges me and not just as a woman. He challenges me to be the best I can be for this company, I just don't always like how he does it, but he is pushing me. He is making me reach higher and I'm not beyond admitting this. I wouldn't think that quota he picked was possible, but now I'm fighting for it.

I close the email and start reading the Walker contract. Once I'm certain I'm up to speed, I end up sidetracked from new money trying to save old money, on the phone dealing with challenges related to a project we've recently closed on for a group of investors. My stomach growls and I eat cookies. At some point, Sallie sticks a sandwich in front of me that I didn't order, but I set aside. I had lunch: her cookies. It's nearly two when I walk out of my office to find Reid's assistant now seated outside his door.

I turn to Sallie with a sudden thought, my father's assistant on my mind. "What about—"

"Resigned," she says, reading my mind. "She heard about the takeover."

"Okay well, that's a solution I guess."

"You know you never liked her," Sallie supplies. "And neither did I."

I don't deny or confirm her words. "How is Reid's assistant?"

"Connie's marvelous. She has a whip she uses on Reid and gets away with it. You'll love her."

A whip. I wonder if it's like my cuffs and before I can stop myself, I glance in Connie's direction, right about the time she heads to Reid's office, her blonde hair streaming down her back. She's pretty, petite, but curvy, in a pink suit. She's pretty and I hate the pinch I feel in my belly over this. I hate that I wonder if Reid is fucking her. It isn't my business and yet, isn't it? I need to know if he's fucking her, considering he's fucking me. Or he did. He *did*. He's not going to again.

I mentally shake myself. "I'm going to walk to the lobby and talk to security about our new security procedures, which I forwarded to you in an email."

"I saw," she says. "You want me to do it?"

"No, I want to make sure they know it's important enough for me to go down myself, but I better grab my phone." I enter my office and grab my phone just in time to find my ex-best friend Crystal calling. I hit decline. She's in Japan with my brother, which wasn't a big deal since they both worked for the same company here. Except that she knows how he treats me and then started fucking him. She can talk to him. I head for the door and Connie appears in the entryway.

"Hi, Carrie. I'm Connie."

And prettier up close. Late thirties I think, around Reid's age. "Hi, Connie."

"You're stunning," she says, shocking me with the compliment "I love it. The next CEO of the company, and you're young, gorgeous, and in control."

"Thank you, but Reid is in control."

Her lips quirk. "Right. Reid is in control." Her blue eyes dance with mischief and some private secret that I find disconcerting. "I'm running to the DA's office to grab a file for Reid. Can I get you anything on my way back?"

"That's very thoughtful, but I'm fine, thank you. I'm headed downstairs. I'll walk with you." I motion her forward and we head toward the lobby.

It's not until we're in the elevator that I say, "I hope that's the settlement for the victims of that serial killer you're picking up."

Surprise lights her eyes. "You know about Reid's case."

"I do," I say. "But he assures me that fighting for the innocent doesn't make him a good guy."

She snorts. "I wonder if he's trying to convince you or him. Actually, I'm surprised he told you about the case."

"I just happened to be around at the right time."

"There's no such thing with Reid. I've been with him for ten years. I know. There is what he lets you see and what he doesn't let you see."

I'm reminded of last night, of me accusing him of being an asshole because I see too much, but I set that aside for now. I focus on her. "Are you two—"

"No," she says. "Never. I'm not beyond seeing his beauty, but I'm not into arrogant alpha assholes. I have enough of those I call family, but that's also why I get him, and why we work well together." She lifts her wrists and shows me the dainty diamond watch on her wrist. "And he buys me gifts."

My eyes go wide. "He does?"

"Well, I buy me gifts after he works me to death, blows a date I might have enjoyed, or he's a big ass in a larger than normal way. I have his AmEx. I use it."

I laugh. "You must get gifts all the time. He's such a big ass."

The elevator dings and she sobers, "You can handle him. I can tell. So can he, and that's a good thing. It's why he respects me. I can handle him." She catches the door. "So can you," she repeats. "I'll be back soon." She heads out of the car and takes off. I follow her, repeating her words: *There is what he lets you see and what he doesn't let you see.* Reid didn't accidentally tell me that I was in his head. He wanted me to know.

I set the thought aside out of necessity and walk to security. After fifteen minutes of coordination, I'm just about to get on the elevator back upstairs when my cellphone rings with a new number that has my eyes going wide. Elijah Woodson is calling me. Elijah, who is a billionaire that I've all but groveled to, to get to invest with us. I step to the side of the elevator to avoid service interruption and answer. "Elijah," I say. "How are you?"

"I hear you're the future CEO over there."

"That's the buzz," I say.

"That works for me."

My heart starts to race. "As in, you'll invest?"

"In you, yes. For the right project. Find it and make sure it's really right, Carrie."

"How much money are we talking?"

"How much are you going to convince me to give you?"

"It's going to be a large sum."

"That I better not lose. Send me a contract. I'll be waiting."

"Wait," I say quickly. "Why now?"

"Because your father is gone." He disconnects and my stomach knots. What was happening with my father that other people knew and I did not?

My stomach knots and I punch the elevator button. I need to set the personal part of this aside. I was just given a gift that makes that financial goal Reid set possible. I need to get the team working on prospects before I consider the implications of the negativity surrounding my father. The elevator doors open and I wait impatiently to arrive back on our floor. My destination is not left toward the lobby and my office, but right, where I enter the offices that house our sales team. Walking down a path between cubicles, I waste no time gathering my best half-dozen to the edge of their cubicles.

"I need your biggest plays for Elijah Woodson and I need them by tomorrow. The bigger, the better, and if you aren't sure it's the right project, get me facts and let me decide. Call the investors that know you. Get them interested in whatever we do with Elijah."

"Hold the name back," Reid says, stepping to my side, and glancing down at me, those blue eyes piercing mine. "There's a development we need to discuss first."

Anger boils inside me but I manage to contain it. I glance at the group. "Get to work. Get me your proposals by tomorrow." I rotate and start walking.

Reid is instantly by my side, keeping pace but neither of us speak. I'm too angry. He's too in control. We exit to the elevator banks. "Let's go to my office," he orders tightly.

"I'll meet you there," I reply without looking at him, aware that I need to cool off before I talk to this man. I cut to the stairwell and exit. I've barely made it inside and Reid is there, pressing me into a corner, his big body framing mine.

"Running again?"

I press my hand to his chest. "I'm not running. I'm sparing your life. You do not want to fight with me when I'm this angry. You say I have the chance to be CEO and yet you pull the rug out from under a huge deal I brought to the table. Me. Not you."

"If you'd hear me out, you'd know your anger is misplaced."

"My anger? Or my attraction to you that is completely misplaced? I must be a sadist."

He tangles fingers in my hair. "Let me remind you what keeps you coming back for more."

"Do not even think about kissing me."

"Too late," he says. "I'm *always* thinking about kissing you. I can't change that. I'm done trying."

"If you kiss me—"

His mouth closes down on mine.

CHAPTER EIGHTEEN

Carrie

Reid kisses me and I know I should resist. I'm furious with this man over the Elijah deal, and yet when his tongue strokes past my lips, I moan with the connection. In other words, I don't resist. I lean into him, I savor the hunger I taste in him, and I tell myself he owes me this. And so I give myself just a few moments to be lost in this man when suddenly, he's on his knees and my dress is gliding up my hips.

"What are you doing?" I demand, trying to catch his hands.

"Reminding you why you don't say no."

"You mean because I apparently like assholes? Anyone could come in here."

His hand slides between my thighs, cupping my sex. "Then I'd better be fast." And damn it, he rips my favorite panties off. I yelp with the force and the next minute, his mouth is on me and I try to resist the drugging effect, but the man is really good at this.

I moan, unable to stop the sound from sliding from my throat, and my head falls back against the wall while he licks and explores. He is without mercy, flicking my clit with his thumb while his tongue is delving in and out, over and around. His fingers slip inside me, stretching me, and traveling my sex. My breath rasps from my dry throat and I reach for him, my fingers tangling in his hair. I am not gentle. I want to punish him. He's punishing me, showing me who owns who and I can't stop it from happening.

His fingers and tongue work magic together, stroking me, driving me wild. Blood roars in my ears and the stairwell fades away. There is only what he is doing to me, and the sweet spot he's touching, and the next. Every place he touches is a sweet spot. My sex tightens into a hard clench, and remotely, I hear my own panting echoing in the small space, seeming to bounce off the walls, but I can't seem to care. Not with Reid's tongue in *all* the right places. I'm mindless and without inhibitions. I arch against him, pump my hips against his hand, and with one more lick my body clenches. I tumble into orgasm, oh God, I tumble hard, and it's over far too quickly. I'm barely back to reality when a door somewhere slams and I jerk. "Reid," I plead desperately. He licks me once more, drags my dress down, and stands, cupping my face. He kisses me, a long stroke of tongue before he says, "I'll leave out the lobby door and come back up."

He releases me and heads for the stairs. "All that did was prove that your power plays know no limits. Elijah is a big business for us."

He's back in front of me in two seconds. "Elijah hates me. He came to you with the full intent of burning you to burn me. Like it or not, you're with me now, and that means he's not just my enemy. He's yours. But I'm not, Carrie. I'm *not* your enemy." He heads down the stairs.

I am struck by the fact that a) after giving me an orgasm in the stairwell, he's actually concerned about discretion, thus leaving separately, and b) that comment about me being with him felt far more personal than professional, but then I'm riding the intimacy of his mouth on my body. And actually, there is a c) which includes questions I need answered.

"Reid!" I call out, racing down the stairs. "Reid, wait. Reid." I'm a full two flights down and working my way past another when he appears at the bottom of that level.

I hurry the rest of the way down the stairs. "I have a question," I say joining him on the landing. "What enemy would come at you this directly? He knows you'll know. He knows you'll stop an attack."

"Which is the point," he says. "He knows. I know. When I turn him down, and I will, the board will want an explanation."

"How can we get burned if he hands us money?"

"He has a plan."

"Maybe that plan is to get you to say no and look bad to the board," I counter. "And you're doing what he wants."

"We aren't doing this deal with him."

"You're good at what you do," I say, stepping closer to him, wanting to shake the man. "You can beat him and take his money. I know you can. If I didn't know you were that good, I wouldn't be here with you."

His hands settle on my waist and he pulls me to him. "We are not taking this risk."

I don't push away from him. Somehow, talking to this man, with his hands on my body, has become more normal than not. "We or you?"

"You're with me now. I'm protecting us both."

"Then we can beat him together, Reid."

"No."

"Yes," I say.

"Woman."

"You said saying it's possible makes it possible."

"No." He backs me up and presses me against the door. "Just because you can doesn't always mean you should."

"Does that include us?"

131

"Yes, but at least we want the same things, including each other. He does not."

It's the first time we've talked about wanting each other without denial.

"There's more to this story than you know," he adds. "We will not do this deal. We'll get a new deal."

"Tell me the story."

He studies me several beats, his expression unreadable before he pulls me to him, kisses me and says, "No," and with that, he releases me and leaves.

I spend the afternoon researching Reid and Elijah, looking for a connection that I can't find. What I do find is details on the case Reid is handling. People died and the DA charged the wrong man, and even after he was acquitted, the DA didn't look for the real killer—who killed again. And Reid is suing the DA. It's not his kind of case—well, not now, but looking back, he represented a lot of random cases that weren't just about money. I am curious about the man who is so much more than all of his money, but tonight isn't the night I find out. By five, my email is already filling with staff ideas for Elijah and I move to my conference table to start working through them because we *are* doing this deal. I'm going to make it happen.

"Have you eaten at all?" Sallie asks, motioning to the sandwich still on my desk.

"Cookies. A lot of cookies and tomorrow it will be a salad."

She shoves blonde hair from her eyes and sits down next to me. "Can I get you anything?"

"I'm good. Go to your Tuesday night yoga class."

"I don't care about yoga. I've been with you for five years. I know what this company means to you. You made it matter to me. And frankly, I'm thirty next month. I don't want to start over somewhere else. What can I do to help?"

"You already are. Really. You are amazing. Go. I just need some time to work on my own."

"You're sure?"

"Positive," I assure her.

"Okay. Can I at least get you food?"

"No food." I point to the bag of cookies next to me, with only one left. "I'm quite well taken care of."

She smiles and hurries toward the door. I quickly get back to work and have a thought. I dial Royce Walker. "Problem?" he answers.

"Why do you always think there's a problem?" I ask.

"That's why people call me."

"Right. Elijah Woodson. I need to know everything about him, how he might burn our company, how we might burn him."

"You want to know how to burn him?"

"That does seem the best way to keep him from burning us."

He's silent for two beats. "I'll look into it."

We disconnect and I feel good about that call. There's a way to do this deal and while I don't like to play dirty, if someone plans to burn me, I have to ensure they can't.

It's at least another hour before Connie pokes her head in the door, a long blonde curl bouncing by her face. Good Lord, I'm surrounded by gorgeous blonde women. "I'm headed out, but Reid wanted me to tell you that your call to Royce was unnecessary. He has it handled."

I am instantly hot under the collar. "Did he now?"

"Yes," she says. "I take it that doesn't please you."

"No," I reply tightly. "It doesn't, but I'll handle it."

133

She laughs. "I'm certain that you will. Good night." She disappears and I am on my feet in an instant. I exit my office and walk toward Reid's open door, the sound of voices lifting in the air. His brother again, and I don't care.

I enter Reid's office and he looks up as I do, those blue eyes lit with expectation. He knows what he did. I know what he expects. For me to back off with Gabe present. I don't. I cross to his desk and stop between them, leaning on the endcap of the desk to stare at Reid. "If you think your brother being here will shut me up, you're wrong."

"There are only a few things that shut you up and we both know it," he replies dryly.

I ignore his reference to us fucking on this very desk. "I had every right to call Royce for the answers you won't give me."

"If you want information, ask me," he says.

"I did. You said no."

"You know what you need to know," he replies arrogantly.

"What you want me to know is more like it."

Gabe clears his throat. "Either you two need to get a room or I need to leave to give you this one."

"Stay," I say, looking at Gabe and then Reid. "We both know we don't communicate when we're alone."

"On the contrary," Reid counters. "Those one-on-one sessions have proven enlightening."

"I think you use anything you can to distract me when we fight, your brother included, because I'm winning. And you don't like to lose. This isn't over. We aren't done." I turn and walk toward the door.

Once I'm in my office, I gather my things and I leave.

Hours later, I've finished a run, and I hate that I hoped to run into Reid. I hate that he's become damn near an obsession. He's all I can think about. Determined to get him out of my mind, I shower and have pulled on sweats to hunt down food when the doorbell rings with what has to be a delivery. No one but security, who brings the packages, can get up here without me knowing. I answer the door to find a small box in the guard's hands.

Curious, and certain this must be from my father, I sit on the couch and open the box to find four pairs of panties inside. My heart starts to race and I reach for the card that reads: *We agree. It's not over and we're not done.*

CHAPTER NINETEEN

Carrie

I don't really spend a lot of time fretting over what to do about the panties Reid just had delivered. I curl up on the couch and call him. He answers on the first ring. "You got my package."

Oh God, why does this man's voice do funny things to my stomach? "And you," I say, "tore my favorite panties today."

"Favorite? Well then, I'll have to give them a closer inspection. I was more interested in the woman wearing them."

"You mean in shutting down my anger. Distracting me from the fight."

"I like fighting with you, Carrie. Every time you get angry, I want to fuck you."

"And yet you, intentionally pissed me off tonight when Gabe was in your office."

"Connie was supposed to leave sooner than she left, and Gabe showed up without warning. Considering that fact, and how much I wanted to be inside you again, Connie did us a favor. Gabe would have interrupted and the office isn't enough. I want you here with me."

"I'm not doing that."

"Why? You don't want me to fuck you out of my system?"

"I don't want to be laying in your bed when you say: 'get dressed and go home,' like you did in your office."

He's silent for two beats before he says, "That's not going to happen."

"I just—*No*."

"Carrie."

"*No,* Reid."

"Then meet me at the railing where we were last night. We'll talk."

"You want to talk?"

"Yes, Carrie." His voice is sandpaper and silk. "I do."

"Why?"

"Meet me." He hangs up.

I press my phone to my forehead. What am I doing with this man? I stand up because apparently what I'm doing is going downstairs to see him because, well, I want to. I slip on sneakers, brush my hair, and spray perfume before I grab my wallet purse I use on occasion. I stuff a credit card inside for no reason other than I don't like to be anywhere without money, slip the strap across my chest, and head downstairs. Once I'm in the lobby about to exit my building, butterflies flutter in my stomach. I'm nervous. Why am I nervous? This man's hands have been all over my body, but even as I ask the question, I know the answer. I'm on dangerous territory with Reid. I'm vulnerable with this man professionally. I don't want to be vulnerable personally, but I fear it's too late. I already am.

I exit the building into the starlit night and travel the sidewalk, ocean air lifting my hair, cooling my skin that only turns hotter when I find Reid standing at the railing, facing the water. He's dressed in sweats and a T-shirt, and he's just one of those people who manages to radiate power and masculinity no matter what he wears. He doesn't have to turn around for me to know this. I've experienced his impact quite fiercely.

I inhale and close the small space between us, stepping to his side. Close but not too close. Reid reacts instantly, pulling me between him and the railing, the ocean at my back, his big, hard body at my front. His fingers tangle in my hair and he doesn't speak or ask permission for what he does next. His mouth closes down on mine, his tongue licking into my mouth, and I don't even think about resisting. I sink into the kiss, my arms wrapping around him, hard muscle flexing beneath my touch. For eternal moments that are still not long enough, I'm lost in this man, in his spicy, masculine taste. The way he consumes me. The way he—

He tears his mouth from mine, his forehead settling against mine, his hand on my cheek. "What are you doing to me, woman?" He pulls back to look at me. "Come home with me. Spend the night with me."

My hand flattens on his chest. "No. I'm not doing that, Reid."

"Because you think I'm going to send you away? I want you there way too fucking badly to be that foolish. But take me to your place if it makes you feel better. You have control there. *You* can send *me* away."

"What are we doing?" I ask yet again.

"We'll figure it out."

"You have everything to gain and I—"

"Have everything to lose," he finishes for me. "I know. I can't change that dynamic, but believe it or not, I now have a lot to lose as well. Come home with me."

"No. That changes things. It feels different from the hate sex in your office."

"So you can fuck me in the office, but not at one of our homes?" he challenges.

"Seems like that's where we're at."

"Then let's go to the office."

I laugh. "We aren't going to the office."

He cups my face and kisses me before his fingers lace with mine. "Then let's go to the coffee shop around the corner and talk. Yes?"

Talk. I do want to talk. I want to understand this man. I want to trust this man. "Yes."

He kisses me again. "Or we can—"

"No," I breathe out, but it takes effort. I want whatever he's about to suggest. I want him to kiss me again. I want to be fully naked with this man and truly know what it feels like to be with him, to *really* be with him, but I don't want to be owned. And Reid *will* own me if I let him.

"Coffee it is," he says, leading me forward, and to my surprise, he folds our elbows and pulls me to him. "I'm holding on," he declares. "I'm not letting you dart away."

"Don't be an asshole and I won't."

He laughs, a low, deep, masculine laugh that I feel in every part of me. "I can't make a promise I might not keep." He lifts our joined hands and kisses mine. "And I never make a promise I don't keep, nor do I say anything I don't mean."

He lets those words linger between us during our short walk, and I decide they're meant to drive home what he's already stated. We are *not* enemies. We want the same things. We want each other. All words that mean more as my connection with this man grows more intimate. That doesn't mean I proceed blindly or without caution.

We reach the door of the coffee shop, that really was just around a corner in one of the buildings along our path. He releases me and opens the door. "Ladies first," he says motioning me forward.

"Honor and manners," I comment. "If you weren't such an asshole someone might think you were a nice guy." I step in front of him, a memory punching at my mind. "But don't worry, Reid. I listened to what you said to me after the call I heard between you and the DA. I won't make the mistake of believing you're a nice guy. If I did, I'd be in your apartment right now, and I'm not." And with that, I walk into the coffee shop.

Reid

I stand at the door for a just a moment after Carrie enters the coffee shop, and I ask myself why I don't want her to expect the worst of me when that's exactly what I wanted only days ago. Hate means we fuck and move on and that's what I do. I fuck. I move on. No one is ever hurt that way because I never claim to be anything but an asshole. But damn it, this woman is not every other woman. She's under my skin. She's in my head. I need to get her out before this becomes a problem, but for once in my life, *I can't* seems to be in my vocabulary.

Entering the coffee shop, I scan to find us being the only patrons before joining Carrie at the counter where we order our drinks, the awareness between us jumping around like a live charge. When it comes time to pay, Carrie reaches for the purse at her hip. I catch her hand, honestly stunned that she's trying to pay after all that she assumes that I've taken from her. "I've got it."

"Thank you," she says, those emerald eyes meeting mine, a hint of something in their depths I don't understand, but I want to. Seems that I want a lot of things with this woman that I shouldn't want.

Reluctantly I break our connection and turn my attention to the register. I pay for the coffees, and together

Carrie and I walk to the end of the bar to wait for our order. I reach for her fingers and walk her to me, stroking a strand of hair from her face.

She catches my hand, her gaze probing, and this time I read confusion in her eyes. I'm confusing her, which isn't a surprise. I'm right there with her, confused as fuck about what I'm doing with this woman. "Let's sit," I say, leading her toward a corner booth with a high back that blocks us from the rest of the room. It may not offer complete privacy, but it's the closest thing we'll get here until I convince her to come home with me.

"Drinks up!"

The shout comes before I even sit down. I cross the small space between me and the counter, grab the coffees and return to the booth where I slide into the seat beside Carrie, setting them down in front of us. "What are we doing, Reid?" she asks, our bodies automatically turning toward each other.

"You keep asking that."

"You keep making me ask it," she counters.

"We're going to talk, though in fairness, I should tell you that I'm one wrong push left or right from taking you into the bathroom and fucking you." I grab her leg and pull her closer. "It would take a very small push."

She covers my hand on her leg. "Talking means answering my question in a meaningful way. *What* are we doing, Reid?"

"Apparently not fucking."

"Because I don't want to get fucked over."

My hand slides to her face. "That's not what this is. This is not about some agenda. This is just us. Not the company. Not a family name."

"My family name is on the line."

142

"Not with me or because of me," I say, wishing like fuck it had nothing to do with my family. I lean in and brush my lips over hers. She rewards me with a shiver that travels her body and radiates into me. "I have no agenda with you, Carrie, besides wanting you."

"Prove it," she says. "No, let me be more specific. Prove that that I can trust you."

I ease back and look at her, and when I would dismiss such a challenge from any other woman, I don't even think about it with Carrie. "What does that mean to you, Carrie? What do you want from me?"

CHAPTER TWENTY

Reid

What do you want from me?

Carrie doesn't even hesitate to answer that question. "Tell me something I don't know."

Something she doesn't know. That's a wide open, widely definable question and for reasons she can't know, I proceed with caution. "Ask me a question and I'll answer if it's at all possible."

"If it's possible?"

"You're an attorney, just like me," I remind her. "You know there are things I can't answer."

"Okay, what don't I know about my father?"

And there it is. The question I dreaded. The one I can't legally answer. "That's between you and your father."

"You tell me. *You,* Reid."

"He's gone. Focus on the company. Focus on you."

She studies me for several beats and when I expect her to push on her father, she hits me from another direction. "Okay then. Elijah. Tell me why you won't do business with him."

She's now hit two of my brick walls. I rotate forward and pick up my coffee. "No." I take a drink.

"No?" she demands.

"No," I repeat.

"*Reid.*"

I set my cup down and look at her without turning. "It's personal."

"Trust me enough to tell me. Because let's be honest. You earning my trust is a façade. You don't have to earn my trust. I've been forced into that trust."

She's right. Professionally she does have to trust me. Personally, she doesn't, and trust is the most intimate and dangerous thing two people can share. It cuts. It burns. It destroys. I know this all too well, and yet, foolishly that's exactly what I want from her. I turn to face her. "You demand that my trust be given freely and yet you say yours is forced."

"If my gut didn't say to trust you, Reid, I'd be looking for a job. I just want you to validate my gut feeling. And I want you to have the same gut feeling about me."

My lips tighten. I'm diving into treacherous water with this woman. I need to pull back. "Elijah hates me. That's what you need to know. You'll lose everything if you get involved with this man. I'll lose millions. You need to understand that. I put my name, my family name, on this deal."

"I can talk to him. I can make him see reason. I can appeal to his humanity. This is my life. This is—"

I grab her arm and pull her to me. "He's like me. He's barely human. I ruin people. He ruins people. It's business, the kind that requires no emotion be present to succeed. It requires no heart. In fact, a heart is a detriment. I am that and he is, too. You are not. He'll cut you, fuck you every which way, and then leave you with nothing. All to cut me. I'm not going to let that happen."

"Because you have too much to lose."

"*We*, Carrie. We have too much to lose."

"But you have no heart. You don't care about me." Her fingers flex where they rest on my chest like she wants to push me away as much as she wants to keep touching me. I know that feeling every damn second that I'm with her. "I know how quickly you could turn on me," she adds, "and thank you for reminding me that I can't let myself forget that."

She hates me in this moment. Hate is what I *need* her to feel and if I told her exactly why Elijah wants to hurt me, she'd hate me even more, and yet, I don't want her to feel those things. And *fuck*. I can't seem to just let her go. "You're different," I say. "You're different from everyone else, Carrie. I'll protect you. I already am." I pull back and let her see the truth in my eyes as I repeat, "I'm protecting you with Elijah and I know you don't understand my decision on this. If my word isn't enough, know this: I stand to lose millions if you fail. I would not let go of a deal that delivers us to our goal. This is not it."

She studies me several beats, seeming to size up my statement before she says, "Okay then, I accept that he's the enemy, but he's the enemy with money. Can we not burn him the way he wants to burn us? And wouldn't using his money to succeed be burning him?"

I release her, but my hand catches her leg. "It's too risky." And then I dive into the quicksand again. "I need you to trust me on this. Set Elijah aside, Carrie. I'll make-up the lost deal. I'll replace it and we'll succeed."

"I don't want *you* to make this happen," she says vehemently. "*I* want to do it. I want to make this happen. This deal with Elijah does that for me and us."

"It doesn't. It's a set-up. It's certain destruction. And as for doing this yourself, if we both bring a deal to the table, we'll win even bigger together. *Set Elijah aside.* Promise me."

"Reid—"

"Promise me."

"Okay. I promise. What about my father?"

"Yes. Set him aside, too."

"So everything I ask you, you tell me to set aside. How is this proving you have no agenda, well, aside from secret agendas?"

"Ask me something else, Carrie."

"Tell me about the case you're handling against the DA."

I don't ask her why this matters to her. I know. It's a character assessment after I just told her I have no heart. "That I can do. I don't know what you've pieced together, so I'll recap. There was a serial killer. The clients I represent, Cole and Lori, are the husband and wife team that represented the innocent man accused of the crimes. When he was found innocent, one of the victim's family members attacked Lori in a public bathroom. Had the DA reopened the case, that might not have happened, nor would the real killer have killed again, but he did."

"How did you end up with this case? I mean, I know you don't like to be called a raider, but you operate in a similar zone. Civil actions again the DA don't seem like your thing."

"It's more Gabe's thing, but in my early days out of college, I played this field, and Gabe wasn't available this go around."

"And you're waiving your fees?"

"Lori and Cole have money. They don't need the sizable settlement they'll receive, so they donated it to the victims' families."

"And out of the goodness of the heart you don't have, you did the same with your fees?"

"Do you know the column Cat Does Crime?"

"Yes. I love that column. Why? What does that have to do with your fees?"

"Cat's my sister, and her husband and Cole are partners. Our firms support each other through a business arrangement. And Lori is a close friend of Cat's."

"So did you do this for your sister, your friends or because you have a business obligation?"

"All of the above, Carrie. Not to mention our firm had a scandal a few years back and the good press from this case helps bury that for good."

"Now you just want me to think you're an ass with an agenda."

"I'm speaking the truth, which is the only way to earn trust. My decisions are not one-dimensional any more than our relationship at this point. Your turn. Tell me something I don't know about you."

She cuts her stare. "I love Cat's column and her books." She reaches for her cup. "She wrote about a serial killer's trial that had to be this case." She sips her coffee but still, she doesn't look at me beyond a cursory glance. "I can't believe I didn't connect the dots to your case. I mean, how many serial killers are there in our city?"

"You're deflecting, talking about my sister. Tell me about you."

She glances over at me. "I am. I follow her writing because I'm a crime buff. I almost went into criminal law. I loved the idea of being a part of real justice. I would have if not for the family business."

"We have that in common."

She gives me a curious, interested look, the kind of genuine interest most women only have for my money or how well I fuck them. "You wanted to go into criminal law?"

"I did." I don't explain to her why. I don't tell her how the system once failed me. How much I wanted to prove it could work, that I could make it work. "The family business made it unfeasible."

"And what made you decide to be an asshole?"

I laugh. "It works for me. It's a profitable position to take."

"It's a good way to keep everyone at a distance," she comments. "And people who do that, have baggage. You have baggage. I see in your eyes. I taste it when you kiss me."

She was right when she said that she sees too much. She does, and this would be a good time to shove her in a corner and fuck her, but with that off the table, I shift the conversation back to her. "Why could Royce find no man in your life?"

"You do know it sucks that you investigated me this thoroughly, right? Why don't you have a woman in your life?"

"I'm an asshole who never married and that won't change. Back to you. Why is there no man in your life, Carrie?"

"It's a choice, but like most of us, I was young and in love once way back as an undergraduate."

"And?"

"And not only did he sleep with my roommate, I found out that I was pregnant three days after we broke up."

I go completely still. "And?" I ask again, my voice softening.

"And I was going to keep the baby. I mean, I had a family with money and a guaranteed job. I decided it must be my destiny."

"Where's the baby now?"

"I miscarried." She looks away. "I don't know why I just told you that." She takes a drink. "Yes, I do." She turns to me. "It tells you who I am. I haven't gone down the emotional path since then. I won't. I'm not that girl. You don't have to be an asshole to keep me on the outside. I like the outside just fine."

Which makes her the perfect woman for me, except that statement doesn't feel as perfect as it should. "There had to be someone since college. What about sex? You had to have—"

"I dated someone for a few years. He wanted more and I didn't."

"Where's he now?"

"He met someone and fell in love, as he deserved."

"Often people want what they can't have. How did you react?"

"I went to his wedding. I was happy for him. He's divorced now, Reid. So is my first ex. And I'm sure you know from your investigation that my mother left when I was five. I speak to her once every five years."

And my mother died miserably married to my father right up until the moment she died of a stroke five years ago.

"Relationships are complicated, messy, and ugly," Carrie adds, as if she's just read my mind. "I don't want any part of complicated, messy, and ugly."

"Then let's keep it simple. Let's go fuck."

"Not tonight," she surprises me by say, and rather easily. Not never, but not tonight.

I arch a brow. "Why not tonight?"

"Because when we hate fuck, it's not complicated, messy, or ugly. That's when we keep everything focused on the sex. But tonight, I almost like you. That's not good for either of us."

"So if I want to fuck you, I need to make sure you hate me."

She reaches up and touches my cheek. "Don't. Don't make me hate you again."

Damn it, I don't want her to hate me. At least not now, and she's right, that's a problem for both of us. "Come on. Let's get out of here." I slide out of the booth and take her hand, both of us forgetting our coffees. A minute later at most, we're outside and I drape my arm over her shoulders. In silence, we complete the short walk to her building where I turn to her, my hands on her waist.

"No fucking tonight," I say.

"Not tonight," she confirms again.

I cup her head. "I have to do this." I kiss her then, a deep drugging kiss that has me hot and hard, and so damn into this woman that I don't want to hate fuck, I don't want that limit, and she's right; that's a problem, that's trouble, the kind that has me tearing my lips from hers. "Goodnight, Carrie." I drag my fingers over her lips, willing myself not to kiss her again before I turn and walk away. Before tonight gets complicated which always leads to messy and ugly.

CHAPTER TWENTY-ONE

Carrie

When I wake in my bed alone, I feel regret. Why didn't I just go home with Reid? We're having sex. That's all. I let myself conjure up some fantasy that there was more happening between us. I can't be emotional. Reid is *not* emotional. The board does not want emotional. Reid will be in my life and out of it in a few short months. And the closer I am to him, the more I understand the man who controls my destiny. He most certainly is using all he knows about me, which is much more than I know about him, a man influencing my future. I need to be as smart as he is and enjoy the ride. I can do this. I am just as capable as he is, and he and the board need to know that.

Therefore, I need to make a fearless statement and when I arrive to work I'm wearing a black skirt and an emerald green blouse. A blouse that matches the emerald green panties I'm wearing, which came in the box Reid delivered to my apartment last night. Obviously, he'll know I'm either wearing those panties or taunting him with the fact that I saw them and chose not to wear them. *I'm* in control. I feel it right up until the moment that I realize that Reid isn't even around to notice. He's gone. I have no idea where and I don't ask Connie for details or call him. Instead, I review all the proposals for growth that I was given by the staff, with disappointing results.

Desperate to find a big deal I can slam dunk, I start making a list of every major investor I've ever dreamt of working with and then isolate the top two. It's nearly three in the afternoon, and I'm sitting behind my desk, talking with Sallie about the research I've had her working on today when Reid barks over my intercom, "My office. *Now.*"

I glance at Sallie. "I'll be back." I stand up and walk around my desk, charging toward Reid's office, which is being guarded by Connie, who's sitting behind her desk.

"Hi, Carrie. Do you need Reid?"

"I got this," I say, walking right to his door and opening it, but not before I hear her laugh. I'm glad one of us is amused.

I enter Reid's office and shut the door. He's behind his desk, looking like Mr. Arrogant Hotness in a gray suit with a blue pinstripe that matches his eyes and his tie. "Is it really necessary for you to continue to be an asshole to me? I thought we came to some sort of agreement last night."

"We did. I can't fuck you unless you hate me. Did you really think that was motivation for me to start being the nice guy I'm not?"

I walk toward him, placing his desk between us as I lean on the surface. "Stop being an asshole. We're a team, remember?"

"Are you wearing the green panties to match that blouse?"

"Reid," I say, "Sallie just heard you bark that command at me."

"Are you going to let her bring me cookies to put me in a good mood?" He stands up, presses his hands on the desk and leans toward me. "Because you sent me to bed with a hard-on, made me wake up with a hard-on, and then wore that fucking shirt to taunt me with what's under your skirt.

So until you come over here, lift your skirt and let me see your panties, I will remain a justified asshole."

I glare at him and then I don't know what happens. I laugh. "Yes. I'm wearing the green panties."

His eyes warm and I swear the hard glint he'd fixed me in moments before fades into a mix of heat and mischief. "Come show me."

"Not here."

"Come *over here* and show me."

"No."

"Come over here and let me lick you under those panties."

"You'll rip them. I like them."

"I promise not to rip them and I always keep my promises." He softens his voice. "Come here, Carrie." The low, raspy command turns my knees weak while my breasts are suddenly heavy, my nipples tight, aching nubs.

"The door isn't locked, and you need to work harder on the whole hate thing."

"Hate is overrated. Especially since I'm meeting with Grayson Bennett tonight."

I straighten. "The billionaire?"

"That's right," he says, pushing off the desk. "He has money to burn and he hates Jean Claude Laurette, who you know I've working with. So I have to do some convincing. Which means that it's going to take both of us to do this deal. He's a relationship person. He wants to know the person he'll work with long-term and that's you."

"Can I go to the meeting tonight?"

"Not yet. He has a problem with one of the board members that I have to get him past first."

"How do you get him past the problem board member if he's a relationship guy?"

"Do you really want that answer?"

My stomach knots. "You'll get rid of the board member one way or the other."

"Yes. I will." His cellphone rings and he pulls it from his pocket, grimacing at the number. "Yes, Nicholas?"

I know the name as one of the board members and I wonder if this is the one he plans to get rid of.

"No," Reid says. "We are not. We *will not*. Yes." His jaw firms. "I'll be there." He rises and stands in profile to me and the desk, more stone than man for a few beats before he rounds the desk.

I turn to face him as he steps in front of me. "I won't hide the dirtiness of this job from you," he says, returning to our prior conversation. "I'll put you right in the pit of hell with me and with good reason. You have to get a stomach for this stuff or you won't make it, Carrie."

"My father—"

"Sheltered you in ways that I won't. In ways that you can't be sheltered and do this job."

"You're saying my father would push out the board members?"

"Yes, Carrie. He would. He's taken these kinds of actions. He's clearly got a side you don't know."

"He's my father, Reid. I worked with him for ten years of my life."

"And?"

"And I know him. He's not you."

His eyes flash. "You mean he's not a heartless asshole? You're wrong. He is."

My jaw clenches. "You're working on that hate again, Reid."

"I'm telling you the truth. If you hate me for it, then hate me."

"He's taken these actions, but you beat him. In other words, you're the devil he is not."

His lips thin. "I never claimed to be a saint, Carrie, but I'm not a liar. Your father was going down. I didn't make that happen. That's the truth. I need to go." He starts for the door and I rotate to watch him leave, wanting to finish about ten things that we've started. I want to grab him and pull him back, but I refuse to stop him. He's the one who stops.

He rotates in my direction and before I know his intent, he's back in front of me, pulling me to him, and his hand is on the back of my head. "If you hate me, then I can do this, right?" His mouth comes down on mine in a brutal, rough kiss that tastes of hunger and anger, even as his other hand cups my backside, and he pulls me hard against his erection. "You're coming home with me tonight, even if I have to carry you there." And with that, he kisses me again, and before I can even process what just happened, he heads for the door, opens it and leaves.

I inhale, my entire body humming with a mix of anger, need, and confusion but I don't linger. I'm on fire in more than one way, which for me, translates to a need for control, a need for action. I follow in Reid's steps, and once I'm in the lobby area, I keep walking. I don't look at Connie or Sallie. I have a purpose I don't want interrupted. I enter my office and sit down behind my desk where I dial Royce Walker. "Problem?" he answers.

"Yes," I say this time. "Since I can't hire you to investigate my father, can you refer me to someone who won't screw me over?"

He does that silent thing he does. "I'm not letting you go elsewhere when we can help. Let me—"

"Talk to Reid. Never mind. I'll handle it."

"We'll help and I won't charge you extra, but I have some confidentiality issues with Reid I need to work out. Give me twenty-four hours."

"Okay, but if you can't work it out by then, I need a name, please. I don't know where to start."

"Fair enough. I'll be in touch."

We disconnect and my cellphone rings, and the number sets my heart racing. It's Elijah. "Carrie West," I answer.

"Carrie," he says jovially. "I'm in your area. Why don't we have drinks and talk about money."

"I'm not ready to present yet."

"We'll speak broadly about my investments and your role in the company versus that of Reid Maxwell."

Unease slides through me. "Okay. When and where?"

He names a time and place and once I hang up, I dial Reid. He doesn't answer, but he could be in the subway. We all take the subway when we're in a hurry and he was in a hurry. "Call me, please. It's urgent. Elijah wants to meet and if I don't leave now, I won't make the meeting. I feel like I need to go. Then I'll know if he's attacking and where he's attacking from. Call me." I hang up and head for the door.

CHAPTER TWENTY-TWO

Carrie

I take the subway to my meeting with Elijah, which is at a popular bar near the courthouse. The minute I exit the tunnel, I check my messages and find nothing from Reid or anyone for that matter. I dial Reid again and end up with his voicemail again. "I really need you to call me back, Reid," I say, ending the connection.

"Damn it, Reid," I murmur, but I remind myself that he has clients. He's doing two jobs and once I'm the CEO of the company, there is no Reid to call for help. I don't need help anyway. This is me making sure we aren't getting sideswiped in some way. I don't want Reid to think that I'm sneaking behind his back. I dial him again and when his voicemail picks up, I say just that. "I'm meeting Elijah. I don't want you to think that I'm sneaking behind your back or breaking a promise. I want to find out what I can so he can't come at you, which like you said, means me. And he said something about my father. I really need to know what he meant. Call me when you can." I hang up.

One block later, I enter the restaurant bar on the bottom floor of a building near the offices of Woodson Cable News Network, which Elijah recently took over after his father's retirement. If I rein in Elijah, I always felt I'd get his father, too, but I've accepted that at least during this window where Reid sits at the helm, that won't happen. The bar is dimly lit, clusters of tables here and there, snowflake-looking lights dangling from the ceiling. I don't really understand the snowflakes as a year-round lighting option, but I guess it's a way to remember this place.

I scan the room to find Elijah sitting in a booth. He spots my approach and stands, greeting me warmly, but then, on our two prior encounters, he did that as well. He extends his hand, expensive cuff links adorning his pressed white shirt that he's paired with a black suit. I accept it and we sit down across from each other. "You look beautiful as always," he comments. "Though please don't take offense. I, by all means, do not mean to downplay your skills, nor my own professionalism."

He's not a handsome man; his features sharp, brown eyes hard, but he wears his age, which I know from my past research to be thirty-nine, with confidence and grace. "I'm not offended and thank you. I am, however, eager to understand why, after I've stalked you for years, you're suddenly willing to do business with me."

"Timing is a big factor," he says without hesitation. "I have a project I've been trying to bring together and the real estate investment firm I was dealing with is dragging their feet."

"What's the project? Because I thought you wanted me to bring one to you."

"I'm open to you doing so, but in this case, I'm looking to develop world-class high-rises in China and Japan, both markets where we're rapidly expanding. We'll run our operation from the building and sell the rest of the space as residential. I'm talking about buildings with such large price tags that we will want to partner with a handful of wealthy investors to make it happen."

Asia. The location and the magnitude of the project do not sit well for me. It's a cesspool of potential legal issues with red tape that can take years to cut through, while tying up financial resources.

"That's a big and exciting project," I say because it is to most. "And as for the timing of this meeting, you mentioned my father, who of course, has manned many Asian projects."

"Correct."

Correct? That's his response? "Why did my father leaving play a role in you coming to me?"

"He wasn't in the game anymore. I could see it in his eyes. He wasn't hungry, but you are."

I reluctantly accept this assessment as reality though it feels like a half-truth. "You knew if you worked with him, you'd work with me. You could have asked for me."

"He was the decision maker and your father didn't instill confidence in me."

"And now Reid's in charge."

"Ah, yes. The elephant in the room. Reid is in charge, but he won't be around for long."

He won't be around for long. I don't like this statement, which doesn't feel matter of fact. It doesn't feel like confidence in me, but rather confidence in Reid's departure. I want to ask how he knows him, but that feels like a betrayal to Reid. I want to hear it from Reid. "He's in charge now and that means I need to run all projects by him."

"Why? You take this to the board, and you take over. It's pretty cut and dry."

"You clearly underestimate my loyalty to those who I'm close to and underestimate Reid's power."

"You mean you're afraid of him."

It's at that moment that my phone beeps with a text message. I grab my phone. "Excuse me," I say, reading the message from Reid: *Get your pretty little ass up and walk to the bathroom. NOW.*

I wet my lips and swallow. He's pissed. He's really pissed, and since he wouldn't know where to find me without listening to my messages, he clearly doesn't care that I tried to communicate. Actually, I never said where I was going. Now, *I'm* pissed. He's having me followed.

"Everything okay?" Elijah asks.

"I have a little problem at the office. Can you give me a minute to make a call?"

"Of course," he says. "Can I order you a drink while you're gone?"

"No thanks," I reply, slipping my purse over my shoulder. "I never drink and talk money, and that's what we're here for. Money."

Approval lights his eyes, though I can't say I welcome his approval when I should. He alone represents enough money to ensure I keep the West family brand. "How about coffee?" he asks.

"Coffee is fabulous," I say, though I am certain Reid's mood right now is not.

Steeling myself for the confrontation the tone of the text message says is coming, I stand and head toward the bathroom sign behind the bar, the idea that I'm trying to create trust with Reid while he has me followed drives my anger and my steps. I enter a narrow hallway and turn right, only to have Reid grab me, and pull me to him. "What the fuck are you trying to pull?"

"Check your messages and you'll know, and really, Reid?" I grab his tie and tug hard. "You're having me followed?"

"I'm not having you followed, sweetheart. This was a set-up. The question is, were you a part of it or not?"

My mind shoots to that comment Elijah made about Reid not being around long. I don't ask questions. Not now, not yet. "Whatever this is, I'm with you. I'm not with them. I swear to you, Reid."

"You can prove that to me later when we're alone. Right now, we're walking out there together, and I'm going to introduce you to the stockholder that just tried to bully me into Elijah's deal. Interesting timing, don't you think? And he chose the location for the meeting."

Understanding washes over me. "It looks like I was plotting behind your back because I was here with Elijah when you just said you wouldn't do the deal."

"Exactly."

"I was not plotting against you, Reid. Have you listened to your messages?"

"I've been with our stockholder."

"And of course, you assumed the worst of me. Your phone transcribed my messages. Read them now."

"I'll read them when we're out of here."

"Of course you will. What do you want to do?"

"We're going to walk out there and say goodbye to both of them and then leave together." He leans in near my ear. "And then we're going to *talk*."

My anger flares hot again. "Oh yes," I assure him. "We're definitely going to *talk*."

"You will tell them both—"

"I know what to say. You made that clear last night."

"And yet, you're here," he reminds me.

"Listen to your messages, asshole." I turn for the door and he catches me from behind, his big body pressed close to mine, his lips at my ear. My body is now as hot as my anger, and he warns, "Do not let them see your anger."

"I'll save it for you."

"Good," he says. "If you can get past mine." He releases me, and I start walking.

CHAPTER TWENTY-THREE

Carrie

Reid and I clear the hallway and he steps to my side, his hand catching my elbow, heat radiating up my arm with the touch. "This way," he orders, the words low, but hard.

We round the bar and bring Nicholas Miller into view, a man I've met briefly through my father. He stands to greet us, his thick hair gray, his suit expensive, and his attention on me. "So good to see you, Carrie," he greets, offering me his hand.

"Good to see you too," I say. "And to deliver an update. As I'm sure you noticed, I was meeting with Elijah Woodson, doing my due diligence as Reid requested."

"Yes," he says, glancing at Reid. "Due diligence." He looks at me again. "How did that go?"

"As Reid warned. Not well. He's luring us in with money, but he has his eyes on a high-risk pet project that I suspect our competitors already passed on. Frankly, I doubt we would see any money but that which he's allocated for the high-risk project."

"This is disappointing," he says. "I met with Elijah and he talked about a couple of high-rise Asia-based projects."

"High-rise Asia-based projects are high-risk," I say. "Believe me. You have to have every duck lined up, and not a feather missing, to ensure you don't lose your ass to regulations, laws, and currency issues."

"And yet Elijah is willing to take the risk."

"Elijah only loses his money," I reply. "We lose the money of those we convince to jump on board and invest, as well as our own money, and that of the stockholders. In the end, a failure would leave Elijah looking like a victim of our mishandling."

"And since I have bad blood with Elijah," Reid interjects, "he could spin his loss as some sort of personal punch from me, which damages my company and family as well. Frankly, I wouldn't put it past him to pull out at the last minute and cause a default of the project that he'd pin on me."

Nicholas arches a brow. "He hates you that much?"

"He does."

"Even if there wasn't something personal involved," I add. "I'd never recommend we take this kind of risk while recovering from two bad hits. Not unless we're trying to sink the ship. That's my two cents, but I'll leave you two to talk this out. I need to go finish up with Elijah."

"Will this be presented to the board?" he asks.

"No," Reid says. "An opportunity to go bankrupt will not be presented to the board."

I try to step away and Reid catches my arm. "I'll go with you. Goodnight, Nicholas."

"Are you sure walking away from Elijah isn't personal?" Nicholas asks.

"Money is always personal," Reid says. "I don't plan to lose mine. If you'd like to pitch losing yours to the board, feel free to formally request a meeting. Goodnight," he repeats and turns us away from the table we never even sat down at.

"Why did he just ask if it's personal?" I ask, softly. "You told him it was personal."

"Elijah told him. He met with him before I arrived and told him we have bad blood in a play to get me unseated."

"He really hates you."

"Yes. He does."

"And you thought I was a part of all of this," I say. "So much for trust."

"We're going to talk trust tonight."

I don't have the opportunity to reply. We step to the edge of the table where Elijah waits on me. He stands and his focus is on Reid.

"Reid," he states, and it's not a greeting but rather disdain on his tongue.

"Revenge is not a game that you want to play with me or Carrie. Consider this a warning. Your *only* warning." With that he snags my elbow again, turning me toward the door, my mind reeling. What went down between these two? We exit the restaurant and cross the lobby of the building, and I open my mouth to ask questions right as Reid softly warns, "Whatever you're about to say. Save it for when we're alone."

"I can wait," I assure him, and when I dare to meet his eyes, he's quick to reply.

"Remember you said that. I sure as fuck will."

He opens the door to the building for me and I exit to the street. I rotate to face him and he snags my hand, leading me toward a black sedan that I assume is a hired car. The heat radiating off our palms and up my arm momentarily stalls my brain, but once I'm in the back of the car with him sliding in beside me, realization hits me.

I face him while he addresses the driver. "Home," he orders the man, and then looks at me. "This is not the place to talk."

"If you were in a hired car," I demand, "why didn't you take my calls?"

"Your calls change nothing."

"Have you listened to my messages?"

"No."

"Why?"

"You obviously don't understand 'not the place.'"

I scoot closer to him, and grab his arm, leaning in to whisper. "I need you to listen to those messages." I look up at him and say the word I've never said to this man. "Please."

"Whatever you said won't change what you did."

"Then I might as well go home because we have nothing to talk about." I scoot away from him and settle into the leather of the seat, aware now that we are already moving.

"On the contrary," Reid says softly. "We have much to talk about and much left unfinished between us."

I don't reply. I'm angry. I'm hurt. I don't know how I got into a place with this man that he can hurt me, but I did. And so we ride, side by side, tension radiating off of us. He grabs his phone and punches a button before pressing the cell to his ear. I don't know if he's listening to my messages. I tell myself I don't care anymore. We are enemies. We always were or he wouldn't assume my actions are those of an enemy. I sink deeper into my seat as well, the space between us feeling wide. He's not touching me. He's always touching me. I'm not sure what this says about where his head is right now. He finishes listening to the messages, whatever messages he's listened to, and slides his phone into his jacket pocket.

He doesn't speak and he doesn't look at me.

And so, I continue to sit here, aware of him in every possible way, inside and out, in a way I have never been aware of another human being. I hate him. I want him. I'm furious with him. It's a theme. I feel all these things every time we're together. I try now though to set aside lust and anger and think about where his head might be right now. He was set up. From there, my thoughts chase every feeling he might be feeling and I come back to trust. He told me to trust him, but he wasn't willing to do the same of me.

The car stops in front of a building that I now believe to be Reid's apartment, where I'm *not* going with him. I open my door and he catches my wrist, following me out of the car. He pulls me to him and slams the car door shut. "Do not even think about running from me right now."

"I don't run. I walk away when it feels appropriate and that's about control. Mine. Not yours. I'm walking away. That's what feels appropriate."

"You're going upstairs to my apartment with me and if you think I won't throw you over my damn shoulder and take you there, you're wrong."

"Why?" I challenge. "So you can fuck me and your anger out of your system?"

"Yes. That is exactly my plan. Now are you walking, or am I carrying you?"

CHAPTER TWENTY-FOUR

Carrie

"What's it going to be, Carrie?" Reid demands, dragging me flush against his hard body.

"I'll go to your apartment with you, Reid, but don't touch me until I say you can touch me. We're going to talk first."

His lips quirk. "You talk. I'll fuck you while you do it." He takes my hand and starts walking.

I fall into step with him because I really have no choice unless I want to make a scene and I do not. "The part where I said don't touch me until I say you can touch me," I say. "That still applies."

He folds our elbows and pulls me closer. "I've got a pair of handcuffs upstairs that says differently."

"You're not cuffing me."

"Tell me that when I'm between your legs licking you the way we both know you like to be licked."

My God, why did that just make me wet? He's crass and almost mean and yet everything about the man turns me on. He opens the door to his building and drags me inside with him like I'm his possession. Or like he just really needs to do what he suggested and fuck me out of his system. That he feels this need because I'm in his head shouldn't please me, but it does. Almost as much as cuffing him and leaving him in that room.

He drags me close again and sets us in motion, waving to the security guard as we head toward the elevators. Some part of me knows this night will change us, and I don't know if that is good or bad. Just that it will, but I can't stop it. It's in motion. It's already happening. Maybe it happened back there with Elijah. Whatever the case, we've been headed here from the moment we met. Reid punches the elevator button and the doors open. Butterflies attack my stomach and in a quick maneuver, Reid has me against the wall of the elevator car, his powerful thighs caging mine, even as he punches in a code on the panel, followed by his floor number.

The doors seal us inside and his hands come down on my waist as he stares down at me, just stares. "Did you listen to the messages?"

"Yes."

I study him for several beats. "It changes nothing," I say, reading it in his face.

"That's right. I was, and am, going to fuck you ten ways to Sunday in my apartment."

"Because that's what you do. Fuck your enemies?"

The elevator dings and halts, and he has my hand again, leading me out of the car. I don't even know what floor we're on. I just know that I'm about to be in this man's private space, and I'm curious about what it tells me about Reid, about the man beneath the stone.

He pulls me between him and the door, his big body hot and hard behind me. He unlocks the door, opening it and presenting me with the entry. I cross the threshold, a light automatically dimming and before I can do more than walk a step or two, he's behind me, turning me to face him, pressing me against the door. "Because," he says, his legs caging mine once more, his hands on the wall by my head, "getting back to your question in the elevator, I can't stop thinking about fucking you and that's a distraction neither of us can afford. It's s distraction that's in my head when it can't be in my head. *You're* in my fucking head."

He says it like he's angry. Like it's my fault. He's blaming me for whatever sins he's decided I created. "You're consuming my whole damn world," I all but growl at him. "Everything I am. No one can claim that, but *you*. And I didn't even invite you to do it."

"And so you tried to take control yourself tonight."

"No, damn it. I *called* you. I thought I could find out the information you needed to know. That *we* needed to know. And Elijah implied he knew what everyone seems to know about my father but me."

"You have plenty of reasons to betray me. Reasons I can't ignore."

"I also have reasons not to," I remind him.

"What reasons, Carrie?"

I'm in over my head, I think. *I need you*, I think, but I don't say those words. They make me weak. I can't be weak. Emotions I don't want to feel well up in my chest. Emotions that are more personal than professional. "Because you saved me. And because..."

"Because what?" he presses.

"I really don't want to be your enemy, Reid. Can we just not be enemies?"

He looks skyward, seeming to struggle with what comes next, or maybe something he knows that I don't know, and there is something before he fixes me in a turbulent stare. "I cannot do this with you. I fuck. I move on. That is what I do."

"Did I ask you to do anything else? Did I? No. No, I did not. I don't want a relationship and I don't know where you get off acting like I do. I'm not that girl. So fuck me or let me off this damn door and out of here." I press on the hard wall of his chest, and his heart thunders under my palm.

He's stone, he's always stone. I'm suffocating in this man. In how he looks. How he smells. How much I want him. How much I keep hating him and not hating him. "You're not going anywhere," he promises. "Not until we fuck this out of our systems, so don't plan on sleeping." He rotates me, forcing me to move, and now I'm in front of him, facing the door and he's dragging my jacket off my shoulders. It's barely off and he's pressing me to the door again, forcing me to catch myself with my hands, working my skirt down my hips. I yelp as he yanks the panties. "You could have at least shown me your apartment before you destroyed my panties."

He turns me to face him, me against the door. One of his hands is at my hip and the other next to my head. "You want to see my apartment?"

"This doorway sex isn't any different than office sex." A sharp pang in my chest has me cutting my stare before I look at him again. "Never mind. Just fuck me here. We don't need different."

"We *do* need different and *more*," he says. "A hell of a lot more." And suddenly he's throwing me over his shoulder and walking down the hallway, my bare bum under his palm.

"Reid!" I yelp. "The blood is running to my head."

"You'll survive," he assures me and one of my shoes falls off.

"That was my shoe," I say, and the other one falls, too.

"I promise not to wear it," he says, and I can see nothing but his legs before he lays me down on a soft gray couch. "Take off your blouse and bra or I'll rip them, too." He kisses me, a deep slide of tongue over too soon. "Now," he adds, standing up.

I love this blouse and I quickly sit up, pull it over my head, and toss it and my bra, with a fleeting awareness of high ceilings and walls of windows. Reid shrugs out of his jacket, his gaze raking over my naked body, before he tosses it away. "My phone was in my jacket in that hotel room where you left me," he comments. "My jacket was out of reach." He reaches for his tie.

I can't help it. I laugh, pressing my hands to the cushions. "What did you do?"

He leaves his tie dangling and unbuttons his shirt, toeing off his shoes, because as I know well, he's quite the multitasker when it come to fucking. "I picked up the whole damn couch."

"How very resourceful of you. Who did you call for help?"

"Royce."

"Of course. A man paid to keep your secrets."

He removes his shirt, and my God, the man is really the definition of asshole perfection, complete with rippling abs and broad shoulders, but I don't get the full package just yet. With his pants still on, he lowers me to the couch and presses me against the cushion, his big wonderful body on top of mine. His lips linger over my lips and the air thickens around us in that combustible way I've only known with Reid. We're fucking, I know we're fucking and it's all I want, but there's something between me and this man, something that is more real than anything I've ever felt. "I can't believe you told me about the jacket."

"I just wanted to make sure you know all the reasons I have to punish you tonight."

There's something in the way he says those words, something that cuts from deep inside him and my hand goes to his jaw. "I didn't betray you," I whisper. "I swear to you, Reid."

"I know."

"You do?"

"Yes. I heard it in your voice in the message. I know, and it would be so much easier if I didn't."

"What would be easier?"

"Everything." He gives me no chance to ask what he means. His mouth closes down on mine, and in the depth of that kiss is the everything he's just declared. Everything he wants. Everything that I want. Everything that he intends to take from me tonight.

CHAPTER TWENTY-FIVE

Carrie

Reid's kiss devours me. *He* devours me. The taste of him. The heavy perfection of his weight on top of me. His hands traveling over my body, cupping my breasts. His lips at my ear as he whispers, "We'll eventually make it to the bed," and those words punch me in the chest.

His bed.

Me in it.

It shouldn't feel like a big deal. We're fucking. He's trying to fuck me out of his system, and who knows how many women have been here, in his bed, fucked and forgotten. That idea bothers me when getting fucked on his desk didn't. I don't want a relationship, I don't *expect* a relationship. I don't—

His mouth closes down on mine again, driving away all thoughts, his fingers tugging at my nipples, and not gently. I moan into his mouth and arch into the touch, wanting more, but he denies me. He tears his mouth from mine and for a moment, he just lingers there, lips just above mine, and he breathes with me. "We'll make it to the bedroom," he repeats, "but not until we get past that punishment I promised you."

I don't even have time to digest that incredulous statement before he's moved, lifting off of me, and when I would rise to follow, he flips me onto my stomach. Suddenly I'm across his lap and his hand is on my backside. I raise up on my elbows and look over at him. "What are you doing?" I ask, my heart racing.

He squeezes one of my cheeks. "Punishing you for making me obsess over your beautiful ass since the day I met you."

"That's not my fault. An ass for an ass and—"

He smacks my backside, not hard, but it stings and I yelp. "Reid!"

"And for tonight," he repeats. "I'm punishing you for tonight."

"I called you."

His hand comes down on my lower back. "Flatten out. Lay down."

"I'm not laying down."

"I'm going to spank you," he says. "*Lay down.*"

"Reid," I bite out, "damn it."

"You can say no," he says. "You can always say no. Do so now and I'll let you turn over."

Do I want to say no? My answer comes shockingly fast. "I'm not saying no. Lord help me, I'm not saying no, but I'm just—I've never—"

He drags my legs out from under me and settles me flat on my hips, one hand settling on my lower back. "Relax," he orders softly, his hand caresses my lower back, his palm traveling up my spine while the fingers of the other travel to my backside, sliding along my sex, and sink inside me. I pant with the intimate invasion that is there and gone. Then he's patting my sex, over and over, and my God, it's good. It's sexy and erotic and it's far more right than I'd ever imagined. I'm aroused. So very aroused. So very on the edge. Some part of me knows the spanking is coming, but I can't think about that when I'm so close to coming. Only I don't come. *It comes.* He stops patting my sex and I have one second of awareness before he spanks me, one fast palm that stings and then his fingers are back inside me, stroking me, teasing me. I'm panting when he spanks me again and then again. And then nothing. His hand just rests where it's settled over my sex.

I suck in air, expecting another palm, wanting it, and wanting more, so much more. "Reid," I breathe out in desperation and that must be what he was waiting for because it's then that he acts.

He drags me off of his lap and then on top of him, straddling him, and before the impact of just being spanked by this man can fully hit me, he's kissing me. A deep, passionate, drive-me-wild kiss and I have never needed a kiss like I need this one. I sink into it, into *him*, molding myself against him. I still need more, so much more. "Hold onto my neck," he says. "Our only condom is in my nightstand. I'm going to stand up."

His bedroom. I don't seem to want to go there. I press my hands on his shoulders, leaning back to prevent him from getting up. "I'd tell you I'm on the pill and that I'm free of all things that might kill you or make your manly parts fall off, but then you'd have to actually trust me." The statement is out before I realize that I'm now staring into those piercing blue eyes of his, and the dim lighting of the room does nothing to diminish their impact.

"You want me to trust you?"

"Yes," I say, "but it's not about this moment. It's about all of them."

His expression is that stone I know this man to be, the stone that is unbreakable, and I don't know why I would think that would change for me. Abruptly, he rolls me to my back, his big body on top of mine and then he just stares down at me again, tension banding around him and us until he kisses me, hard and fast, and then orders, "Don't move or I swear I'll spank you again."

He stands with that threat and I don't disobey simply because I'm trying to catch my breath. But I can't catch my breath. He's undressing and is one hell of a specimen of a man, all sinewy muscle and perfection, and in about sixty seconds, he's naked and returning to me. He comes down on top of me, the thick ridge of his erection jutting between my legs.

"Trust is a dangerous thing," he says, his cock sliding along the slick line of my sex before he presses inside me, driving deep, burying himself to the hilt, as he adds, "You understand that, right?"

"And yet you're not wearing a condom."

"I keep breaking rules with you." He rolls to his side and drags me with him, pulling my leg to his hip.

"I'm pretty sure getting spanked was my unknown, never-considered rule before now, as was not fucking assholes."

He strokes hair from my face and tilts my face to his. "Did you like the spanking, Carrie?"

It's in that moment that I realize after all of my fears of this man owning me, I laid across his lap and let him spank me, and have zero regrets. "Yes," I say. "But that's not the point."

He shifts inside me and then pumps his hips. I pant and arch my back. "Then what *is* the point?"

"You," I whisper because it's my only coherent thought. "You push me, and I don't know if I love it or hate it. Both. I think both."

He drags my lips to his. "The feeling is mutual." And with those words that I don't even understand, his mouth closes down on mine again. His tongue presses past my lips and it's a slow caress, a savoring, a shift in the mood. The anger is gone. The push and pull between us is all pull now. I don't even know the moment we start moving, our bodies swaying, molded close, hands all over each other. I am lost in this man, in the contrast of the man who spanked me to the man that cradles me to him even as he thrusts inside me. I can feel him everywhere, goosebumps on my skin, my body hyper-sensitive to his every touch.

We build into a sudden urgent need, our bodies moving faster, his hand on my backside lifting me into the pumps of his hips and I both want what comes next and resist it at the same time. I don't want this to end, but he cups my breasts and squeezes and I'm over the edge. My body stiffens and then I begin to quake. He moans, a deep guttural moan, and rolls me almost to my back with a hard thrust of his cock, and he too shudders and shakes.

I don't know how long we are lost in that place of utter release and complete escape. I come back to the present, with me on my back, and him completely on top of me. And now comes that moment after, the one we've shared once before. The one that ended with him telling me to put on my clothes and leave. It's what I expected of him then. It's what I should expect now. Reid is Reid. No matter how good we just felt, I cannot let myself get emotional. He will hurt me. It may already be too late and I don't know how I let this happen.

Feeling as if I'm suffocating in my own stupidity, I press on his chest. "I need up."

CHAPTER TWENTY-SIX

Carrie

"I need up, Reid," I repeat when he doesn't move.

"Hold on, baby," he murmurs, the endearment rolling off his tongue in this intimate, warm way, that does crazy things to my stomach, and feels nothing like his arrogantly delivered "sweetheart" references.

He reaches over me and before I know his intent, he's pressing tissues between my legs, and as silly as it seems, it feels more intimate than anything we've done so far. It drives home the absence of the condom, the undertone of asking for and giving trust between us. "*Baby?*"

He eases back to look at me. "Did that bother you?"

"Since when do you care what bothers me?"

"*Answer*, Carrie."

"No," I say. "It didn't bother me. I just—we're—just—I need a bathroom." I roll away from him and sit up, tossing the tissue in a well-placed trashcan.

Reid is sitting next to me in a flash, snatching up my blouse as I reach for it and tossing it out of reach. "What are you doing?" I demand.

He grabs his shirt and settles it over my shoulders. "Making sure you stay."

I glance over at him. "I don't like an awkward morning after, and all of my things are in my apartment. I should just go now."

"It won't be awkward because this isn't some drunken mistake. I was an asshole in the office."

"Yeah, you were."

"I was pissed at you."

"Pissed at me?" I ask incredulously. "For what?"

"Because I was sure once I fucked you, my obsession with fucking you would end, but it didn't."

"So you were an ass to me," I supply.

"Yes. I was pissed. But—*I'm sorry.*"

I blanch and rotate to face him. "Did you just apologize? And, with a bonus of you being naked while doing it?"

"I did, in fact, apologize while naked." He reaches up and strokes hair behind my ear, the touch remarkably tender, his voice softer now. "We'll get up early and I'll walk you to your place so you can get ready."

I catch his hand, needing to control what I can about where this is headed. "If I stay, then tomorrow morning, it's over. We don't do this anymore."

"No," he says. "I'm not going to say that. I'm not going to make you a promise I can't keep. I already know that I'm not only going to want to touch you tomorrow. I'm *going* to touch you tomorrow, Carrie."

"We're supposed to be fucking each other out of our systems," I remind him.

"And so we'll keep trying."

"You're confusing me, Reid."

"You and me both, baby." He leans in and kisses me. "Stay. I want you to stay, and I want you to *want* to stay."

He wants me to stay. I want to stay. I can't seem to say the words, though. I can't seem to get my head around what I'm doing with this man. But I'm staying. We both know that I'm staying. "Are you going to feed me if I stay?"

He laughs, and I'm not sure I've ever heard him laugh, not like this, not natural and at ease. "Yes. I'll feed you. I'm starving for food and you. There's a sandwich place I love around the corner. They deliver."

"Jersey's?" I ask.

"Yes. Jersey's. I can't believe you knew that."

"I love it, too."

"Well then. You go to the bathroom. It's to the left by the stairs. I'll order."

"Great. Thank you." I stand up, holding his giant shirt closed around me and I start walking, only now aware of the long, rectangular-shaped room with windows that literally climb the room to the second floor.

"What do you want?" he calls after me.

"Tell them to make Carrie's usual," I say over my shoulder without turning or looking out the window. I just want a bathroom and a few minutes to myself.

I reach the door, enter, and shut myself inside. I lean on the door, taking in the long mahogany cabinet beneath a shiny white countertop with a mirror above it. I look down at myself in Reid's shirt and I have a come-to-Jesus moment. I like being in his shirt way too much. I like being here with him way too much, but I'm not a relationship person and neither is he. Reid and I connect professionally and sexually. There is no reason I can't just enjoy this ride. That's how you enjoy a man like Reid, as an adrenaline ride that can be sustained. I'm not falling for him. I'm living the high of the ride. The end. I will not go anyplace else with this.

I drop the shirt, pee, wash up, run my fingers through the wild mess that is my hair, and that's it. I'm not going to give myself a chance to think beyond the logic I've established. I'm going to enjoy Reid. I want to know Reid. I can learn from this man. I have never been with a man who I admired and wanted, to learn from. It's sexy. It's part of his allure. I pull his shirt back into place the best I can and when I open the door Reid is standing there, wearing nothing but his unzipped pants, beautifully naked from the waist up. He lifts a T-shirt in his hand to show it to me. "This won't be so big on you and you can actually use your hands to eat."

He brought me a T-shirt? "Thank you," I say.

"Drop the shirt you're wearing."

"Just like that? Drop the shirt?"

His eyes burn hot with challenge. "Just like that."

"Fine. Just like that." I let it fall from my shoulders and pool on the floor behind me. I am now naked but for my thigh highs, and Reid sweeps my body, his gaze hot and heavy, my nipples puckering beneath the inspection. He groans low in his throat and drags me to him. "You're beautiful. *Really* fucking beautiful."

I can't breathe with the intensity in his voice that is almost anger. Like he doesn't want to feel whatever he feels, and I wonder if we're headed toward him suddenly wanting me to leave, but then he's kissing me, a sultry stroke of tongue before he says, "I'm not even close to done with you, woman."

"And if I'm done with you?"

"I'll lick you until you aren't."

Heat rushes to my cheeks. "You say—"

"The truth. I told the truth. That's what I'll do. And if we don't get you dressed, I'll be fucking you when the food gets here." He kisses me again and pulls the shirt over my head. I shove my arms inside right about the time his phone rings from the living room.

He grimaces and runs his fingers through his hair, leaving it in a spiky sexy mess. "For once I'd like to ignore that damn thing," he says. "But I have to get it."

"Of course you have to get it."

"And you understand that," he says, and this must please him because his hands come down on my waist and he pulls me to him, kissing me hard and fast before releasing me to chase down his phone somewhere near the couch.

For just a moment, I scan the room I've barely noticed because of the man that consumes it and me. The large gray cloth couch a shade darker than the floor, the one where I just had an orgasm, is the entry of the room, framed by cream-colored chairs that are leather to contrast the gray. There's a gray rug under the couch. The coffee and end tables match the chairs. Cluster lighting dangles just above the seating area, resembling diamond raindrops in the sky. It's appropriately Reid in its simple masculinity while I don't believe there is anything simple about this man beyond this room.

I move forward, intending to join Reid where he's now standing by the couch on the phone. Instead, I find myself stepping to the window just in front of the living area, staring at the Statue of Liberty alight in the center of a now black sea. My stomach knots with about ten emotions, all personal, all about where I am in life right now at this moment.

"Tomorrow," Reid says to whoever he's talking to. "No, Gabe. I'm not dealing with this tonight. Tomorrow. I'm hanging up now." I sense rather than know that he does just that, and in a few beats, he is standing beside me, his hand stroking down my hair.

"Problem?" I ask, glancing over at him.

"My fucking brother is always a problem."

"Gabe?" I ask, turning to face him.

"Yes Gabe. He has no limits. Not where I'm concerned."

"It's just him and a sister, right? You don't have any other siblings?"

"We have a younger brother, who lives in Texas. He's also completely removed from the family business. He's a civil engineer which is a blessing. Gabe manages to be a pain in my ass enough as it is." He pulls me to him, hands shackling my waist. "Forget Gabe. What were you thinking when I just joined you?"

"I don't think I'll share that," I say, my hand settling on his chest.

"Why?"

"It's my own personal baggage. It's not for you, Reid."

"What if I want it to be?"

"But you don't. You just think you do because we're in the moment. Tomorrow changes everything."

"We had this discussion. Tomorrow changes nothing. What were you thinking?"

"I love your view, Reid," I say.

He narrows his eyes at me. "And you're comparing my view to yours?"

"Yes," not sure how he reads me this easily but maybe that's part of how he's made so much money, and he's under forty. He's a good poker player. He reads people.

"I have years on you, baby. You know that, right?"

"Yes. I do. I know."

His hand goes to my face and he tilts my gaze to his. "You don't have to sell your apartment. You aren't going to lose your job. We're going to make a lot of money together."

"I really hate that you had me investigated."

"It was before we were personal. You know that, too."

"That doesn't mean I like it."

"You aren't selling your apartment."

"I am, and I'll buy another later," I say, "more like this one."

"I'll make your apartment part of the deal when they sign you as CEO. We'll pay it off."

"No," I say immediately. "No, I'm not some sort of kept woman, Reid. I will earn what I get."

"Kept woman? The board will award it to you and you take every perk you can get. You think that you won't be earning it?"

"I think *you'll* earn it. I think you'll make it happen. You thought I betrayed you tonight for a reason."

"What does that mean, Carrie?"

"You know what it means. I had the chance to sweep control and I didn't take it, but you would have and that's why you have this apartment and I'm selling mine."

"You're seeing this with the wrong eyes."

"Exactly," I say. "If you were me, would you have taken it?"

His expression hardens. "Not with you."

"But with someone else?"

"Not with you."

The doorbell rings. "That's our food." He kisses me. "We're doing this together for a reason. I can't do it without you. I'll teach you how to swim with the sharks and win. And no, you don't have to be as brutal as I am."

"Why wouldn't you demand that I be exactly as brutal as you?"

"Because I want you to stay you and you'll be better for it." The doorbell rings again. "I'll be right back."

He heads toward the door in nothing but his unzipped pants and I focus on three words he spoke. *Not with me.* He's heartless. He's brutal. He's spared me. It's not comforting. What happens if he turns on me? And why am I not running? Because I'm not. I'm not even close to running.

Reid

I walk down the hallway toward the door, out of Carrie's sight, and before I answer the door, I press a hand on the wall next to it and let my chin dip. What the fuck am I doing? I'm acting like I want things with Carrie that I swore I didn't want in my life. More. Like I want more than sex when sex is the zone where I keep women. I need to reel this in, but instead, I'm not going to. I'm going eat sandwiches with Carrie and talk to her. I won't even consider letting her go home tonight.

The doorbell rings again.

Fuck.

I open the damn door.

CHAPTER TWENTY-SEVEN

Reid

I enter the living room with the take-out bag in my hand and Carrie meets me by the couch, my T-shirt swallowing her whole, but damn I like her in it a little too much for comfort. And yet, I pull back from where we're headed tonight. "Let's go upstairs."

Her eyes meet mine. "As in, to your bedroom?"

"Yes," I say, sensing the tentativeness in her over my room and not sure where that is coming from. "To my bedroom. My favorite place to eat is up there."

"Now you have me curious," she says, the tentativeness fading quickly.

Pleased that we jumped that hurdle quickly, I motion her forward. "Then onward to the man cave."

She laughs as we head to the stairs. "That sounds dangerous considering this is you we're talking about," she teases.

Dangerous.

That word hits about ten nerves, all connected to my past that I don't intend to think about tonight, not with this woman, *with Carrie*, in my bed. We climb the steel stairs that lead directly into my master bedroom through an archway. "No door?" Carrie asks as we approach.

"It's just me," I say. "And I like to be able to see and hear everything at all times."

"Talk about a control freak," she teases as she passes under the archway directly in front of me, to halt a few steps inside the room.

I step to her side, taking it in with her as if I've seen it for the first time. The room is a V-shape with a fireplace to the right, and dark gray flooring throughout. Directly in front of the fireplace and several feet away, there's a step up to the master bed, which has a gray leather headboard beneath which I plan to fuck Carrie until we can fuck no more.

"It's very you," Carrie says, glancing over at me. "Very powerful and masculine."

I'd like to see that as a compliment, but it also tells me that despite all her pushing back against my every demand, the power thing is on her mind, it's between us, and it's a problem I need to deal with now rather than later. I motion to the pillars framing another archway just beyond the bed. "That's our dinner location."

She moves ahead of me to enter the round room wrapped in windows, with a gray sectional in the center, and a tree trunk-style gray coffee table set in front of it. "This is my favorite place in the apartment," I say, as I sit down on the couch and pat the cushion next to me.

"I can see why," she says, claiming the spot I've patted. "It's like a little escape." She indicates the bookshelves to our left and right. "What would I find if I explored?"

"A collection of law reference manuals, as well as fiction, and non-fiction pleasure reads. I come here to relax but also to think through big decisions." I set two bottles of water on the table and then remove our sandwiches, setting hers in front of her. "I ordered our regulars." I rest my elbows and glance over at her. "What's yours?"

"Egg salad. What's yours?"

"Egg salad," I say, surprised at how many things I really do have in common with Carrie.

192

She smiles, and damn I love her smile. "They must have thought it was odd that two regulars ordered together tonight. How long have you been here and ordering?"

"Five years," I say, opening my sandwich as she does the same. "You?"

"Six years for me. I can't believe we haven't run into each other, as in literally, while jogging. I mean, we're on opposite sides of the plaza, but the running thing. We must have run right by each other for years."

"It wasn't our time to meet," I say softly, thinking about the different place we'd be in had we met before I read that letter from my mother, and even before that debt with our parents was paid. "Eat," I say, winking. "You're going to need your energy."

She gives me a shy smile and slides onto the floor before she takes a bite. *Shy.* This woman who cuffed me and left me in a hotel room is such a perfect contradiction. I dig in as well and for a few minutes, we eat in comfortable silence. That's something I don't remember having with another woman but then I never wanted to try. "In darkness there is light," she says of the dark sea and starless night, illuminated only by the Statue of Liberty.

"Exactly what this room is to me."

She tips back her water and sets it down before abandoning the rest of her sandwich to join me on the couch again. "Your father retired?" she asks, curling her legs on the couch, turning to face me.

I finish off my sandwich and settle back on the couch next to her, angling toward her. "Semi-retired. He has a hard time letting go."

I expect her to push on my father, but she doesn't. "And your mother?" she asks instead.

"Died four years ago, going on five that feels like ten."

"You had her growing up and then you lost her. I'm both envious and heartbroken for you. Were you close to her?"

Most people say they're sorry for my loss, but not Carrie. She dives into the heart of the matter and dives deep, and yet, when I would normally pull back, I find myself answering her without hesitation. "I thought I was."

"What does that mean?"

"It means that I found out that I didn't know what was going on in her life. There was a side of my mother I didn't understand, but I should have."

"Like me and my father, it seems."

"I don't think so," I say, wanting to avoid her father at all costs and that cost is me making confessions I never make. "I idolized my father. I chose to be blind to my mother's pain because he created it."

"I'm not sure if I should ask what that means."

"My mother wrote my sister a letter that detailed her miserable life with my father. He cheated often, with many, and treated her like shit. I had no idea. I knew he was a bastard in the boardroom, so to speak, but I thought she was the person that kept him human. I was wrong." I meet her stare. "My mother also wrote of her fears that I was so close to him that I would become him."

"But you're not," she says. "You know that, right?"

"Says the woman who is always calling me an asshole."

"You *are* an asshole," she says. "But we both know that's a choice, or rather a persona. I don't believe you're him. Not the way you describe him. Not from what I know of you."

To allow her to believe that I'm not that asshole she's called me would be a selfish mistake. That's how she gets hurt. That "persona" as she calls it, is what keeps people at a distance, it's how I keep from actually getting close enough to anyone to hurt them the way he hurts people. And yet, what do I do? I reach for her and pull her closer. "I don't talk about my family, Carrie. I don't bring women to my apartment. I have never brought anyone to this room."

Shock flickers over her face. "Then why am I here, Reid?"

I drag her onto my lap. "Because I want you here. Because I can't seem to stop breaking my own fucking rules with you."

Her hands plant on my shoulders. "And you're mad at me again? You're blaming me."

"Yes. Stop making me break my rules." I cup her head and kiss her, my tongue pressing past her lips, stroking us both into a needier place, where rules don't matter.

She moans and sinks into the kiss, and damn it, I love those moans, I'm addicted to those moans. I'm addicted to this woman, and all my good intentions to sate that addiction, fail. I pull my T-shirt over her head and toss it, and my gaze raking over her breasts, her nipples puckering under the inspection. My hand slides between her shoulder blades, and I mold her close. "This is definitely your fault."

"Is this where you decide to kick me out again?"

"No," I say. "This is where we fuck." I drag her mouth to mine, and kiss her, telling myself that fucking is all this can be, reminding myself of the debt and the secret I legally cannot share. The secret that she'd never stay silent over if she knew.

I tell myself to get lost in the taste of her, defiant and yet submissive at the same time, in that way that defines this woman. I tell myself to just enjoy the moment, and I do. I waste no time getting naked and pulling her down the throbbing length of my cock. I waste no time driving into her. I waste no time getting lost in her touch, her kisses, her moans. And later, much later, when I've laid us down and pulled her next to me on the couch, I hold her, listening to her breathing slow and even out. I'm acutely aware that she is a woman caught in the middle of a debt that has to be paid, destined to hate me. It's why this has to stay just sex. It's why no matter how deep I go with her, I cannot get too close.

CHAPTER TWENTY-EIGHT

Carrie

"Carrie."

I blink to the sound of my name and an awareness of Reid behind me washes over me, his big body wrapped around mine, his lips at my ear. "You awake, baby?"

"Yes," I whisper. "Are you trying to get rid of me?"

"Not even close," he says, nuzzling my neck, his lips near my ear as he softly orders, "Look out the window."

I blink again and bring the window into view, my lips parting with the sight of a golden sunrise lifting the darkness from the sky. "It's beautiful," I murmur.

"How's that for your awkward morning after?" he asks, his hand flattening on my belly.

"It depends on what comes next," I say, rolling over to face him, my hand settling on his jaw, the dark blond of morning stubble rasping my palm. "We kind of blew your plans to stay up all night. We never made it off the couch."

He catches my hand and kisses it. "Then we can try again tonight."

"You want me to stay again tonight?"

"Yes," he says. "I do. And let me give you some incentive." He rolls me onto my back and the next thing I know, he's spreading my legs, settling between them, and his mouth is on my belly. "I want to add a little something to your awkward morning after." His lips curve and he slides lower, settling his shoulders between my thighs and then he licks my clit.

I suck in air as sensations spiral through me, my hips arching toward his mouth. He licks me again and my sex clenches with how badly I want him inside me. "Reid," I whisper, intending to tell him just that, but his mouth closes down on that oh so intimate part of me and I forget everything but what he is doing to me. He suckles and licks, his fingers stroking my sex, pressing inside me and I am on edge that quickly. I can't help it. He seems to naturally know my body, and I'm at the arousing disadvantage of an overwhelming erotic and somehow romantic experience, of being woken up to Reid Maxwell's mouth on my body with a sunrise as a backdrop. Already the build to that sweet blissful place is upon me and there really is no climb to the top. I'm just *there*. My body clenches around his fingers and then I'm spasming, my entire body trembling with release. It's hard and fast and I melt into the cushion, a complete limp noodle.

"My God," I whisper, looking down at him, expecting him to come to me, but he does not.

He kisses my belly again and stays where he's at. "That's how I'll wake you up in the morning if you stay again. *I promise.*"

I raise up on my elbows and study him, wondering if he realizes that he's a very generous, selfless lover. Actually, he's generous in many ways, a contradiction to the hard-ass that he shows the world. But not me. He's let me see beneath his stone exterior and I've never wanted to know him more. "I'll stay," I say, "but tomorrow morning, it's my turn to wake you up properly and I will. *I promise.*"

His eyes light in a way they rarely light. "Is that right?"

"Yes, but we can practice tonight to make sure I get it just right. Or now. We could practice now."

That's all it takes and he's on top of me. "Not now. *This* now." His mouth is on mine, his cock pressing between my thighs, and then inside me. And there is no kink or play or teasing to this. It's need. His. Mine. So much need. We are fast and hard, him thrusting, and me arching into each movement he makes. It's wild and hot and like my orgasm, too fast. We shatter together and he is pure raw male perfection as he reaches beneath me, cups my backside and lets out a low, guttural moan as he shudders into his own release. He relaxes into me as I sink into the cushion, but we are only there for moments before he rolls us to our sides, facing each other.

"You, woman," he growls.

"What does that mean?"

"It's a synonym for 'I wish the fuck I knew.' Fuck." He squeezes his eyes shut and then looks at me. "I'm not the guy you marry and have kids with. You know that, right?"

"I'm not the girl that wants those things. Why are you even saying this to me?"

"I'm not my father. I'm not, but I am hard, cold. I'm brutal, even. I'm *not* the man for you."

"O—kay." A knot twists in my gut. "So much for avoiding the awkward morning after." I try to pull away.

He snags my leg with his leg, his hand settling on my waist. "I'm not the man for you, but I can't seem to care. I can't and I should." Relief washes over me as he adds, "I don't want to let you go. I don't want to stop touching you. I don't want to share you."

He doesn't want to share me? I don't want to share him, either. "Then don't," I whisper.

"I'm not," he says. "That's what I'm telling you. I'm not sharing you. I'm not walking away, but you should. You should, Carrie, and—"

I lean in and press my lips to his. "I'm not and I should. I get it. You've warned me. I've warned me, but I don't break easily."

"One day you'll hate me all over again. It's not what I want but it will happen. Remember this moment. Remember that it's *not* what I want."

"We've already been at hate, Reid. That's not where we're at."

"Not now," he says, lacing his fingers with mine and kissing my knuckles before he seems ready to move on. Like he's said all he can say. "Let's go shower."

I want to push him to talk to me, to understand where all of the hate comes from, but I sense this isn't the time. "I have to shower at home with all my products. Maybe you can walk me there?"

"We'll go get your things and come back here."

"Reid—"

He kisses me again. "Let's go get your things." There is a hard push in his words that I could read as a demand, but I don't.

I pull back and study him, and I'm right. It's not demand. It's more need. *For me.* This powerful man that I know could teach me so much, show me so much, *needs me.* At least for now. I don't know when that ends or how it ends or if that's with hate, but there is more to Reid Maxwell than meets the eye. And right now, I need him, too.

"Yes," I say. "Let's go get my things."

He smiles. This man of stone smiles. And so, I smile, too.

Reid throws on sweats and I knot his T-shirt over my skirt, and we walk to my apartment, with his arm around my shoulders. We enter my apartment and I motion to my windows. "It's not an ocean view, but the windows are cute and perfect." I glance over at him. "I love them."

"They, and this place," he says, scanning our surroundings, "are very you."

I laugh at the play on my own words about his place and step in front of him. "I'll bite. What does that mean?"

"It's unique, feminine, and powerful."

"Just not as powerful as you, but I'm okay with that." I press my hand to his chest. "Knowledge is sexy and so is power and even money, but don't worry, I don't want yours. I want to make my own."

His hands close down on my arms and he pulls me to him. "And you will. You already are." He kisses me. "Go get your things. I still need to have coffee and you before we leave for work."

"You already had me."

"And it never seems to be enough." He turns me and smacks my ass. "Go."

Heat rushes over me with that smack, memories of me across his lap flooding my mind and body as he intends, I'm certain. I don't give him the satisfaction of knowing it worked. I hurry forward and up my black steel winding stairs, which I also adore. I love this place. I don't want to lose it. Maybe I don't have to lose it. I might not be as cold as Reid, but he said he could teach me ways around that. Maybe he can. I refuse to believe destroying others is the only way to succeed and it's a testament to my state of mind that I allowed myself to slip into that point of view.

Feeling more positive than I have in a month, I enter my bedroom and make my way through the bathroom to the walk-in closet in the back, a luxury in this city. I pull out a pale blue suit dress that travels well and hang it to the side before grabbing my overnight case and setting it on the stool in the center of the room. I'm just filling it with heels, hose, and lingerie, including a red silk slip gown, when I hear, "Pack for the weekend."

At the sound of Reid's voice, I glance up to find him leaning on the doorframe, his blond hair a sexy, rumpled mess. "Weekend?"

"I'm trying to fuck you out of my system, remember? How can I do that if you aren't with me?" He delivers that statement in a deadpan voice, but I know he's joking.

"Maybe an extra night is all it will take for me," I say, going along with him. "I'm not committing to more."

He's around the stool in a heartbeat, dragging me to him. "You think you can get rid of me that easily?"

"We'll find out soon, now won't we?"

He kisses me, a deep drugging kiss that makes my sex clench. "We already know it's not that easy, for either of us. Pack for the weekend. That's an order."

"And outside of work, I should take your orders why?"

He kisses me again and this time his hand cups my backside and he pulls me hard against him, the thick length of his erection pressing to my belly. "Pack for the weekend, baby," he says, his voice low, rough, affected.

The "baby" wins me over, that and knowing he doesn't invite women to his apartment for a night, let alone a weekend. "I'll pack for the weekend."

CHAPTER TWENTY-NINE

Carrie

I change into sweats and Reid and I drop my stuff off at his apartment with time to spare, which we don't spend naked. We walk to the coffee shop and back again. "How many days a week do you run?" he asks.

"Every workday," I say, "and I go to the gym in my building three days a week. What about you?"

"Same," he says, "but I have a gym in my apartment."

"Of course you do," I say. "Right along with the perfect sunrise view."

"Both of which you can share," he says, sliding his arm around my shoulders.

"In between fucking me out of your system?"

"Exactly," he says, laughing. "In between fucking like rabbits, we'll watch sunrises and work out. What more could you want for a weekend?"

Not much, I think, especially if he's going to laugh like that. I like that he laughs. It feels like a goal I need to achieve more often. Make Reid laugh. His cellphone buzzes with a text and he glances down at it and types a reply, grimacing. "My damn brother," he murmurs as we step onto his elevator. "I need to run by my office and deal with him before work."

"I don't know how you run your company and mine, too, or, well, it's not mine."

He pulls me in front of him, his hands on my shoulders. "It will be again."

"I know," I say. "And not because I think you're on my side. Because I'm going to go in there today and find a better version of Elijah."

"I am on your side. You know that, right? This thing between us, it's not some way for me to read you or control you."

I push to my toes and kiss him. "I know."

He molds me close and cups the back of my head. "Just don't forget, and yes, that's an order." He kisses me and the elevator dings. "Come on," he says, lacing my fingers with his as he leads me out of the elevator to his door.

Not long later, we're in the shower, and I'm pressed against the wall with him inside me, that ends with us on the shower floor, me straddling him. I have a moment when we manage to stand with me still in his arms that I remember telling him that he's taken over and consumed my whole life. And he has. Completely. He's taken over my life completely.

That feeling only grows as we step out of the shower and I slip on my robe, and I end up at a sink next to him getting ready for work. At one point, he's shaving and I just watch him, but I don't feel nervous or uncomfortable. One thing I decided years ago is that I'm me. I can't be anyone else. I can be a better me, yes, but still me.

I'm still flat ironing my hair when he steps out of his closet in a three-piece gray suit with a red pinstripe that matches his tie, looking like sex and sin and every woman's fantasy, when his phone buzzes on the counter. He grabs it and glances at the number, smirking as he answers. "Mr. District Attorney. You're early this morning." He listens a minute and then says, "You're closer. You're not there." He hangs up.

I blanch. "Did you just hang up on the district attorney?"

"I did."

"My God, Reid. That takes balls."

He steps behind me, his hands on my waist, his eyes meeting mine in the mirror. "Yes, Carrie, it does. Just like you making me your bitch in that hotel room."

I laugh. "You are no one's bitch."

"You beat me that night, Carrie. That's why I convinced the board we should rethink the future. No one beats me. That's not arrogant. It's a fact."

His cellphone rings and he grabs it from his pocket, winks at me in the mirror, and then answers the call. "Yes, Mr. District Attorney?" He listens a minute. "That's closer and yes, I'll come meet you, but it won't change the number. I'll be there in half an hour." He disconnects and turns me to face him. "I'll meet you at the office."

"You're leaving me in your apartment?"

"Yes. I am. I trust you."

"Just give me a minute and I'll leave with you."

"Stay. Take your time."

"You don't even bring women here, Reid. You can't leave me here alone."

He pulls me to him and kisses me. "I'll see you at the office."

He releases me and heads for the door. "Reid!" I call out.

He turns at the door.

"The settlement is for the families of the murder victims, right? In the serial killer case?"

"Yes."

"*Destroy* him."

His eyes sharpen. "I plan to. And you—have a look around, Carrie. That's an invitation." He turns and leaves me in his bathroom, in his home. I'm overwhelmed with the trust he's given me when I believe this man trusts no one. When just last night he questioned my loyalty, or maybe that's what's behind the hate. He expected of me what he expects of himself with anyone but me, he'd said. Something is happening between me and this man, and I react.

I rush after him. "Reid!" I exit the bathroom and he stops at the bedroom door, turning to face me and my God, the man is hotness personified.

I cross to stand in front of him, push to my toes and kiss him. "What was that for?"

"Because. Just because. Good luck. That's all."

He cups my head and kisses me, a real kiss, deep, sexy and fast. "You, woman," he says and then, reluctantly it seems, he sets me away from him and heads down the stairs. I follow him and stand at the railing, watching him depart, his stride confident, predatory even, but underneath his killer persona, he's human, he's damaged. He's a man surrounded by a stone wall meant to hide that damage and keep everyone away. And yet, I'm here. I know this man could ruin me. I know he could hurt me. I know he controls much of my future and that I need him. And yet, for reasons I can't explain, I feel like he needs me, too.

Reid

I step onto the elevator, leaving Carrie behind in my apartment in my private space where I want her. At some point last night, I accepted that my obsession with Carrie isn't going away. This isn't about her perfect ass, or how much I want to fuck her. It's more. This woman is under my skin in ways I didn't think any woman could be under my skin. Beyond reason, I need her with me when I know all the ways this could end badly, but I can't seem to care. I've never walked away from anything I wanted, no matter how hard the challenge, and I'm not starting with Carrie.

She was right. I want to own her, all of her. She's mine. That very premise defies the way I've lived my life and all the reasons that being alone serves me well, but it's too late to cut this off. Those reasons don't matter now. It's too late for me to walk away. But I'm done trying to save Carrie from me. Everyone else, yes, but not me.

CHAPTER THIRTY

Reid

I play the district attorney's game and listen to his offer, right before I tell him to fuck off, quite literally, and walk out. I've made it halfway to the Maxwell offices when my phone rings and he ups the offer. "Still too low," I say and hang up. He doesn't call back right away, but he will. Sometimes, being an asshole to assholes really is the icing on top of the cake with this job. He needs to pay. People died and suffered because of him.

My minds goes to Elijah and I dial Royce Walker. "I need to control someone without ruining him but I'll ruin him if I have to."

"Why would you ruin him?"

"Because he tried to ruin me."

"Why would you save him?"

"Because he took an emotional bullet I didn't intend for him to take but I'm not taking a financial bullet to dry up his tears."

"Name?"

"Elijah Woodson."

"Give me a couple of hours. Anything else?"

"Yes. Do you know who Grayson Bennett is?"

"If you mean the billionaire businessman, yes. What about him?"

"This is out of your realm of services, but I need to win him over. I want to show him that I can find out what he likes, by way of a gift, and deliver that item to him today."

"And this wins him over how?"

"It shows him I do my research. I find out what makes people tick and pleasure is part of what makes us all tick."

"The John Walker, which will run you four thousand a bottle."

"And you know this how?"

"We've done private security work for him for a charity event. I had the opportunity to talk with him over a bottle of that particular whiskey."

"You are worth your money, Royce Walker."

"Remember that when I raise your rates. I'll be in touch." He disconnects and my head starts to throb, as in literally, the way it used to when I was recovering from yet another too hard hit when I played football in school. I ignore the pressure at the back of my head and dial Connie and arrange to have the whiskey delivered with a note I custom dictate. By the time I'm done, the car pulls to the Maxwell offices. I enter the building, with one goal in mind: get my fucking brother off my ass. I enter the executive offices and ignore his secretary, Lulu, a thirty-something redhead with an attitude, and I do so based on principle. I don't like any attitude that isn't Carrie's, and who the fuck is named Lulu anyway?

Gabe's door is open and I walk into his office to find him on the phone. I shut the door as he glances up and eyes me. "Yes, father. I know, father. I know. You told me that three times." He glances at the receiver and hangs up.

"What the hell is the crisis?" I demand, crossing to his desk and sitting down on one of the burgundy visitor's chairs.

"Our father is the problem," he says. "That's call number three. He feels you've undone the effect of the debt payment between him and West. He threatened to walk away from the consulting job he's doing in Europe and return home."

My jaw clenches. "You mean because of Carrie."

"Exactly."

"I only got involved because of his fucking stroke and the state he and our dear uncle left our reputation in the first place. And I made a deal with West and our father. They get out of town. This wasn't Carrie's debt or ours and yet we're the ones paying for it."

"Her father tried to make it ours," Gabe reminds me. "You know that."

"They both did and they failed. I didn't let them make this about the younger generation of our families. I won't let them. This isn't our war. I thought you agreed."

"I do," he says. "Just making sure I know where we stand. I thought maybe Carrie had become a weapon for you."

"No."

"That's a short answer. What's the story here on you and Carrie? The real story?"

I rub the back of my neck and look at him, my brother, who outside of what is blooming with Carrie, is the only person I actually trust in this world. "I don't know," I answer honestly.

He leans forward. "I don't remember ever hearing you say those words."

"Because I *don't* say those words," I bite out.

"Are you sure she's not the enemy?"

"Yes," I say. "I am." I scrub my jaw. "If she was, it wouldn't matter though. I'd turn her."

He studies me a few beats. "I get it," he finally says. "More than you know. The question is, does she know about the debt?"

"Hell no. You know we have a gag order. You know what's on the line if this leaks and she'd confront her father if I told her."

"Of course, she would. I sure the fuck would."

"And honestly, man. As much as not telling her is killing me, I think of mom's letter. I think of how much I didn't want to know what I know. Carrie is a good person, too good for me. I don't want her to go through the awakening I did."

"But you're glad you did. I know I sure the hell am."

"I needed to get my shit together. She doesn't."

"Her father will always hold this secret over you."

"And ultimately he'll use it and she'll hate me. I know, but what the fuck am I supposed to do, Gabe?" My cellphone rings and my jaw clenches. I grab it and look at the number, standing up and walking to Gabe's window as I answer, "Yes, Mr. District Attorney. I'm going to break a rule and say please, do not make another insulting offer."

"Three o'clock. My office. My final offer."

"Tell me now."

"No," he says, and hangs up.

Gabe steps to my side. "No deal?"

"There's a deal," I say. "He's just being a pain in my ass to get there," I say the words, but my mind is already back on Carrie.

Gabe knows too, returning to her with me. "You just met Carrie," Gabe says, joining me. "Right now, you can't say anything."

"Thank you, brother," I say, looking at him, "for confirming, my fucked-up situation."

"What's a brother for," he says, "if not to ground you in reality of just how fucked your life is right now?"

Carrie

I arrive to work feeling motivated and smelling like Reid. Literally. I forgot my perfume, and without really thinking about the potential fallout of spraying myself in "him" I doused myself in his cologne. After which, I'd inhaled with the brutally perfect spicy smell of me because, well, I love how he smells. I'd proceeded to head to work feeling motivated to score that big number goal Reid has inspired me to achieve. He saved my company. He gave me a chance to lead its future. He made me think big, and I need to think big to be CEO.

I walk by Sallie's desk, offer her a cheery "good morning" and claim my seat behind my desk. She then dashes into my office, stands in front of my desk and says, "Who is he?"

I blink up at her, hating the rush of heat to my cheeks. "What are you talking about?"

"You smell like a man and you have a glow about you."

"I smell like a man," I say, and with a completely straight face, continue with, "as in sweaty and I need a shower?"

She smirks. "You know what I mean. Like cologne."

"In other words, my new perfume is a no-go."

"That's perfume? It smells manly."

Because Reid is manly, I think, before I reply with, "Like I said. Ditch the new perfume."

"What kind is it?"

"Some sample in my makeup order." I change the subject. "Anyone present any grand ideas for Elijah?" I ask, despite the fact that Elijah is a no-go, because no one knows that yet, and I can use the ideas elsewhere.

"None you want to see I promise you," she says. "And on that bright note, I'm going to get coffee at the coffee shop. Want one?"

"Yes. Please."

She departs, leaving me wallowing in my dissatisfaction with our team's performance, despite the fact that Elijah is out of the picture. Had he been in the picture, we would have failed to provide him with an enticing investment. Elijah who Reid and I never finished talking about, a man on a mission for revenge, that could land right here with this company. I need to know what that's about. Reid has to tell me.

For now, I set that aside, and I think about the comments about my father. Some people really wouldn't do business with him, and I think hard about who else is on that list. I look down my prospect list, highlighting contacts that were far warmer to me than my father. Somewhere in this process, Sallie brings me coffee and the little egg white quiches I eat often.

Once I've downed my breakfast, I home in on one name: Marcus Phelps, one of the money men behind the New York Rockets baseball team comes to mind. He seemed like he wanted to do business, but something held him back. I dial him and leave a message. He calls me right back. "I was going to call you," he says, his voice flirty as usual, because he flirts with everyone. He's a real player. He can't even stop himself. "I hear you're up for CEO to replace your father."

"I am," I say. "Does that change things for you?"

"Maybe. Let's have lunch. I'm headed out of town for a week. Let's set a date for when I get back."

We set our date and disconnect. I'm about to call through a few other prospects when Reid calls. "Hey, baby," he says softly.

My stomach flutters with the endearment, and my reaction tells a real story. We've gone from me calling him an asshole, to here, and we've done it quickly. I wait for this to feel uncomfortable, but I let the man go down on me the night I met him right before I cuffed him. I'm pretty outside any supposed boundaries with Reid.

"Hey," I reply. "How are things? Did you settle?"

"Not yet. I'm meeting him again at three but we're close."

Noting the strain in his voice, I ask, "What has you worried?"

"Who says I'm worried?"

"Worried or weary or something. I hear it in your voice."

He's silent several beats and then says, "I'm headed to one of the stockholders' offices to head off a problem."

"About Elijah?"

"Yes," he confirms. "About Elijah."

"Are you going to tell me what's between you two?"

He's silent another two beats and then he says, "We'll talk," and moves on. "I won't be in until after my meeting at the DA. How are things there?"

"Good. I got a meeting set up with a big prospect."

"You can tell me all about it tonight, naked, in my bed or anywhere in my apartment that suits you. Location is optional. Being naked is not. Did you look around?"

"No. I wanted to wait for you. I want you to show me what you want me to see."

"Did you now?"

"Yes. I did. I do." I hesitate. "Reid."

"Don't swing this conversation back to Elijah."

"What if I can pull him out of revenge mode?"

"No."

"Reid—"

"No, Carrie. I need to go."

"I'm not done with this topic."

"But I am, at least, until you're naked."

"You're obsessed with me being naked."

"I'm just obsessed with you, Carrie."

My stomach flutters again. "You are?"

"Yes. I am. Everything about you. One partial obsession you've stirred in me comes to mind."

"What obsession?"

"My desire to cuff you to my bed, with the very cuffs you cuffed me with the night we met. You're going to let me."

Heat rushes over me. "No."

"Why? You don't trust me, Carrie?"

The words tease, but my brow furrows with the certainty that there's more beneath their surface. "Actually, Reid, I do trust you."

"Those words will be tested, Carrie. I have to go. Call me if you need me." He hangs up.

Those words will be tested. He's not talking about the cuffs. He's talking about his certainty I will soon hate him again and I want to know what that means. Actually, I want to know a lot of things. Like what's the story with Elijah and what does everyone but me know about my father. Maybe I'm the one who needs to cuff Reid Maxwell again, but this time, he'll be naked first, and I won't be leaving.

CHAPTER THIRTY-ONE

Carrie

It's nearly four in the afternoon and I'm sitting behind my desk with Sallie in front of me again, when my intercom buzzes and I hear, "My office. Now." It's Reid, of course, announcing that he, and the asshole persona he slips into at work, are now present and in the building.

"Why are you smiling?" Sallie demands. "The man bosses you around like you're his slave."

I didn't actually know that I was smiling, but I don't miss a beat. "I'm smiling because he's doing it to piss me off and that's the entire point," I say, standing up. "He wants me to lead among all the assholes like him. I get it. I get him. And he doesn't get to upset me." I head for the door.

"Kick his ass!" she calls after me, and I laugh. I love this woman who would be horrified and then asking for details that I wouldn't give her if she knew about me and Reid.

I cross the office where Connie is presently behind her desk. "Beware. He's in some kind of mood."

"Really?"

"Really, and I don't say that often. I get him. I know him. Something is wrong."

I immediately think of Elijah, but then my mind goes to the DA and his settlement. "Thanks for the heads up," I say.

"I don't give a heads up about Reid," she says, obviously prompting me with the question I ask.

"Then why did you just warn me?"

"I have a gut feeling about you."

Her gut feeling could mean many things, and for all I know, she thinks I'm too weak to handle his mood. She doesn't give me time to ask. "Do you want me to buzz him or are you going to retreat?" she asks.

"I'll just go on in," I reply, heading for the door and when I open it, she laughs, a kind of gloating laugh that has me thinking I just did exactly what she hoped I'd do.

I enter the office and shut myself inside. Reid is behind his desk, looking his normal ten shades of hotness, and he arches an expectant brow at me. With those blue eyes of his fixed on me, I cross to his desk opposite him and lean on the wooden surface. "Are you really going to be a bossy asshole to me at work?"

"Yes," he says. "Because I've seen you naked and my plan to keep you naked all weekend changes nothing here."

His reply is what I expect from Reid, but Connie's warning still rings in my mind. "Did you deal with the stockholder?"

"Was there ever a question that I would?"

"Did you settle your case?" I ask.

"Yes. For twenty million."

This seems like good news, but he's so matter-of-fact, that I don't assume. I dig deeper. "Did you ask for more?"

"I asked for fifteen."

"Then," I say, still being cautious, "you won and helped a lot of people today."

"As best as you can help someone who's lost someone they love."

I push off the desk and round it to join him on the other side. He's on his feet to meet me by the time I'm in front of him, but neither of us touches the other. "You did a good thing and you did it bravely."

He pulls me to him. "The last thing you should do is to decide that I'm a nice guy with the moral compass you want me to have."

"Is this where you're an asshole again because I see too much?"

His fingers tangle in my hair and he stares down at me. "Because you want to see something that isn't there. Don't do that to me or us."

"So I should spend the weekend with an asshole I hate?"

"I want you to see me for who I am."

"You don't have to be an asshole to keep me from asking for a ring and a commitment, Reid. I'm not that girl, but I don't want to hate you. I *don't* hate you. Not anymore, so just stop—"

The next thing I know he's kissing me, that earthy wonderful scent of him drugging me right up until the moment he groans. "That sound wasn't pleasure," I say, pulling back to look at him. "What's wrong? What was that?"

He rests his forehead against mine. "Nothing." He inhales and sits down, pressing his hands to his head. "Damn it to hell. I do not have time for this."

I go down on my knees in front of him. He looks up at me. "Don't go down on your knees in front of me right now when I can't take full advantage of it."

"Being crass isn't going to piss me off and distract me. In other words, you aren't getting you out of this. Tell me what's wrong."

"You're on your knees and I can't take advantage of it, is what's fucking wrong," he grumbles testily.

"Reid," I command softly.

"You don't give up, do you?"

"No, and you wouldn't want me here if I did. Talk to me."

"I do not want this going past this room or I swear—"

"It's just you and me," I say.

He studies me a long moment that feels like an hour. "I played football in college. I had a few concussions. I used to get migraines."

"Used to or do?"

"Nothing for five years."

"Until now," I supply.

"Yes," he confirms. "Until now."

"Do you have medication?"

"Not anymore."

"Okay, well, you're rich," I say. "We'll get a doctor over here."

"Did you just stay I'm rich and we'll get a doctor over here?"

"Yes. I did." I stand up and reach for the phone. He rolls toward me, his hands coming down on my hips.

"Don't."

I turn to face him. "You need—"

"Elijah and who knows who else are having me watched. These takeover roles are high-profile and high-pressure. I cannot have this problem now."

"It's a headache, Reid."

"It's more than that. I cannot have someone dig up my concussion history and decide I'm going to go off the deep end."

"It's one migraine in five years. You're human, Reid."

"Outside of my brother Gabe, you're about the only person who really believes that. I need to keep it that way."

I don't miss the fact that he left his sister and his other brother out of that statement. I focus on a solution. "Then you need to get rid of the headache."

"I use a combination of Advil, Excedrin Migraine, and Sudafed. If I get that rotation in me and take a twenty-minute nap, I'll be fine."

"Oh," I say. "Okay. We can do that." I try again to turn and he stops me, his fingers flexing at my hips.

"What are you doing?" he demands.

"I was going to get Connie to pick it up."

"No. Connie doesn't know about this. No one knows."

"Not even *Connie*?"

"Not even Connie."

"She's worked for you for ten years?"

"Yes. She has."

"Okay. I won't comment on that while you have a migraine. On to Plan B." I try to turn again and he holds me still. "Reid. Let go."

"What are you going to do now?"

I reach out and cup his cheek. "I know you don't trust easily. I see that now more than ever and I even understand it, but on this small thing, I'm asking you to trust me. You said you don't want anyone to know this, and they won't."

He shuts his eyes and draws a breath before looking at me and giving me a tiny nod that actually makes him grimace. "Okay," he murmurs.

"I have Excedrin," I say. "Let me start by getting that down you. I'll be right back." I step into him and kiss his temple before I can stop myself.

He catches my hand and looks up at me with hard, unreadable eyes and then to my surprise, he flips my hand over. His lips press to my palm and those unreadable eyes are suddenly etched with pain that he allows me to see when moments before he had not. *He lets me see.* He chooses to be human, to trust me, and it steals my breath. "Hurry back," he orders softly, releasing my hand.

"I will," I say, rounding the desk and heading out the door, my knees wobbling slightly with the impact of whatever just happened between me and this man. *What did just happen*? He happened. That's the answer to every question in my life right now. Reid Maxwell happened.

CHAPTER THIRTY-TWO

Carrie

I hurry out of the office, avoiding Connie's gaze. I can't invite her questions when I'm trying to answer my own about me and Reid. About Reid. About what he's making me feel that I can't even name. He's not stone. He's a man hiding beneath stone and I just saw a little piece of that man. It was enough to convince me that I want to see more, not that I needed much convincing.

I stop at Sallie's desk, certain that she will help me without any unwelcome questions. "It's going to be a long night, and I have this sudden sinus pain in my face that I was hoping would go away. It's not."

She perks up, eager to help. "What do you need?"

"Advil and some Sudafed would be great."

"What about some sort of cold medicine?" she offers.

"I called my doctor earlier and he said Advil and Sudafed should work."

She grabs her purse. "I'll go next door and get it."

"Thank you. Just set it on my desk. I'll sneak out and get it soon. We're about to be on a conference call." I hurry into my office, reach in my desk and grab the Excedrin and pour a few in my hand for fear the bottle is too obvious. Snatching up the bottle of water on my desk, , I hurry out of the office and back toward Reid's.

"Everything okay?" Connie asks.

"Seems his normal asshole self to me," I say, "but I haven't known him ten years like you. However, the asshole part of him wants me to review some paperwork *now*."

She laughs. "Now is one of his favorite words. Maybe he is normal today after all."

"Wish me luck," I say, entering the office without giving her time to ask another question, and shut myself inside.

Reid's still behind his desk, on the phone. "Monday," he says. "Ten AM. Be ready for all hell to break loose." He pauses a beat. "Saturday night? Doubtful. In fact, no. Call me Sunday night." He disconnects as I round the desk and hand him two Excedrin. He pops them in his mouth and I offer him the water.

He downs them and I pull open his top drawer and stick about ten more inside. "I didn't bring the bottle. I thought that would be obvious."

His hands come down on my hips and pull me to him. "Thank you."

"Did you, Reid Maxwell, just say *thank you*?"

"Yes," he says looking up at me. "Apparently, for you, I'm capable of manners and apologies."

"And crassness."

"That you like," he counters.

I don't deny or confirm this statement but rather reach for one of his hands. "Come and lie down." I tug on his hand.

"Believe it or not, I'm not going to argue."

He stands up and his hands come down on my shoulders, his head resting against mine for a moment that I'm pretty sure is about pain, not me. "Come on," I urge again, walking backward and holding onto him, taking him with me.

I manage to get him moving and he sits down on the couch, but he doesn't lie down. "There will be a press conference for the settlement on Monday. It's going to bring a media craze. They'll hunt me down here. We'll need extra security. I would say I'll stay away for a few days, but until they explore every piece of my life, the press won't go away." He lies down. "They suck." He says those words bitterly and shuts his eyes.

I sit down on the stone table right next to him. "We'll handle it. I'll alert the appropriate people."

He looks over at me. "I'll be accused of being a press whore, trying to sweeten my sins. My father and my 'uncle' who isn't really a fucking uncle dragged the company into an insider trading mess a few years back. It haunts me."

"I read about that, but clearly you're well-respected."

"It still comes up. Often. I get past it, but it infuriates me to have to explain myself. That's why I was even at that bachelors' auction. It keeps coming up and my sister felt she could work magic and rework our reputation."

"Why did you take this case?"

"Not for the press."

"Why?" I push.

"Because I could win."

He's not giving me what I want. I rephrase. "Why'd you forgive your fees?"

"The same reason my client, Cole Brooks, isn't taking the money. Because we don't need the money and the victims do. And before you ask me if I did it for our reputation, no. I did not. It's just going to drag out the press again and that always drags up the past."

Now he's given me what I was looking for. "Then you did a good thing, for the right reasons. That's all that matters."

He pulls me down next to him. "You're the good thing." And with a quick shift, I'm underneath him and he's pinning me in a blue-eyed stare. "Too good for me."

"Does that tie into my destiny to hate you?"

"Yes. It does."

"Why am I going to hate you, Reid?"

"You ask too many questions." Before I can stop him, he's kissing me, a drugging, almost brutal kiss, his hands sliding up my sides to cup my breasts. "Reid," I hiss, covering his hand with mine. "Not here."

"We fucked on the desk, baby. Lighten up. What's different?"

There is something about how he says this that hits ten nerves. He makes it sound so dirty and this time it bothers me. It feels like he's trying to make me feel like I'm some sort of call girl. "I need up." I shove at his chest. "Take your nap."

He raises up just enough to search my face. "What just happened?"

"Let me up, Reid."

"No," he says, as his phone starts to ring. "I'm not letting you up."

"Answer your phone."

"What just happened?" he repeats, ignoring the call.

"I don't want to do this. I need up and I need to go to my office. And I don't like you trapping me like this."

He rolls us to our sides, but his leg cages mine. "Talk to me."

"Now you want to talk?"

"Yes. I do. I'm not letting you up until you tell me what just happened."

"It's like I challenged you to make me hate you so you have to prove yourself right. I can't do this. I can't feel—*this*."

"Don't say that. Whatever I just made you feel, whatever 'this' is, I didn't mean to make you feel it."

"Says the man who wants me to hate him."

"I don't. I don't want you to hate me. I don't want you to push me away."

"You're the one pushing."

"I'm going to say this again because I want you to know I mean it. Whatever I just made you feel, I don't want to make you feel that ever again."

"I don't think you can help yourself."

"I can. For you, I can."

"I'm a strong person."

"I know you are." He strokes a strand of hair behind my ear. "And it's sexy as hell."

"I'm strong because I know what makes me tick. I don't even date, in order to stay focused on my career. I can't mix this and that. I can't be what you want me to be, what I need to be for me, in the boardroom, with you fucking with my head."

"Carrie," he says, his hand settling on my face. "I don't want you to push me away. We'll do this together." His thumb strokes my cheek. "We'll work out rules this weekend."

"You're going to follow rules?"

"I want you, baby. I want to know you, not just fuck you, and the migraine is not an excuse, but it makes it easy for me to slip into old ways."

The phone on his desk buzzes. "Reid, you have Grayson Bennett on the phone."

"Tell him I'll be right there," he calls out and looks at me. "Don't move. *Please.*"

"Go get the call."

"Tell me you won't run for the door."

"Reid, damn it, get the call. We need his business. I won't leave."

He kisses me and rotates, walking to the desk and grabbing the phone. "Grayson," he answers. "Good to hear back from you." He listens for a moment. "We'll be at the chopper pad in two hours."

I'm standing at his desk across from him when he disconnects. "He wants us to have dinner with him at his Hamptons home. Tonight, baby. Let's go pack for an overnight stay and then go nail the deal of a century. He wants to get to know you before he talks about a project he has brewing." He rounds the desk and pulls me to him. "But not the way I want to get to know you." He cups my face. "I want to know you, Carrie. I'm obsessed with knowing you, woman. I know the smartest thing for you to do is to walk away, but I already told you last night—I can't let you."

"Instead you'll just push me and push me until I do it for you?" I don't give him time to reply. "No. In or out, Reid. Isn't that what you told me? And before you answer, I don't want asshole-Reid. I want *you*. The real you. I won't tell that he exists if you don't."

"You might not like what you discover," he warns.

"Does that mean you're going to let me find out?"

"Apparently it does. In, baby. I'm in with you."

"No more warning me away or promising me that I'll hate you and then trying to make it happen to get it over with."

He narrows his eyes at me. "That's what you think I do?"

"I know you do, Reid."

"As I said. You see too much."

"I don't see enough."

"Well, that's about to change." He kisses me. "Let's get out of here."

CHAPTER THIRTY-THREE

Reid

My plan to get Carrie out of the office and all to myself after announcing the Grayson Bennett meeting fails. We head for my office door, exit, and Connie is immediately on her feet.

"Where exactly are you going?" she demands.

"We're headed to the Hamptons for a meeting with Grayson Bennett," Carrie replies before I have the chance, excitement lifting in her voice as she adds, "This could be huge for us. The deal of all deals." She's animated, her beautiful eyes alight with anticipation.

This matters deeply to her, and it matters beyond pleasing the board. I can't remember the last time anything mattered to me on that level. Until now. She's making this matter to me on a level I didn't know anything could matter ever again. I set that bombshell aside for further analysis later.

"Hold all calls that aren't critical," I add, "and we'll need a chopper ready to go in an hour."

"You mean like your four o'clock conference call with Mercury Bank?" Connie asks. "And before you tell me to cancel it, I'll remind you that he refused to talk to Gabe and wants you to prove you're still his man."

"Right," I growl, the thundering in my head that comes and goes, hitting me all over again. "That man needs a woman. Maybe then he'll get over this hard-on for me."

Carrie laughs, the soft mix of sweet and sexy stirring my impatience to get us the hell out of here and someplace where I can use her as my remedy, "Why the hell did we book that for Friday afternoon again?" I ask.

"You know why," Connie reprimands, the only damn person other than Carrie, who ever reprimands me, "your client is leaving for Europe for a month tomorrow."

"In other words," I say dryly. "I'm taking the call and pushing back our departure." I glance at Carrie. "It'll be at least an hour."

"Let me grab that file I wanted to review with you really quick," she replies. "Then I can handle the problem while you take your call." She hurries away.

I have no idea what the hell she's talking about, but since this is Carrie, I have no doubt, she'll be making it loud and clear in the near future. I head back into my office and by the time I'm behind my desk, Connie appears in my doorway. "I'll take care of the chopper and hotel rooms for you both. Do you want me to coordinate a time with Grayson?"

"Let him know the situation. I'll call him the minute I'm out of my meeting. Do what you have to and then go home. There's no reason for you to hang around."

She doesn't move. "Anything I need to know?"

"Be prepared for press hell on Monday," I say. "We're holding a press conference on the Brooks' case Monday. The deal closed."

"For a good number?"

"Yes."

"I'd say congratulations, but the press is your punishment," she says. "They'll demonize you in some way, I'm sure. It never ends."

"Who'll demonize who?" Carrie asks, joining us again.

"The press comes at Reid no matter what good he does," Connie explains. "I hate them. I really do hate them."

"Hate them at home," I order. "Get out of here, but be in early Monday."

"Got it, boss." She heads out of the office and Carrie crosses to set the folder in front of me. "The items you needed are inside."

Her cellphone rings and she snakes it from her pocket while I open the folder to find four Advil and two Sudafed taped to a piece of paper; her extreme discretion appreciated. She'd been right. I don't trust easily. I don't ask for trust either. I've done both with Carrie.

"Elijah," Carrie says, drawing me back to the moment and indicating her phone. "He's calling me. Reid, I think I should take it and feel out his position. To protect you and us. He might talk to me."

He will talk to her. He'll run his mouth and that's not an option. I'm simply not ready for the hate he could earn me with Carrie. "Talking to him offers him hope that he can turn you," I say, downing the pills with water before adding, "That empowers him in ways we don't need him empowered."

Her phone stops ringing and she purses her lips. "Have more faith in me than you obviously do," she says. "It also might tell us where his head is now."

"You know I believe in you," I say. "You *know* I do. I know you know that at this point. I've shown you that by way of my actions, but you *don't know* Elijah like I do. Don't talk to him."

"I know this is personal for him and that is always where things get dirty." She leans on the desk. "If you get hurt, I get hurt. If that doesn't make you trust me, I don't know what will."

"I'm not going to let that happen, Carrie. It's my turn here. I need *you* to trust *me*."

"I do trust you, Reid, or I'd be gone already, but I need us to do this together."

"We are. Deep breath, baby. I got this, and I got you."

"I don't want you to have me or this. We do this together."

Connie buzzes in. "Your call is live."

"I'll grab it," I say, and when I'm certain she's hung up, I refocus on Carrie. "Let's win over Grayson and we'll deal with Elijah when we come back."

"This weekend," she insists. "We deal with Elijah this weekend. Promise me."

"I promise we'll talk about Elijah."

"This weekend," she repeats.

"This weekend," I agree.

"Promise."

"Promise," I concede.

"And you never break a promise," she reminds me, giving me no time to reply. Her, and her perfect backside track across my office and exit, shutting me inside alone.

I reach for the phone, but not without a vow to shut Elijah up no matter what it takes. I'm not losing the only woman I've ever wanted to call mine over that asshole.

The call lasts every bit of the hour I'd predicted, and the minute I hang up, I dial Grayson Bennett. With the six o'clock hour upon us, we coordinate a nine o'clock dinner at his beachfront home, and I grab my briefcase and head for the door. I find Connie and Sallie already gone, and make my way to Carrie's office, stepping inside the doorway, to discover her fretting over something on her MacBook screen. I lean on the frame. "Problem?"

Her gaze jerks to mine, the connection between us punching me in the chest. She feels it too, her lips parting, her breath hitching a moment before she recovers. I can almost see her mentally set her reaction to me aside, before she says, "Yes. I have a problem. The numbers on a European project we're involved with aren't adding up. I need to go over them with you. Reid, I think it's a problem."

"The Westbrook Project?"

"Yes," she confirms. "That one."

"I think it might be, too. I was going to talk to you about it. I did some work on it already."

"You did?" she queries.

"I did."

She inhales and breathes out on her reply. "I guess that's why you're CEO."

"You're at the same place I've landed on this, baby. I have some ideas we can debate." I motion with my head. "Let's go pack up. We have a chopper waiting on us."

She shuts her MacBook and stuffs it in her briefcase. "I hope your ideas are better than mine. I've been worried over this for an hour with no answers." She stands and crosses the room to stop right in front of me, but she doesn't touch me. Those emerald eyes search my face. "You're still feeling—" She catches herself as if she's afraid we might be heard. "How are you doing with that *situation* we were dealing with?"

There's concern in her face, in her tone. It sideswipes me and hits me as hard as that look we'd shared. When has anyone, since my mother died, worried about me? Why have I let this woman close enough for it to happen? Why do I not want to push back? And I don't. I say simply, "I'm okay."

She doesn't leave it alone. She pushes for more. "Okay?" she prods.

"The edge is off," I say. "And thanks to the drugs you got me, it happened quickly. That usually means it's not going to get worse."

She motions toward the outer office. "Are we alone?"

"Yes. We're alone."

She closes the small space between us, lowering her voice, as if "alone" doesn't make her quite feel alone. "Then I was thinking that surely Royce could get you medication under an alias."

I pull her to me. "I'm better. It's under control."

"This time," she says, "but what if this means your headaches are coming back? It would be good to be prepared."

"You've given this a lot of thought, it seems."

"Yes, actually. I have. I mean, how are you going to beat Elijah at his game, win over the stockholders, fight the press, and give me unlimited orgasms while battling migraines? That's impossible, even for a machine like yourself."

She delivers the words without even a smile, but I laugh. God this woman makes me laugh and I don't even know what to do with that. "Unlimited, huh?"

"Yes," she confirms. "I *do* deserve quite a lot, considering what an asshole you've been to me, but I'll trade you one for one. Maybe if I give you your fair share, you'll forget how to be an asshole."

"Maybe," I tease. "Or maybe not."

"Probably not," she says. "But I have to try."

I sober quickly with her determination, stroking a lock of hair from her face, a crazy, unfamiliar tenderness for this woman overtaking me. "There's a lot of things I could forget with you, Carrie West, but you might wish I didn't."

She catches my hand. "But you're not going to make that decision for me, remember?"

"I remember. All too well." I kiss her and force myself to release her for the walk to the elevator. I don't remember ever having to force myself to let go of a woman, not until Carrie.

CHAPTER THIRTY-FOUR

Reid

Carrie and I step into the elevator on our way to the lobby and out of the West Enterprise offices, where I will have her to myself. The doors shut, sealing us inside the confined space where we stand side by side, our bodies close but not touching. The floral scent of her teases my nostrils, and I swear I can almost taste this woman on my tongue.

Floors click by and I have never in my life wanted to touch a woman the way I do this one. "Do you want to know what I'm thinking?" I ask without looking at her.

"Does it involve you ripping my panties yet again?"

"Yes," I say, as we turn to face each other. "But only after I hit the stop button and shove you against the wall. Then I'd yank your shirt up, rip your panties off, and fuck you."

The car lands on the bottom level and the doors start to open, the sound of voices on the other side lifting in the air. "Another time?" she asks as if I've just invited her for coffee.

"Another time," I promise, winking at her as we face forward to be greeted by two elderly women appearing before us. I hold the door.

Carrie glances over at me, offering me a mischievous smile before she exits the car. I allow the ladies to enter, give them both a nod and then I exit. Carrie is waiting on me nearby, and together we fall into step and depart the building. "Your mother really did teach you manners," she comments as we start our walk toward our neighborhood.

"Yes," I say. "My mother really did teach me manners."

"And your father taught you to be an asshole, or was that just practice because practice makes perfect? You are pretty perfect at it."

We round the corner into Battery Park, our private space, and I snag her hand, bending our elbows, and pulling her close. "I'll save that skill for everyone else."

"Try," she says. "Really try."

"Try?" I ask, halting us beside my building and pulling her in front of me. "What does that mean?"

"It means I know that you push back when you feel like I cross an invisible line. We both know that it'll happen again."

"And you'll push back like you did in the office."

"I push back because you push back."

"And now I'm trying to pull you close, baby. You'll see." I kiss her. "*You'll see,*" I repeat and when I lean in to kiss her my cellphone rings. I grimace. "Of course," I say.

"It could be Grayson," she warns.

I nod, reluctantly abandoning the kiss to grab my cell from my pocket, glancing at the caller ID, "Connie," I say to Carrie to put her mind at ease, holding the door to the building for her, even as I answer the line. "Yes, Connie."

"Grayson offered you one of his private rentals," she says as Carrie and I start the walk past security and toward the elevator. "I canceled your hotel and I'm emailing you the rental property details. Additionally, I have a chopper booked for your return Sunday night at seven, but that can be changed. Text me and I'll handle it. What else do you need?"

"A secretary without an attitude."

238

"She'd never survive your all-mightiness," she says. "Knock 'em dead, but don't get dead. I've always imagined that's for me to do." She hangs up.

Carrie and I step into the elevator, I punch in the code and pull Carrie to me. "Grayson offered us one of his private rentals for the night."

"Us? As in he assumes we're staying together?"

"I doubt he gave much thought to which bed we'd choose to sleep in, and he won't unless we start costing him money. He'd much rather us be fucking than fighting. Love not hate, baby, and I'm going to give you every reason not to hate me while we're there. That's a promise." The elevator dings and I kiss her. "Come on." I take her briefcase from her, and lace my fingers with hers, leading her into the hallway, a rich awareness between us.

"Did you look around my apartment?" I ask as we reach my door.

"You asked me that," she says. "My answer is the same as it was. I didn't."

I give her a curious look. "As in, at all?"

"At all," she confirms.

I pull her in front of me, leaning her against the door. "Why?"

"Still the same answer, Reid. I didn't want you to wonder about what I saw or thought. I wanted you to know."

"You wanted me to know," I repeat, but I don't wait for a reply. I open the door, and walk her inside, kicking the door shut, rid myself of our bags, and press her to the wall, my legs framing hers. My hands are on her waist. "Did you want to look around?"

"Very much," she says, her hand settling on my chest. "But it felt like an invasion of privacy. I waited for the personal tour."

Any other woman would have been all over my apartment. "You are never what I expect, Carrie."

"Is that bad or good?"

I cup her face. "Good, baby. Really damn good." I kiss her and run my hand over her hip, cupping her backside and pulling her to me, a portion of this day coming back to me and not in a good way. "You were right. I did learn to be an asshole from my father, Carrie, but I'm not him and I hate the idea that I made you feel like I did today. I hate the idea that I made you feel what I know my mother felt."

"Then don't do it again," she orders, her hand closing around my tie.

"I won't. I promise you. I will never make you feel that way again." I seal the promise with a kiss, and I let her taste how much I mean those words, and I do. Holy fuck, I do. I want this woman. Some part of me needs her, and when she moans and arches into me it's all I can do to drag my mouth from hers. I squeeze her backside, inhale before releasing her, catching one of her hands with mine. "No more now. Come help me pack."

"What?" she asks, breathless. "Now?"

"Yes, now."

"But we—"

"Want to fuck? Yes. We do, but we're going to wait."

"Why? I mean we—" Her eyes go wide and her hand goes to my face. "Your head. Oh God. I'm sorry, I—"

I cup her hand where it rests on my cheek. "I'm not worried about my head. This is about us. It's about us leaving for the Hamptons with you knowing that I want to know you beyond fucking, though plenty of fucking is just fine by me."

"I do know, Reid. I knew when you left me here alone this morning."

"You don't know," I say. "Not after what happened in my office today, but you will by the time this weekend is over." I lean into her, a hand on the wall, one on her face, while my cheek presses to her cheek, my lips near her ear. "But when I do finally get you alone this weekend, I *will* own you, Carrie West, and I'm going to make you like it." I stroke her hair back from her face, forcing her gaze to mine. "You don't get to run, and I don't get to push. We're seeing this through. We're seeing where this goes."

"Are you sure you want to do that?" she challenges. "Maybe it's you who'll get owned."

"Own me, baby. If you can," I say, heat pulsing through me just thinking about the battle for control before us. "Consider that another invitation. I'm looking forward to you trying."

I link my fingers with hers again. "Now." I start walking backward, down the foyer of my apartment. "Let's got to my bedroom where we will not fuck, no matter how badly we want to fuck. That's for later." I turn to walk forward and pull her to my side. "I still can't believe you didn't look around."

"Thankfully I had to get to work, so temptation couldn't kill me, and as it turns out, I won't have that problem this weekend either." We start up the stairs. "We won't be here."

"We'll be back sometime this weekend," I say. "If we finish up with Grayson tonight or even tomorrow morning, we can stay or go." We enter the bedroom and I motion for her to follow, before heading to the closet by way of the bathroom. "Have you ever been to the Hamptons?"

"I have," she says from behind me. "A couple of times, but never for pleasure."

I flip on the closet light. "Then we should stay. I've considered buying a place down there, for business and pleasure." I grab a suitcase and set it on the stool against the wall.

"The business side of things is why I think it's hard to go there for pleasure," she says, leaning on the doorjamb. "Everyone is floating in money, and there are all kinds of expectations. That's not a vacation. That's a normal day at the office."

"I'll show you the pleasure side when we're there. You just have to step outside the plastic world which exists here, too. Do you have anything you need to pack at your place?"

"I packed for the weekend."

"Did you bring the emerald dress?" I ask.

"Do I need a dress?"

"You might," I say. "Actually." I close the small space between us, catching her waist with my hands. "You need that dress."

"You liked the dress?"

"It got me cuffed and obsessed, so yes. I'd say it's safe to assume I liked the dress with you in it, which will make me want to take you out of it. Wear it this weekend."

"Why? So you can try to work me and the dress out of your system?"

"I already tried that," I say. "It didn't work. I'm done trying to work you out of my system. I'm keeping you."

"If I let you."

"I'll convince you."

"Good luck."

And just that easily, I am hot and hard and tangling fingers into her hair. "You really know how to make me want to fuck you, woman. But I won't. Not yet. We need time to go get that dress." I kiss her and set her away from me. We'll wait until later, but the cuffs are going in my suitcase.

CHAPTER THIRTY-FIVE

Carrie

Once our car arrives to take us up to our chopper, Reid and I head downstairs. I toss my bag in the trunk of the black sedan and I listen as Reid instructs the driver to pick us up at the front of my building. Reid motions me toward the sidewalk. "Let's go get that dress."

I laugh. "You really are determined."

He drapes his arm around my shoulders and we start walking. "We'll have a do-over," he says. "I brought the cuffs."

"You aren't cuffing me, Reid," I promise him, "but if you want me to wear the dress and cuff you again, I'm in."

"Quid pro quo," he says. "This for that. It's my turn but I'm willing to work for it, and I'm pretty sure we both have a few ideas as to how I could do that. My tongue on your nipple. My tongue on your—"

"Stop," I warn.

He laughs, a low sexy, masculine sound that tingles along my nerve endings, as he says, "Until you don't want me to stop."

The sexy tease of his words and laugh, do more than awaken nerve endings. They do funny things to my belly and undo me in inexplicable ways. I just don't think Reid laughs much, but he does for me and it becomes a goal of mine: make him laugh as much as possible this weekend. "Handcuffs aside," I say, laughing. "I really do wonder how many times we've walked by each other. What's your routine? What are the places you go to around here?"

We compare our regular spots and have four out of six in common. "I guess you were right," I say as we enter the elevator in my building and punch floor three. "It wasn't our time to meet or we would have before now."

He wraps his arm around my waist and drags me to him, holding me intimately against his hard body. "*Now* is our time." He kisses me, and then the short ride is over, signaled by the ding of the car and the doors opening.

He strokes my hair, tender in a way I'd once thought him incapable of being before he glances at his Rolex. "We have an hour and twenty minutes," he says, holding the door so it won't shut. "We better get moving."

I exit the elevator and he joins me, and the talk about our neighborhood that just happens to be right by the office triggers fresh concern. "What if someone sees us together, Reid? Are you sure this isn't an issue with the board?"

"I told you. Money matters. No one cares who is fucking who. They just don't want to be the one getting fucked the wrong way. You sign Grayson to a contract this weekend, and your deal is sealed."

I grab my key and he takes it from me, unlocking my door, always in control. I see this in him, and I wonder why with Reid it doesn't bother me when I know it would if it were someone else. I set this aside, deciding it's something I need to revisit later. Reid opens the door and motions me forward. "Can we even talk about strategy in the car?" I ask, instead of entering the apartment. "I know we can't talk on a chopper and I don't really want to talk in front of driver and we need to talk."

"That talk is fast, easy, and now. Grayson knows me. He wants assurances I won't drag him into business with Jean Claude Laurette that I'll give him, but more than anything he wants to know you." His hands come down on my arms and he pulls me to him and kisses me. "Be you. Don't question who that is. You won me over. You'll win him over, too." He turns me and places me in front of him. "Grab the dress and let's go make some money." He smacks my backside, as he has before, and I head inside, hurrying through my living room, my butt cheek well aware of his palm. I'm aware, and I know why he did it. It's not just about a promise that he will spank me again, which I have no doubt he will. It's about control. It always comes back to control.

I rush up my stairs and enter my bedroom and I decide Reid really needs control, not just wants it. It's a part of him. It's the stone that covers the man. It's survival for him on some level that I don't completely understand, and I wonder what created that in him. He's a master of control. He owns every room he enters, and the truth is, he's managed to own me. I said he would not, and yet he has, and I can't look back. I can't change this. I don't know if I ever had the chance. Now I just want to know what damage is beneath the beast that he shows the world, and I find myself hoping this weekend begins to reveal the real Reid.

I enter my closet, grab the dress, toss a few extra items into a garment bag, and suddenly I'm even more eager to get to the Hamptons than before. I waste no time, rushing back to the stairs. The minute I bring Reid into view, I freeze. He's sitting on my couch with a photo album open on the table, with shots of a vacation I took with my father—a safari a good ten years ago. I don't know why this has my belly clenched, but it does. I know he and my father have issues. I know that will eventually be an issue for me if Reid and I were to become more than fuck buddies, but isn't that an issue already? Aren't we more than fuck buddies at this point? We all but agreed to be more, whatever that means, back at his apartment.

"I'm ready," I say, starting the walk down the stairs.

He shuts the album but holds up a small three-by-five shot of me and my mother that I forgot was shoved in the back of that book. He stands and takes the garment bag, setting it down on the couch. "She looks like you," he says.

"Technically, I look like her," I say, taking the photo from him and damn it, my hand shakes. I hate that she still gets to me.

"She doesn't get that distinction," he says. "She left. When was the last time that you talked to her?"

"Years. Five. Seven. More, maybe."

"How many?" he asks again, obviously sensing that I know the real number.

"Seven. It will be eight in two months."

"Is she alive?"

"Yes. I get a postcard here or there, from her travels." I toss the photo onto the album.

Reid steps into me and cups my face. "I'm here now. You know that, right?"

My chest tightens with emotions I don't want to feel. He's tearing down some wall I didn't know was there. He is. I feel that. I like it a little too much, too. "For now," I say. "Yes."

He pulls back to look at me. "Because you still think I'm going to fuck you out of my system?"

"Some version of that, yes."

"I'm not the one that will walk away, baby. I told you that." His thumb strokes my cheek and he kisses me. "Let's get out of here." He laces his fingers with mine, grabs my garment bag, and heads for the door with me in tow. And for now, I really do know I can depend on this man. I trust him, perhaps beyond reason, considering how we came together, but trust adds merit to his claim that I will walk away, that I will hate him. He believes I will and that's hard to ignore, which means I need to understand where this certainty comes from before his prediction comes true. I need to use this weekend and chip away at the stone. I need to find the man beneath.

CHAPTER THIRTY-SIX

Carrie

A sense of raw vulnerability suffocates me as Reid and I exit my apartment. I was right when I said that this man has a hand in every aspect of my life, quite literally, now that we've gotten personal, and that is the kind of control I have not allowed anyone in my adult life. And it *is* control. He could hurt me as easily as he saved me professionally. We step into the hallway and I can't look at him. I'm angry at myself, and I'm not even sure why. It's not about trusting Reid. I made that decision when I decided to stay and fight for the company by his side.

We step into the hallway and Reid shuts my door, making sure it's locked up; protective, I decide. It's not controlling, not at this moment. When he turns back to me, he is suddenly cupping my face, kissing me deeply, like he can't help himself, like he can't wait until we're alone again, and it helps. I needed to feel his need, not just mine. "I will never use that information you just told me against you," he promises. "I told you about the letter from my mother. You're not out there on a ledge alone. I'm right there with you. This is all new to me, too."

I'm stunned that he is this in tune with what I'm feeling that he even verbalized it in ways I had yet to do in my mind. "Is that where we're at? On a ledge?"

"Yes, and we've decided we're jumping together." He strokes my kiss-dampened lips with his thumb. "Come on. I can't wait to get you alone in the Hamptons, and to watch you charm Grayson." He laces his fingers with mine and starts walking toward the elevator; his confidence in me affects me, pleases me, but it also feels like pressure.

"I hope I can," I say as he punches the elevator call button.

"You not only can, you will," he says. "He doesn't have a chance to even think about saying no to working with us," he adds, as we reach the elevator and the doors open to display a group of people crammed inside.

"We punched the wrong floor," one of them says. "But join us for the ride down." They make room.

Reid glances at his watch and nods, indicating time is an issue. We step inside and he pulls me in front of him, his hands on my shoulders, his big body framing mine. In this moment, I have this sense of us being a couple, not just fucking, for the first time. Are we a couple? Jumping off the ledge does mean that, right? The ride is short, and my unanswered question is left for later review, perhaps with Reid, not without him. The doors open and with Reid still holding onto me, we hurry out the front door, rather than the rear of the building where the car waits for us on the street. Once we're inside, Reid pulls me close, our legs aligned, his hand on my knee, a warm sense of belonging together, wanting each other, between us. That vulnerability of minutes before is still here as well, but what I don't feel is the resistance I've felt to falling for Reid. It's too late. It happened somewhere in between him being an asshole and an asshole I started falling for, and it's too late to stop it. Whatever this is happening between us has a life of its own, and it will not be stopped. I just pray "the end" isn't hate. I don't want to hate Reid ever again.

Once we arrive at the chopper site, Reid and I are quickly escorted to our ride and airborne in no time. The airtime is short and when Reid and I land in the Hamptons, a car is waiting on us. "Tell me more about Grayson," I say, as our driver pulls us out of the small airport.

"He's rich as fuck, demanding, arrogant, and honest."

"He sounds like you."

"He has about a hundred times more money than I will ever dream of having," Reid says. "And I have a lot of money."

"Wasn't he on the Forbes list?"

"When wasn't he on the list? He inherited his family fortune of ten billion, which he's turned into twenty." He squeezes my knee where his hand has settled once again. "We'll settle for a one-billion-dollar investment."

"In what project? I have nothing on the table that I think will entice him and that makes me nervous."

"With his money, you find him a project, and promise him a thirty-percent return, that you turn into a fifty-percent return, so that he sees us as over-performing. Over-performing is the key."

It's at that moment that my cellphone rings. I grab it from my purse to find my father's number on caller ID and as much as I hate to take it with Reid present, I need to talk to him, too. I need to know where he is now and what he's doing. "Hello," I say.

"Good news," he says. "The land development deal here in Montana looks like a done deal."

"What does that mean? What are we developing?"

"That's what I want you to come here and talk about. This is not the traditional land development deal we've typically done. It's a new twist on our old business."

"I can't go there. You know that."

"Because you're working with Reid Maxwell," he says. "I told you—"

"This means everything to me," I say. "Saving the company means everything to me."

"And if he's taunting you?"

"He's not and I need you to trust my judgment on that. I need to make this happen. I need you to support me. I can still support this new endeavor of yours, but support me in this. Please. If you love me—"

"If? You're my daughter. You're everything to me."

"And yet, you have secrets," I say, letting that comment, better spoken in private, slip out with my frustration. "Secrets that impact me."

"Everyone has secrets," he says without the denial I'd hoped to hear.

"I don't," I say. "I don't have secrets." That frustration balls in my chest. "I have a big meeting. I have to go, but we need to have a real conversation."

"I'll come there."

"No," I say quickly. "No, *don't* come here. If you do that right now, it could complicate things in ways that aren't in any of our best interests. Close your deal."

"Our deal."

"Okay. *Our deal.* I love you. Good luck and wish me luck."

"Yes," he says. "All the luck in the world, daughter. I do love you." He disconnects and I stick my phone back in my purse. "Never promise more than you can deliver, and always deliver more than you promise," I say, going back to my prior conversation with Reid, but the comment isn't about that conversation, but rather the one with my father. "I get it," I add, looking at Reid, his blue eyes already fixed on me, "My father said the same. My father was good at his job, Reid." I cover his hand on my leg. "I need you to tell me

252

what you haven't told me. I need to know what you know and I don't know."

He lowers his voice. "This isn't a conversation for here and now, or before our meeting."

"But it is a conversation we have to have," I reply, softer now myself. "We have to have it."

The car halts in front of a sprawling white mansion illuminated in the dark. "We'll talk later," he replies, opening the door, and then he's stepping outside, offering me his hand.

I fight frustration over him putting me off for logic. Of course, he put me off. We're at Grayson's mansion. I slide my hand into his palm and he pulls me to my feet, and out of the way to shut the door. A moment later, his hands are on my waist. "Your father doesn't know me. He knows of me. You know me and I'm not taunting you."

"You heard."

"The entire conversation. You can trust me, Carrie."

"I know that," I say without hesitation.

"I don't think you do, and I don't expect that you can yet, but I'm going to change that. Consider that a promise." He turns us toward the mansion, his hands settling at my back, and in contrast to the word "trust," the word "secret" plays in my mind. I'm not sure how he thinks his vow of trust works when we both know he knows my father's secret, just as we both know that he's not going to tell me.

CHAPTER THIRTY-SEVEN

Carrie

Grayson Bennett's beachfront property is a complex, sprawling property that somehow manages to be understated with a wood finish and numerous steeple tops. Reid and I start up the front steps, and I'm aware of his hand resting on my back, hyper-aware of his touch, as well as that secret and promise between us. I'm also aware of the confidence that he has in my ability to impress Grayson. That's pressure, not from him alone, but from myself as well. I *want* to impress Grayson and I mentally shove aside that call with my father, and all the questions and emotions it clearly has stirred.

"Just do you," Reid says, reaching out to ring the bell, only to have the door open before he even presses the button.

A slender woman in a navy-blue pantsuit, with raven hair and blue eyes, appears in the doorway. "Welcome, Reid and Carrie," she says. "I'm Leslie, the household manager, which is a fancy way of saying that I'm Grayson's godmother. I look out for the house while he's gone, and him while he's here. As I will the two of you tonight." She smiles and steps back, waving her hand in our direction. "Come in."

This warm greeting has an unexpectedly intimate feeling and I find Leslie quite charming. Reid's fingers flex on my back, urging me forward first, and I step ahead of him to enter the open-concept foyer distinguished by a table to the right and a chandelier above. The entrance opens wide into a beautiful room with dark gray floors, high ceilings, and dangling elegant lights. And of course, as would be expected, there's a wall of floor-to-ceiling windows, and a fireplace, that together frame a living area that's a mix of gray and cream furnishings.

Reid steps to my side, and while he doesn't touch me this time, I have this sense of possessiveness in him, like he's ready to stake a claim, a contrast to anything he's made me feel about this meeting up until this moment. I don't understand why he would feel this, and perhaps it's simply protectiveness, but whatever the case, it's fierce, radiating off him and crashing into me. I want to ask him, to understand, but Leslie is quickly in front of us. "Grayson is on the back patio," she says, motioning us forward as she leads the way.

Reid leans in close and whispers his prior words. "Just do you."

"Does that mean you're going to just do you? Are you going to be an asshole?"

His lips curve and he winks. "You know it, baby."

I laugh, and somehow that exchange eases my tension, and his too, I think. We both settle into the challenge before us and start walking, following a path along the edge of the sleekly decorated kitchen of gray marble and the living area, to an exit with a glass door. Beyond it, a cozy, enclosed patio complete with a fireplace and a view of the ocean greets us. Immediately to our left is a square table for four where Grayson sits, his dark hair wavy and thick, his goatee neatly trimmed.

He stands upon our approach, towering a good bit over six feet tall by my estimates, his attire of black jeans and a simple black T-shirt, as unassuming as everything about this encounter thus far. "Reid," he greets, and the two men exchange a firm handshake before Grayson's intense, deep green eyes land heavily on me, an assessment in their depths. "Nice to meet you, Carrie."

"Nice to meet you as well," I say, "and thank you for the invitation to your lovely home."

"I'm pleased to have you here," he says. "And what better way to get to know each other than in private, and outside a formal setting." He motions to the chair beside him. "Make yourself comfortable."

Reid holds out my chair and I sit down before the men join me, Reid to my left, and Grayson to my right. "We have lasagna for dinner," Leslie announces, joining us. "But I can accommodate any special needs or requests."

"Lasagna sounds wonderful," I say quickly.

"My first home-cooked meal in years," Reid adds.

"That's too long," she says, scoffing in disapproval. "And no better meal than Grayson's mother's lasagna to fix that problem. Ann might be gone, but she keeps our bellies full." She glances at Grayson and then quickly changes the topic. "What can I get everyone to drink? We have about every choice you might wish for: wine, brandy, scotch. The list goes on."

I glance at Grayson's glass of wine. "I would say I'll try what you're having, but I'm afraid that in an effort to not take advantage of your hospitality, I don't want to choose something outrageously expensive."

He laughs. "I'm actually drinking an excellent hundred-dollar bottle of pinot I found while in Sonoma." He fills my empty glass with the bottle sitting in the center of the table. "The most expensive wines are like all things in life, not always the best *and* I have a lot of money because I don't throw away what I have." He glances at Reid. "I believe we share this trait."

"Indeed," Reid agrees. "We do, and a few others we might not brag about quite as readily."

"Are you an asshole too?" I ask Grayson.

Grayson laughs. "I can be, but I'm more selective about when and where than Reid."

"Would you like a glass of pinot as well, Reid?" Leslie asks, still hovering to await his choice.

"Scotch on the rocks for me," Reid replies. "The most expensive option you have. He owes me ten grand."

Grayson eyes Leslie. "Bring him the bottle and we'll call it even."

I want to ask about the debt between them, but Leslie disappears inside, while Grayson refocuses on us, already leading us elsewhere, on Reid specifically. "I see she's not afraid to call you on your shit, Reid."

"She most certainly is not," Reid replies, "but she made that statement loud and clear from the moment I met her."

"How *did* that go?" Grayson asks, looking at me. "He fired your father. That was brutal. You must have hated him."

"I was angry," I agree, feeling honesty to be my best path with Grayson. "I actually hated Reid quite a lot."

"And yet, here you are by his side," he comments, watching me closely.

"She worked her anger out of her system," Reid replies for me.

"And without regret," I say, glancing in his direction. "You deserved what you got."

"Is that right?" Reid challenges, his lips quirking, and that spark between us flares, impossible to hide, impossible to deny, and I'm certain Grayson will notice. Thankfully, Leslie reappears, and I hope breaks up the connection enough to downplay it to Grayson though I know Reid says it doesn't matter. My gut says it might.

She sets a bottle of whiskey on the table as well as a glass of ice. Reid glances at the bottle. "That's five thousand. You still owe me another five."

I see another opening to ask about their debt, and when Leslie walks away, I intend to take it, but once again Grayson steals my thunder, and this time in a big way. He leans forward and speaks to Reid. "You're fucking her. Is that why I'm supposed to believe in her?"

CHAPTER THIRTY-EIGHT

Carrie

"Apparently you are a bigger asshole than Reid," I say, reacting to Grayson's crude question, which he hasn't even bothered to direct at me, considering it's about me. "He believes in me because—"

"She bested me right out of the gate," Reid finishes for me. "She beat me when no one beats me."

Grayson sits back and looks at me. "Now I'm intrigued. How did you best him?"

"Without blinking," I say, not about to tell the story. "I beat him and walked away without blinking. He came to me afterward and you're still an asshole."

"*How* did you best him?" he presses.

Reid answers. "She bought me at a charity bachelor auction and then cuffed me to a couch in the hotel room and left me there. And, for the record, wholly unsatisfied."

I'm stunned that Reid has told this story that most would feel make him look bad. Grayson narrows his eyes at me and I pick up my wine, taking a long swallow before saying, "It's good. Really good. Dry and woodsy."

"You did that?" he asks, ignoring my wine commentary.

"Yes. I did do that."

"What did you think you would gain?" he asks.

"I wanted to remind an asshole that he was human."

He laughs. "Priceless."

"Exactly," Reid says, his gaze catching mine. "She is. She's fearless, but smart." He looks at Grayson. "And those two traits are hard to find."

"As is the ability to put aside ego and get over the cuffs," I say of Reid, but my focus is on Grayson. "I can't believe he just told you that story."

"The food is here!" Leslie announces, her timing less than perfect, but she's unstoppable, as is the interruption. Soon we all have plates in front of us, and I cave to the moment, inhaling the spicy scent of the wonderful food. We all take a bite and various satisfied sounds lift around the table. "How spoiled is Grayson to have you here to cook," I say, dabbing my mouth with a napkin. "This is the kind of special meal that money can't buy. It's love. Family. Home."

"It is," Leslie says, glowing with the compliment. "I keep hoping Grayson will marry and build those things for himself, but he's all business."

"I wish the same for you, Leslie," Grayson says, "and perhaps if you'd stop worrying about me, you'd find them."

She purses her lips. "Another argument for another day." She waves her hands at us. "Enjoy," she says, and then walks away.

I lift my fork again and I find Grayson's attention on me. "What do you know of family and love?" he asks.

"My father and I have our version," I say easily. "His place is home to me."

"And yet you're dating Reid, the man who took his company."

"He made bad decisions, Grayson. I knew he was making them. I couldn't stop it from happening."

"Tell me about it," he says, lifting his fork.

Reid's phone rings and he grabs it from his jacket and grimaces. "I have to take this." He doesn't apologize to Grayson. He simply states a fact and looks at me. "The DA.

I'll be right back." He stands up and walks away, entering the house, but not before I hear, "The ink's dry, Mr. District Attorney, but if you're calling to offer an added cash bonus to the families of the victims, we'll take it." And just like that, he's inside the house, and I'm alone with Grayson, and the impact of that vulnerability isn't as forceful as I expect. He's really an easy personality, his intensity more in his cunning than his force.

"He negotiated the settlement for the families of that serial killer that was in the city," I say. "He donated his fees."

He arches a brow. "Did he?"

"He did."

He changes the subject. "What does your father think about what you're doing with West Enterprises?"

"He knows this is important to me."

"And will he reinsert himself into the business?" he asks.

"No. He's moved on and I want it that way."

"And he's okay with you taking over his creation?" he presses. "That seems like it would be hard for him."

"Yes. It will be, but for now, he doesn't think it's real. He thinks Reid is scamming me."

He doesn't blink. "Does he know you're seeing Reid personally?"

"No," I say and this time I don't blink. "And I'd rather he not, which is an easy achievement since he's presently chasing a land deal in Montana."

"Montana?"

"Yes. Montana, and no, I would not be taking your money to Montana."

Grayson glances at Reid through the window, shares a look with him, and then refocuses on me. "Do you think Reid is scamming you?"

"No," I say without hesitation.

"Do you want to know what I think?" he asks.

I narrow my eyes at him. "Why does that feel like a trick question?" I ask because it does. And if it's not a trick, it's a test that I do not want to fail, and yet, I do want to know his answer. Perhaps too much.

CHAPTER THIRTY-NINE

Carrie

I don't know why I want this man's opinion of Reid. I don't, actually. He momentarily drew me into the web he cast, and I know why. It's not his charm, good looks, money or power. It's not about him at all. It's about Reid, all Reid. I'm falling hard for him. I feel vulnerable where he's concerned, exposed, but that's on me, that's personal. This conversation is not, nor was my decision to stay on board at the company under Reid's supervision, personal. And so I set the personal aside, and focus on what matters here and now.

"To suggest that Reid is scamming me is suggesting a lack of confidence in my skills and leadership," I say. "Those things are not lacking. You have to decide if you're willing to gamble on me, I understand, but ask me questions about those things, not about my agreement with Reid."

"He needs you to get me. Did you know that?"

"I do," I say. "He told me you don't like his past history with Jean Claude."

Surprise flickers in his eyes. "Did he now?"

"He did."

"Are you comfortable with that association?"

"I am. He's not. He told me about his past with Jean Claude and his shift from then to now."

"You believe that shift is real?"

"I think my recent transition from following my father to becoming my own person makes me understand it well. So, yes. I believe that shift in Reid is real." I think of his mother's letter to his sister. "For reasons beyond what I'm willing to share with you. Why does Reid's past with Jean Claude matter this much to you? Reid is good at what he does."

"Agreed, but how he gets there matters to me because he takes me with him if I'm in business with him."

"As he does me. If I felt he cheated my father, or anyone else, I wouldn't be here."

"There are many that feel differently about Reid."

"Are you going to tell me that you've become this wealthy without pissing off one single person? Is there no one out there that would say you betrayed them to succeed?"

His eyes sharpen, darken. "Who have you betrayed?"

"Myself."

He arches a brow again. "Meaning what?"

"I knew when my father was making bad decisions, but I let him convince me I was wrong and he was right. I didn't stay true to my instincts."

"And that should instill confidence in me why?" he asks.

"I'm honest. I don't make excuses. My gut feelings are right."

"And you consider Reid honest?"

I don't like the way he keeps pushing against Reid. "What do you want to say to me?"

"The two of you are not alike."

"If we were then you'd only need one of us, but you don't know me."

"I know enough," he says.

"Enough to do business with me?" I ask, taking an opportunity where I find it.

His lips quirk. "I didn't say that."

"You should do business with me."

"Yes, you should," Reid says, crossing the patio to reclaim his seat. "Why aren't we eating?"

"Why indeed?" Grayson asks, picking up his fork he'd abandoned, as had I, during our talk. "We should eat and enjoy the company."

"Everything okay?" I ask of Reid's call.

"All is well," he says, and there is a hint of warmth in his eyes at my question, an intimacy between us that I no longer try to hide from Grayson. He knows we're together. I'll own it. *We* will own it.

We all dig into our food and the mood shifts. Grayson seems to settle into our company and conversation, these two powerful, handsome, confident, and yes, arrogant, men talking stocks and the financial market, which isn't my cup of tea, but they make it interesting. They make me want to know more. These two savvy minds often collide in debate, and in the process, both men intrigue me. The topics vary only slightly, but they stay focused on financial gains, and I use this time to try to size up Grayson who is thoughtful in his communication rather than dogmatic, asking questions, listening. I have a sense that there is a cunning hardness beneath his surface, but he tames it, using it when and how he sees fit while Reid remains himself: direct, hard, cautious, but informative. I like this about Reid.

Much later, we've finished our meal, and have moved to a circular lounge area around the fire, our glasses graciously refilled by Leslie, and the conversation remains casual. Grayson actually tells us the history of the mansion, which he inherited from his father, right along with the law firm his father founded. "And your mother?" I ask. "Was she involved in the firm?"

"No," he says. "She was a teacher, and an angel on earth gone too soon. She left me five years before my father."

Left him.

I cling to those words that feel more like they belong to my story, as my mother did, in fact, leave, thinking they tell a story that helps me work with him. I'm about to dig for more information, but he's now refocused on Reid. "How's your father? He had a stroke a while back, correct?"

Reid's expression is implacable, but I can feel the shift in his mood, the tension radiating off of him. "He did," Reid confirms, "and he's no less a bastard now than he was before if that's what you're asking."

"It does take a real bastard to work with Jean Claude," Grayson replies dryly.

"Are you referencing me or my father?" Reid asks.

"You raided right along with them," Grayson reminds him, apparently unwilling to let go of the Jean Claude situation.

"I trained beneath my father," Reid says, and as if he heard my earlier conversation with Grayson, he adds, "I cultivated my own self and I get it. He hits all the wrong nerves with you, but I'm not him."

"He breaks people."

"He makes money," Reid says.

"He made you a lot of money."

"And now," Reid says, "thanks to that money, I have the ability to make cautious, thoughtful choices about what I do and with who."

"And Carrie is one of those choices?"

"Yes," Reid says, his voice absolute. "She is. The board wanted her father out. They wanted her to stay long enough for me to sell the business for fast, big money. I even had an offer on the table, but then I met Carrie and I knew we could do better and she most certainly deserved better. If we can hit certain goals, she'll take over the controlling interest that was once her father's. Carrie is a worthy investment for us both. And I might not be Jean Claude, but I have enough of him left in me not to make a decision based on who I'm fucking."

"Just who you can fuck?" Grayson challenges. "Because Elijah has plenty to say about that. He wants you out and her in, now." He looks at me. "What do you think about Elijah's claims?"

This question hits a nerve or really two. Reid hasn't told me what he knows about my father and he shut me down over Elijah and it must show on my face. "You don't know about Elijah's claims," Grayson assumes.

"Elijah came to me and tried to take down Reid," I say quickly. "He was unethical and unprofessional, driven by personal vendettas that he'll use to destroy Reid and my company with him, and he won't care. He just wants revenge."

"Revenge for what?" he presses.

"A problem of his own creation," Reid states.

"Does it matter?" I add. "He's after the wrong thing and he doesn't care who it hurts. And you just keep hitting Reid over and over. Why did you even meet with us?"

"As you said, Reid *is* good at what he does. And I believe him when he says you can make me money. He wouldn't risk his credibility."

"And yet you want to find a reason to say no," I point out.

"On the contrary," he says. "I want you to be the reason I say yes, so let's talk about what yes looks like. I've been on a mission to place my firm in every state and beyond, starting with Asia."

Asia again, I think, already concerned.

"I'm buying complexes and buildings to develop around the firm," he continues, "I don't want the firm to be the only revenue in each state. I've completed the set-up of ten properties in ten states and two in Asia. I'll consider letting you take over one location in the US and one overseas, to start, as a test."

"What locations?" Reid asks.

"Japan and Austin, Texas," Grayson replies. "I'll need a proposal. I want to see how you will handle domestic and international locations. Analyze what we've done thus far, tell me what you'd do differently, and we'll go from there, but you should know I have a proposal I favor."

"Can I see it?" I ask.

"No, you cannot see it," he says. "Give me your best foot forward, not someone else's. I'll provide you with details on what we've done thus far."

"What about budgets?" I ask.

"What about return?" he replies. "That's what I want. Returns. Make that number right and the total investment will land where it needs to land."

"Fully funded by you?" Reid asks. "Or will you want investors?"

"I'll consider all proposals," Grayson says. "It's all about the big picture and the returns. We can meet next week when I'm in the city if you're ready."

"We will be," Reid replies and we all stand up. "We'll get to work right away."

"Work is good," Grayson says, "but enjoy the weekend."

"Thank you for allowing us to stay at your property," I interject quickly and the three of us make small talk as we enter the house where Leslie greets us. I'm just raving over our meal when Reid motions to Grayson and the two men step back outside.

Leslie keeps talking, but I'm distracted. This private meeting between the two men, instigated by Reid, hits those same nerves the Elijah conversation with Grayson hit and it's all I can do to keep chatting properly. When finally, after five minutes that feels like an hour, Reid returns without

Grayson, this visit is over. We head for the door where we graciously thank Leslie for dinner, while tension curls in my belly and tightens every muscle in my body. I'm angry with Reid over the secrets he's keeping that make me have to question him and I'm nervous about what just occurred. Maybe he was just asking Grayson what he thinks about me, which is reasonable, but it feels more like the Elijah thing, like something he doesn't want me to know, and I don't like it.

I fight the urge to explode at Reid when exploding really isn't my thing. That tells me that the secrets just aren't working for me. That tells me that I'm a hundred shades of over my head emotionally with this man. Once we are finally on the porch alone, I don't look at Reid or speak. I know there could be cameras filming us and I need what comes next for us to be private, not part of some test Grayson Bennett is giving us. I know this entire night is just that: a test, and my actions now could be a reflection on my control and Reid's presumed character.

We start walking down the stairs. "He likes you," Reid says. "You won him over."

My reaction is one-part relief while that anger I'm feeling stays firmly in place. I don't respond. Nothing I say will come out right at this moment. Reid is smart. He says nothing else and side by side we walk down the sidewalk toward our car, where the driver waits at the car door. Reid motions to him and he climbs inside the car, leaving us to our approach alone. I charge forward and reach for the rear door, but Reid is behind me, his big body framing mine, his hand on my hand on the door. "Talk to me before we're in the car with a driver."

I don't turn. "You're my boss right now. You don't have to tell me anything you don't want to tell me professionally and I have to live with that. If we're fucking, just fucking, you don't have to tell me anything at all. But if this is a relationship, I don't want secrets or lies between us. Decide which it's going to be, Reid."

Several heavy beats pass, and I sense an internal battle in him, and I think he will say something, but he doesn't. He releases me and steps back. I open the car door and get inside, not sure what to expect when he follows, and most certainly not when we're finally alone. I just know what I want and that's him. I want this man and I'm not sure just fucking is enough anymore.

CHAPTER FORTY

Carrie

Reid joins me in the car and shuts us inside, the earthy woodsy scent of him teasing my nostrils, the power that is this man consuming me and the small space, and yet, he doesn't touch me. In fact, he doesn't even attempt to close the space between us. He settles in next to the door and taps the driver's seat, which triggers the driver's reaction. Without a word, the car is in motion, and with every inch we move, the space between me and Reid seems to widen. Somehow, despite this, I feel this man in every part of me. I have never in my life been so hyperaware of another human being. I want him to touch me. I *want* to touch him, but those secrets between us keep me in place, and him too, I suspect. Or perhaps I've scared him with my list of options right before we got into the car. Maybe he doesn't want a relationship over fucking if that translates to transparency, while I don't want a relationship over fucking that translates to secrecy. All I know is that I can't continue on like this and I don't even know what that means. Maybe we're over. Maybe we're just fucking, but again, I just don't know if I can do that anymore and when my gaze catches on his hand on his knee, and I notice the way his fingers are digging into his leg, I know that he's just as on edge as I am right now. I hate that I think of those hands on my body, too, but I do. I have it so damn bad for this man.

I'm not sure if it's relief or distress I feel when only minutes later, the driver pulls us to the front of a navy-blue beachfront cottage illuminated in outdoor lighting. Reid doesn't look at me. He simply reaches for his door and I spare us the awkwardness of him helping me exit. I don't slide his direction, but rather open my door and get out. I meet Reid at the trunk where the driver unpacks our bags and Reid tips him before grabbing our luggage all himself before I can offer my help. "I have the key," Reid says, his gaze meeting mine with a hard punch of tension between us. "Grayson gave it to me before we left."

I nod and when I try to reach for my bag, he holds onto it. "I have it," he murmurs, turning away to move ahead of me and up the sidewalk with a brisk enough pace that he's already unlocking the door when I reach the porch. He shoves open the door and the light flickers on, be it by his efforts or a motion detector, I don't know. Whatever the case, he enters the cottage first, and I follow him into a narrow hallway, black wood flooring beneath my feet. Reid sets the bags down by a wooden table, and I shut the door, turning to lock it, the very act one of claiming the control that feels so damn out of reach.

By the time I face forward again, Reid's back in control. He's in front of me, pulling me to him, his fingers tangling in my hair, those blue eyes staring down at me, and the fact that he's touching me is a blessed relief. I need this man and it's addictive and terrifying at the same time.

"Reid," I whisper when he doesn't immediately speak, asking for answers, asking for more.

His answer is not in words. His mouth slants over mine, his tongue stroking deeply, and that's all it takes. I'm lost and found again in this moment and this man. There are no questions, no secrets, no need for control. There's just this kiss and I sink into it, my arms wrapping around him, under his open jacket, my body pressing to every hard inch of him I can manage, a soft moan sliding from my lips at just how good he feels. But when he tears his mouth away, his lips linger a breath from mine, vulnerability, and presence of mind has me challenging him for answers and myself for sanity.

"Was that a fuck you kiss or a relationship kiss?" I demand. "Or maybe just a distraction, a way to forget the secrets?"

"What did it taste like, Carrie?" he demands, his voice low, rough.

"Like that answer," I say. "Indecisive."

Tension flexes a path through his body beneath my touch and he releases me, pressing his fists to the wall on either side of me. "I fucked Elijah's wife."

I gasp at the unexpected answer. "What?"

"She wasn't wearing a ring and I didn't know who she was, but Elijah and I were rivals on a deal at the time, and I damn sure didn't apologize." He pushes off the wall and starts walking away, but when he would disappear into whatever the next room is, he half turns and adds, "I told him that if he knew how to satisfy his wife, she wouldn't have come to me. I've done a lot of hard things in my life, Carrie, and I'm not sorry for most of them." And with that, he turns and leaves me standing in that hallway.

I inhale and try to process what just happened. He didn't know but he wasn't sorry. He *isn't* sorry. I repeat those words in my head about three times and my emotions land on anger. I charge after him, reaching the edge of a wide living room with cream-colored furnishings, Reid's jacket and tie lying on the couch that faces a wall of curtains, of which one flaps in the wind, indicating an open door. I kick off my heels and follow him, exiting to a wooden porch overseeing the inky-black ocean waves crashing in the distance. Reid stands with his back to me, his hands on a wide wooden railing, the muscles of his broad shoulders bunched beneath his shirt.

I close the space between us and I dip beneath his arm and step between him and the railing. "You aren't sorry?" I challenge.

"No," he says. "I'm not sorry."

"You say I'm going to hate you."

"You will," he says. "Maybe it's already starting."

"Maybe you're trying to push me there. Maybe that avoids the relationship side of this. Maybe you want to make it happen. Is that it? You want me to get on to the hate so you can just fuck me? So you can backtrack all the rest of the talk and—"

His fingers tangle in my hair. "I don't want you to hate me," he bites out. "I dread the day you hate me, woman, but I can't change who I am or what I've done. It's already done."

"I'm not asking you to change who you are."

"Because you don't know who I am, and I keep telling myself to walk away before you do."

"Then I'm right," I say. "You just want to push me to hate. You want a reason to walk back—"

"I don't want to walk back anything," he says, his fingers tightening in my hair, "and this isn't just fucking." His mouth closes down on mine, his tongue licking into my mouth, devouring me, consuming me. "How do I taste now?"

"Angry."

"I am angry," he says. "And I'm not hiding from that."

"Why are you angry?"

"Because the hate will come and I can't stop it. Because no part of me is not right here with you, Carrie. What about you?"

"I'm here," I whisper, but I don't say more. I can't. He's already kissing me again, as if he's testing that claim of "I'm here" on my tongue, on his lips, turning me to press me against the wooden railing, his hand sliding around my hip to cup my backside. "You're never all here with me," he says. "You always hold back and that's not good enough anymore. If this has to end, you're mine until it does. You're mine now."

I don't push back against that claim of ownership. I welcome it in a way I didn't believe I was capable of welcoming such words. His mouth closes down on mine, the taste of him demanding and possessive, but there is also regret and the certainty of "the end" that I don't want to exist. I want to drive that piece of his emotions away. I need to drive it away and I'm not sure I have ever been as aroused in my life. "This time is hard and fast, baby," Reid says, his lips finding my ear, his hand caressing my breast over my silk blouse. "I need to be inside you."

"Yes," I whisper, and already he's turning me to face the pole, forcing me to catch my weight with my hands, and already he's unzipping my skirt and dragging it down my hips, right along with my panties, not ripping them away this time. I don't even care that I'm outside, on a beachfront, naked from the waist down but for my thigh highs. I just want Reid and when his arm wraps my waist and he lifts me, kicking away the material, I turn easily in his arms, eager to feel him next to me. Eager for his mouth on mine again. Hungry for more, so much more, and I'm not sure it will ever be enough.

Nothing is ever enough with this man and yet I fear the day that it's too much, and that has me tugging at his shirt, trying to drive away anything but the here and now.

CHAPTER FORTY-ONE

Carrie

I want Reid inside me and that's exactly where this is headed, hard and fast fucking, but some part of me pushes back, not on being owned by this man, but at the idea that I don't own him. That's the control issue. That's what I've been trying to avoid with Reid, but it's not about power. It's about him letting me in, him letting down that stone wall, and while sex isn't the way either of us owns each other, it feels like a good starting place. It *was* our starting place.

All is grand in the "I need control" scheme of things, but this is Reid Maxwell, and he wants to go hard and fast, and that's exactly what he's doing. His shirt is gone, and I'm pretty sure in between kissing him and touching him, I had something to do with that. His hands are all over me and my blouse and bra are short-lived, gone in a few quick movements. I'm now naked on a porch, on what I hope is a private beach, but considering I'm shoved against a pole, his powerful legs framing mine, his hands on my breasts, it's hard to care. His fingers tug roughly at my nipples and I moan with the pain and pleasure of it, his cheek finding my cheek as he whispers, "I'm going to fuck you right here and now on this porch."

Yes, please, I think, and my fingers flex on the hard muscle of his shoulders, and his mouth is on mine while he unzips his pants and my sex clenches with how soon he will be inside me, but that need to go deeper with Reid, to make him let go, stays with me. I reach down and help him with his pants, my hand wrapping his shaft and freeing him, but his hand covers mine, while the fingers of his other hand slide between my thighs and stroke the line of my sex, pressing inside me.

I pant and his mouth lowers to mine once more. "God, I love the sounds you make," he murmurs before kissing, and it's all I can do not to melt right here and surrender to whatever he wants. I press my hands under his waistband and tear my mouth from his. "Why are you still dressed?"

He reaches for his pants and that's when I try to go down on my knees, but Reid catches my arms. "What are you doing?"

"I'm pretty sure you can figure that out."

"As many fantasies as I've had that involve your mouth on my body now is not that time. This is about us, feeling us, not me feeling you." He melts me with those words, even before he kisses me again and that's it. I'm done. I can't fight this anymore. He squeezes one of my butt cheeks and smacks the other. I yelp and he's kissing me, lifting me as he does, setting me on the waist-high railing, and then just that quickly, he's pressing inside me, stretching me, driving me crazy in all those indescribable ways he and he alone does. There is just something about the intimacy with this man, something that has always been there, but feels different now like it's changing, like we're changing.

He presses deep, burying himself as far inside me as he can and then tilting me back to look in my eyes. "If I die anytime soon, I'll die a happy man. God, woman, what are you doing to me?" His mouth closes down on mine and his hands close around my backside, squeezing as he lifts me and then we're in this frenzied, grinding, thrusting, insatiable dance of pure lust and need. Reid's hands are at my waist and I lean backward as he lifts me and pulls me down, thrusting into me, and I trust him to hold onto me. I know he won't let me fall. His gaze rakes over my breasts, hot and heavy, but it's not enough. He seems to feel the same, and he sits down somewhere, a large chair I think when my knees hit the cushion, and then I'm straddling him, my hands on his chest, our eyes locked, the connection between us a living breathing thing that consumes me and us.

He cups my face, closing his fingers around my hair. "We might be fucking, but this is not just fucking." He drags me to him, kissing me hard, deep, roughly even, his hand on my lower back, molding me to him, moving to the center of my back to press our bodies together, the press of my naked breasts to his naked chest undoes us both. I rock against him, and he thrusts into me, and we are suddenly wild, frenzied, trying to get closer, trying to crawl into each other's skin it seems. I tumble into the hotspot that is the edge of orgasm, my nails digging into his shoulders and then I'm there, my body spasming around the thick pulse of his erection.

"Oh fuck," he murmurs, groaning as I drag him along with me, and I can feel the hot, wet heat of his release, the tension in his body going from intense to a softer, gentler place. I collapse against him, my face buried in his neck, the earthy wonderful scent of him all over me and around me. He holds me, his hand firmly on my back and my hip, neither of us moving, and I try not to think about the secrets he holds or the return to reality that comes next, but there is no escaping the dampness between my legs.

Reid must feel it too. He strokes my hair and whispers in my ear. "Hold on." He shifts, and before I know his intent, he's adjusting his pants that he never took off, and standing up with me in his arms.

He walks inside the cottage. "Where do you think the bathroom would be?" he murmurs.

I try to look, but I really can't see anything. "The bedroom has to have one," I say.

"And since I don't know where that is, the kitchen it is."

I laugh. "The kitchen?"

"Sure. There are paper towels, we hope, and we can fuck on the counter while we're there."

"Even you can't be ready for that yet," I tease.

"You underestimate me with you, baby, but I see a door that might be a bedroom. We're going for it."

He walks in whatever direction he walks and I just hold on, which works out well. Soon I'm being set on a pale gray and white swirled bathroom sink, and Reid is pressing a towel between us. It's a few beats later, when I've tossed the towel in a hamper, and I'm sitting naked on that counter. With him still in his pants, I feel the absence of my clothes.

Reid presses his hands on the sink beside me. "If I wanted you to hate me, I would make you hate me and it wouldn't be subtle, or by way of Elijah. I have that in me. You know that."

I know instantly that he's not trying to shock me or drive me away. He's being honest in a way that is raw and real, which matters to me. *He* matters to me. "Yes," I say, "I know, and no, it doesn't scare me, or I wouldn't be here. Neither does the Elijah confession."

"It wasn't a confession," he corrects. "It was a statement of fact."

"That you didn't make from the beginning," I counter. "That says you didn't want to tell me."

"Because I wasn't after your hate, as you accused me when we got here."

"There was no reason for you to hold that back. I need you to shoot straight with me and trust me to handle even the rough stuff. I'm not unreasonable. I'm not sensitive or emotional. You didn't know she was married. I believe you."

He studies me for several beats, his expression indiscernible, his jaw hard, before he says, "Let's put on some comfortable clothes and take a walk on the beach."

I know instantly that I'm not the only one who feels naked right now. The walk isn't about romance or conversation. It's about escape, but it's not a shut door, or he wouldn't be taking me with him. And I'm coming to believe that I'm about the only person Reid Maxwell hasn't shut out of his life and I hope that one day soon, he'll trust me enough to tell me why.

CHAPTER FORTY-TWO

Carrie

"A walk sounds good," I say, and I swear I feel the relief wash over Reid. I'm right. He's suffocating right now, but it still doesn't feel like it's about me. It feels like it's an internal war he's battling now, and perhaps for a long time. That I see it at all, matters. He's letting me. I wouldn't see it if he wasn't letting me.

He kisses me and helps me to the floor, surprising me by grabbing a big towel from beside a huge, claw foot tub and wrapping it around my shoulders, but he doesn't let it go, even when I grab hold of it. "I'll grab our bags," he says.

"Okay. Thanks."

"Thanks?"

"For the towel."

His eyes warm. "One of the few times I'll ever cover you up, so don't get used to it." He releases me and walks out of the bathroom.

I follow him, entering the master bedroom, which is stunning, with the same black wood floors, and a massive bed with a unique navy-blue leather frame. Two blue leather chairs sit in front of a large patio with parted blue curtains. I stare at that window and I think about the lower level patio and replay that moment when I'd tried to drop to my knees and he'd stopped me: *As many fantasies as I've had that involve your mouth on my body, now is not that time. This is about us, feeling us, not me feeling you. If there has been*

285

any moment with Reid where I felt like we were more than sex—ironically considering we were having sex at the time—it was that one.

He walks back into the room with the bags in hand and I swear when his eyes meet mine, I feel like I'm punched with emotions. He feels it, too. He pauses just a moment in the doorway, and it's like the world stands still for us. Just us. I'm going to fall in love with him and I've never said that about any man ever and so soon, to top it off. I cut my gaze, afraid he can read this in me and I'll freak him out because Lord only knows, I'm freaking myself out.

I start to walk toward the bathroom, and before I make it two steps, Reid catches my arm and turns me to him. He doesn't speak. He just cups my head and kisses me, a deep, drugging, drive-everything-else-away kiss, before he says, "How about that walk?"

I think he knows what I was feeling, and I'm not sure what to make of his reaction. "I think that would be good," I whisper.

"In more than a towel," he teases, turning me toward the bed, where he's set my suitcase. He unzips it for me and opens it before he steps to his suitcase right beside mine to do the same. Side by side, we go through our things and I pull out clothes while he tugs a snug black T-shirt over his head, and I'm reminded of how good he looks in pretty much everything. Feeling uncharacteristically shy, I grab my stack of clothes, walk to the bathroom, shut the door and I don't give myself time to think. I quickly pull on boyfriend-style sweats and a tank top, minus a bra, that I cover up with a sweat jacket. My socks and sneakers are next, as is a quick trip to the bathroom. Once I've washed up, and am fully dressed, I press my hands to the sink and look in the mirror. "What are you doing, Carrie?" I breathe out, letting my chin fall to my chest. Reid's not the guy a girl falls for, and yet I'm rolling right down a hill that has no bottom.

Reid knocks on the door and I inhale, I swear I can smell him everywhere, all around me, and on me. I love the way that man smells. I walk to the door and open it to find him standing immediately in front of me, big, broad and gorgeous in that snug shirt, and sweats, his hair mussed up, his jaw lightly shadowed. I like this Reid, the casual, real man. He rests his arm in the doorjamb above my head. "Everything okay?"

My hand dares to settle on his chest, and his heart thunders beneath my palm, suggesting the casualness of that question isn't casual at all. "Yes," I say. "Everything is great."

"Yeah?" he presses, and I almost think I sense uncertainty in him. This confident, gorgeous, take-no-prisoners man feels insecure? It can't be, but yet, I think—I think, *yes*.

"Yes," I repeat again firmly. "Everything is great."

His hand covers mine on his chest, and he closes his around it, dragging me closer, his hard body a warm shelter I find nowhere else, with no one else. "Let's walk."

"I'd like that very much," I say, deciding not to let fear steal a moment I have with this man. No matter what we are or what we become, I have now. I *want* now.

I push to my toes and kiss him, a quick peck on the mouth. "Yes. Let's walk."

He's stiff for a moment as if he's stunned in some way, or that's what I feel since the man shows no exterior emotions. And then suddenly, he's cupping my head and kissing me again, a deep, drugging wondering kiss, before he laces his fingers with mine and leads me forward. Together, we walk down the stairs through the cottage and exit the house where we'd made love earlier and of course, my bra is lying smack in the middle of the patio.

I tear my fingers from Reid's and scoop it and the rest of our clothes up. Reid laughs. "It's a private beach, baby. No one is going to see our patio."

"Oh. No?"

"No."

I drop our clothes onto the chair we'd occupied earlier, and Reid slides his arm over my shoulders and pulls me close. It's intimate. It's what a man does to his woman, and I've really never wanted to be that with any other man. I mentally reprimand myself, telling myself to enjoy the moment, live in the now. We're conquering the world together but as we step onto the starlit beach, a full moon our lantern, Reid's emotions beat at me. He need to escape, and yet somehow it takes me with him, suffocates me.

We walk to the shoreline and cut left, the ocean crashing on the shore, the rush of water filling the air, but our words do not. We don't walk far though before Reid stops walking and motions to the ground. "Elijah's wife knew I was his rival," he says, breaking the silence. "That's why she picked me."

"That was between them, Reid," I say, halting and stepping in front of him. "You know that, right?"

"Exactly," he says, but he turns away from me, facing the ocean. "It was between them." His hand drags through his hair, an act that is more out of control, than in control, when he is all about control.

I have this sense that he needs to ground his emotions, so I decide to help him do that in a literal way. I sit down and grab his hand urging him to join me, relieved when he does so with no hesitation. He not only sits next to me, he sits close, both of our knees in front of us, our hips all but touching. Seconds tick by and I don't push him. "I didn't care," he says without looking at me. "I meant what I said to him. He should have treated her right. He should have pleased her. And it was easier to take that stance because he and I were rivals after a contract."

I take this in, weighing his words and his mood. I decide that he's not trying to make me hate him. That's not what this is. I'm just not sure where he's headed but I think he needs me to understand. I *want* to understand. "What are you trying to say, Reid?"

He looks at me then, and even in the shadows, I can see the torment in his eyes. "That letter my mother wrote my sister. The pain she felt over my father's infidelities was deep."

"I know that letter changed you. I feel that every time you talk about it."

"I didn't know I was fucking Elijah's wife, but I dug that knife deeper, and now he's coming for West Enterprises. You need to know that I told Royce to find a way to back him off, something I can use against him."

"To ruin him?"

"I won't ruin him unless he forces me to ruin him, but I won't let West Enterprises go down because of a personal vendetta. Too many people lose too much, in too many ways, for that to happen, you included."

This is that part of his job that he does well, that I fear that I can't stomach. "A lot of people would lose a lot of money."

"Yes. They would and I—we—have a responsibility to protect them. I could have handled this without telling you, but—"

"I'm glad you told me," I say, taking his hand. "I needed to know. I told you, I can handle the truth, even when it's bitter to swallow. I just have to know."

"That statement you made earlier is why I'm telling you." He reaches up and strokes the hair from my eyes. "I didn't want you to know about Elijah. I have never cared what anyone thinks of my actions, or how they judge me, but I do with you. And I have never shared my decisions and explained myself to anyone but you, Carrie."

"Why me, Reid?" I ask, not sure I've ever needed the answer to a question more.

"Why isn't the question I've asked. How is the question." His hand cups my face. "*How* did you do this to me?"

"How did I do what?"

"Become the one obsession I can't beat." He doesn't give me a chance to reply or even process a reaction. He kisses me and takes me down on the sand with him.

CHAPTER FORTY-THREE

Carrie

Reid's lips part mine, and we're now lying in the sand, our bodies aligned, his leg hooked over one of mine. "How, Carrie?"

"I could ask you the same."

"You're obsessed with me?" he asks, caressing my cheek.

"Depends on how you define obsessed."

"I can't wake up and not think of you. I can't go to bed and not think of you. I wanted to tell you about my settlement. You're in my head, Carrie. I don't even want to get you out anymore."

"You couldn't if you wanted to," I tease, but there is a twist in my gut as I add, "Because we have Grayson to close and a board to satisfy." I hate this convenient side of our relationship when that should be exactly what I revel in. It represents the freedom to live in the moment, to avoid emotional investment, and yet, I haven't. It's too late for that kind of thinking. I'm invested in all ways with Reid, and I roll to my back before he reads that in me.

Or I try to, but he doesn't allow my escape.

He rolls with me, his leg still between mine, those blue eyes are staring down at me. "What just happened?"

"Nothing happened."

"You think this is all about the company. That we're here and now and gone when this is over."

"I didn't say that."

"It's not about any of those things," he says. "I told you, Carrie. I don't want to share you. I'm obsessed with you and it's not the kind of obsession that goes away. You're with me now. I'm with you now. Say it."

"Reid—"

He kisses me, a silky caress of his tongue before he orders, "Say it."

I'm in deep with this man, so very deep because I do it. I say it. "I'm with you now and you're with me."

"Do you know how many women I've said that to?" He doesn't give me time to reply. "None. No one but you. This isn't about a deal or a company. This is about you and me and us. How many men have *you* said that to?"

"None. Just you. You know that. I told you my history."

"I wanted to hear it again." His hand slides under my shirt, settling warmly on my belly. "I *do* want to own you, Carrie. I can't seem to stop myself from wanting to own you."

"You'll never own me, Reid, but as you said to me, you can try."

His lips, those sexy lips, quirk on the sides. "And we'll enjoy trying, now won't we?" His hand slips under the back of my sweats. "Let me show you how much."

I'm instantly aware of what Reid quickly discovers; I didn't actually put on underwear. He breathes out heavily with the realization that his hand meets no resistance. "God, woman," he says cupping my face, "you make me crazy." His lips touch mine, his tongue stroking deeply, even as his fingers stroke a line down the wet seam of my body, and I moan with the sensations rippling through me. He answers that moan by deepening the kiss, and his fingers are doing this crazy wonderful thing to my clit and then they're inside me and his thumb is in just the right spot. I'm lost in the sensations rolling through me, and almost embarrassed by how fast I'm headed to that sweet, sweet escape. So very fast that I tear my mouth from Reid's and press my face to his chest, my fingers curling around his T-shirt as I fight what is too far gone to be stopped.

"Reid, I'm—I'm—" I tumble over into bliss and my entire body quakes. It comes over me hard and fast, and then it's over and I'm panting. "That was—"

Reid cups my face and forces my gaze to this. "So damn sexy." He kisses me again. "And for just a few minutes, I *did* own you."

"Was it that long? I think you owned me pretty quickly."

"I like that you were that turned on," he promises. "I *love* it."

Love.

That word.

It taunts me despite the context. Could I fall in love with this man? Am I headed there?

He lies back on the sand and pulls me close. For long minutes we just lie there, listening to the ocean, breathing together until he flexes fingers on my back and murmurs, "Tell me something I don't know about you."

I smile without looking at him. "I can have an orgasm in about sixty seconds flat if you're the one giving it to me."

He gives a low, deep sexy laugh and kisses my forehead. "I said something I don't know."

I think of my father, and what I still don't know, and how much I want to push him to tell me, but I don't want to lose this time with Reid. He's relaxed, and I don't know if he's often in this kind of casual way with anyone. "My favorite food is macaroni and cheese and I could take you to all the best places in New York City to get it."

"It's a date," he says. "How many places?"

"Half a dozen."

"Even better," he says. "My favorite food is a hamburger and I can take you to all the best places. Another half dozen."

"It's a date," I mimic his reply.

"Where in the world have you traveled?" he asks next.

"Asia and inside the United States," I say, aware of Reid really trying to get to know me, as I want to know him. "Nowhere else."

He glances down at me. "Your family had money. How is that even possible?"

"After my mom left, my father did trips for business and that's all. What about you?"

"All over the place," he says. "That you have not—we have to fix that."

"We?" I ask, leaning up to look at him.

"Yes, we. Let's go to Italy to celebrate your CEO promotion when it happens. You like pasta, I assume since you love macaroni and cheese. You'll get lots of great pasta there."

Italy. He wants me to go to Italy with him. My stomach twists a little with just how confusing and complicated this thing with us is getting. "Reid—"

"Don't overthink it, Carrie," he says. "Just live in the moment. Just say yes."

Live in the moment, only Italy months from now isn't in the moment. *Just say yes.* He makes it seem so simple. Is it? "If I even become CEO," I say.

"You will," he assures me. "Are you still going to sell your apartment?"

I sit up with a sudden twist in my belly, pulling my knees to my chest. "I want to sell it."

Reid sits up and moves to sit in front of me, his hand settling on my knees, those blue eyes probing. "Why?"

"I don't feel secure. I won't for a long time after this mess with the company. And since I know what you're thinking, yes, I'm aware that my need for security stems from my mother leaving, but it's a need that exists to be fed. I'm going to feed it."

"Don't sell yet. I promise you, Carrie, *promise you*, that you'll feel secure when this is over."

"I won't," I repeat firmly. "Not for a long time."

"You will, baby. Trust me."

I want to trust him. I want to believe this man could hold my heart and my life in his hands and he wouldn't crush them both. But Reid is not the guy I could take home to my non-existent mother, as he himself proclaimed quite adamantly. He's the guy I will end up hating, and that is not a good thought right now.

"Let's go back to the cottage," he says, and when he tries to stand up and take me with him, I have this sudden need for control. I push him back and into the sand.

"You don't get to get up yet," I say, shoving him until he's lying flat, and twisting to my knees beside him, my hand on that perfect, hard chest of his.

"And why is that?" he challenges.

"Because I'm not done with you here," I say, and when I would kiss him, he wraps his arm around me and pulls me against him.

"What are you going to do with me now that I'm here?" he challenges.

"Wait and see," I say, reaching down and stroking the satisfyingly thick ridge of his erection. I turn him on. I like that I turn him on. I like so many things with this man that I might even love those things, but not him. I'm not going to fall in love with Reid Maxwell. I'm going to enjoy every inch of his hard body with my hands and my tongue, and own him like he did me.

Inspired, I straddle him and lean down and kiss him. He tangles rough fingers in my hair, and I moan with the lick of his tongue, but I don't let myself get lost. Not in the kiss. There's too much more of this man for me to enjoy, to *own*. I push away from him and slide down his body, settling between his legs to shove up his shirt and kiss his stomach. "You want to know what I'm going to do, don't you?"

"Show me," he orders gruffly, affected, and the very idea that he's aroused, that he wants this, turns me on. I'm wet. My nipples ache. My body burns for this man, but I want him to burn for me.

I slide lower, and kiss and lick the line above his waistband, my hand stroking his cock through his sweats. His lashes lower, his hard body harder with the tensing of his muscles, and I know how on edge he is, how much he wants my mouth on his body, and I want it there, too. I drag his pants the rest of the way down and then my hand is wrapping his shaft, and I look up at him as I lick the pooled liquid at the tip of his erection.

He jerks slightly and I'm inspired to do more. I drag my tongue around the soft head of his cock and then suckle him into my mouth. He moans and arches his hips, and I draw him deeper, sucking on him, my tongue working the underside of his cock. His hand comes down on my head and that's what pushes me over the edge. That's what has me wet and hot and sucking harder and deeper. He's in need. *He needs*. I need his need. I want that burn I felt to burn him and it does. He starts pumping harder, pushing into the movement of my mouth, and when he murmurs, "Carrie, baby," and releases my head, I suck him harder and deeper until his hand is back on my head, and he's shuddering, shaking and groaning as the saltiness of his release fills my mouth and I don't stop. I take it and him and go all the way, slowing as he slows, easing my mouth only when he's collapsing into the sand. I give him one final lick and then drag his pants back into place.

"Carrie," he whispers, dragging me up his body. "You know—"

"That I owed you. And never say I don't pay my debt. I owned you and owed you."

Suddenly I'm on my back and he's on top of me, his hands on the sand on either side of me. "You owe me nothing, ever. That is not what we are. You never owe me. Say it."

"Reid—"

"Say it, Carrie. That's not who we are."

"I don't owe you. That's not who we are."

"Say it again."

"Reid—"

"I'll say it. We don't owe each other. Ever. That's not who we are. That's not who I ever want us to be."

This matters to him. Really matters and it makes me feel like *we* matter. It makes me fall harder for this man. He pushes to his feet and takes me with him, his hand under my hair on my neck as he drags my mouth to his. "And now, I vote we go to bed—together."

And just like that, he owns me again.

CHAPTER FORTY-FOUR

Carrie

Reid drags me close under his arm, and we walk back to the cottage. We don't speak, a new intimacy between us that is comfortable in the silence. So much so that when we enter the cottage and head upstairs, we still don't speak. We end up on opposite sides of the bed staring at each other, and what passes between us is intense, intimate, and like nothing I've ever experienced. We understand each other. We know each other in ways no one has known us. I don't talk about my mother, but I have with him. He knows about my challenges with my father. He knows my weaknesses. He knows when and how I am strong. In turn, I know about his struggles with his father, his guilt with his mother, his intimacy issues. I know about his migraines. I know about Elijah. We know what we want and that's the space out from in between us.

We undress and once we're under the blankets, we're instantly in the center of the bed, together, kissing, touching, and when he's inside me, I'm not sure it's fucking. It's more than fucking. It's tender and intense and it just feels different. We are starting to feel different again, the way we had when we'd kissed by the water between our apartments.

At some point Reid turns me, pulling my back to his chest and his hand is on my breast, his entire body wrapped around mine. I don't know how having him behind me is more intimate, but it is. It's like he's sheltering me and protecting me in some unexplainable way. When we both tremble into release, we don't move. In fact, he pulls me closer and murmurs my name before the heaviness of sleep and satisfaction wins. My lashes lower and sleep claims me.

I wake with Reid still wrapped around me and it's a surreal moment, lessened only by the fact that I have to pee so badly I'm about to burst. I've never woken up in a man's arms, which at my age is probably a bit screwed up, but I just—I don't, or I didn't, have anyone that made me want to wake up in their arms. Even when my ex stayed the night, I ended up with a pillow hugged to my chest, not him. Reid's cellphone rings and he groans. "I'm going to ignore it," he says, his hand sliding to my belly, the thick ridge of his erection sliding between my legs. "So I can tell you good morning properly."

My hand covers his. "Take the call. Good morning has to come after I pee."

He rolls me to my back and ignores his call and my bathroom request. "I don't wake up with women in my bed, Carrie. I don't do this."

"I don't either, Reid," I say, my fingers curling on the thick stubble on his jaw. "*What* are we doing?" I ask yet again.

"Everything, baby, and I'm not sure that's enough." His cellphone rings again. "And apparently, everything includes answering my phone while you use the restroom." He kisses my temple and then rolls off of me.

I roll in the opposite direction and grab my clothes on the way to the bathroom. I'm pretty sure Reid's phone stops ringing again before he answers. I hurry to do my thing, and then pull on my clothes, with that word "everything" in my head. What does that even mean? What do I want it to mean? I don't let myself get too in my head about it. Instead, I look at my wild hair and smudged makeup that I never took off, and decide I need my overnight bag, and most definitely the toothbrush inside.

I open the bathroom door to find Reid pulling on his pants, and since his back is to me, I have just enough time to appreciate the perfection of his backside.

"I'll let you know in the next hour," he says and whoever is on the line must be talking because he runs his hand through his hair and just listens, his shoulders bunched with obvious tension.

I walk to my suitcase that Reid set on the floor at some point, I really don't remember when, and pull out my toiletries about the same time he says, "I'll call you," and disconnects.

He turns to face me as I stand up with my pink bag filled with makeup and miscellaneous items. "Problem?" His phone rings again and he grimaces. "Why can I not just take you to eat mac n' cheese after fucking you good morning? And no, nothing is wrong." But he doesn't seem like nothing is wrong. He answers the call and I walk back into the bathroom, brush my teeth and take off my makeup. I've just put on a little moisturizer, despite the fact that I'll likely wash it off in the shower, when Reid walks in, sets his overnight bag on the sink, and grabs his toothbrush from inside.

"That was Grayson," he says, putting toothpaste on his brush. "He has a proposition for us." He starts brushing his teeth.

"Did you really just say that and stuff a brush in your mouth?" I demand, while wondering how he manages to look so damn sexy while brushing his teeth, and decide it's all the muscles flexing here and there and everything.

"Patience, baby," he says, rinsing his mouth and then his brush.

"Reid!"

He gives a low, sexy chuckle, and snags my hips, placing me between him and the sink and despite my impatience, I'm pleased with his laughter. "I needed to do this." His fingers tangle in my hair as he adds, "and have you actually enjoy it." His mouth closes down on mine and I'm thoroughly kissed before he says, "We need to go back to New York City."

"What?" I don't like the instant knot in my belly that follows or the sense of rejection that cuts a little too easily.

"My sister is holding a surprise party for her husband. She's really pushing hard for me to be there tonight."

"Oh. Well, you should be."

"I'm not going unless you go with me."

"You—you want me to go to the party?"

"It's the only way I'm going," he says firmly. "I don't like these kinds of events, but I do respect Cat's husband. Say yes. Get me through this or I'm going to call and tell her no."

"Okay, you're not saying no. This is *your sister*. That's an order."

"Then you're going with me," he insists.

I'm confused. So very confused with this man. "We don't do white picket fences and family, Reid."

His fingers flex at my hip, his voice turning low, rough. "Ask me the question again, Carrie."

I know what the means. I know what question. "What are we doing, Reid?" I ask, and I swear my voice trembles.

"Everything and that might not be enough."

"I don't know what that means."

"Neither do I, but I've never been one to let fear get in the way."

"Fear? *You're* afraid."

"Damn straight, baby. In ways you don't understand, and I really don't want you to. Come with me to the party."

He's scared. This is not an admission that I expected from this man, but he's proving to be so much more than anything I believed him to be when we met. I want to push him for more, but I decide just to give him more instead. "I— okay. I'll go with you."

"Good," he says, tension easing from his body as if he feared rejection. "We'll eat that mac n' cheese on our way to the airport. Right now, we're taking a shower together."

He wants me to have my mac n' cheese. Why does this hit so many right buttons for me? It's mac n' cheese and yet, it's more. It's this hard man I've called "asshole" over and over, caring what I want and like. "Shower," he repeats. "Together." He lifts me off the counter and starts walking backward, taking me with him.

I catch the band of his sweats. "Wait. What about Grayson? How have you still not told me about Grayson?"

"He had a falling out this morning with our competition. He's taking bids next week for Asia. Texas is on hold until he gets that property under control. I don't personally think he's taking bids. I think he's waiting to see what we can do, but keeping us on edge."

"You know how I feel about Asia. That was my biggest worry talking to him."

"I have some ideas on that, and we can talk about them over lunch. I have contacts, a few people I really trust."

"Reid, this project will be going on when you're gone. I'll be stuck with it and the fallout. I don't want to get on top to fall again by making the wrong move now."

He cups my face. "The moment I resign from the board and cash out does not mean I leave you, Carrie. Trust me," he says again.

"You keep saying that, but you also keep promising I'll hate you. That makes me very uneasy."

"I know," he says. "And it should." He releases me and walks toward the shower.

"What does that even mean, Reid?" I say, following him, only to have him turn on the shower and slide off his pants, which means he's now standing in front of me fully naked, beautiful with his cock thick, hard and between us. Which also means, that I'm wet, warm, and having a hard time remembering what I was about to say.

"What does that mean?" I repeat, thankfully I've found my brain again. "*I know and it should*? I should be uneasy about trusting you?"

He drags me to him. "You can trust me. Absolutely trust me. What it means is that we need to fuck and you need to stop overthinking everything. We'll figure it all out. I will make it work out. And like it or not, you're going to have to trust me." He kisses me and then drags my shirt over my head, and his hand on my breast distracts me enough that my pants are quickly off as well.

"Reid, damn it," I murmur as he pulls me in the shower and shoves me in the corner, his big body protecting mine from the spray of water at his back. "Fuck me like you hate me," he says, lifting my leg and pressing inside me, his hand cupping my face. "Then hate will feel so damn good, you'll forget why it matters." His mouth closes down on mine, and he thrusts into me again.

I decide that if this is his version of hate, I'll take it.

CHAPTER FORTY-FIVE

Reid

I'm just finishing off the last swipe of my razor at the bathroom sink, Carrie next to me at the second sink, when her eyes meet mine in the mirror. She gives me a shy smile when she is so far from shy, but it's these contradictions in Carrie, the small little things that make her *her*, that draw me to her. She glances away and runs her fingers through her wet hair. I'm starting to think obsession isn't the right word for what I feel for this woman. It's more. It's so much more.

I wipe my face and she turns on the hairdryer, this kind of intimacy with a woman is not something I'd have considered in the past, but there is no hesitation in me to be here with her like this. I don't want to be without this woman. She's changing me, and I don't even care. I've stopped asking myself why everything is different with Carrie. I'm not even going to ask how this happened anymore. It just did. She happened. And I've stopped trying to save her from me. It's too late. She can't be saved. I won't let her be saved. Not from me.

I walk over to her and kiss her despite the hairdryer blasting and brush my thumb over her kiss-dampened lip. I don't say anything. I like that I don't have to say anything with Carrie. She doesn't need some false sense of security in words. She doesn't force me to say things I'm not ready to say. She doesn't force me to be anything but a better man, and that's what this is. I'm better with this woman. I know this. I think she does, too. The problem is that she doesn't know what I am without her. She'll know if she ever finds out the truth of that debt.

Feeling that certainty like a punch in my gut, I leave her to finish her routine and walk into the bedroom to dress in gray Diesel jeans and a gray Diesel T-shirt and boots, trying not to think of that debt. I fucking hate the way I'm legally bound not to tell her, but if I do, she'll go to her father, and he'll come at my family. I fucking would if I were her. It's too personal. She'll be too upset not to react. I run my hand through my hair. The hairdryer turns off and I walk to the bathroom door and just seeing her there in her robe, looking beautiful and just so damn her, guts me for one reason: I want her and I'm going to lose her, and I can't stop it from happening.

"Hey, baby," I say when she looks at me with those perfect emerald green eyes. "I'm going to check in with Royce on Elijah and see what this place looks like in daylight."

"Okay," she says softly. "I won't be long."

I cross the room and pull her to me, all her soft curves pressed to every spot I can get her. "Good." I stroke her cheek. "I want you with me, Carrie. You know that, right?"

"I'm starting to figure that out."

"Say what I want you to say."

"I want to be with you, Reid, but don't make me hate you. *Please*. Stop trying to make me feel hate. I don't want to feel whatever it is you're making me feel and then have it turn into that."

I want her to tell me what I make her feel, but then I'd have to tell her what I feel and I'm not ready to name this feeling. I don't think she really is either. What I want, so damn badly at this moment is to tell her everything. "Hurry downstairs," I urge, kissing her firmly on the mouth and then turning away, a plan to expose all I can legally to Carrie tonight now in my mind. Somehow she doesn't know our fathers are enemies. She deserves to know, but I know this will convince her I came at her company as an enemy when that's simply not the case. I can only hope that once she's around Cat and Gabe together, she'll see that isn't the case. I won't let my father, or anyone else, hurt her or her company.

With that in mind, Elijah is back in my thoughts, and I head downstairs, pull my phone from my pocket to dial Royce, who answers on the first ring. "What do you have for me?" I ask, walking through the living room to exit onto the patio.

"If you mean about Elijah, we're still working, but he has a couple of offshore accounts that look shady. More soon, but that should back him off if needed."

"Excellent," I say, leaning on the railing. "Exactly what I need. Get me proof as soon as possible."

"Will do," he agrees. "One thing before we hang up. I've been trying to catch up with you on a situation. Carrie wants me to help her investigate her father and I'm past due responding to my promise to follow up with her. I told her I'd do it, but I also told her I had to clear any conflict with you."

I consider this a moment and decide my only hope that Carrie finds out what I can't tell her is Royce, and I'm telling her what I can tonight. "I'd tell you to bill me, but there are some legal reasons some of the information you give her can't be connected to me."

"You want her to know," he assumes.

"Hell yes I do, but I can't tell her."

"For legal reasons," he assumes.

"Exactly."

"I'm pretty good at finding out what no one else can."

"It's buried," I say. "Good luck."

He laughs. "I'll tell my hacker brother Blake how little faith you have in him and the truth shall be found."

"Warn me, man. I need a warning. She's going to feel like I betrayed her."

He's silent several beats. "That sucks, but understood."

We disconnect and my phone buzzes with a text message from Gabe: *Get your ass to the motherfucking party.*

"Reid."

At the sound of Carrie's voice, I happily ignore motherfucking Gabe and stick my phone back in my pocket. Turning, I find her standing in the doorway, looking good enough to eat in tight black jeans and an emerald green V-neck T-shirt. I'm instantly hot and hard, but then, this is Carrie. She keeps me hot and hard. "How much do you like macaroni and cheese?" I ask.

"I told you it's my favorite. I love it. Why?"

I cross to stand in front of her, but I don't touch her. Yet. "Then you shouldn't have worn those jeans, because I'm going to have to take them off of you now." I reach for her, my hand on her hip, dragging her against my own hips, the thick pulse of my erection at her belly.

"Oh no," she says, catching my hand. "You promised me mac n' cheese. You better deliver."

"We can be fast and still have mac n' cheese."

"I'm starving, Reid. I'll have to lay there and let you do all the work."

I arch a brow. "And that's a problem why?"

"The part where I said, *I'm starving.*"

"Right. You need food. Okay then. As long as we're back here by five, we'll have time to fuck before we head to the chopper."

She laughs. "You're crazy."

My voice lowers, a rasp in its depth. "For you, baby, yes I am."

"Reid," she whispers softly and then smiles big. "Because I'm the only one not afraid of you."

"Maybe you should be," I say grimly, hating that reminder.

Her hand flattens on my chest. "Stop trying to scare me off, Reid. I knew your reputation when I cuffed you to the bed. You didn't scare me then. You won't scare me now."

"You haven't met my family yet," I joke, but I'm thinking about my father, not Gabe and Cat. I'm thinking about the fact that she's just mimicked my thoughts. She did know my reputation. But she didn't know who I was before I met her. And she damn sure didn't know that my father hates her father like hers hates mine: passionately, vindictively, and with such perfect hate that it's driving us right there with them.

CHAPTER FORTY-SIX

Carrie

The restaurant has a balcony with a stunning ocean view and Reid and I claim a cozy corner table that will allow us to eat and work, as is the plan we determined we'd follow right before leaving the cottage. We order what the waiter declares to be "world famous" macaroni n' cheese, as well as a wine Reid wants me to try, which he favors. Soon we have our glasses filled and I decide I too love this wine. "Do I dare ask how much it costs?"

"Don't," he says. "Just enjoy it." His voice is warm and his eyes warmer.

"I am," I say, the spark between us damn near igniting. "Very much," I add, and when I'd once felt perpetual anger toward Reid, I now feel connected. On some unspoken level we understand each other and yet, I understand too little about Reid. "But," I add, setting down my glass, "I better drink cautiously. I'm meeting your family tonight. I can't imagine a room with three Maxwell siblings."

"You know Gabe, and Cat's someone you'll get along with. She's independent, hard-headed, intelligent, and fiercely protective of those she loves. In other words, you two are alike."

"And yet you and I are—compatible. I get the idea that you and your sister aren't close. Actually, you made it sound you aren't close to anyone."

"If there was anyone who knows me, it would be Gabe," he concedes. "We're alike in ways that aren't obvious on the surface."

"What ways?"

"What makes us tick."

"Which is what? Money? Power?"

"It's deeper than that, and I know you know that."

He means the parts of me that are about my mother. I don't push him to explain. Those are the inner demons we all battle privately. "And Cat. Does she get you like Gabe does?"

His jaw sets and he reaches for his wine. "We've had problems."

"For how long?" I ask.

"A decade."

I blanch. "Ten years? You've had problems for ten years?"

"Give or take. I'll spare you the questions. I was an asshole to her and that's how we got where we are now."

"Were?"

"I remain an asshole."

"Have you apologized? Because I know you know when you're wrong, Reid."

"I have not."

"Why?"

"I have my reasons," he says, giving me nothing more.

The waiter appears. "Hot plates!" he announces and then sets a monstrously wonderful looking entrée-sized macaroni n' cheese in front of each of us.

We chat with the waiter just a minute and when he finally leaves, as much as I want to try my food, I don't want it as much as I want to say something else to Reid. "Fix it with Cat," I say. "She's your sister, and like your mother, you could blink and she could be gone."

His jaw sets hard. "That's the point. That's always been the point."

My brow furrows. "What does that mean?"

He studies me for a few beats. "I'm going to the party, Carrie," he says, avoiding the question. "*We're* going. I wouldn't have in the past—attended, much less taken anyone with me. Let that be enough."

"Right," I say. "I'll leave it at that then."

His knee connects with mine under the table and he reaches out and covers my hand with his, "*For now*, Carrie."

His expression is hard, jaw firm, but there is a softness to his voice, a plea that promises his shutdown is not forever. And this right now is him telling me I'm pushing his limits, but he's not unwilling to be pushed. And so I say, "For now."

"For now," he repeats. "Tell me what you think of the macaroni n' cheese."

"I can't wait to try it," I say, picking up my fork and poking the bubbly, wonderful layer of cheese.

Reid picks up his fork too and I have this moment of realization; this is our first restaurant meal together. His eyes meet mine and I read the same in him. We are no longer hate-fuck buddies. We are something more, something I cannot name, but I don't feel the need to either. He motions to my food and together we take a bite. "Mmmm wow. Okay. I believe our waiter now. This must be world famous. This is amazing."

His eyes warm with my reaction. He's pleased. I'm not sure Reid is ever pleased, but he is now. "Good," he says softly. "I wanted you to like it."

"I do," I reply. "I mean, this is the kind of dish you come back for."

"Then we'll come back. Just you and me. No Grayson on the menu. We'll finish the weekend we planned."

"I'd like that," I say, warmth spreading through me. "And for the record," I reach for my glass, "I like your wine choice more than Grayson's."

He laughs as the waiter reappears to check on us and by the time he's gone, Reid and I have managed to down half our glasses of wine, and the macaroni is now cool enough to eat more heartily. We dig in and start eating and for a few moments, we both watch the ocean crash against the shore. "It's beautiful," I murmur.

"It is," he says. "I like the city, but it's been a while since I remembered the benefits of just getting away. Maybe it's time to remember. Tell me something else I don't know about you, Carrie."

"I'm not complicated. I live for my job. Despite working for my father, I'm not one to lean on him or anyone. I make my own way and I like it like that. West Enterprises is everything to me. It's where I always knew I would be."

"Then we understand each other, as all of those things apply to me with our company. Let's win Grayson together for both our families."

"With Japan? I don't like Japan, Reid. You know how Asia's burned me and no, that has nothing to do with my brother living there, as well as presently fucking my ex-best friend, or any past history with him. The regulations and money are both hard to manage from afar."

"I have a couple of investors who eat up the Asian markets that I trust completely and they represent big money. Because of my work with them, I've invested an exceptional amount of time into the understanding of the regulations there and enlisted a variety of insiders to aid my efforts. I can protect us, but then I need you. We need a project that entices them and Grayson."

I hesitate and he notices.

"What?" he asks, pushing his food aside.

"This is an unconventional investment to pair with a law firm and it's really not an option anyway."

"Carrie," he prods.

I sigh. "Okay. Right before the takeover, I was emailed a lead about the investors in a major event center—as in sports, concerts, you name it are held there—wanting out."

"And?"

"And I dismissed because a) timing, we were in trouble. B) Asia is tricky and in light of the trouble, that seemed bad at the time, and c) the lead came from my brother who only told me because he wants some sort of payout for finding the deal. And neither one of us has a high opinion of my brother."

"He wants to make money. We'll make sure it makes money together."

"Then you like the idea?" I query.

"It's an option," he says. "It's thinking out of the box."

"It's not a for sure thing though," I remind him, "and we have to present to Grayson next week,"

"Be honest with him," he says. "He knows the short timeline. I might bite when I need to bite, but I play devious where devious is needed, but I do that with people who deserve it. Grayson is an honest man. He's hard. He's demanding. He will cut you if you cut him, but he won't cut you just to cut you. He'll appreciate that you don't fluff it up."

"But if I work this, I may not have time to come up with something else."

"Then don't," he says. "Just give him an idea of how you think. He can decide if he wants to be on board with that or not. And he will."

"You don't know that."

Reid leans forward. "You won me over and believe me, baby, I didn't want to be won over. You'll win him over, too.

But leave out the cuffs. Those are for me, right along with the emerald dress, I'm not going to get to see this weekend after all. Just another reason to bring you back here next weekend."

"Next weekend?"

"You have a problem with that?" he challenges.

"No," I say. "I don't think I do. Are you going to be an asshole and change my mind between now and then?"

"Let's make a bet. If it's no more than three times, I get to cuff you next weekend."

"And if it's more than three times, I just don't come with you next weekend?" I challenge.

"In which case, I'll have to cuff you to my bed and make you come so many times that you can't help but forgive me."

Heat pools low in my belly at the many ways he could do just that, but I stay focused on the conversation at hand. "You're obsessed with cuffing me and I think I know why."

"Do you want to tell me why?" he asks, leaning closer, his hand sliding up my leg under the tablecloth.

I catch his hand. "You don't like me one-upping you. It feels unbalanced."

"More like I owe you."

"You want to taunt me like I did you?"

"No, I want to finish you like you didn't me, but that doesn't mean be finished you. No, Carrie. I'm not going to ever be finished with you. I told you. It's you who will walk away." He releases my leg and leans back.

We're back to planning for me to hate him again and it's getting to me in a big way. I'm suddenly angry and attacked by emotions I can't name and don't want to feel. Not after what he just said. I toss down my napkin and stand up. "I'm going to the bathroom." I don't look at him or wait for a reply.

I start walking and enter the restaurant with its beach-style low ceiling, and boat-like structure, a waiter directs me to a hallway behind the wooden bar. I can't get there quick enough. The tiny walkway, the seclusion of it, is relief that is ironic considering I feel as if I'm suffocating in all that is Reid Maxwell. I pass a turn down another hallway when suddenly, Reid is with me, pulling me into it, pressing me against the wall. His big body crowds mine, legs caging my legs.

"What just happened?" he demands, his hands coming down on the wall next to mine.

"You just had asshole moment number one," I bite out, all the emotions I can't name, or won't name, spewing right from my mouth. "You said we were done with the doom and gloom. And yet, what do you do? You say things like you did just now at the table that infer that it's inevitable that I hate you. I can't keep doing whatever this is if that's where you are driving us."

"That's not—"

"I can't feel whatever it is that I'm feeling when you keep pushing us there."

His fingers tangle in my hair. "What do you feel, Carrie?"

"Too much, you're too much, if we're spiraling into hate. Just fuck me and let me go."

"No," he says. "No, I'm not letting you go. It's not too much. It's not enough. No more of those statements. They're irrelevant because if you try and walk away, I will just cuff you to the bed like I said, and make you orgasm until you don't want to leave."

"I already don't want to leave, and with you that scares me, Reid."

"The idea that might change is what scares me, Carrie."

"Why? Why would I hate you?"

"I told you that I'd let you figure that out on your own, remember?"

"Then let me. Stop pushing me into the quicksand."

"If you're in quicksand, baby, I'm right there with you so let's make a deal. No more fear. We're in this all the way, good and bad. Say it."

"I don't have a choice but to agree. I'm in. You already made that happen."

"No running," he adds, and then he's kissing me, a deep stroke of the tongue that I feel everywhere. It drugs me into momentary submission and then there are voices, headed in our direction. Reid pulls his mouth from mine, his thumb stroking the dampness from my bottom lip, before he says, "Let's go pay the bill and get out of here." He takes my hand and we start walking, but his words are in my head: *No running*.

He really does think that I'm going to run and suddenly I'm not angry at him anymore. I realize at that moment, with his hand firmly around mine, that he's allowed himself to be vulnerable with me when Reid Maxwell, the king of assholes, is vulnerable to no one, proven by him admitting fear. He's invited me inside the walls of his private life, to meet his family even.

He's torn down walls and trusted me not to hate him, even when he believes he deserves the hate. That's his walls coming down, and that means I have to meet him halfway, and let mine down, too, but some part of me knows he's going to hurt me.

But it's too late to turn back.

CHAPTER FORTY-SEVEN

Reid

As eager as I am to get Carrie back to the cottage in time to actually have her to myself for a decent amount of time before we fly out, I find her insistence that we wait for boxes, and take home her mac n' cheese and mine for that matter, adorable. I watch her interact with the waiter who is scooping our meal into the takeout container, her brown hair tangling in the wind, her lips curved in a smile; those emerald eyes seeking mine often, telling me how engaged she is with me even when she's talking to someone else. That's the thing that I can't explain. I've had beautiful, smart, sexy women just as engaged, but they didn't stir what she does in me. I need her just as in this with me, and I'm in all the way. Right, wrong, everything in between, I'm in this and if I have my way, and I will, I will soon be in *her*.

I tip the waiter an extra chunk of change and give him a look to go away. He glances at the cash I've palmed him, gives me a look, and seems to get the idea. He leaves. "Let's get out of here," I say, reaching for Carrie's hand. "We have plans before we leave." I lower my voice for her ears only. "I need you naked and on my tongue right now."

Her cheek flushes pink, and holy hell that little shy moment has me so damn hot and hard I might have to take her to the bathroom. "Reid Maxwell."

At the sound of my name, I glance up to find a tall, dark-haired man with wild, curly dark hair, and brown hawk eyes.

"Eli Matthews," I say. "I didn't know you had left your tower in the city."

"One could say the same of you." He glances expectantly at Carrie and I grind my teeth and force myself to face facts. Eli could be useful. We aren't leaving.

"Carrie, this is Eli Matthews, as you already heard. We went to college together and you should care about him because he's half the asshole I am, filthy rich, and connected."

"Oh," Carrie says, laughing. "At least you're only half the asshole. And rich and connected works for my line of business."

"Which is what?" Eli asks.

"Sit down," I order. "The wine we were drinking is expensive, just like you like it. I'll order another bottle. Unless you're tied up."

He glances at Carrie's mouth and I want to punch the asshole. "I just finished up a meeting," he says, grabbing a chair. "I'll stay."

He's across from Carrie and next to me. I motion to the waiter, order the wine, and then as the waiter steps away, I lean in close to Eli. "There's nothing but money at this table for you."

He eases back to give me a surprised look. "That's new for you."

I don't acknowledge that comment. I ease back into my seat fully, settle my hand on Carrie's leg and give her my attention. She gives me a curious look, but then her hand covers mine and understanding settles in those beautiful eyes. "Is time an issue? We have to get to your sister's party. We could let him know the details, and see if he fits later."

She's coy. She's just told him that she's with me and made him think we have a big opportunity that we might not let him in on. "I know how you are," I say. "You like to trust people you do deals with. Eli is honorable."

She hesitates for a few beats and then looks at him. "Then it's nice to meet you, Eli."

For the next hour and a half, we talk to Eli about his company, where West Enterprises is headed, and a potential Asian investment, holding back Grayson's involvement. When I finally draw the line on time, Carrie has charmed Eli, who's a little too attentive to her as far as I'm concerned, but he's also pledged to open his wallet, and since he wants to impress her as well, I know we'll be hearing from him. Carrie is happy and excited by the time we're in the car and rushing to grab our bags.

Once the driver sets us in motion, I pull her close and whisper in her ear, "Eli wants to fuck you."

She leans in close, twisting toward me, her hands resting on my chest and my upper thigh, her lips at my ear. "I want to fuck *you*."

My cock twitches and she presses her hand over it, stroking the hard line of my now throbbing erection. She's teasing me because she thinks we don't have time for this, but she's wrong. The motherfucking chopper can wait. I cannot. I cup her face and pull her mouth to mine, nip her lips and kiss her. She doesn't hesitate. She kisses me back, hungry, just as damn hot as I am. She's in jeans but I don't let that deter me. We're behind the driver's seat, and I mold her close, stroking her breast.

She catches my hand, but when she would pull it away, I slide my hand under her T-shirt and tear down the top of her bra to pinch her nipple. She buries her face in my neck. "Stop."

But I don't. I won't ever stop where this woman is concerned. I stroke the line of her sex through her jeans and squeeze her breast. "Reid," she hisses and I kiss her, a deep stroke of tongue against tongue, and she arches against my hand on her breast and between her legs.

The car halts at the cottage and I tear my mouth from hers. "We're here."

Her teeth scrape her bottom lip. "Thank God," she whispers, reaching for the door.

I catch her hand, delaying her escape, while I pat the driver's seat. "We'll be twenty minutes."

The driver smartly says nothing. He lifts a hand in compliance and now I scoot Carrie out of the car, shutting the door behind us and folding our elbows; pulling her close to me. "Do you know what happens when you tease me?"

"You get hard and hot and I get all the rewards?"

Well, she's not wrong on that, but she left something out that she won't leave out next time. I unlock the front door and pull her inside, and before she can get away, it's shut again, and she's facing it, her hands on the door. I step into her, my hands on her hips, my lips at her ear. "You get punished." I reach around and cup her breast.

"Is this supposed to be punishment?" she asks, all but daring me to go further but I don't need a dare. She's my woman now and I feel the edge of telling her about the war between our fathers. I feel the need to ensure that when she walks into that party tonight, she feels owned. She feels like she belongs to me and with me. *Fuck*. I need to feel like I own her and can't lose her.

I reach around her and unbutton her jeans, dragging the zipper down. Her pants follow and when I would slide them all the way down, I don't. I tangle them at her knees, and move to her side, my hand on her naked backside, which is naked because she's not wearing any panties. I cup her backside and her sex at the same time. "Do you know what I'm going to do to you?"

"Punish me," she says, looking at me. "I know what you're going to do, but do it naked."

I smack her backside, just a light smack. "I'm not getting naked. Not now." I slip my fingers along her clit, flicking it back and forth.

She pants, a sexy, raspy drive-me-out-of-my-fucking-mind sound that has my cock throbbing against my zipper. "I'm going to spank you. For teasing me. For making me watch Eli flirt with you."

"I don't want Eli. Not even a little bit."

"I know that." I slide fingers inside her. "That doesn't mean I liked how he looked at you. I'm the only man who gets to fuck you now."

"You are. You are the only man, so do it. Why aren't you—"

"It's not time." I smack her backside and this time not gently.

"Reid," she pants out.

I spank her again and my fingers move inside her, my thumb stroking her clit. I pat her backside now, fast but not hard, working that friction against that of my hand stroking her to orgasm. "Oh God," she whispers. "Reid, I need—"

I spank her again because that's what she needs. I figured that out the first time I spanked her. She likes it. It's an escape, a release, the one time she doesn't have to think. So I give it to her. Harder this time. Not once. Not twice. Three times and she locks up around my fingers, spasming into orgasm, her entire body quaking. I wrap my arm around her waist, twisting her around to face me, my mouth coming down on hers, my fingers easing as I sense she needs them to ease until she collapses into me. I turn her and press against the door, giving her that extra support as I pull up her pants.

"What are you doing?"

"We have a chopper to catch."

"No, we didn't—"

I cup her face. "We will, but we're waiting."

"I don't want to wait." She presses her hand to my erection. "And you don't want to wait."

I inhale on the need burning through me and catch her hand. "It'll be better because we waited. And believe me, I need to be thinking about fucking you when we're at that party. I'll need to fuck you when it's over."

Her expression softens instantly. "Talk to me. Tell what that means."

My hands go to the door on either side of her. "It means we'll fuck and talk afterward."

"You'll talk to me."

"Yes, Carrie. I will talk to you and only you."

"Reid—"

I tangle fingers in her hair and kiss her. "Whatever you're going to say, say it when we're naked and in my bed later tonight. Okay?"

She studies me a moment before her fingers find my jaw. "Yes. Okay." She presses to her toes, pushes her lips to my lips and kisses me before whispering, "Right after we fuck whatever this is out of your system. And in case you were wondering, I love everything you do to me."

Holy hell, this woman is trying to make me fuck her right now. No. She's trying to make me fall in love with her.

CHAPTER FORTY-EIGHT

Reid

The ride is short and loud, which allows me time to get inside my own head when I'd rather be in Carrie's. I'm thinking about family, both hers and mine. They've brought us together in ways that Carrie doesn't even know and I'm hoping like hell that I'm right and my siblings will help ensure my father doesn't tear us apart. Cat and Carrie really are alike in many ways, most especially in how unlike our fathers they are. I need Carrie to know that while my father might be the patriarch of the Maxwell clan, it's Cat who's at our core, leading the way to change. Ironically, and not in my favor, it's Cat who would call me the most like my father, which makes my strategy today a dangerous one.

Once we're on the ground, I help Carrie out of the chopper, lifting her off the ramp and setting her on the tarmac, but I don't let her go. I don't want to let her go. Wind gushes, and her long brown hair blows into her face. I brush it away, barely recognizing the tenderness in the act as within my capacity, but like Cat in different ways, Carrie's changing me and I'm not sure that's good for her. My past is still my past. What I learned from that is still what I learned. And yet, I can't turn back. That means I need to protect Carrie. I *will* protect her.

"Talk to me," Carrie says, her hands settling on my face. "What are you thinking right this minute?"

"That you should run away, and yet if you try, I'll just come after you."

One of the airport staff chooses that moment to step to our side. "We have paperwork for you to fill out, sir, just inside."

I kiss Carrie and lace the fingers of one hand with hers. "More later," I promise, both dreading and looking forward to the moment I clear the air with her to every extent possible.

Once we're inside the terminal, I release Carrie to sign the necessary paperwork. I'm just turning to reach for her when she grabs my hand, and the intimacy and comfort level this action suggests in her and between us, washes over me as unfamiliar but not unwelcome. I want her to be comfortable with me. I want her to be in this with me. "Everything okay?" she asks, and the concern in her eyes says that she's not talking about the document or the airport attendant.

"You're going to be in my bed tonight," I say. "So yes, everything's fucking fabulous." I kiss her hand and start to walk, but she tugs against me and steps in front of me.

"Is there something I need to know right now?"

"Everything is fucking fabulous," I repeat, avoiding a direct answer, or a lie, to slide my arm around her and set us back in motion. And I am fucking fabulous and I'll stay that way as long as she doesn't turn the war between our fathers into a war between us. I sense her desire to push me for more, but she already knows me well enough to know now isn't the time to push. I've never let anyone close enough to read me that well, to know me that well. But then, she doesn't know everything about me. She doesn't know how easily she really can hate me and I don't want her to know.

Exactly why when we settle into a hired car, I pull her close where I plan to keep her the rest of the night, my hand on her knee, our legs aligned. The car begins to move and I'm relieved when Carrie and I fall into a comfortable silence, both of us deep in our own thoughts; hers most likely trying to figure me out, while mine are all about what she knows, needs to know, and cannot know, at least through me.

We're nearly to my sister's place when the growling of her stomach erupts into the silence. "I didn't come close to eating all of my food." She laughs, a soft, sexy and yet somehow sweet sound that drags me out of the hell of my thoughts and into the moment with her. "I'm starving," she announces. "In case you didn't notice."

"I did, in fact, notice," I say, and remarkably, just this easily, I'm laughing as well. "They'll be food at the party, but we can order food at my place where I want you right now." My fingers flex on her knee and the driver manages to stop at our destination at that very moment. "But that will have to wait. We're here." I tap the driver's seat. "I'll text you before we come down."

"Yes sir," the man replies, and I open my door, exit, and help Carrie out as well.

"I've been to the bar inside this building," she says, surveying our location. "It's a hot legal spot. No wonder your sister, the crime writer, and her attorney husband live here."

I open the door to the building for her. "Reese chose this location. He was here first."

"Cat moved in with him then?" she ask as we cross the lobby.

Seeing an opportunity to show the divide between my father and the rest of us, I share with Carrie what I would no one else. "When Cat met Reese she was living in the apartment our mother left her. Reese's mother moved into Cat's place a few years back."

She casts me a sideways look. "How do you feel about that?"

We stop at the elevators and I punch the call button. "According to my mother's letter, she went there to get away from my father," I say. "I don't want any part of a place where she suffered. So how do I feel about Reese's mother being there? Happy that Cat's out of there and with someone that isn't like my father."

"I love the way she covers his cases when he's at trial, like now actually. I've been reading about his recent murder trial in her column. I think I, like so many others, are looking for the inside scoop." She meets my stare and asks, "Do you read her column?"

"Yes, but if you tell her that, she won't believe you."

The elevator doors open and we enter. I punch in our floor and the doors shut. Carrie steps in front of me, her hand on my chest. "I don't know why you and Cat are broken, but if that's why you're on edge right now, I get it. If had to go to a party with my brother, I'd be just as tense as you are right now."

"You know how Cat feels, Carrie. Because your brother and I are alike. I'm the ass in this equation."

"Why?"

"Because it felt like the right thing to do."

Her brow furrows. "I don't understand."

My jaw sets hard. "You don't need to know that part of me. Ever. Because I'm not driving you toward hate, remember?"

"You've mistaken me for someone who wears rose-colored glasses. I know how hard you are. I also know that's not *all* you are."

She's right. It's not, but that doesn't make what's there good and right either. I turn her toward the door and pull her against me, my lips at her ear. "You've mistaken me for someone who deserves you," I say. "I don't, but it doesn't matter. I'm not letting you go. That's the kind of asshole I am. I'm also the asshole who's going to cuff you to my bed and keep you there this weekend if you go home with me."

"Cuffs will require negotiation in advance," she says as the elevator halts and then opens.

"I'll negotiate with my tongue."

"While using it to talk," she retorts without missing a beat and then tries to dart forward.

I hold onto her, but I walk us both into the hallway and pull her to me as we start down the long hall. "You aren't going to ask what I want to trade for those cuffs?"

"Not until you're naked and I'm holding the cuffs."

"Those negotiation terms could work for me if you're naked as well."

And there it is. Exactly what I have to do to keep this woman: bare it all. She told me just last night she wants no secrets and lies between us, and the problem is that there will always be a secret between us.

If I don't deal with that, it will destroy us. The hammer will not fall without me in control. I won't let it.

CHAPTER FORTY-NINE

Reid

We stop at Cat and Reese's door and right after I ring the bell, Carrie says, "She'll believe you if you tell her."

I don't have to ask what she means. She's talking about me reading Cat's column. She's talking about me pulling the walls down with Cat the way I am with her. She's pushing me to forget all the reasons I have lived alone and kept everyone, including Cat, at a distance. "It's complicated, Carrie. Really fucking complicated."

"And regret is unforgiving."

Now she's talking about my mother and the regret I have for not seeing all there was to see with her and my father, but I'm thinking about the regret I already have with her. The door opens and Carrie whirls around as Gabe appears in the doorway. And damn it, he's paired his black jeans with a black T-shirt that reads Maxwell, Maxwell, and Maxwell, which drives home the connection between us and our father.

I pull Carrie close, holding on, rejecting regret. Gabe looks at me, narrowing his eyes at me, understanding in their depths that his words don't match. "Holy hell," he says. "You came." He glances at Carrie. "And you came." He winks, acting like the player he pretends to be, his way of keeping everyone at a distance. He's a loner, just like me, and no one ever knows the real him any more than they know me. Until Carrie.

He backs up and motions us forward. "This way to the party."

My hand settles at Carrie's back and I urge her forward, resisting the urge to leave, and reminding myself that the best way for Carrie to see the disconnect between us and my father is to get to know my family, Cat especially. Of course, Cat hating me doesn't exactly help my case, but I'll make it work.

We cut right into another hallway and voices sound ahead and to the right, which is where we travel. Just before we clear the archway leading to the living area where the party is taking place, I lean in close to Carrie and whisper, "Food, drink, cake, my bed."

She gives me one of her beautiful smiles, and a moment later we're in a room wrapped in windows with a high ceiling that encases a good twenty people, more no doubt, just beyond the open patio door. Gabe is instantly engaged with some blonde while I scan the crowd filled with familiar faces, but Cat and Reese are nowhere to be found. "Let's look for my sister," I say, taking Carrie's hand and leading her forward, only to have us run smack into Lauren, Royce's wife, and one of Cat's closest friends.

"Reid," she says with obvious shock. "You're here."

"I am here," I say. "And so is Carrie." I introduce the two women, hoping to talk to Royce as well, with no luck.

"Royce has his hands full at the moment," Lauren comments. "I doubt he'll make it tonight." She gives me a coy look. "Cat will be happy that you came. She and Reese just walked to the kitchen right behind us, if you were trying to find her. They didn't see you."

"We'll go find her there," I say, giving her a nod, and guiding Carrie in that direction.

We enter the room to find my sister, looking as blonde and beautiful as ever, standing next to Reese behind the granite island, a chocolate cake in front of them. "I say we cut it now," Cat says. "Don't you want cake?"

"I'd rather have you," he says, at the same moment he looks up to find us entering. He clears his throat, alerting Cat to our company. "Reid," he greets.

"Reid?" Cat asks, blinking as if she can't believe she really sees me.

I urge Carrie forward again, my hand on her back as we step to the island. I'm across from Cat, and Carrie is across from Reese, who I look at now. "Happy birthday, man."

"Thanks," Reese says. "Glad to have you here and with a date."

"This is—" I begin but Cat cuts me off.

"Carrie West," she supplies.

"I told them about Carrie," Gabe says, entering the kitchen and walking to the fridge.

"I'm a huge fan, Cat," Carrie says. "And Reese. I'm following your case through her column. I missed today's."

Cat and Reese look at each other and laugh. "Today was—loaded. I don't like the DA any more than Reid does."

"What about the DA?"

Cole walks into the room and joins us at the endcap. "He's a piece of shit," I say, and then quickly introduce Carrie. "Cole, meet Carrie West. Carrie, this is Cole Brooks, Reese's partner. His wife, Lori, works at the firm as well. Cole's the one—"

"Who sued the DA and gave up the settlement. Congratulations on the settlement."

"Thanks," he says. "News conference Monday."

"And I can't wait to write about it," Cat says as Lori, a pretty brunette, joins us.

"Reid," she says, stepping to Cole's side. "Thank you for kicking the DA's ass."

From there, we fall into conversation and Cat and Carrie end up on the opposite side of the island talking while Reese, Cole, and Lori stand with me, talking about the press conference. Somewhere in the process, I grab a whiskey sour from the bar, and Carrie ends up with a glass of champagne. We both munch on some sort of taco a waiter brings us, and while we both chat with other people at a distance, we catch each other's eyes. I have never been as present with another person in my life.

"What about the cake?" Cat says. "We need to cut the cake."

Cole is wrangled into carrying it to the living room to a special table that's set up and everyone gathers around. "Birthday wish!" everyone shouts.

"That Cat gives me her birthday surprise she's been teasing me with for weeks," Reese says.

"After the party," Cat says, linking her arm with his. "When we're alone."

"Everyone leave," Reese calls out. "Party over. No, no, just kidding. Kind of. Everyone eat cake. My wife is going to give me my gift now. Lauren!" He grabs her where she stands next to him and places her in front of the cake. "Give the people cake." He then scoops up my sister and starts walking.

Carrie laughs. "They seem very much in love." Her eyes meet mine as they have so many times tonight, but never with the fierce awareness that pulls us together at this very moment.

Love.

Marriage.

Those two words are in the air between us and I cannot say that I have ever had them in the air with anyone else. And I know, I know in that moment that if I don't stop this now, I'll fall in love with Carrie. I know all the reasons that's wrong and can't work, and yet, I don't want to stop.

I pull her to me. "Carrie—"

"Cake?"

We look up to have a waiter hand us each a plate. I stroke Carrie's hair behind her ear. "Later."

"Later," she whispers.

We both accept a plate, and neither of us are shy about digging in. "I love Cat," Carrie says. "And Lori, too, but Cat, just—we connect. Really connect."

I reach up and wipe chocolate from her lip and lick it from my finger the way I'm going to lick her tonight. She seems to read my thoughts, pink flushing her cheeks in one of her demure moments, which contrast the many bold. I'm hot and hard, and ready to get her out of here when Cat and Reese return and Gabe steps to our side.

"What do you think?" he asks. "Was the gift what we think it was?"

Reese is now standing behind Cat, arm around her hip, hand on her belly. "Look at his hand," I say. "Yes. She is."

"Pregnant?" Carrie asks.

We both look at her. "How did you guess that?" Gabe asks.

"A gut feeling," Carrie says, "But the hand on her belly, on top of the fact that she refused champagne, also makes it a good guess."

It's right then that Cat catches our attention and motions us to the kitchen. "We're about to confirm," I say.

"Should I stay here?" Carrie asks, tugging my hand as Gabe moves on ahead.

"She'll ask to see us alone if she wants to see us alone," I say, turning to face her, "but Cat's probably more comfortable telling you than me."

Her hand settles on my chest. "She wants you in her life, Reid. Whatever went wrong, you just have to reach for her."

"It's—"

"Complicated. I know. Let's go hear her news." She links her arm with mine and my cellphone rings. I snake it from my pocket to find a client, who's a hundred feet deep in legal issues, calling.

"Go on in," I tell Carrie. "It's a client I need to talk to."

"How important is that call?" she asks. "This is not just some party. It's your sister in there waiting and this could hold up her announcement."

She's right. I stick my phone back in my pocket. "You're right. I'll call him back."

Approval warms her eyes and she pushes to her toes and kisses me. "You might not be the asshole I thought you were after all."

I mold her close and those perfect curves press to mine, my lips near her ear. "Don't go weaving fairytales unless they include me spanking you while you're playing dress-up, preferably in something see-through. And handcuffs."

"After tonight," she says, "I might just trust you enough to let you, Reid Maxwell."

Trust is exactly what I wanted to earn tonight, with the handcuffs as a bonus. "Now you're just trying to make me drag you into the bathroom and fuck you."

"That would be bad manners," she says, tilting those full, kissable lips in my direction, and tempting me ten ways to Sunday.

"And?"

She laughs. "Maybe after another slice of cake." She twists in my arms and tugs me forward, with me enjoying the view of her perfect ass in those jeans, while hoping like hell that trust is really where we're headed. The kind of trust that will endure even the most wicked of storms.

I urge her ahead of me to enter the kitchen. Carrie steps to the endcap between Cat and Lori, and I'm just joining her when the unexpected, and unthinkable happens: my father, who never attends family events, walks into the room, inappropriately dressed in a three-piece ten-thousand-dollar suit.

"What's she doing here?" he demands, claiming the endcap directly across from Carrie and staring her down. "What are you doing here?"

CHAPTER FIFTY

Reid

"Who are you?" Carrie asks, staring across the island at my father, because while my father has been obsessed about her father and anyone connected to him, Carrie's been sheltered, even by me.

"Just like your daddy," my father says. "Playing coy, but really a cobra."

"Let's go to the other room and talk, father," I bite out, motioning toward the door.

"Father?" Carrie demands, whirling to face me, but I'm already rounding the island to stand beside my father. "Let's go talk." I can't look at Carrie. I can't invite conversation that will allow my father to flatten her and destroy me with her.

But my father won't look at me. He's looking at Carrie. "You aren't welcome here. No West is welcome in a Maxwell house."

"She's welcome in this house," Cat snaps, "but I'm a Summer now, and you're giving me yet another reason to be proud of that fact." Cat turns to Carrie. "Ignore him. This is our house, not his."

"You're welcome here now, and you have an invitation to return," Reese adds and Cat whirls on my father again.

"Why did I invite you?" she demands. "Right. You never come. That's why. Leave."

I feel those words like a punch, like it's what she feels about me, but right now, I have to deal with the beast that is

339

my father. He turns to me, finally giving me his attention. "Did you bring her here?" His voice is pure accusation and hate.

In this moment, looking into my father's hard eyes, I know that if I don't convince him that her presence makes sense for his reasons, not mine, he'll target her. He'll go after her because he thinks I'm not. "Carrie and I work together," I say. "We're an investment, making money for both families."

"Investment?" Carrie demands. "You brought me here to make me more committed to the investment? You really are an ass, Reid Maxwell." She looks at Cat and Reese. "Thank you for the invitation and the lovely evening up until this point." She eyes Cat. "You're most definitely a Summer, not a Maxwell."

She turns and darts out of the room, which is exactly what I want and need, but it's gutting me to let her go for even a moment. My eyes lift and meet Cat's fiery stare that tells a story. She's angry with me. She thinks I used Carrie. She thinks that I am no better than my father. "It's not what you think. *I promise.* I'll explain." I don't wait for her reply. Fuck my father. I can't let Carrie go. I'll protect her. I'll back him down.

I'm already walking, rushing in the direction where Carrie departed into the living area. "Reid!" my father calls out, but I ignore him. I got Carrie away from him. I got her out of the range of his nastiness that would have buried me and her with me. Now I need to explain myself. Now I need to make this right.

I exit the kitchen to scan the crowd and catch a glimpse of her turning the corner toward the door. I cut through a group of people, and all but run after her. She's in the hallway halfway to the elevator when I exit the apartment. "Carrie! Wait."

She disappears around the corner leading to the elevator banks. I break into a run. I bring her into view as she waits for an elevator. "Go away, Reid," she hisses the moment she sees me. "We're done."

"No," I say, stalking toward her.

She points at me. "Do not even try to come near me," she warns, her voice quaking with emotion.

I hold up my hands in surrender. "Okay. Just hear me out. Our parents hate each other, Carrie. I was going to talk to you about it after the party, after you saw that we are not a part of that war. That's what tonight was. I wanted you to know that we, that I, am not your enemy. My father is another story. He is."

"In other words, you did his bidding. You did what you told me you didn't do. You went after our company to go after my father."

"No," I say, closing one of the at least five steps between us. "I didn't lie to you, Carrie. That is not what happened and when I realized you didn't know about our fathers, I knew you'd say just that when I told you."

"You just told your father that I was a business deal."

"That's not what I said. I said we were making money together. I spoke his language, the only one that can get him past his hate. The only way I could pull him back in the middle of that party, one which was supposed to be special for Cat, and good for us, Carrie."

"Do you know how that made me feel?" She shoves a hand through her hair. "And poor Cat. Tonight *was* supposed to be special for her and Reese." The elevator opens and I'm beside her, shackling her arm, her in an instant. "Carrie—"

"I thought we were—I don't know what I thought we were—it doesn't matter. I don't trust you, Reid. I can't be with you."

"I could just as easily have thought that you were setting me up because I'm my father's son, Carrie, but you aren't your father and I'm not my father. We're us. I want you and us. I swear to you, I was going to tell you about their war tonight."

"War? It's a war and you didn't think you needed to tell me?"

"I thought your father would have. When I figured out you didn't know—"

"You hid it from me? Why? To get me to perform with Grayson Bennett, who didn't trust you?"

"Glad to see I caught you both."

At the sound of my father's voice, I grimace and whirl around, quick to put Carrie at my back, where I can protect her from his direct onslaught of verbal abuse. "You need to step away, father. Now."

The elevator behind me dings and damn it to hell, I know Carrie is about to leave, and I have to let her go. I still can't risk him twisting his war into mine. "You need to explain yourself and her," my father bites out.

I step toward him and I can hear Carrie step into the car. "You need to back out of this," I say.

"I told you—"

"I'm sick of you telling me how to do anything," I say as the elevator door shuts behind me, the idea that Carrie is gone igniting my anger. "Back away from this," I repeat.

"I told you to ruin West and that means his offspring, too."

"I never told you I'd ruin West. I made sure the debt was settled and it is. A debt that has nothing to do with Carrie."

"It has everything to do with her. That man came at me, and us, after my stroke. He tried to sweep the stocks in four of my investments and two of yours. There's no mercy here.

You are my son. You will do this. You will ruin him and his daughter."

"If you go after Carrie or her company, you will regret it. I am your son and you taught me *far* too well. I will make you hate life and regret the day you hurt Carrie and mom, for that matter. Mom's biggest fear? That I would become just like you and I'll make that fear come true in order to hurt you. Walk away now, and I don't mean back to Cat's apartment. You hurt her tonight." I punch the elevator button and a car opens instantly. I hold the door. "Leave."

He snorts. "You'd ruin me? You really think you have that in you, boy?"

"We both know you don't really doubt that I do. Sacramento, father," I add of the secret he never wants revealed, a dirty deal he did that not even Gabe knows about. "I'll use it."

He charges at me and pokes a finger at my chest. "You dare to go there?"

"With a smile on my face and I don't smile much."

He huffs out a breath. "That would hurt the firm."

"The firm is about me and Gabe now. Not you. I want you out."

"I'm not retiring."

"Sacramento."

"I'm not fucking retiring. You think I don't have anything on you?"

"You don't, asshole, because I don't break laws."

"This isn't over," he says, but he gets on the elevator. I wait for it to shut and then turn for the stairwell with one thing on my mind: getting to Carrie.

CHAPTER FIFTY-ONE

Carrie

My taxi is stuck in stand-still traffic and it's all I can do to hold it together. Reid keeps calling my phone and I can't talk to him. I don't want to talk to him. I don't even want to listen to his messages. I'm going to melt down and cry. I'm not a crier or a fool, but Reid apparently wants to make me both. I trusted him. I was falling in love with him while I was an "investment" to him. I feel so foolish. I hurt. God, this hurts. How did I get to a point this quickly that this man could hurt me that badly? And his father—well, I know where the asshole in Reid comes from. Two peas from the same pod.

I dial my father for the fifth time, and this time when I get his voicemail I don't hang up. "You need to call me back. Now. Stop dodging my calls. This is important. I need to talk about you about Maxwell Senior. I need to talk to you about you." I disconnect.

The cab hasn't moved in five minutes. Unmoving traffic surrounds us. I can't sit here like this, with my emotions clawing their way out of me. I can't do it. I only took the cab in the first place to be able to use my phone, which isn't doing me any good. I eye the meter and throw a ten at the driver before opening my door and getting out, the crush of fumes and that dirty city smell Manhattan is famous for attack my nose and lungs. Once I'm outside, I dart for the nearest subway and replay Maxwell Senior saying "You aren't welcome here" in various ways, over and over. By the time I'm in a subway car, my thoughts go to a place that my mind is avoiding, to the place I know I can't get past; Reid and his "investment" comment. Reid letting me leave when his father arrived at the elevator. He could have gotten into the car with me. He had that opportunity, but he didn't. Just like he didn't come to me in the kitchen. He went to his father.

He was using me for some financial mark. He still is, and I have to let him. I want the company back. I can't walk away and he knows it.

He was just plain using me.

When finally the subway ride is over, I exit to the street, and I scan, making sure Reid isn't anywhere in sight. If I see him, he'll try to pull me back under his spell. It won't work. Not this time. But he's not here. He's not. I don't know why this upsets me. I don't want to see him. Anything he would say now will not erase what just happened. I hurry into my building and wish for my things that are in the hired car, where I'd left them. There are things in there I need and now I'll have to buy them again.

I enter my apartment and press myself against the door, the only thing holding me up right now. I was falling in love for the first time in my life, with someone using me. I really don't know what to do with that. Tears leak from my eyes and I swipe them away. He doesn't deserve my tears. And as for my father? Why would he not warn me about a war? He never said there was a war. Reid called it a war and after what just happened, on that, I believe him. My cellphone rings again and I grab it from my purse to find Reid's number, not my father's. I hit decline. My phone buzzes with a text from Reid that reads: *Please talk to me. I can explain. I want us. I need you.*

My heart squeezes. *He can explain.* I don't even know what "us" means and as for needing me, I get that now. I'm part of his investment. My phone rings again. It's him again and I want to take comfort in him trying to reach me, but nothing with Reid feels real anymore. I walk to the couch and sit down. Being home alone feels off. How is that possible? I love this place. This is *my space*, but mentally, I was ready to be in his, perhaps more than I even realized. My phone buzzes with another text from Reid and I lay down and hold my phone above me to read: *I'm downstairs. Come down. Let me come up.*

I type one word: *No.*

It hits me then that Reid has the money and wherewithal to get past security and when my phone rings, I answer this time. "Go away," I breathe out.

"Never," he promises, his voice low and gravelly. "I'm not ever going away. Let me come up."

"No."

"Carrie, *we need* to talk."

"You said it all with that investment talk with your father, who is my enemy, and I didn't even know."

"I was going to tell you tonight."

"After I met the family and you made sure if I bolted I'd stick around professionally?" I shut my eyes, emotion welling in my throat.

"That's not how it is. Please. I need to see you. I need you to look into my eyes and see the truth."

"Of course you need me to look into your eyes. When I'm with you, you're the snake charmer, but then that makes sense. I'm the cobra. I'm just like my father, and we both know there are things about him you could tell me, too, but I guess that doesn't serve you well."

"I'm not leaving. I'll stay here until you come down."

"Then you better ask them to bring you a pillow and blanket." I hang up. He calls back. I dial my father.

He answers this time. "Carrie," he says. "What's happening? I just heard your message. I was about to call."

He's lying. I realize now that I know this. That he has this weird pitch to his voice when he lies that I've always ignored. "You and Mike Maxwell are enemies."

"That is, in fact, accurate."

"You didn't think I needed to know that?" I demand.

"I've been that man's enemy for years. It's never affected you."

"I'm working with his son."

"Who I told you was a problem. I told you to get out."

"And you knew I wasn't. You should have been specific. He hates you. Why?"

"We go back a long way."

I think of Elijah and how easily personal hate drives professional anger. "You've gone after him. You've tried to hurt him."

"Of course I have. Every fucking chance I got."

"And his family?"

"Carrie—"

"That's a yes. I'm *working* with his son. You didn't think I needed to know that you'd tried to hurt him?"

"I told you, you need to come here. Now."

"No. No, I have a chance to save the company and I'm going to."

"He won't let you."

"I have a contract," I say. "He will. He has to."

"There's a loophole or a plan to destroy you after he gets whatever he wants out of this. I promise you."

"You underestimate my legal expertise and my ability to hold my own with anyone."

"This isn't about your skill. It's about your morals. You have too many to survive a Maxwell."

"In other words, you don't? Who are you?"

"A man who holds his own, even with the nastiest of them all."

A man I don't know, I think. "What else don't I know?" I ask.

"I have no idea what that means."

"There are people who will work with me now that you're gone."

"We all make enemies."

"*We all make enemies*? I never knew we had enemies."

"I have enemies."

"Apparently, that means I do, too. Can I get a list or is it too long?"

"You're going too far with this."

My phone buzzes with another call that I ignore. "What's in Montana?"

"Money. You know that."

"*My money*," I say. "I put so much of my money into your investments and I'm tired of not knowing what I'm really getting. Blinded, I trusted you. No more. I love you, but I clearly don't know you. Are your morals why mom left?"

"That's uncalled for. She left. She left you, Carrie."

"Right. It was my fault."

"I didn't say that."

"I want details on the Maxwell war."

"You're not getting them."

"They took over our company."

"Walk away, Carrie."

"This is my life."

"*I will* take care of you."

"I'll take care of me. I need to go."

"Not yet. Talk to me."

"Now you want to talk? Are you sure about that? You avoid me."

"What happened? Because obviously, something did."

"I met Mike Maxwell. I'm waiting to meet you, too. The *real* you. When this is over, when I get the company back, I need that to happen."

"You're blowing this out of proportion."

"We lost the company to a hostile takeover by your enemy. I'm not blowing this out of proportion. I need to go."

"Carrie—"

"I've already said things I'll regret later, even though you deserve to hear them. Don't push me to say more. I'm not in a place to show my normal restraint right now. We'll talk later if you actually take my calls." I hang up.

My phone buzzes with a text from Reid: It's not our war. I didn't go after your company to destroy it. The stockholders were taking him down anyway.

I don't answer. I now know that he is a part of the war. My father tried to hurt him and his family. I flashback to the party and the kitchen and squeeze my eyes shut as the tears start to flow.

CHAPTER FIFTY-TWO

Carrie

I don't know how long I lay on the couch, weeping away my emotions but when it's over, it's over. I have to pee. As crazy as it is, that's what brings me back to the present, to me. The need to take care of myself on some level, I guess. I stand up and without any real decision to do so, go upstairs to the bathroom. I go pee only to discover that I've started my period, because of course it's early. I'm a ball of stress, that must have been a trigger. And yes, this has to happen right now and of course, I don't have enough of what I need to manage this new-found problem until morning.

I contemplate ordering online, but I don't even have my computer. Reid does and he also has my bag with important items, most of which I can buy tomorrow but I need my MacBook. Actually, I have my old one that I kept for emergencies when I upgraded. So yes, I could order online, but tampons, aren't exactly something I want the delivery boy delivering. Leaving, however, means potentially running into Reid. Is he still downstairs? No. Surely not. It's been about forty-five minutes now.

I fix my face the best I can and decide that I'll run to the corner store but to be safe, I dial the security desk. "Is the man that was waiting on me still there?"

"He left about fifteen minutes ago."

He left. Of course he left. I knew he would. "Thanks." I disconnect, slip on a hoodie and head for the door. The coast is clear. The man I thought might be falling in love with me while I fell in love with him, left.

Once I'm in the elevator I hold my breath anyway. He won't be in the lobby. I was just told that he's not. I don't want him to be there. I *so* want him to be in the lobby, and that's a problem. I can't trust him. I need to remember that I cannot be with a man who I'm sixty seconds from falling in love with who I can't trust. How can I even fall in love with someone I don't trust? Does that mean I *do* trust him? Or that I'm just a fool who wants to trust him, therefore, I'm convincing myself that I can trust him? Why am I thinking these things? He was horrible to me at the party. No one who cares about you acts like that. I'm business with a side of sex. I press my hands to my face with anger and pain. The doors open and my heart thunders in my chest, adrenaline surging through me.

I exit the car and scan the lobby to find no signs of Reid, a discovery that stabs me in the heart because I'm one big self-destructive mess right now, apparently. Or I will be if I don't watch myself. The man not only kept something huge from me, I know he's got another secret. I know he knows something about my father and he won't tell me. Obviously it's something he believes will turn me against him.

I hurry out of the door and my eyes land on the railing where Reid and I had met that night, not long ago, because as he pointed out, we have not been together long enough for it to be long ago. He's not there. Of course, he's not. Why would he stand there when I'm inside?

I rush down the sidewalk and hurry to the store. I grab a pint of Ben and Jerry's, a candy bar, skittles, and almost forget my tampons because I'm on my period and heartbroken, which apparently makes sugar a critical need, and brain cells optional. I can't be heartbroken. Reid was right. We haven't been seeing each other that long. I need that ice cream. Which will mean, I'll then need to work out in the building gym twice as long next week because I can't run, since I've bumped into Reid doing just that before. I really need to call the realtor. I have to move. If I give up everything, no one can take it from me anyway. I need to stop. I'm rambling in my own head. I'm having a rambling conversation with myself.

Ben and Jerry's, here I come.

I'm almost back to my building when my gaze falls on that same spot by the railing this time, but this time, Reid *is* there and my heart explodes into a charge at the sight of him. He's leaning forward, his head bowed, and even from a hundred feet away, I can feel the torment radiating off of him. God. I want to go to him. I want to kiss him and touch him and tell him I trust him, but how do I know his torment is about me and us? How do I know it's not about letting his grand plan go awry? I have a random flashback of us on the beach and Reid telling me how into me he was.

"I can't wake up and not think of you," he'd said. "I can't go to bed and not think of you. I wanted to tell you about my settlement. You're in my head, Carrie. I don't even want to get you out anymore."

"You couldn't if you wanted to," I'd teased, but I remember the twist in my gut as I'd added, "Because we have Grayson to close and a board to satisfy."

It's like some part of me knew he was using me. I'd even tried to tell myself to revel in living in the moment because I knew there wouldn't be more. But he'd been so good at convincing me there would be more. He'd sensed I was worried about the business side of our relationship. I go back to the beach again, to how he'd gotten me past those feelings:

He'd rolled with me, his leg still between mine, those blue eyes staring down at me. "What just happened?"

"Nothing happened."

"You think this is all about the company. That we're here and now and gone when this is over."

"I didn't say that."

"It's not about any of those things," he'd said. "I told you, Carrie. I don't want to share you. I'm obsessed with you and it's not the kind of obsession that goes away. You're with me now. I'm with you now. Say it."

"Reid—"

He'd kissed me, a silky caress of his tongue before he'd ordered, "Say it."

I blink back to present, I'd known then that I was in deep, so very deep, and so I'd done it. I'd said it. "I'm with you now and you're with me."

And then he'd gone in for the kill and added, "Do you know how many women I've said that to? None. No one but you. This isn't about a deal or a company. This is about you and me and us."

Us.

He'd convinced me there was an "us" that reached beyond business until his father blew it all for him.

I turn away and run toward the building, entering the lobby and forcing myself to walk to the elevator. I step inside and the doors are shutting as I hear, "Carrie, wait!" And for just a moment, he's standing across from me, our eyes connecting, as the door finishes sealing me inside. We're divided, broken in every possible way.

CHAPTER FIFTY-THREE

Reid

I wake Sunday morning on the couch with a bottle of scotch next to me and a bitch of a hangover, the likes of which I've not experienced in a decade. The fact that I didn't go to bed because Carrie was supposed to be there with me, only makes me want another drink, which I won't take. I don't have the luxury of being drunk, not with my father to deal with. But holy hell, when in my entire life have I wanted a woman in my bed, no, in my life? Now. That's when. *Fuck.* I drag fingers through my hair and stand up, walking to the kitchen where I grab the Excedrin and down two pills with a bottle of water. I'm going to get another fucking migraine thanks to this hangover. I can feel my temples throbbing. I grab my phone from the pocket of the sweats I put on after I showered last night and check it for a message from Carrie, one I know won't be there. I'm right. It's not there. I can't get to her until Monday. I know this. She's not going to talk to me before then. She doesn't understand my father. She doesn't know what was in my head and I can't even make her understand. I need out of here. I need to run. I down another bottle of water and head to my bedroom. By the time I'm there, I'm dialing Carrie instead of dressing.

She answers. She fucking answers. "Reid."

Damn, I like my name on her lips. "Let's meet."

"No. And I'm going to work from here tomorrow."

That pisses me off. "No," I say, hardening my voice. "You are not. Because that's not what CEOs do. And I'd say this to anyone else, too. You want to run this company, you need to step up, no matter how personal or rough it is."

"Right. I need to step up and make your investment worthwhile."

"Damn straight. You protect everyone's investment. That's what CEOs do, and the staff needs to see you there making that happen. If you want my support with the board, you come to work tomorrow. Do you understand?"

"I'll be there."

I lower my lashes, hating that I just had to do that, but it was for her own good. She wants this. I know she does and I'm not going to let my father, and me for that matter, get the best of her. "I'll see you then." I disconnect and shove the phone into my pocket, about to climb out of my skin. My phone rings and I snatch it up, hoping for Carrie, but it's my father.

I grimace and answer the call. "Father."

"We should meet."

"After I draw up your retirement papers. I'll let you know when they're ready."

"Or you'll ruin me," he states.

"Yes. With a smile on my face."

"I made you, boy."

"I couldn't be more aware of that fact right now. I'll be in touch." I disconnect and call Gabe.

"We need to talk. I'm on my way there."

"I had a feeling that was coming," he replies.

"I'm running. I'll be there in under an hour."

"Running. That tells me you and Carrie didn't make up."

"Not even close."

"Man, Reid. That sucks. What are you going to do?"

"Make him pay." I disconnect and head to my closet. A few minutes later, I've brushed my teeth, and I'm now dressed in running shoes, a T-shirt, and a hoodie. I walk to the front door, snatch my keys from the entryway table, and stare at Carrie's bags on the floor right beside mine where I left them last night. I open the fucking door and exit. I need out of here.

A few minutes later, I'm running, music blaring in my headphones in an effort to block out everything but the run, but it doesn't work. I'm replaying that kitchen scene with my father. He's such a little bitch. In the moment, standing in that kitchen, all I could think of was to contain his attention on Carrie and get her out of there. A strategy I blew when I went after her, which means it was all for nothing. I could have just wrapped her in my arms, ushered her out of there and forced my father out. I need to tell her that. I stop running and pull my phone from my pocket, but shove it back inside. I need to tell her in person and if that means waiting until tomorrow, I'll wait.

I start running again and this time I don't stop until I reach the high-rise where my brother lives, several miles away. I pass security without a need to sign in; I'm on his list and security knows me well. I'm at his door just as quickly. Knowing Gabe will leave the door open for me, I enter and head through the living room, a room framed with brick on two walls and a floor-to-ceiling window spanning another. Everything in his place is brown and tan, the décor masculine, the statement screaming: Bachelor forever. I get it. I felt the same way.

Until Carrie.

I walk up a set of stairs that leads to the upper-level kitchen to find my sister standing at the wood-finished island with Gabe, both in sweats and T-shirts like me. "Let me guess," I say, leaning on the door jam. "You're here to tell Gabe your big news. Are you—"

"If I had a secret," Cat says. "I wouldn't tell you two. At least not right now."

"So she's pregnant, but not announcing it yet," Gabe says, leaning on the island. "An assessment I make by the fact that she won't say she's not."

"Good grief. I'm not on the stand in a courtroom." She folds her arms in front of her. "What happened with Carrie?"

"You saw what happened. She fucking hates me now."

"You made her feel like you were using her, Reid."

"I know, fuck, I know, Cat. In my mind, at the time, it felt like the best way to get her out of there and try to get her off his radar."

"I know," she says. "You told me that, but if it were me, if I were Carrie, I'd be hurting right now."

"Sounds like a six-dozen roses apology is needed," Gabe says.

"No," I say. "She thinks I took over her company to hurt her and her father. She thinks I'm using her for some endgame. Roses will feel fake."

"Agreed," Cat says. "They might actually make it worse. What are you going to do?"

"I told dad I'm forcing his retirement." I look at Gabe. "Has he called you?"

"No, and Cat told me what you said to him, but how the fuck are you going to force him out?"

"I know something he did that he doesn't want anyone else to know."

"Then why the fuck haven't we gotten him out before now?" Gabe says. "Let's do it."

"You're really going to do it?" Cat asks.

"Yes. I've wanted him out since I read that letter from mom."

"You have?"

"Yes, Cat. I have. I didn't know who he was. I'm not him. I'm really not him after meeting Carrie."

"Do you want me to talk to her?" she asks.

"No," I say. "Not yet. Maybe, but I don't want you being connected to this. I want her to know you as you. She needs to know we aren't like him. I know she saw the real you yesterday, at least."

"He needs to know we're united," Gabe says, drawing our attention back to our father. "The three of us. That's not something he's used to. It'll let him know our role in his bullshit is over." His cellphone rings, and when he answers his lips curve. "Send him up." He disconnects. "He's here. How well-timed."

"Yes, it is," Cat says. "Because I'm still angry about him making a scene at Reese's party."

"Anyone want a drink while he comes up?" Gabe asks, looking at Cat.

"Stop trying to make me announce that I'm pregnant," she says. "And why would I drink? I need to be here and present for this."

"I'll go get him," Gabe says. "He should be at the door any minute." The bell rings. "And there he is." He rounds the island and I step further into the kitchen to allow him to pass. Once Gabe is gone, I look at Cat. "Let's go to the living room. I don't want us all trapped in this small space with him. I actually think he will find that empowering, a place he can throw his power around and have it bounce off the walls onto us."

"Good idea," she says, hurrying forward and out of the kitchen, down the stairs.

I follow her and right about the time we're standing on the far side of the couch facing the door, Gabe and our father walk in the door. They join us, the two of them facing us until

Gabe steps to the opposite side of Cat, the three of us facing him. "Isn't this cozy," he says. "My three children, whom I love."

"They're with me," I say. "You're out."

His lips twitch and he looks at me. "I'll leave the firm, but my payout will be substantial."

"It'll be what I say it is," I say. "And we both know why."

"I don't think you have the balls to act on that threat."

"You don't believe that or you wouldn't be here trying to recruit Gabe to your side. You're out."

"Maybe later, when work isn't everything to you," Cat says, "we can try to be a real family."

He looks at her. "You have no place in this conversation. You walked away from the firm. Stay out of it."

"Perhaps the only one of us that was smart about her life," Gabe replies dryly.

"All this for West's daughter?" my father demands, turning his attention back to me.

"It's for all of us. It's for mom and yes, for me, it's also for Carrie. The war is over. There's closure. West Senior is out and so are you. A new generation now runs both companies."

He stares at me, his eyes glinting hard. "I'll send you my terms. Meet them and I'll leave quietly." He turns to walk toward the door but stops short turning to pin me in a stare. "But I'm never out, boy. Remember that." This time he rotates fully and leaves.

When the door is shut, the three of us stand there, seconds tick by before Cat says, "A new generation. Mom is cheering from above."

I scrub my jaw, thinking about Carrie. "I need to go."

"To Carrie?" Cat asks.

"No, but I have an idea to get her back."

I head for the door, and then the elevator. The minute I'm on the street, I call Carrie's father. He doesn't answer. I leave a message. "I want to make a trade. Call me." I start running for the return home and I'm halfway there when he calls back.

"If that trade involves my daughter, forget it."

"If I push my father out, you tell her everything."

"Never. I did this the way I did it, so she'd never know everything and I will never let you be with her. Never."

"I'm giving you my father's demise in exchange for you telling her everything."

"You won't admit it, but you wanted his demise. I gave it to you. Thank me by staying the fuck away from my daughter." He hangs up.

There's only one way I can force Carrie's father to talk. I'd have to get new dirt on him and blackmail him and he deserves it, but I can't do it. Not if I want her back and I do. I'm damned if I do and damned if I don't.

CHAPTER FIFTY-FOUR

Carrie

I wake Sunday morning on my couch, where I ended up after tossing and turning in my own bed. I actually couldn't sleep in my own bed alone. I tried. I even took a double dose of melatonin because why wouldn't I let Reid turn me into a druggie? Not that melatonin is really a drug, but still. I'm not a person of excess, unless it's related to that man. Which is why I had laid in my bed thinking about being in his bed and all the things he would have done to me, including just sleeping with the man. Then, thinking about him standing with his father on the other side of that kitchen island. The two versions of Reid contrast in my mind to such an extreme that it's confusing me.

Sitting up, I cup my head, which is throbbing from all the crying, and I head to the kitchen where I start a Keurig pod brewing and then pop two Excedrin with a swallow of water. I reach for my phone in the pocket of my sweats that I wore to bed—because I just needed to be ready to do something, though I have no idea what—and I remove it. I actually check it for messages from Reid because I'm the pathetic girl who is obsessing over the man who's using her and who humiliated her less than twenty-four hours ago.

I grab my coffee and pour a ton of Reese's Peanut Butter Cups creamer in it because I never ate the ice cream last night. I deserve the splurge. I head back to the couch and decide that work and a hard workout is the only way I can survive today. Since it's the middle of the night in Japan, I email my brother about the event center, hoping the contact he has for the sale is as good as he promised. I then head to my bedroom, throw on workout clothes, and head to the gym on the fifth floor, since awkwardly running into Reid during a run is not on the agenda.

I'm just leaving for the gym when my phone rings with Reid's name on the called ID, and I don't hesitate to answer. I need to work from home for a few days. I need space and I tell him just that. The asshole lectures me about doing my job and how my role as CEO means putting aside personal baggage. And he's right. No asshole, in other words, *him*, should keep me from my goals and my job. I'm now almost as pissed at myself as I am at him. Almost.

Once I'm in the gym, I burn off a lot of emotion, then run to the store to grab all the items that are in my suitcase which Reid still has. I return to my apartment, check my email to find nothing from my brother, and then I shower. I settle onto my couch and start looking for a backup plan if the event center bombs. Every hour that passes is torture. I think of Reid. I want Reid. I hate Reid. I might be in love with Reid, which makes me hate him all over again. And isn't this just what he promised? He knew I would end up hating him because he knew he'd done me wrong.

"Asshole," I whisper.

By evening, when it will be morning overseas on a workday, I've just ordered Chinese food when my brother calls. "I'm walking into a meeting, but I want my percentage on this."

"I'll pay you a finder's fee, but not a percentage."

"How much?"

"Nothing if I don't do the deal, which means I need the number."

He actually hesitates but gives it to me. Our goodbye is curt. I dial the business office for the event center and connect with the man I need to speak with. His English is good and he confirms that yes, they are considering a sale. We talk about what he needs from me and the starting bid is a huge number, but he emails me financial data to justify the sale.

I spend the next few hours working through that data, putting it in presentation form, and it does look good. I email it all to Reid and then I fall asleep on the couch with my MacBook beside me and my phone beside it. I shouldn't want it to ring again but I do. "I hate you, Reid Maxwell," I murmur into the darkness.

❧

Reid

I want to call Carrie, but I can't take her shutting me down again. I need stand in front of her and make her listen. And so I work out long and hard, and finish with a cold shower and memories of fucking Carrie in this very shower. I then call the contacts I need to call to get the money together for Grayson, which leads to a dinner I really don't want to have. After hours with the "money men" as they love to call themselves, I arrive back to my apartment, with the promise of an investment so damn large, it even makes my head spin, and I've done my share of mega-deals. This project Carrie came up with for the event center is hot. I hope she can pull it off. I hope *we* can pull it off.

I walk into my godforsaken, big-ass empty apartment. Why did I want this place? My phone rings and I dread looking at the screen. I want it to be Carrie, but I know it's not. I pull the damn thing from my pocket and read the caller ID. "Hello, Cat," I say, walking to my bar and pouring a whiskey because I'm apparently over the hangover and ready to do it again.

"What's happening with Carrie?"

"Not a damn thing. Not until tomorrow when I can force her to listen to me. If she will. For all I know, I'm dead to her."

"No," she says. "I saw how she looked at you and I saw you looked at her. Reid, I've never seen you look at a woman like that. She's—changing you or maybe healing you in some way I can't know. We just aren't that close."

"Cat—"

"We're going to work on it. I sense that now. I'm—willing, Reid. There has to be some way you can earn Carrie's trust. Just tell her whatever it is you say you can't tell her."

"I'll lose my stock in the company if I do, which means Gabe will be destroyed right along with me, and then Dad will destroy Carrie's company, and we're all fucked."

"Oh my God. It's that bad?"

"Yes. It is. I'm protecting her, too. Dad did some stuff that I'm connected to that I didn't have any idea about. I'm guilty by association. That's how I got pulled into it."

"Gabe?"

"Doesn't know. I don't want him to be guilty of anything. He doesn't know. He can't know."

"My God, Reid. What a burden you're carrying."

"I had it under control until Carrie. She's a game changer. I called her father. I tried to get him to break the contract, but he wants me out of her life. He won't do it. The irony is that the old me would burn that bastard to the ground, but he's her father, Cat. She loves him. Her mother left her years ago."

"You love her."

"I—it's too soon to say that word."

"You know," she says. "It's crazy, but when it's the person you're meant to be with, you know fast. It matures, but you know early. Make her listen. I know you can. She wants to. She just needs to feel safe."

"Safe," I say, that word resonating. Her mother left. Her brother is gone. Her father lied to her. "Yes. I think she does."

"Be her safe place, and that's a big order right now, but she needs you. Let me know if you want me to talk to her."

"Thanks, Cat." I hesitate and then say, "I missed you."

"Well, we'll talk about why you ever had to at some point. Right now, you need to get your woman back."

We disconnect, and I down my whiskey, processing Cat's words, my mind starting to work. I walk to the living room, open my MacBook on the coffee table and find an email from Carrie that reads: *Event Center sale info.* I read through the numbers that are a slam dunk to entice Grayson. I dial Grayson.

"Reid. I hope this is good news."

"We have an amazing opportunity in Japan and money to bring to the table with it. Carrie brought the deal to the table. I just supported it with money."

"It's not something I can do on my own?"

"No. It's that big. We can't guarantee you can get this deal over another bidder, but we can guarantee you'll want to, and we'll fight for it."

"I'm intrigued. I'm throwing a party for the opening of my new hotel Wednesday evening at seven. Meet me at my business office in the hotel at five and plan on attending the party. My assistant will send you the details."

"We'll be there."

I pull up my email, but I can't do it. I have to call her. I dial her number. "Hello," she says, answering on the first ring. "You got the numbers."

"Yes. They look good. The best thing that's happened to either of us professionally, ever. I did my part. I secured a hundred million today that I believe can be turned into three hundred million."

"Oh my God. Grayson is going to be floored."

"I teased him without details. I just hung up with him. We meet him Wednesday at five right before a party he wants us to attend. His assistant is emailing us the details."

"That's perfect. We have plenty of time to prepare."

"Yes." I hesitate. "Carrie."

"Yes?"

I have so many things I want to say but I know I'll get one more shot and I need to take it in person, where she can't shut me down. "I'll see you in the morning." I start to hang up.

"Reid," she says, her voice lifting urgently.

"Yes?"

She's silent a moment. "I—I'll see you in the morning."

She doesn't hang up. I don't hang up. Finally, she says, "Can you hang up now?"

"Because you can't?" I ask.

"Just hang up, Reid."

Fuck.

I hang up and it about kills me, but I know after that call that I still have a chance, but a chance isn't enough. I have to go after her father, but not to destroy him. I'll make him rich as fuck if that's what it takes to get him to tell Carrie the truth that I can't.

CHAPTER FIFTY-FIVE

Carrie

I don't remember going to sleep, but the alarm on my phone wakes me after what I think is about three hours. Not only did I work most of the night, I kept thinking about that last call with Reid. I know I'm not overreacting to what has happened, but I want to be overreacting. His voice made me want so very badly, on so many levels. Knots form in my stomach at the idea of seeing him today. I'm going to have to face up to who we are, not who I thought we were. And I will. Maybe that's just what I need. To see him, to look into his eyes, and see the truth.

I shower and slip into a black dress with a neckline that goes all the way to my collarbone. I use the products I bought yesterday. I wear panties that I bought myself that he will never touch. I pack my backup briefcase because Reid has that, too.

I arrive at work with coffees in hand, one for me and one for Sallie. "Morning," I say, eyeing Reid's closed door, with Connie already at her desk.

He's not here.

I am.

I walk into my office and claim my desk. My cellphone rings with Royce Walker's number and I answer immediately. "Hi, Royce."

"I'm late getting back to you, but Reid told me to get you whatever you want on your father."

"He did?"

"Yes. He did. What do you want to know?"

"Everything, because I now believe I know nothing."

"Then you'll get everything. I'll be in touch."

"Wait. When did he tell you to do this for me? Before the weekend?"

"Yes. Before the weekend."

"Okay, thanks." He disconnects and I lean back in my chair.

Reid told him to do this for me and it wasn't motivated by what happened this weekend. It matters. The timing matters. That he did it matters. It says he's not trying to keep whatever is going on with my father a secret. He just doesn't want to be the one to badmouth my father.

Sallie appears in my doorway. "You okay?"

"Yes. Why?" I try not to look guilty as charged.

"You didn't even look at me when you gave me the coffee."

"Sorry. I was up dealing with a Japan deal and barely slept."

"Japan? You hate Asia deals."

"This one is different, and Reid has investors he's confident in."

"But are you?" she asks, perching on the edge of the visitor's chair.

"If Reid believes in them, I do. I trust him." The words are out before I can stop them. *I trust him.* How can I trust him on this and nothing else? *Money*, I think. He won't let himself get hurt financially.

"What can I do to help?" Sallie asks, grabbing my attention again.

"I'm about to email you a list of research items."

"Got it. I'll watch for it." She heads out of the office and I stare after her, thinking about my words, "I trust him." I'm very confused. I don't spend much of my life confused. I'm decisive. I have goals. I know what I want. I'm focused, and I need to focus now. I dig into my work and I keep expecting to hear, "My office. Now," from my intercom any minute. Some part of me craves that moment, while another dreads it.

It's nearly nine and Sallie is at my desk going over data with me. "This all looks good," Sallie says. "Incredible. But it's Asia. You're sure you trust Reid on this?"

"I do. I trust Reid."

At that moment, Reid appears in my doorway, his big, perfect body eating away the doorframe, his blue eyes meeting mine. I feel so many things in this moment, too many things. "My office," he says. "Now." He turns and leaves.

I swallow hard. Sallie looks at me. "When he does that in person looking all hot and dominant, it's not nearly as offensive as when he does it on the intercom, don't you think?" She narrows her eyes at me. "Carrie?"

"I need that data quickly. I need to be ready to show it to investors as early as this afternoon."

Reid buzzes my office. "Now means now."

Now means now. I want to be pissed, but I'm not. I'm ridiculously nervous. I stand up and round my desk, marching out of my office, across the open office area and I don't even look at Connie. I open Reid's door and the next thing I know, I'm pressed to the hard surface. "Yes. I'm pushing you against a door again." His fingers tangle in my hair. "And yes, I've wanted to do this for twenty-four painful hours." His mouth closes down on mine and I try to resist, I do, but I'm back to thinking he owes me this. He humiliated me. He hurt me. He owes me the damn kiss. It doesn't matter that thinking is what got me to this place with him. I just want him to keep kissing me.

I sink into the connection and I forget everything that happened between us. I need him. I want him. My hands are on his body and his are on mine and it's not until he's tugging my skirt up that I come to my senses. I catch his hand. "I'm on my period," I pant out.

"Ask me if I care right now."

"We're at work, Reid."

"Then let's leave now."

"No. No, we—this—it changes nothing. I don't know why I just let that happen."

"Because we're good together. Because we *need* to be together, Carrie."

"I can't just fuck you and let you fuck me. I'm not you, or my father, or your father. I don't want to hurt you. I can't do this. I'm getting too—I'm just—I can't."

"Too what?"

"Emotionally involved, and you will hurt me. You already did. You—in that kitchen—God. Please leave me out of this war. I just want out of it."

"I would never hurt you, Carrie. *Ever.*"

I shove against his unmoving chest. "What do you think that was in your sister's place? What do you think you did to me?"

"My father's brutal. If you had lashed back at him, he would have come at you hard at the party and beyond. I was protecting you."

"If that's your way of protecting me, I'll stick to protecting myself. I can't do this."

"I have never asked a woman to trust me. I am asking you. Trust me. I won't let you down."

"When this is over, maybe. But not now, and I get it. You're you. You can't wait. You can go fuck whoever you want, and I'll fuck whoever I want and—"

His fingers return to my hair, tangling roughly. "You do not have permission to fuck any other man. I do not want another woman. We're together. That isn't changing."

"I'm afraid to trust you."

"I know, baby. I know you have reasons, and I'd feel the same in your position, but I need you to look at everything I've done to earn your trust." He brushes his lips over mine. "I need you to think about how we feel. That's real."

His intercom buzzes. "Your car is waiting and our flight is scheduled for two hours from now."

"I'll be right there," he calls out.

"Flight?" I ask, my heart racing. He's leaving? "You're leaving?"

"I have a problem I have to deal with. It can't wait. I'll have internet on the plane. You can reach me. We aren't over, baby, and neither is this conversation. And if you don't leave now, I will pull your skirt up and fuck you. I will forget this trip and I can't. Not this trip." He releases me and steps back. "Go, baby."

I don't immediately move.

He arches a brow.

"Carrie?"

"This doesn't mean we're still us."

"Just tell me you'll listen when I get back. Alone. Be with me long enough to really hear me." He steps to me, his hands on my waist. "I don't know if there was another way to handle what happened in that kitchen, but I swear to you, I meant to protect you. I hate leaving right now. Promise me—"

"I will. I'll listen."

He breathes out in relief and cups my face. "I'm not letting you go." He kisses me and turns me toward the door. "Go, baby, before I don't let you."

I don't want to go but I do. I exit his office, and I know that I'm in a quicksand of my emotions with this man. I know that I'm in dangerous territory with Reid, but I have nothing to go on but what I feel. And I trust this man. I want this man. I'm going to risk everything for this man.

CHAPTER FIFTY-SIX

Reid

I'm on my way to the airport for my trip to Montana when one of the investors I met yesterday calls and wants to meet. He has another investor he needs to introduce me to who is leaving town in the morning. I can't refuse, not with this Grayson deal in play and I change all my plans. By the time, I'm finally through with the meeting, it's nearly seven at night when I reach the airport and board the private jet. The first thing I do when I'm settled into my seat is dial Carrie. "Hey, are you wherever you're going?"

I read the question. She wants to know where I'm going, and I don't want to lie, which is why I don't offer it up. "Actually, I'm just leaving. One of the investors needed me in a meeting. The good news is we landed more money, and considering how vague I've been about this project, we're looking good."

"That's wonderful and the vague thing is good. I don't want the competition trying to put together a group of investors to beat us on this."

I love how damn smart she is. "Exactly. Listen, baby, I'm about to take off. I'll land really late. I won't call you and risk waking you up. And I'll be up early. I won't likely have much of chance to talk tomorrow, but if you need me, call or text."

"I will. Are you going to make it back for the meeting?"

"I'll fly back late tomorrow night, in the middle of the night if I have to. Just remember that my silence means nothing, but I am trying to get back to you. Okay?"

"I'm okay. I'm going to listen to you and I'm not thinking of more reasons to doubt you. I did plenty of that on Sunday."

"I'm working on a way to fix those doubts."

"What does that mean, Reid?"

"When I get back we have a lot to talk about. No confessions. Don't read into that. I haven't done anything to confess. I'll see you soon." I disconnect and hope like hell my plan works.

I finally land in Montana, at nine local time, and eleven back home. Once I'm inside the rental car, I dial Royce, "What do you have for me?"

"I'm texting you the address where he's staying. From what I can tell, he's sleeping with a woman who inherited a horse ranch from her father, which just happens to set on top of oil. Obviously, he's after the oil. She's younger, pretty, and widowed. I'm not sure she understands the implications of the oil beneath her land or just doesn't care. She's all about the horses. What else do you need?"

"That's all."

"No dirt or ammunition?" Royce asks.

"No. I just need a sit-down with the man. I have what I need from there. I'll be in touch." I disconnect, and in a few minutes, I'm inside my shitty hotel, which is all this area had to offer. I'm exhausted, but now that I'm here I decide to find the address for where I'm going tomorrow. The drive is half an hour, and the ranch is gated and locked up. It'll be open tomorrow for the ranch crew to go in and out and I'll be here.

It's nearly midnight by the time I grab food and return to my room, crashing in the crappy bed. Tomorrow, I'm going to end this war once and for all.

I'm up at six, and already my phone is going off. At nine, I call Connie. "I need radio silence. If someone calls you, tell them I'm giving a presentation and will call them when I'm out."

"What are you doing, Reid?"

"Is Carrie there?"

"Yes. Do you want to talk to her?"

"No. I don't."

"She seems good, Reid. She's excited about whatever you're working on."

"As we all should be," I say, not giving her that hint of what's between me and Carrie that she wants. That's for us to reveal, at some point. And I'm going to make sure that point exists. "I'll call you later." I hang up and an hour later I've had black coffee and some sort of pastry I could have done without but I'm at the ranch and the gates are open.

I drive down the dirt road, and when I reach the sprawling white mansion that is the main house, I'm greeted by a ranch hand who informs me that Mr. West is gone for the day. He won't return until tonight. It's clear he's living here. Interesting. I tip the man a hundred-dollar bill, with the promise he'll call me when he returns.

I drive to a diner nearby and pull out my MacBook. I want to call Carrie, but I don't. She'll ask where I am and I want to tell her about this in person after I secure a truce. I'm at the table a good two hours when West slides into the seat across from me. He's my father's age, late fifties, and he wears those years just as arrogantly and well. "Obviously my hundred-dollar bill to the ranch hand didn't earn me any loyalty," I say.

"This is my territory," he says. "You had to have known that."

I study West, search his eyes for some part of Carrie to connect with, but I see nothing that resembles the woman who has come to mean so much to me.

"What are you doing here?" he demands.

"She matters to me. We aren't a part of your war."

"You're his son."

"We had an agreement. I did what you wanted."

"And I gave you what you wanted."

"Tell her."

"Never," he says.

"Tell her I didn't destroy you."

"Never," he repeats.

"What's it going to take?"

"You will never be with my daughter."

"Money? I'll give you money. I'll make you a rich man."

"I am a rich man."

"And yet you took Carrie's money."

"To make her more money. And my money is locked up and substantial. She'll inherit well and you won't see a dime."

"I don't need her money. I need *her*. What's the number?"

"There is no number. I don't want money. I want out. I want peace. I want this place and the woman who's here."

"And the oil under her land?"

He smirks. "Of course, you know."

"Carrie wouldn't want you to displace those horses for the oil. I'll make you the money. Five million in two years."

"This oil is worth four times that."

"Is that the number? Twenty million?"

"There is no number. I won't ever do business with a Maxwell. I hate your father. I hate the Maxwell name."

"Why?"

"You signed away everything and he didn't even tell you why. Oh, right. He didn't have to. He put your name on the line with illegal activities you didn't even know about."

"You're one to talk. We both know the lines you crossed."

"Go home, Reid." He stands up and walks away.

"I'll give up everything and tell her," I call out. "I can remake the money."

He turns around and walks to the table, pressing his hands on the surface. "You won't do that for Carrie."

"Do you want to take that risk?"

"If I ruin you, your father ruins Carrie. If you really do care about her, you're smart enough to know that, and you won't do it. I've got you by the balls, and apparently, so does she." He pushes off the table and walks away.

I sit there for a good twenty minutes, processing what to do next. I want his head. I want to hurt him. I stand up and go back to my room and change clothes. I go for a run. Once I've blown off steam, I go back to my room and pace. I dial Royce. "What can I do for you?"

"If I wanted to ruin him, do you have the ammunition?"

"Don't do it," he says. "She won't get over that."

"Thank you."

"What?"

"I called you because I knew you'd say that. I needed to hear it."

"Give me time to hand her a file with the research on her father. It'll be hard for her to read, but it'll do that for you."

"You can't get to the information I need you to get to."

"You'd be surprised what we can get to," he says. "And I'll get to enough. Trust me. Come home before you do something you'll regret."

"I'm going to stay."

"Why?"

"Because I don't want to be on a plane when I come up with a proposal he'll actually listen to."

I hang up.

I drag my hands through my hair and spend most of the afternoon into the evening coming up with nothing. Finally, I take a shower, pack and charter my plane for tonight. I want to be back in New York City. I need to talk to Carrie. I'm sitting in my rental car when I decide I'm operating without facts. If I know the core problem, then maybe I can talk to West again. I dial my father. "Reid," he answers coldly.

"Why does he hate you?"

He doesn't ask who I'm talking about. "At this point, I see no reason not to tell you. I fucked his wife."

"As in Carrie's mother?"

"Yes. Carrie's mother."

"Holy fuck. While you were married to mom?"

"Yes. That's what started the war. I fucked his wife and he told your mom."

"You're such a bastard."

"And you, son, are a chip off the old block."

I hang up thinking of Elijah and decide I need to deal with him. Twenty years of two families destroying each other is a lesson I can't ignore. I also decide that talking to West won't matter. I need to hope Royce finds what I need him to find and tells Carrie. Right now, I'm worried about Carrie's father getting to her before I do. I need to get home now, tonight.

I drive to the airport.

CHAPTER FIFTY-SEVEN

Carrie

Reid hasn't called all day and even though he warned me he might not, we're so broken right now that it feels bad. I'd just suck it up and call him, but two in the morning isn't the time to make that decision. He's probably asleep like the rest of the world, while I haven't even tried. The fact that I'm working on the Grayson numbers, sitting at my island in the kitchen, pumping coffee down me like it's my lifeline at this hour is a testament to how much our current state of broken is affecting me. I stand up. It's time to try to sleep. I'm not even in my nightgown. I'm still in the sweats and T-shirt that I put on after a workout and shower, which isn't the way to convince myself to sleep.

I shut my computer and it's as if it triggers my cellphone to ring. I grab it and the minute I see Reid's number I hit answer. "Reid?"

"Yeah, baby. I'm downstairs. Come get me. They won't let me up."

The sound of his voice, rich and masculine, washes over me and awakens and warms me inside out. "Wait. Did you say you're here? As in my building?"

"Yes. I flew home to see you."

He didn't call because he was coming back to me.

"Carrie?"

"I'll come get you. That guard is new. I won't convince him to let you come up." I disconnect and head for the door, and despite everything that has happened, I just want to see him. I just want to feel him. I can't get to the elevator soon enough and nerves flutter in my stomach as it arrives in the lobby. The minute the doors open and I step into the lobby, Reid is in front of me, looking like sin and satisfaction in dark jeans and a navy T-shirt, his fingers tangling in my hair. "I missed the hell out of you, woman," he says, his voice gruff, affected, his mouth closing down on my mouth, his tongue licking deliciously at mine.

I sink into him, my arms wrapping his body and I remember his words about feeling him, about feeling us, and how real it is. And it is. In this moment, I feel how much he wants me, I feel that I mean something to him. "Let's go upstairs," he murmurs, brushing fingers over my cheek, his lips parting mine with a reluctant lift.

"Yes. I need to wave at the guard. Did you sign in?"

"Yes. Do the wave."

I lean around him. "He's with me, Kevin."

"Have a nice evening, Ms. West."

I ease back in front of Reid and he laces his fingers with mine and punches the elevator button. The doors open immediately and we enter. He punches in my floor and then turns to me, his hands settling on my waist, pulling me close. My palm settles on his chest where his heart thunders beneath my touch. "You didn't hesitate to let me up," he says.

"No. No, I didn't."

"Why, Carrie?"

"Because despite the fact that you hurt me, I missed you, too."

He lowers his forehead to mine. "I didn't want to hurt you. I don't ever want to hurt you again."

"Then don't."

The car halts and the doors open. When Reid tries to exit, and take me with him, I tug against his hold. "Wait." The minute he looks at me, I say, "Right now. I really want to pretend the broken part of us doesn't exist, okay?"

He drags me to him, and into the hallway. "We aren't broken and when we walk out of your apartment tomorrow morning, you're going to know that." He kisses me, a delicate brush of lips I feel in every part of me before he leads me to my door.

"It's open," I say, and the minute we're inside, he shuts the door and locks it. The next minute, I'm in his arms, my body pressed to every hard part of his perfect one, and he's kissing me. God, he tastes so good. I want and want with this man and I don't even care how he might crush me right now. I cling to him, sinking into the kiss, my hands all over him and I just want to feel.

"Carrie," he whispers, cupping my face. "Baby, I need to tell you something."

"Don't tell me now. Don't ruin this."

"I need to tell you before we wake up in the morning to a call."

That jerks me back to reality. "What does that mean?"

"I went to see your father. I tried to get some sort of truce. I wanted him to tell you that I didn't do this to you or him, but he wouldn't. He said I'd never be with his daughter."

"You went—that's where you were?"

"There's more, but—"

"To try and convince me to trust you?"

"Yes."

"To Montana?"

"Yes. I can tell you all I found out there. Do you want to hear now?"

"No. No, I want you to kiss me again."

"You're not mad?"

"You went for me. You flew back for me. That doesn't make the kitchen scene with your father go away, but it comes really close."

"I didn't know how you would react. I was—"

"Reid, kiss me already."

His mouth closes down on mine, and I swear I breathe him in, my hands pressing to his back, my body molded to his. He went to Montana for me. I don't even consider this to be business. I taste the emotion on his tongue. I taste the relief, the need, the passion. This isn't about sex. This isn't about money. His hand, his warm, big, perfect hand slips under my T-shirt and cups my naked breast. I moan into his mouth and he tears his lips from mine. "If I can't have you in my bed, we need yours. And before you warn me, I don't care about your damn period."

"It ended. It was early and nerves—it's not an issue."

His mouth closes down on mine, a quick lick of tongue against tongue before he scoops me up and starts walking. I cling to him, and right now, in his arms, I feel one of those shifts in our relationship. We are not as we were. We are not broken.

The light is on in my bedroom, and Reid carries me to the bed and lays me down on the mattress. "I'd give up everything for you, Carrie." He brushes his lips over mine. "I need you to know that."

"I wouldn't ever ask you to do that. I wouldn't want that."

"I know because you are good and pure in ways I will never be, but I'm a better man with you and because of you. I need you to know that, too. I'm not after money. I don't want anything from this but you."

My hand presses to his cheek. "I believe you. I have questions, but I believe you."

He kisses me, his lips brushing mine and then trailing down my jaw and over my neck before he presses his cheek to mine and whispers, "I'm not going to fuck you this time. We can fuck later. I'm going to make love to you."

CHAPTER FIFTY-EIGHT

Reid

Inhaling the sweet floral scent of Carrie, my lips linger at her ear. Never in my life has a woman affected me like Carrie. I find myself having this thought yet again with this woman. I could savor her forever in every way. My mouth settles above hers, our breaths mingling, as she whispers, "Reid," and damn it, I should not be this affected by a woman saying my name, but I am.

I kiss her again, and just drink her in, in no rush to fuck anything out of my system. She's under my skin, in my mind, in my damn heart when I didn't think I could feel such things. My hand presses under her T-shirt, palm caressing her ribcage, and up to cup her breast, my fingers teasing her nipple. She arches into my touch, and I nip her bottom lip before dragging the shirt over her head. Her hands press under my shirt as well, her tongue stroking against my tongue, igniting a fire in me. I want her hands and her mouth all over my body.

I drag my shirt over my head and Carrie shoves against me. I roll to my side at her obvious request, and her hand settles on my zipper, fingers closing over my erection. "I owe you something."

I tangle fingers in her hair. "We've talked about that. You owe me nothing, Carrie."

"Then I want my mouth on your body. On a certain part of your body." She tightens her grip on my cock. "How is that?"

My cock throbs with the suggestion, but that's not where I want to be with her tonight. I roll her to her stomach and settle over the top of her. "I'm making love to you, Carrie. I need you to know we're more than fucking."

"I do," she whispers.

"No," I say. "You hope we are." I caress down her shoulders, goosebumps lifting on her arms and I love that she responds this way to me. "You don't know that we are, but you will. You don't really know what you do to me or what you are to me, Carrie." I kiss her shoulder and scrape my teeth over the delicate flesh, my tongue laving the offended skin.

I move to the other shoulder and repeat, my hands sliding underneath her to cup her breasts as I kiss a path down her spine, and then slowly caress her sides until my hands are on her hips, my lips finding the small of her back. I slide my hands under her waistband and slowly drag down her pants until that beautiful bare backside of hers is exposed. That's enough to make me impatient and I scrape my teeth over her backside. She makes a soft, sexy sound and arches her hips. I press my hand on her lower back again and then order, "Don't move," before I release her and pull her sweats all the way down, lifting off of her long enough to finish undressing her and myself.

My hands come down on her ankles, caressing a path up her legs and I don't stop until I'm slipping my fingers under her and stroking her sex, the wet slick heat beneath my touch telling me how ready she is for me. My hand goes to her belly, lifting her hips to slip a finger inside her and then lean in to lick her. She looks over her shoulder at me. "Come here. Please."

"Not yet," I say.

"Reid. I want to touch you."

I lick her once more and then slide up her body, settling on my side and rolling her to me, lifting her leg to my hip. My hand on her face, my cock nestled in that wet heat where I was just licking her. I brush my lips over hers. "Is this what you want?"

"Yes. This is what I want."

I kiss her, or maybe she kisses me. Our lips collide and our tongues lick and stroke in a seductive dance that has me rubbing my cock along the seam of her body, and then pressing into her. She gasps another soft, sexy sound that has me driving into her fully, my hand cupping her beautiful backside to find that deeper spot we both want. That's all it takes. I am now in that place of need that has me deepening our kiss and pulling back to thrust into her. She moans and arches into me, and there is this wildness between us that isn't fucking. It's about needing and wanting on an entirely different level. We are trying to crawl underneath each other's skin, to be one in some indiscernible way and it's all fire and heat, passion and yes, lust, on a whole new level.

I press my cheek to hers, my lips at her ear, my hand on her breast. "Do you feel how much I missed you now?" I thrust hard.

She pants. "Show me again."

I smile, when I never fucking smile, and damn sure not during sex. I thrust again. "How's that?"

"Again," she breathes out and I swallow the sound that follows, licking into her mouth as she arches into me and then stiffens. A moment later, she's spasming around my cock, and that's my undoing. I pump into her harder, and there is a tight spasm in my balls, and then holy hell, I'm groaning with the way she milks me into complete, utter oblivion. We collapse together, holding on to each other, our breathing softening, slowing.

I stroke hair from her face and drag her gaze to mine. "You really do rock my world, woman."

"Yeah well, you're not so bad yourself."

I press my forehead to hers. "I hate this, baby, but we should talk a little more before morning."

"Do we really have to?"

"Yes. We do." I reach over her and grab her a tissue and press it between her legs before I pull out. "Where's your robe? I can't focus when you're naked."

"I'll get it. I need to go to the bathroom anyway because you know, that's what us girls do after sex. We pee."

I laugh. "Is that right?"

"Yes. That's right." She rolls away from me or tries.

I catch her and kiss her. "I have no confession to make. It's nothing like that. Just a few details about my trip you need to know."

"I didn't think you were making a confession." She caresses my cheek and then rolls away before standing up and walking toward the bathroom.

I'm momentarily distracted by her naked body but that comment that she didn't think I was going to make a confession doesn't sit right. I don't know if it's about trust or something else. I stand up and pull on my sweats, sans the underwear, since I don't plan to stay dressed. Carrie exits the bathroom in a knee-length silk robe with her nipples distractingly puckered beneath the silk.

"What are we doing, Reid?"

I close the space between us and link our fingers. "Making sure what happened at my sister's house doesn't happen again by getting everything on the table before someone else does it for us."

"If this isn't a confession, why I do feel dread in my stomach?"

"Because it's not all good, baby." I lead her to the bed and sit us down. "I now know why our parents hate each other, and I know what your father is doing in Montana. Which do you want first?"

"Oh God. I don't know. Pick my punishment for me."

"The worst first then. Why they hate each other. You won't like this, Carrie."

"Just tell me. Did my father tell you?"

"No. I called my father and told him I needed to know. He decided that considering what I now know, which means, considering I read my mother's letter, there was no reason not to tell me."

"What does your mother's letter have to do with this?"

"Our fathers were friends. My father fucked your mother."

"What?" she gasps.

"That's right and your father told my mother. And so the war began."

She presses her hands to her face and then looks at me. "How can we be together?"

"We're not them, baby. We have nothing to do with this and it's not like we're going to have family events with my father. He won't be invited ever again."

"You're right. It just feels weird. I want to blame your father for her leaving us, but I can't. She made her choices. She cheated. She left and never looked back." She swallows hard. "What else? I need it all now. Montana. Tell me about Montana."

"Montana," I repeat. "He knows I'll tell you what I'm about to tell you. That's why I know he'll call you tomorrow and tell you I tried to convince him, or threatened him most likely, to lie to you. I need to know you aren't going to believe him."

"I'm here. I'm with you. I trust you." She shifts more fully toward me. "What is he doing?"

"Fucking a young pretty widow who owns a horse ranch she won't give up."

Her brow furrows. "He wants to buy a horse ranch? Is there money in a horse ranch?"

"There's oil under the land. He wants that. She wants to protect the horses. I think he might go so far as to marry her. He didn't say that, but that's my gut instinct." I think of his comment about cash stashed away and the realization hits me. "I'm speculating, but something he said makes me think that he looks at that land as a retirement plan."

"And he's using my money for this? Surely he knows I won't think that's acceptable. He wants me to go there."

"I'm sure he planned to convince you the horse ranch was a good long-term investment. He wants you to fall in love with it."

"But now you know and so I know."

"Yes. I'm sure he'll have a backup plan and tell you I'm full of shit. Royce found out about the oil."

"My money is basically gone."

"No. We're going to make a fortune with Grayson, both of us. You. Your own money and, Carrie, it's enough to never need another dime."

"We are far from closing this deal."

"We will. I feel it, but I need to know that when he calls you, you're ready for what he'll say."

She lays back on the bed. "I can't do this anymore."

I lower myself to her side, resting on my elbow. "Carrie—"

"Not us." Her hand goes to my face. "I'm sorry. I didn't mean us or you. I meant everyone going at each other and me being in the middle. So I choose to trust you and what I feel with you, until you, not someone else, gives me a reason not to. But please don't make me sorry."

Relief washes over me. "I'm not going to make you sorry."

She rolls to face me, propping herself up on her elbow. "Be honest with me no matter how bad it is, because I get it. There was stuff that happened before we knew each other. I'm not stupid. Just be honest like you were tonight. No secrets. No lies. Promise me."

"I promise," I say, and I mean those words despite the fact that I have a secret and therefore I just told a lie.

One lie, one secret, to protect her and my brother.

CHAPTER FIFTY-NINE

Carrie

The minute Reid says, "I promise," I climb on top of him and let my robe slide from my body. His gaze rakes over my body and he grabs me, rolls me, and in an instant, he's undressed and pressing inside me. And this time, we fuck. Hard and fast, with my legs on his shoulders and then my knees in his chest. When it's over, we end up under the blankets with me curled into his side, my head resting on his chest; his heart thrumming beneath my palm.

"Tomorrow's the big day," I say.

He leans up to look at me, his gaze cutting through the haze of the room lit by open curtains and starlight. "It'll go well."

"Yes. I think it will."

"Tell me something I don't know about you," I say as we have in the past.

"I'm a movie buff. I love going to the movies and eating popcorn. I even go alone."

I lift my head. "Alone?"

"Yes. Alone."

"Well, I like movies. So you don't need to go alone anymore."

"I won't," he says. "It's a date. Many movies. Your turn. Tell me something I don't know about you."

"I want a cat, but I fear I work too much."

"I want a dog, but I fear I work too much."

I roll to my stomach to look at him. "You want a dog?"

"Yeah. I do. I had one as a kid and I loved that damn dog."

"What kind?"

"German Shepard."

"I had a Pomeranian I lost a few years back, it feels like yesterday. I think I'm ready to have another fur baby. I was actually thinking about getting a cat. Do you like cats?"

"Yes." He laughs. "I feel like we're having the 'do you want kids' conversation." He rolls me to my side and pulls me against his chest, with that comment lingering in the air.

"I don't," I say as if he asked. "I don't want kids. I just don't want someone to disappoint."

His curls his arm more fully around me. "You understand me better than you think, Carrie. And I don't know if that's a good thing. Go to sleep, baby. Tomorrow's a big day."

I shut my eyes, my hand settling on his arm, and just like that the warmth of slumber overtakes me.

I wake naked, in my bed, with Reid wrapped around me, sunlight beaming through the window, announcing the new day I'm starting with him, and it really is heavenly. He smells good and I feel safe. I don't remember any human being except my father, and of course, in a different way, making me feel safe. But as I lay here, I realize at some point my father stopped giving me that feeling. I guess I assumed it was being an adult and independent. But it was more. I sensed something in him and only now does everything Reid told me last night start to sink in.

"I can hear you thinking some pretty heavy thoughts."

I roll over and face him. "Not about you."

He brushes what has to be my wild morning hair from my eyes. "Your father."

"Yes. My father."

"I get it, you know. It wasn't that long ago that I finally saw my father for what he is."

"The letter?" I ask.

"Yes."

"I think I knew, but I was in denial," I reluctantly admit.

"As did I. The fairytale of my mother keeping him human was obviously a lie. It doesn't get easier, Carrie. You want them to be more."

"You forced your father's retirement. That had to have been hard."

"Easier than you think. I was about to do it when he had his stroke. You'd think that would tame the bastard in him, but it didn't."

"How does Gabe feel about it?"

"Happy as fuck. He's the one who convinced me to read the letter."

"You needed convincing?"

"Yes. I did. I'm not one to do the out of sight, out of mind thing, but I didn't want to know what I couldn't change."

I press my hands to his chest and listen to the thundering of his heart, absorbing how very human Reid "the asshole" has become. And I know from the thundering of his heart that while he seemed to speak easily, he has not. He doesn't share these things about himself, but he has with me. "I've failed you."

He arches a brow. "What does that mean, Carrie?"

"I was supposed to wake you up properly." I press him to his back and slide down his body, kissing his chest, his cock already hard and pressing to my belly. "Good morning."

"It most definitely is a good morning," he says, as I ease lower and wrap my hand around his hard length.

I lick the tip of his cock. "Holy fuck, Carrie," he murmurs, his voice low, gruff, affected.

I like affecting this man. I like making him feel as out of control in all the right ways as he makes me feel. I lick him again, and he draws in a subtle breath. I don't want subtle. I suckle him, draw in just the soft head of his cock, and he lifts his hips. I don't give him the "more" that action requests. I swirl my tongue around him and move my mouth from side to side. His hands go to my head, tangling in my hair. "Stop teasing me, Carrie." It's an order, but there is a desperateness to the low, rough command that's exactly what I'm looking for.

I glance up at him and slowly take more of his shaft, my tongue traveling the underside of him as I do, sliding all the way to my hand that still grips him, and not gently. The look on his face is pure lust and arousal, and it affects me. I'm hot, wet, and my nipples ache. I suckle him and then start pumping my mouth, adding a little side back and forth movement, and his hand tightens on my hair, his hips lifting. His thigh where my hand rests tenses. He begins to thrust into my movement, and I can feel his urgency, his approach to that place of no return and yet he tries to pull me back.

"Carrie, stop or I won't be able to," he says. "*Carrie.*"

I don't even think about stopping. He wouldn't stop when I needed more. He wouldn't stop when he wanted to please me. I feel the moment he stops fighting. The moment he is right there, and then over the edge. He spasms beneath my palms and the salty taste of his release touches my tongue and throat. I don't pull back. I slow down, I ease him into completion, and when it's over, when I know he's completely sated, I let my hand fall away and my mouth leaves his body.

He drags me to him and under him. "Carrie."

"Reid."

"Come shower with me at my place. Stay with me tonight after the party."

I feel no hesitation. "Yes. I just want to gather a few extra things."

My cellphone rings on the nightstand. I shut my eyes. "It'll be him," I say, knowing he'll know I mean my father.

He presses his forehead to mine. "Yes. It'll be him." He kisses my temple and rolls away, grabbing his clothes and heading to the bathroom. My phone stops ringing and I grab it, confirming that yes, it was my father. I throw away the covers, find my own clothes and dress.

Reid exits the bathroom and we stand on opposite sides of the bed. "Call him back, baby. You need to hear what he has to say, and I need to know you see me, and us, despite that."

"I'm not sure I want to deal with this today. We've barely slept and tonight is important."

"All the more reason we need this behind us."

I hate that the bed is between us. I hate that I finally have someone in my life I want here, and my father is between us. "You're right."

"I'll go downstairs and make us coffee." He rounds the bed and kisses me, fast and quick on the lips and then leaves. I watch him disappear out of the door and the fact that he offers me this privacy matters. It's him telling me that he needs my trust. It's him telling me that I have his.

CHAPTER SIXTY

Carrie

I walk to the navy-blue lounge chair by my window and sit down. Inhaling, I hit redial. "Hello," I say when my father answers.

"He's with you, isn't he?"

"If you're talking about Reid, I'd like to know what you and Maxwell Senior have against each other."

"That doesn't even come close to answering my question."

"You're right. It doesn't because a) I wouldn't tell you who was in my bed ever, b) I wouldn't give you the satisfaction of knowing he wasn't here, because you and his father split us up, and c) It's none of your business. Which while a and c might be one and the same, I still needed to say them both. I'm that irritated right now."

"In other words, you've been fucking him or there wouldn't be anything to break up."

"Contrary to popular belief, a woman does not believe fucking is a relationship. You have to have a relationship to have a break-up."

"So are you fucking him or dating him?"

"Refer to a, b, and c."

"He came here."

"Okay."

"That's it? Okay?"

"Yes. Okay."

"He told you."

"You tell me."

"He wanted me to tell you that he didn't force the takeover and ruin me or us. He offered me money. Millions of dollars and you know why. That convention center deal you're working on. He can't have that go south. He needs to sweeten you up and keep you in his bed until he gets that payday."

I wait for that to hit home and feel real, but it doesn't happen. "Because there's no way I could possibly matter to him? Why? Because I'm not pretty enough? Because I'm not smart enough? Because I'm not what? Not good enough?"

Reid reappears in the doorway with two cups in his hand, his eyes meeting mine, and what passes between us in that moment is full of promise, full of trust, a part of a growing bond that this call with my father has not broken.

"Carrie," my father says. "You're a beautiful woman, but he is an evil bastard."

The evil bastard sits down next to me and hands me a cup of coffee that smells like Reese's Peanut Butter Cups. I take a sip and glance at Reid. "He's an asshole, not an evil bastard."

Reid smiles—God, I love his smile—and he follows it with a wink. "What's happening in Montana?" I ask.

"He told you, didn't he?"

"Should I ask him?" I retort, avoiding a lie.

He's silent a moment that becomes two. "I want you to come here. I want you to see the horse ranch I'm staying at. There's real money in stallions. With your charm, we can lure in some professional riders, stable their horses, give them a place to train."

He didn't tell me about the oil. He's hoping Reid didn't. "I don't even know what to say to that, father. I really don't. How long does it take for that to get my money back?"

"It's a long-term investment, but a stable one. We need a stable business this go around and there's a bonus. There's oil under the property, so if the horses stop delivering profit, we have a fallback that protects them and us."

"And how much will all of this cost us?"

"Nothing, Carrie. I'm going to marry Stella, the woman who owns it. Well if she accepts. I haven't proposed yet."

"Marry?" My eyes meet Reid's and he nods, his expectancy at this announcement. "Who is she?"

"A retired school teacher. Forty-four. Widowed. She inherited the ranch. She loves the horses."

"And you get the oil."

"It's not like that. It started out that way, yes. But Carrie, honey, she's special."

Reid's hand settles on my leg, grounding me as I listen to my father ramble for several minutes about this woman, but he never goes at Reid again, which tells me he's so nervous over the woman, the oil, and my money, that he's hyper-focused on his defense, not Reid's execution.

We disconnect, without him asking one question about the convention deal he's thrown out as ammunition against Reid. That bothers me, but of course, he's in that hyper-focus mode. I set my phone down and sip my coffee. "Thanks for this."

He sets his cup on the floor and then takes mine and does the same. "You're too beautiful, too smart, and too perfect for me, but I am never letting you go."

I drag my fingers over the one-day stubble along his jawline. "And you are such an evil bastard, but apparently I like you that way."

He leans in and nuzzles my neck, his lips by my ear as he says, "I'll show you just how evil if you ever let me use those cuffs."

I smile, but don't reply. I think tonight would be a good night to show him I do indeed trust him by letting him have his wish. "I'll think about it."

He pulls back. "That's more than I've gotten before."

"Yeah well, I'm trusting you, remember?"

"I do," he says, pulling me to my feet. "Just make sure you do."

I don't question why he makes this statement. I just heard my father call him an evil bastard.

A few minutes later, Reid and I are in his apartment, in his bathroom, and he walks to his closet, flips on the light and sets my bag inside. "Claim your space."

"What?"

"I plan to keep you here as much as possible. Claim your space."

He walks forward and catches my hand, guiding me into the closet where his suits are neatly lining one wall and his casual clothes another. He points me toward the empty center rack. "It has your name all over it. And there's never been a woman's clothes inside these walls."

My stomach flutters and I rotate to face him. "What are we doing, Reid?"

"Everything I can convince you to do. I'm just that kind of evil bastard." I laugh at the reference to my father's remark, and he drags me to the shower with him and it's not long before I'm against the wall, and he's fucking me into a very good morning. By the time we're dressed, me in my lucky navy-blue dress, and him in a gray pin-striped suit with a gray tie, it's nearly nine, and we're walking to work, the hell of the weekend behind us.

"Does it look bad if we walk in together?" I ask.

"It would look bad if we fucked on the receptionist's desk, though I'm all in, if you are." He jokes but then turns serious. "We're working together on a deal that secures everyone's future. The staff and stockholders better hope we fucking walk in together."

"There's the Reid I know. So warm and fuzzy and diplomatic."

"I tell it how I see it."

I laugh and we enter the building. Once we're in the elevator alone, Reid glances over at me. "I don't believe I saw what color panties you wore today."

"Perhaps I didn't wear any panties," I say, as I did when we did this before.

"I'll find out for myself," he warns. "At the most unexpected time today."

The elevator opens and an older lady steps on, standing beside me. I scoot closer to Reid. "I'll spare you the work. I'm not."

He glances down at me, his eyes hot. "You're not?"

"No. I'm not."

"Why?"

The elevator dings. "It's just something I do every now and then." The doors open and I dart forward. I can feel him at my back, watching me, wanting to pull me to his office and yank my skirt up and see for himself. Connie is at Sallie's desk when I approach and they both look at me with keen eyes that see too much. "You look happy," Connie says, and when Reid stops beside me, she eyes him, "Wait. You look happy, too. Who are you?"

"A man about to close a deal so big they'll be talking about it for fifty years." He looks at me. "We need to be at the meeting, dressed for the party, by five." He walks away.

I turn to the ladies. "He brought so much money to the table there's no way Grayson can't be impressed. And he's barely gotten started."

"Then you two are working well together?" Connie asks, her eyes searching mine.

Sallie snorts. "He orders her around like she's his plaything."

My cheeks heat and Connie smiles. "And that only goes well for him when she lets it go well for him." She winks and walks away.

I quickly bypass Sallie's curious look and enter my office. I claim my seat, ready for tonight. I want it to be here. That's when I hear Sallie say, "Sir. Sir, you can't be here."

I stand up and hurry to the door to find Reid's father walking toward his office, because apparently the hell of the weekend is not behind us, and neither is the hate.

CHAPTER SIXTY-ONE

Reid

I've just hung up with one of the investors I'm working with who's demanding a meeting, and promising fast cash when Connie buzzes my office. "Your father is charging toward your office while Sallie runs after him."

"Holy fuck," I murmur. "Get Sallie out of this."

"Done."

No sooner does she say that word then my father walks into my office in one of his expensive suits, and he doesn't bother to shut the door. He saunters toward me like he owns the place and sets a folder on my desk. "I saved you the work. My retirement terms and contract."

"You aren't here to give me your retirement contract. You're here to drive home the fact that you and I are in Carrie's father's old office. You want to cut her because she's his daughter. Or you're afraid she'll marry me and get the family fortune."

"Marry? You're going to *marry* that woman?"

I said those words with no hesitation and I don't back down now. In the back of my mind, I've known Carrie was it for me, the final woman, from the beginning. "I could be so lucky as to have Carrie agree to be *my wife*," I say, "which should tell you how deeply I will cut you for her."

He presses his hands on my desk. "How did you become what you are right now?"

"My mother wrote a letter that told me who you really are, and do you know her worst fear? That I would become you."

He stands up and for the first time in my life, outside of the day we buried my mother, he looks stricken. "She didn't say that."

"She did. You hurt her. You *cut* her. She wasn't a business conquest. She was your wife and my mother."

His lashes lower and he cuts his gaze. "Read the contract," he says and then he turns and leaves.

I don't believe what I just said to him will change him, but it affected him. There is still something human in that man and I can only hope that means he's capable of a real truce. I round the desk and I exit my office, crossing the offices and entering Carrie's office. She's standing at her window and she turns as I shut the door.

"What are you thinking right now?"

"I'm not. I'm waiting for you to tell me what that was."

I cross to stand in front of her. "He brought me his version of his retirement contract and he did it to taunt you with the idea of him in your father's office. And me in your father's office. He's afraid of you, Carrie."

"Why would he be afraid of me?"

I shackle her waist and pull her to me. "Because you have a bigger hold on me than he does."

Her hands settle on my chest, tiny, delicate, and yet her touch undoes me. "And my father," she says, giving me what I want, what I was looking for, "fears that you have a bigger hold on me than he does."

"Yes, Carrie. They're afraid of us. We're the generation that ends a war they've lived for years. It became a chess match, and they didn't care who they hurt to win." I drag her dress up and cup her naked backside.

"You had to find out if I was wearing panties, didn't you?" she challenges, her hands settling on my arms.

"You know it, and damn, baby. I wish I had the time to lick you properly right now, but I have to meet one of the investors and then take this contract my father dropped off to Gabe. I don't want to wait and get sideswiped in some way. I'm going to meet you at the apartment at three-thirty."

"Do you have a tux?"

"I own one and it's pressed and ready to go."

I release her and reach into my pocket, grabbing my keys to remove my extra apartment key. "For you."

She tugs her skirt into place and the minute she looks up, and spies the key, her eyes go wide. "You're giving me a key to your apartment?"

"Yes." I press it into her hand. "I am. Is that a problem?"

"No," she says softly. "No problem."

"Good." I cup her head and kiss her. "I'll see you soon." I turn and exit the office, and a few minutes later, with my father's agreement that I haven't even looked at in my briefcase, I leave the building, but I have no doubt there's something in it that I won't like.

Fifteen minutes later, I'm in my office at the firm, looking over the agreement and I pinpoint exactly what my father wants me to see. The clause that says he retires with the understanding that no West marries into the family, works for the company, or benefits in any way from a Maxwell or Maxwell enterprise. It seems Carrie's father and my own, are of the same mind, to keep us apart. I stand up, walk to Gabe's office to find him behind his desk on the phone. He hangs up. "What's wrong?"

I shut the door, cross to his desk, and toss the contract in front of him, with the clause circled. He laughs. "He's such a bastard you can only laugh. I have a gut instinct for our move. What's yours first?"

"We'll sell our stock and get out and it's all his or whoever outbids him."

"My thought exactly."

I dial my father. "That was fast."

"Here's my counter. I'm standing with Gabe. You sign my version of the contract, which will come over today, or we put our stock on the market to the highest bidder on Monday morning." I hang up.

Gabe's lips curve. "Five, four, three, two, one."

My cellphone rings and I answer, "Yes, father?"

"You will not sell Maxwell stock to someone else."

"We'll give you first right of refusal to a fair offer."

"You'd never walk away."

"We'll survive and thrive without this firm, because despite all the attorneys that work here, we *are* this firm. You have until Monday." I disconnect and eye Gabe. "I'll draft it and send it to you to review."

Carrie

It's three-thirty when I arrive at Reid's place and I've just stepped off the elevator when he calls. "I'm running late. I'll be there by four-fifteen."

"You're cutting it close."

"I know. Believe me, I know. I'm leaving my meeting now and all is well. I'm taking the subway to get there faster. I'm going underground. See you soon." He disconnects and I walk to his door and pull out the key he gave me. A key. To his apartment. It feels like a message, an invitation to know him more intimately and be a part of his life. I smile and open the door. I want to be a part of his life.

I hurry inside, not lingering. I haven't unpacked and once I'm in the bedroom, I dare to do as Reid suggested. I hang up some of my clothes in his closet and stare at the space with our things hanging together, butterflies in my belly. I think I'm falling in love. I probably am in love, but it feels too soon to say such a thing. How can I already feel this? I have never used that four-letter word with a man. And we went from broken to sharing a closet. I might be crazy, but I can't seem to care.

I pull out my emerald dress and then hop in the shower because I want to feel fresh for tonight. I'm still in my robe and have just finished flat ironing my hair to a long, sleek, brown finish, which will be destroyed in the Manhattan humidity when Reid finally walks in. I glance at the time. Four-twenty. "You're pushing it."

"I know, but us men are fast." He kisses me and then enters the closet. I stand up and turn to watch the door, thinking about my clothes hanging with his. Seconds tick by and Reid appears in the doorway, his eyes warm, his voice husky. "You claimed your spot."

"Yes. I did. It was still okay, right?"

He closes the space between us and pulls me to him. "It was what I wanted, Carrie. And," he cups my naked backside through the thin silk of my robe, "you're wearing the emerald dress. You have it pulled out."

"Yes. I am."

His eyes burn hot. "If you wear panties under it, I'll spank you when we get home. If you don't, I'll lick you. You don't get both. You decide."

Oh my. I'm suddenly wet and hot and tingling all over, and before I can even recover from that onslaught of sensations, he smacks my ass hard enough that I yelp, and then turns me to face the counter. "Let me give you something to think about." He yanks my robe up. "I'm going to spank you now."

"What? Reid—"

"Count. One. Two. Now." He spanks me, one, two, three times. He then turns me around, sits my tingling ass on the counter and kneels between my legs, and licks my naked clit. And that's all. He teases me. He stands up and says, "That was a taste for later. For me and you. You decide how we end the night." And with that, he turns, walks to the shower, strips naked, and gets inside, leaving my backside burning and my sex clenched. Because Reid Maxwell knows how to make me want more.

CHAPTER SIXTY-TWO

Carrie

Reid is as stunning in his tuxedo as he was the night I met him, and perhaps memories of his tongue that night are what solidify my decision on the panties or no panties topic.

I'm not wearing panties, because while I like that man's hand on my backside, his tongue is magical. The only problem with that state of undress is that October has reared its head this evening and fall has arrived. My dress is not much of a defense for the chilly eve, even without the straight stream of air up my skirt which I found out in our short walk to our hired car.

Once we're settled into the backseat for the short ride, the driver talks parking and pick up details for a full two blocks. When finally, that is over and done, Reid pulls me close, offering me a big dose of that big, hot body of his to warm me up, and while it works, it just makes me want more of his big, hot body. "You looking as stunning as ever in that dress, Carrie." His fingers slip under my dress and inch up my thigh, and he clearly has no intention of stopping.

I catch his hand. "You wait."

"Waiting's overrated."

"Not tonight when I have to be focused."

"I can take the edge off." His fingers flex on the lace of my thigh high.

"Stop," I whisper.

His eyes dance with mischief, but the driver announces, "Your destination, sir."

Reid inhales and then cups my face, bringing his lips to my lips. "Waiting is really fucking overrated." He kisses me. "But it appears I'm waiting."

I laugh and he presses his cheek to mine. "I'll make you pay for that laugh. Perhaps you get the spanking to go with my tongue, because we both know you aren't wearing panties." He doesn't give me time to reply. He opens the door, exits the car and helps me out, pulling me flush to his hard body. "I'm right here with you, Carrie." He strokes my hair. "We're going to win Grayson's business." He takes my hand and starts to walk, but I tug against him.

He turns to look at me and I don't know why I need to say it or why I feel he needs me to say it, but I add, "I'm right here with you, too, you know that, right?"

Something flickers in his eyes, some unknown emotion, but warmth follows. "Stay that way. I want you to stay that way." He kisses my hand and shuts the car door.

The driver arrives to see us off, apparently obsessed with our arrangements. "I'll be close by, sir. Just text me."

Once we're inside the luxurious hotel that is all sleek white tiles that contrast the dark furnishings, beneath a high ceiling with dangling lights, I don't miss the way several beautiful women walk by us and gape and whisper about Reid. He, however, doesn't seem to notice, though of course, this is Reid Maxwell, and he notices. He knows. He's simply focused on me, his arm around my waist, hand on my hip. There is not a fleeting moment where I feel he is anywhere but one hundred percent with me.

We are met by security, who lead us to a second-level conference room. Inside, we're greeted by Grayson, and another man, both in tuxedos. Grayson's particularly handsome in his, quite able to inspire the tall, dark, and handsome cliché, while the other man, who is in his late thirties I estimate, has wavy light brown hair and looks that inspire more of a ruggedly good-looking observation.

"This is Eric Mitchell," Grayson says, indicating the man. "He's my right-hand man, and considering he's made himself a millionaire many times over managing my investments, I want him in on the meeting. I trust him."

There is the traditional shaking of hands, and I note that Eric has a black and gray tattoo sleeve peeking from his jacket. My gaze meets his and he arches a brow as if wanting me to ask about it. I don't. I simply find it interesting. Grayson isn't the ink kind of guy, at least I didn't think he was, and I actually think Eric's obvious differences make both men more interesting.

"Let's sit," Grayson says, indicating the large rectangular table.

My next surprise is that Grayson doesn't choose the endcap, but rather a spot across from me and beside Eric. "Ask the question, Carrie," Eric says.

Reid glances down at me. "What's he talking about?"

"Me looking at his tattoo sleeve." I shift my attention to Eric. "An observation doesn't require a question. I don't have one."

"Just a judgment."

"So you want my judgment, not a question. Is that what you're used to getting?"

All three men just look at me and then they all laugh. "I told you she's priceless," Reid says, looking at Grayson and squeezing my leg under the table.

My hand covers his and the knowledge that he has spoken positively about me confirms the trust I have in Reid and contradicts all those words my father spoke this morning.

"Indeed," Eric agrees. "What is your judgment, Carrie?"

"That you and Grayson are different, but alike in ways that make you both interesting."

"As are you, Carrie," Eric says.

"Tell us what you have for us," Grayson says.

"An opportunity of a lifetime," Reid says. "A deal that was brought to Carrie, but she's nervous about Asia."

"I've been burned there," I chime in. "But Reid has brought solid financing to this deal. He has contacts I don't, and I feel like that can balance this project out. It's a convention center in Japan." I glance at Reid to see if he wants to continue.

"It's your baby," he says. "You explain it all."

I dive into my pitch and we all chat for a good hour or more. Grayson glances at Eric. "I could fund it myself."

"Why? Limit your liability, spread out your assets." Eric looks between us. "I need to do due diligence but it's intriguing."

That's when Reid takes over. "How intriguing? This is hush-hush and time-sensitive. I've brought big money to the table. We're doing this with or without you. If you want another proposal—"

"No," Grayson says. "We'll let you know in twenty-four hours, but on first glance, I'm in. No matter our decision, we'll grant you a number of test cities outside this project that you can grow upon."

"I'll put together the agreement," Eric says. "We'll do this other deal separately."

I want to jump for joy, but Reid remains cautious. "Twenty-four hours. We need to move on this."

Grayson's lips quirk. "Understood."

We all stand and the shaking of hands begins again. "Please enjoy the party," Grayson says, while Eric holds onto my hand and doesn't let go.

"Military and then Harvard."

He releases me. "Interesting," I say, and he laughs.

A few minutes later, Reid and I are walking down the hallway. "We're going to make our goal."

"Yes, baby, we are."

"We did good."

"Yes. We did. And you," he adds, "charmed the room."

"We do the good cop, bad cop thing pretty well."

He laughs. "Yes, we do."

I revel in his laughter that I know now has not been frequent for Reid, and while I still don't know why, I feel one day I will. We arrive at the party, a huge ballroom with chandeliers and tables filled with clusters of people in formalwear everywhere I look. Reid and I accept champagne and toast to our success. "Panties or no panties?"

"You have to wait to see."

"Then drink up. We made a showing. Let's get out of here."

"We have to stay a respectable amount of time."

He groans. "Right. That respectable time thing I hate so fucking much." He downs his bubbly. "Let's mingle."

It's an hour later and Reid and I are on the dance floor, our bodies closer than is "respectable," but I don't care.

His hand caresses my back. "Let's go home."

Home.

His home, but the word is spoken as if we share a home, and it does funny things to my stomach. "Yes. Let's go home, but do we need to find Grayson and say goodbye?"

"Grayson has the deal of a lifetime. That's all he gets. We're leaving."

He takes my hand and guides me toward the exit, and in a matter of minutes we're in the car, and he's pulling me close, his hand under my skirt again. "The wait is over," he murmurs as firetrucks start to push through the traffic and sirens sound.

"Something is going on," I murmur as even more sirens seem to encroach upon us.

Reid's cellphone rings and he frowns. "Gabe, who would not call me on a night like tonight, unless it was something important." He answers and listens a moment. "You're sure? Right. We're going there now." He disconnects. "We'll walk. It's not far." He opens the door and helps me out.

"What's going on?" I ask as he starts all but pulling me down the sidewalk.

"There's a fire in Battery Park. Gabe can't tell where yet, but it's close to our apartments and both of our offices."

"Oh God." It's all I manage. Neither of us speaks. We just walk as fast as we can with me in my heels. It takes us ten minutes, and through a parade of emergency vehicles, to reach our office which is fine. Reid's phone rings again, and he answers it. "Yeah, Gabe." His hand tightens on mine. "Yes. Okay."

A horrible feeling settles in my chest and when he disconnects the line, he turns me to face him his hands on my shoulders. "It's your building, Carrie."

"My building. Mine?"

"Yes, baby. It's yours, but—"

I have to get there. I twist out of his arms and start to run. I'm halfway across a crosswalk when Reid catches my hand. "Stay with me. They aren't going to let you in the area."

"I need to know details. I need to talk to an emergency worker." I motion to a policeman at the entryway to our walkway. "Him. There."

Reid folds our arms at the elbow and pulls me close. "We'll talk to him."

I tug against him and rush toward the uniformed man. "I live in the building. Is the fire contained?"

"Yes, ma'am, but we are asking residents to report their whereabouts if they live on floors one through three."

"I live on three. What happened on three?"

"I'm sorry to tell you that it's a full loss, ma'am."

Emotions rock my body and my knees go weak. Reid drags me to him and I don't know how but I end up near a bench out of the walkway. "I lost everything. *I lost everything*. I have no home." Tears burst from my eyes and Reid folds me close, his lips at my ear. "Live with me, Carrie. Move in with me."

"No," I hiss, shoving at his chest. "I'm not your charity case. You're not getting stuck with me."

"Stuck with you? There's no stuck with you, Carrie. Now or ever." He cups my face and thumbs away dampness. "I gave you a key. We were headed there anyway. A few more weeks of back and forth was all I was going to be able to endure. Live with me."

"How do I even know it's what you really want?"

"It is what I want. Is it what you want?"

"I want to make the choice, and I want you to ask me not when my apartment is burning down. Not like this."

"I would have asked that way and still, it wouldn't be enough. Baby, I need you with me. I need you, Carrie." He folds me in his embrace. "You're safe with me. I got you. I really do, even if you don't know it yet."

I stop fighting what he offers, that safe place I need. I sink into his embrace and wrap my arms around him and it does feel like he has me, like he's holding me up. I've never given anyone this kind of power, the power to hold me up or crush me. But I've given it to Reid because I know, in this moment, that I love this man.

CHAPTER SIXTY-THREE

Reid

If my father did this to Carrie, *I will kill him*.

An hour after we found out about Carrie's apartment fire, the police are talking to Carrie. Cat and Gabe are standing with me a few feet away, but my eyes are on Carrie, watching her shove a shaky hand through her hair and the very idea that my father might have done this has me fighting fury. And damn it, the way Carrie reacted to the idea of moving in with me with such instant resistance is killing me and has me wondering if she blames me, if she thinks I did this to her, took everything from her; her company, her home.

"Reid?"

At the sound of Cat's voice, I force my gaze in her direction. "What can I do? Can I get Carrie anything to get her by?" she asks.

I pull out my wallet, handing her my black AmEx. "Buy her everything and anything she could need. Spend thirty-thousand if you need to. I have plenty of money. I don't care. She has to have nice work clothes. She needs to feel like she has things of her own."

"She'll want to pick out her own things," Cat says. "And I can't get much tonight." She glances at her watch. "Very little, actually."

"Get what you can. She can exchange what she needs to, but she won't want to spend my money. I want to do this before she makes me promise not to do it. And I want the insurance money to be a nest egg. And buy yourself something for doing this."

"I don't need payment," Cat says. "Money doesn't make me feel loved, Reid."

My eyes narrow on her and I know she's not just talking about herself. "I know, Cat, but I need her to feel safe and that means having what she needs at my place, which is now her place."

Her expression softens and she nods. "Safe is good right now," Cat says. "And you do have a point. I'll do what I can. There's a boutique that is owned by a fan of mine. She'll open for me. I'll see you soon." She takes off and I focus on Gabe, my voice now low, gritty. "Do you think—"

"I don't think dad did this. This drives Carrie closer to you and he doesn't want that. That agreement he drew up made that clear, but I'll go pay him a visit. I'll know when I look into his eyes."

Carrie steps to my side. "There are people missing. I could have been one of them."

Just that idea guts me and I wrap my arms around her and pull her close. "But you weren't. Do they know what caused it?"

"The restaurant on the main floor. A short in some machine they were told to replace."

Gabe whistles. "Sounds like a criminal act to me. Someone is in trouble," he says, his eyes meeting mine, and I give a barely perceivable shake of my head to tell him that no, I'm not convinced that machine caused the fire.

"It's right over my apartment," Carrie adds and looks up at me. "They said the outlook for saving anything in my place is grim. I guess I won't have any personal items to bring to your place."

"You're alive, baby. We have to focus on that."

"I'm going to take care of a problem," Gabe says. "Carrie. Put my number in your phone. If you need me, you know how to reach me."

She reaches for her purse, but she's trembling too hard for her to open it. I catch her hand. "I'll do it later." I look at Gabe. "I got this."

"I'll call you both," he says and then takes off.

"They want me to stay close," Carrie says, stepping in front of me, shivering and hugging herself as she does. "And we can't get into your apartment, but it's cold and I'm so very tired."

I wrap my arms around her and pull her against me. "I'll keep you warm," I say. "And safe. You have a home now with me."

"I know."

"Do you?"

"Yes." She nestles in closer to me, but I sense the tension in her reply that I want to drive away. "I want to be there now or just stay just like this wrapped in your arms," she adds, "but I can't even do that. I need to call my insurance company. And my father." Her voice lifts with urgency. "Should I call my father? Why is that my instinct when he's acting like he is?"

"Deep breath, baby. It's your instinct because he's your father, the person who took care of you when you couldn't, and no matter what, we assume our parents will worry about us. And he does worry about you."

"Maybe he does. I don't know anymore, but I can't deal with him now, though. I just can't, but I don't want him showing up here when we have so much going on."

"Just text him and tell him that if he hears about the fire, you're safe."

"Yes. Good idea. I'm not thinking straight. I'll text him." She reaches into her purse for her phone, her hands a bit steadier, enough now that she snags it easily, types the message, and then reads it to me. "If you hear about a fire in Battery Park, I'm safe." She eyes me with uncharacteristic uncertainty, but then, her apartment just burned down.

"Perfect," I say.

She hits send.

"You'll have to tell him you lost your apartment eventually."

"I know, but not now, even if he calls. I can't handle him pushing me to go there to him. I'm not going there."

Because she's staying with me, but I don't say that, and the divide between her and her father that represents. I just hold her and help her ride out the storm. A storm I feel growing more intense for both of us, as her father doesn't reply to her message, and I simmer over the idea of my father causing her this pain.

Carrie

I'm so cold that I can't stop shaking.

It's ten-thirty when Reid and I are allowed back into his building, my building now, but I just can't digest that at the moment. I'm in emotional overload, and the minute we step inside Reid's apartment, it's as if the wind falls from my wings. My knees are weak and my mind is exhausted. My head spins and for a moment I think I might drop. Reid seems to know this, and he scoops me up and starts walking, his strong arms and body warming me. I rest my head on his shoulder and it's only a minute or so before we're in his bedroom and he's sitting me on the bed.

I kick off my shoes and just sit there on the edge of the mattress, a nightstand to my left. "My only photo of my mother was in the apartment," I say, as Reid sits next to me and shrugs out of his jacket. "I haven't seen her in years, but it represented a part of my life that made me who I am today."

"I could tell you we'll find another or find her," he says, tossing his jacket on the bed, his hand coming down on my leg, "but I know that's not what you want to hear. That photo had a special meaning for you."

I cover his hand with mine. "You understand things I don't expect you to understand."

He kisses my hand. "I want to understand everything, Carrie." His voice is low, gravelly, and yet warm.

I study his handsome face, searching for confirmation or perhaps a lie? Why would I search for a lie? But I know why. It's not our parents. It's not business or money. This man affects me, understands me, connects with me, but now, now, if I move in with him, he controls every part of my life. To allow such a thing requires vulnerability and trust. "Everything?" I ask.

"Yes." He strokes hair from my eyes, the light touch sending goosebumps down my spine. "Everything," he repeats. "I want to know everything about you. I want everything, Carrie."

"Everything is so much."

"Too much?" he asks.

The doorbell rings and his hand falls away, the moment shifting away from the intimacy of the one before it. "That's Cat. She brought you some things."

"She didn't have to do that. I have enough to get by here." I shiver and Reid walks to the closet, rather than out of the room, and returns with his big navy robe.

He stops in front of me and wraps it around my shoulders, the lines of his face harder now, tension in his voice. "I'll be right back." He kisses my head, a tenderness to the act that defies that tension, tenderness I'd once thought him incapable of, but it's welcomed now. I'm strong, I am, and I'll come back fighting tomorrow, but tonight, I just need permission to only survive.

He exits the room and I lay back on the bed, Reid's bed that could be mine now if I say yes to moving in with him. *If I say yes.*

"Hello, hello!"

At the sound of Cat's voice, I sit up, wrapping the robe more tightly around me to find the gorgeous, sweet blonde bombshell standing in the doorway with bags in her hands. "I have Chanel and much more. I know someone. She opened her store for me."

"What? Thank you, but with what money?"

She sets the bags down and settles her hands on her jean-clad hips. "Reid's black AmEx. He told me to spend an insane amount of money on you. He wants you to feel like you have your own things."

"I don't want his money." My throat constricts. "I don't want him to do that." My hand goes to my throat now. "God. I don't want to be here."

Cat blanches. "What? You don't want to be here?"

"No. Yes. I do. I really do." I go back to my first reaction to Reid's invitation for me to move in. "Not like this, though. I just don't want to feel like I forced myself on him."

"You didn't. You aren't." She sits next to me. "That man wants you here. The way Reese wanted me with him almost immediately."

I barely know Cat, but I like her, and I just need to say what I feel, to get it out and understand it. "I want to believe that, but our parents hate each other, and it wasn't that long ago that Reid was an asshole to me. And then suddenly he's becoming everything to me and it's wonderful and scary and—he's in control. Now, here, living with him, he has all the control and it's terrifying."

"You're wrong."

At the sound of Reid's voice, Cat and I turn to find him standing in the doorway with his jacket, vest, and tie gone. "For the first time in my adult life," he says, "I don't have the control."

Cat squeezes my arm. "I'll go. I'll check on you tomorrow." She stands and hurries toward the door, and Reid steps back to allow her to pass before walking toward me, and sitting down next to me. His hands come down on my face and he tilts my gaze to his. "You have control, Carrie, in ways I never thought I'd let anyone have control." His voice is low, raspy. *Affected.* "And I understand the argument that I might have the control, I do, but it's you who does. All you." He rests his forehead on mine. "When I think of you in that building, and how easily you could have died, it tears me apart." He pulls back to look at me. "Stay, Carrie. I want you to stay, but I'm not going to pressure you. I need you to *want* to be here. And I hate that the war between our fathers makes you distrust me and us to this degree."

I shiver with the impact of his words, and all the emotional punches this night has given me, but there's so much I want to say to him. I never get the chance. "I'll run you a hot bath," he says, and then he's standing and walking away, as if he shut down, pulled back in some way.

It's that wall he puts between us, even as he confesses to needing me, that makes me hold back. That's what scares me. It makes me think there's more to all this hell around us where he's concerned than I know. I want to live with Reid, but I can't live with secrets and lies.

CHAPTER SIXTY-FOUR

Reid

I walk downstairs, after having started Carrie her promised bath, when Gabe calls, "It wasn't dad. I'm certain of it. You should have seen his face when I told him Carrie was moving in with you. I also called a friend who works at the fire department to verify what we'd been told. It was a machine in the restaurant and Carrie's floor is a complete loss."

I wait to digest that, to feel relief, but I'm not capable of that emotion at present. "Thanks, Gabe."

"How is she?"

"As expected."

"Right. I'll check in."

We disconnect and I'm standing at the damn bar in the corner of the living room and don't know how I got there. That doesn't happen to me. I press my hands on the cushioned counter and let my chin rest on my chest. I just blamed my father for her not trusting me when it was me who was the asshole in the beginning. Me, who still hasn't told her why because it had nothing to do with her being a West and me a Maxwell. I have to tell her. If I want her to stay, I have to tell her what I've never shared with anyone. I have to trust her that much. There's no escaping that reality and I really don't want to escape, not if it means losing Carrie, and it might. I push off the counter and grab a bottle of wine and two glasses and head back upstairs.

Carrie's not in the bedroom so I set the glasses on the nightstand and fill them both before entering the bathroom. Carrie is neck deep in bubbles that smell like my body wash, and damn, I like her in my tub and using my soap, which only drives home the conversation we need to have. Her lashes lift when she hears me enter. "Hey."

"How's the bath?"

"Good. It's amazing how a hot bath can solve so much. Just getting rid of that chill helps so much."

I sit down on the ledge next to the tub. "Wine?"

"Yes, please." She lifts her wet, bubble covered hand and accepts it. She sips and nods her head in approval. "Good. Don't ask the price, right? Just enjoy." She sets the glass on the other side of the tub.

"Exactly. Gabe called a friend at the fire department."

"And?"

"It really was a machine in the restaurant."

Her eyes narrow. "You thought it was your father." It's not a question.

"I was plotting his certain death quite literally, yes."

"I didn't."

"Why?"

"Maybe I haven't known his evil to the extent you have, but I saw the intelligence in his eyes. An act that hurts others, that would come back on him, would put him in jail. And then he wouldn't get to wear his suits at inappropriate times."

I laugh, and considering my state of mind, only this woman could make that happen right now. "Very true. Very true." I lean in and kiss her, but I pull back, the laughter fading into my mission, into the truth. "I know I was an asshole to you, but it had nothing to do with the company or our names."

"Then what? What are you telling me?"

"That's a complicated answer, but one you deserve." I lean back. "Enjoy your bath and your wine. We can talk later." I exit the bathroom and I grab the bottle of wine and my glass before walking into my escape room off the bedroom, where I sit down.

Carrie is smart and intuitive. She knows I'm holding something back. She probably thinks it's about the takeover, or my intentions toward her father, or even her. But she's still with me because she also senses how damn much I care about her. I want her to wake up tomorrow morning and make my bed her bed. I fill my glass, trying to prepare myself mentally for this conversation. Fuck. Maybe it needs to wait. Her apartment burned down tonight. Or maybe that's why it has to happen tonight, so she knows I mean it when I say I want her here.

I'm on my second glass of wine when Carrie joins me, sitting next to me, her body draped in a pink silk gown. She sets her wine glass on the table in front of us and I do the same. She scoots closer, her leg next to my leg, her hand on my knee. "Do you want to talk about it?"

"Never before, but with you, yes. I think you need to know why I am how I am. Or was. You've done a lot to change me and even now, at times, I'm not sure that's a good thing. Embracing that change is going to take a while. You need to know that, too." I reach for my glass and down my wine.

"We have to do this now."

I set my empty glass down and look at her. "We do, because I know how this affects me, how it's shaped me, but you don't, and that makes you afraid to let your life become completely entwined with mine. And that decision is upon us, Carrie. I want you here and you have to decide if you want to be here with me."

"I'll tell you the exact thought I had when you left the bedroom: I want to live with you, but not with secrets and lies."

"Then I was right. You need to hear this." My hands go to my knees and I lower my chin to my chest. "When I was a first-year law student, I was dating a girl who was really into me. I wasn't really into her, but you know, I was young enough to want a convenient fuck." I look at Carrie. "That's the truth, as shitty as it sounds, but I'm not holding back."

"You can tell me anything. I promise."

I puff out a breath. "I finally decided I had to break it off with her. She said the L-word and I knew that meant that the situation was out of control. I decided that particular night. We stopped in a convenience store on the way back to my place." I stretch my neck left and right. "It was being robbed."

"Oh God," Carrie whispers.

I rotate to face her because I need to own this. "I've never told anyone this. Gabe doesn't know. Not beyond the outcome. Cat doesn't know at all. No one knows."

She takes my hands. "I'm listening."

"The guy had a gun and he was going to shoot the clerk. I yelled and I took a step toward him to try and stop him. He turned and pointed the gun at me and Kelli—that was her name—threw herself in front of me. And she died."

"Oh my God. Oh my God. Reid."

"I led her on and she obviously really loved me. And what did she get for it? Dead."

"And that's when you considered criminal law."

"Yes. I wanted to do something to make a difference, but the system is fucked with limitations and I'm sure you know by now, that I don't do well with limitations. And rolling around in that kind of criminal law hell, wasn't allowing me to move on. I refocused on corporate law and stepped away from pretty much everyone. I didn't want anyone caring enough to end up hurt over me. Even Cat. She's the kind of person who would throw herself in front of a bullet for someone she loves."

Tears pool in Carrie's eyes. "The pain and guilt you must still struggle with."

"I found a place to put it. I don't think about it anymore except for random moments and yeah, they still gut me. I hated when Cat went to work for the DA right out of school. I knew she was putting herself in the sights of criminals. That's when she and I really hit a wall. I wanted her with us, where I could protect her."

"Did you tell her you felt that way?"

"No. I just drove at her like a bulldozer."

Carrie pushes me against the couch and climbs on top of me, her hands on my cheeks. "Thank you for telling me. I understand so much now."

"I don't think you do. I didn't want to care about you, but there was something about you from the moment I met you. I knew you were a West, but I didn't stay away. I knew that would cause us both grief, but I didn't stay away. It wasn't to punish you or to hurt you. It was because I couldn't." I roll her to her back and lower myself over her. "I can't, Carrie. Because I love you too damn much."

"You love me?"

"Yes, baby, I love you. So damn much. I know it's probably soon to say that, but I've never said it to anyone. I—"

"I don't hate you like you predicted, but I get that now. I love you, too. And, Reid, I did need to hear this. I needed to understand why you were an asshole and why you are who you are."

"Then you'll move in with me."

"Yes. I will. I want to. I wanted to. I just needed—more. And you gave it to me."

"More," I whisper. "That's the word that defines every moment I am with you. I want more. I am more because of you. Do you know what I want the most right now?"

"Dinner?"

I laugh. "Dinner would be good, but how about we eat it in my bed that is now our bed?" I stand up and pick her up, carrying her to the bedroom and laying her on the bed and setting on top of her. "Our bed, baby."

Her arms wrap my shoulders. "Our bed."

Our bed and our life. I'm going to marry this woman. She just doesn't know it yet.

CHAPTER SIXTY-FIVE

Carrie

I wake to Reid's hands all over my body, and his thick erection pressed between my thighs, and despite losing so much last night, I feel like I gained so much. I found Reid, really found him, the real man. I found us. *We found us.* "Are you awake now?" he asks, his breath warm on my cheek, hand cupping my breast, fingers teasing my nipple.

I pant out a breath. "Yes," I whisper, covering his hand with mine. "I'm awake."

"Not awake enough," he says, rolling me to my back, and then the next thing I know he's between my legs, his shoulders easing them apart and I'm grabbing the sheets as he licks my clit. "What about now?" he asks, those blue eyes brimming with heat and challenge. "Are you awake now?"

"If I say yes, are you going to stop?"

He presses his lips to my belly. "I'm not going to stop until you come."

His tongue teases the sensitive flesh on my belly and then he's back between my legs, twirling my clit with his tongue, a slow, sexy tease while his fingers stroke the line of my sex and then slip inside. He licks, strokes, caresses and teases and pleases in random wicked ways that has me pumping my hips, moaning, and then crashing into orgasm way too quickly. I've barely collapsed into the mattress when my cellphone rings.

I groan. "Come here," I plead, wanting him inside me. "I don't care who it is."

He slides up my body and grabs my phone. "Grayson."

My eyes go wide. "My cell is on my business card. He must have gotten it from there."

"Answer it," he says, handing me the phone and rolling to his side, his hand on my belly.

"Good morning," I greet.

"She greets me politely, with high energy, and ready to make a deal despite her apartment burning down hours before. You only solidify my decision, Carrie. I'm in on the convention center, but find out what it's going to take to keep it off the bidding table. I want it closed quickly."

I look at Reid and nod. He smiles and kisses my temple. "I'll make the call now," I promise Grayson. "It's the middle of the night in Japan, but I have a cell number for my contact."

"Good. Now, about your building."

"About that. How did you know?"

"I have everyone I consider doing business with checked out. I knew your address."

"You had me checked out and quickly. Of course you did. You're a billionaire and while I am not, I thankfully have good insurance."

"I can offer you a luxury apartment for six months free of charge."

I blanch. "That's incredibly generous Grayson, but I'm fine. I'm with Reid."

"Interesting. Well, if you change your mind, the offer will remain on the table. Let me know on the offer."

"I'm on it." I hang up and look at Reid. "Did you hear the conversation?"

"Every last word, including the apartment."

I kiss his cheek. "That I don't need. I have a home with you and we're about to be very rich together thanks to that clause in my contract that gives me a percentage of anything above a certain threshold."

He covers my hand with his. "You know I don't care about the money, right?"

"Why? It's a lot of money. I care. This is my first time ever to make this kind of money. I'm excited. It's okay to want to make money with me, Reid." I think of the hours we sat and talked last night, even after his confession and I easily say, "I trust you." I smile. "Now, are you excited?"

He laughs. "Yes. Now I'm excited. It is a shit-ton of money."

"I need to call Japan." I sit up and start looking through my cellphone contacts. "Got it." I punch in the number and listen to it ring and end up with my contact's voicemail. I leave a message and then throw away the covers. "We need to get to work. You should shower with me. It'll save time." I dart toward the bathroom and then turn and point at Reid, who's clearly about to pursue. "Wait a minute though. I have to pee, and we aren't at a place where you get to watch that."

He laughs. God, I love to hear him laugh and it means even more after what he confessed last night. I pee and turn on the shower. "Ready!" I call out only to have Reid already behind me, his big body walking me into the shower and pressing me against the wall.

"This isn't the way to make the shower faster," I tease.

"Sure it is. We fuck and shower at the same time. It's the definition of time management." He lifts my leg and presses inside me, drilling hard and cupping my backside to angle my hips. And then he's thrusting, his gaze raking over my breasts as they sway to his pumps, and I forget everything but how good he feels. How intensely he looks at me, how perfectly he fucks me and kisses me.

Yes.

I will live with you, Reid Maxwell, I think, and enjoy every minute.

Much later, we're both dressed, me in a pink suit, and him in a navy suit with a blue tie the color of his gorgeous blue eyes, sitting at the island in the kitchen drinking coffee and eating eggs that he made us. Yes, Reid Maxwell does cook. The beast has a human side and that's why I decide to breach a difficult topic. "Have you thought about telling Cat what you told me last night?"

"I don't want her to know," he says, and I'm pleased with how quickly he answers, how easily he's let down his guard, though I doubt it felt easy to him. "But I need to make things right with her," he adds. "I've been working on it, but I need to do more."

"I think I'll invite her to lunch, just to get to know her. Are you okay with that?"

"Of course. Why wouldn't I be?"

"I just wanted to make sure."

"Which reminds me." He grabs my phone. "I'm putting her number and Gabe's in your phone." He keys them in and offers me my cell. "You know they'll be there for you, Carrie. For all the hell my family has been through, my siblings are still loyal."

"They know you are, too, even if you don't get warm and fuzzy with them. I knew there was more to you, even when you were barking orders at me."

He arches a brow. "You think that's over?"

"No. Because it apparently turns me on since it always ends with us fucking."

"Exactly."

My phone rings and I glance at the caller ID. "Japan." I answer the line and thirty minutes later I hang up. "It's a huge number, but I got it. He's emailing me a written declaration. I'm going to text Grayson."

"Do it," he says.

I punch in the message and then sigh. "It's gonna happen, Reid. I feel it. I want to go to Paris to celebrate."

"Paris it is."

My cellphone rings and I glance at the number, and eye Reid. "Grayson," I tell him and then quickly answer the call. "Hello," I say.

"What's the number?"

"It's big," I warn.

"Number, Carrie."

"Two and a half billion."

"Tell him it's done. Get it in writing and then close it."

"Oh," I say. "Yes. Done." I hang up. "He said to make the offer."

Reid rounds the island and pulls me to him. "Paris, baby. You and me and a whole lot of money. But just remember, there will be so much negotiation of this contract that it's going to take weeks if not months to close."

"But it's going to close."

"Yes," he says. "It's going to close."

My cellphone, still in my hand, rings and this time when I glance at the number I'm not as eager to answer. "My father," I say tightly.

"You don't have to take it."

"I do," I say. "I want it over with and right now on this high, I can deal with him better than otherwise."

"Okay, baby."

He releases me, and I hit the answer button. "Hi, dad."

"Was the fire in your building?" he asks.

"Yes, it was."

"And?"

"Total loss for me."

"As in your apartment?"

"Yes, but I have insurance."

"Okay," he says, "so obviously you're meant to be here with me. Come here now."

My lashes lower and I grab the island. "Did you really just tell me that my apartment burned up so that I could be there?"

"Things happen for a reason. I came here and I belong here. You'll feel the same."

"You're right. They do happen for a reason. I moved in with Reid."

"What?" he growls. "You did *what*?"

"I love him. He loves me. I'm living with him. I'm with him." I turn to face the island and Reid, who's now directly across at the opposite endcap. "And you need to know that any action against the Maxwells is now an act against me. Do not go after Reid or his family, who, with the exception of his father, I really like."

"You have no idea how that family affected our family."

"I actually do. I know about mom and Maxwell Senior, but she left me and that speaks of her character. You didn't leave me. She wasn't worth the war you started over her. She wasn't worthy of us, but you're making yourself unworthy of anyone by engaging in this kind of war. Please be bigger than that."

"Reid told you about your mother?"

"He didn't even know until this week. It's not our war, but you two want to make it our war. You don't get to pick my enemies."

"It's too late. It's about more than your mother now. We *are* enemies. He's your enemy."

"No. Please don't do that. The company is safe. I saved it and Reid helped me."

"You don't know what you're talking about. I'm coming there."

"Don't. Don't come. I won't be here. I'm going to Asia." I hang up.

Reid joins me and his hands come down on my shoulders. "Are you okay?"

"Yes. Was it okay that I said I knew? It just kind of came out."

"Of course. I would have told you to keep it between us if that was necessary, but I still would have told you, Carrie."

"I know that. We're not enemies."

"No. We're not enemies."

CHAPTER SIXTY-SIX

Carrie

Reid and I are about to walk into the West office building when he stops me, pulls me to the side, and around the corner into a small alleyway. "Where are you going to say you're living? Because people are going to find out about your apartment."

"I—well, where should I say I'm living?"

"With me, Carrie. We've nailed a huge opportunity for the stockholders and the staff. We're living together. That's not something easy to hide and I don't want to."

My hand goes to his chest. "You don't?"

"No, I don't. What about you?"

"Me either."

His eyes warm. "Good. We'll stay professional, but we won't hide our relationship either. Agreed?"

"Agreed."

He pulls me to him and kisses me. "Then let's go up."

He takes my hand and leads me toward the door, but releases me when we enter the building. And it's a good thing we just had that conversation because the minute we step off the elevator and into the executive offices, Sallie and Connie, who are both at Sallie's desk, bombard us. "We heard about your building," Connie says. "Oh, hon, I'm so sorry."

"I tried to call you," Sallie says.

443

This goes on for a good two minutes, before I say, "My apartment aside, we've all but closed on the Japan deal and we're signing on with Grayson Bennett's company for more work. So I have to put the apartment thing behind me and dig in."

Both women show appropriate excitement, and when Sallie's phone rings, Reid eyes Connie, "I'm expecting a document from my father today. Call his office and check on the status."

"Oh right. What documents?"

"He'll know what it is," Reid says and then looks at me, motioning to my office. "Let's talk."

I nod and head that direction. He's on my heels and shuts the door behind him. I round my desk and set my briefcase, which had thankfully been at Reid's place during the fire, down. Reid walks to the window and offers me his back. I frown and join him. "What's up?" I ask.

He turns to face me, or really tower over me. "Our lives are merged now."

"Yes. They are."

"Then you need to know something."

"Okay," I say cautiously.

"My father tried to make his retirement contract contingent on no West having any personal or professional involvement with a Maxwell."

"In other words, me moving in with you means he's not retiring," I assume.

"It's more layered than that. Gabe and I came together and gave him papers that officially withdraw us from the firm should he not sign my version of the retirement plan by today."

I blanch. "Wait. Maxwell and Maxwell would leave Maxwell, Maxell, and Maxwell?"

"Exactly."

"You can't leave your firm for me. Reid, no."

He pulls me to him. "Gabe and I will start over. I'm not against the idea and Gabe and I both have plenty of money and connections to make this work."

"What about this Japan deal? I assume as CEO, you, and your firm, receive a percentage of this sale. How badly does leaving cut you out of your profits?"

"I'm operating as an extension of the firm, but I'm on the front line and a managing partner. I'll get a nice payday as will Gabe. He's a co-managing partner. I have plenty of money, Carrie. You can feel secure with me. I know how much you need to feel that stability."

I swallow hard, shocked at how well he really does get me, but I don't want him to feel that motivates me in negative ways. "I feel secure because of you and what we're becoming, not because of your money."

"I want you to feel secure and comfortable with me *and* my money." He kisses me. "But we have plenty of time to talk about that. I need to run to the office and meet with Gabe. Call me when you know anything about Japan."

"Yes. Of course, I will."

He caresses my cheek. "See you soon."

He walks toward the door and my cellphone rings at my desk. "Leave it open, please," I call after him as I race to answer my phone.

Once I'm behind my desk, I snatch my cell from my purse to find the number labeled "Cat" that Reid input for me. "Hey, Cat," I say. "Thank you so much for last night."

"You sound good considering everything."

"This huge deal Reid and I have been working on is about to close. It's exciting and, well, Reid and I are good. I'm going to live with him without hesitation."

"That's wonderful. I wasn't so sure last night that was going to work for you."

"We talked for a long time. Cat, do you know he and Gabe might pull out of the firm?"

"Yes," she says. "Gabe told me and honestly, if they make that decision, they'll make it work. They're incredible together and all around incredible at their jobs."

"I noticed," I say. "It seems to run in your family. And on that note, I'd love to take you to lunch soon and fan girl over your column."

She laughs. "You're too kind I'd love to have lunch, but Reese has a huge trial going on that I'm covering. Well, you know that. You read my column. It would need to be next weekend."

"That works. I'll call you later in the week."

"Perfect, and Carrie, you're good for him. My mom would approve." She hangs up and Sallie appears in my doorway. "What do I need to do?" she asks.

I motion her forward and she claims the visitor's chair in front of my desk. "I need to have you fight my insurance company to get me paid. I need to focus on Japan."

"Of course. Do you need them to advance you for clothes and a place to stay?"

"Get them to pay for all you can, please," I add.

"Do you need a hotel or a short-term rental?"

"No, but brace yourself," I warn. "I'm staying with Reid."

She blinks. "What? You hate each other."

"No. No, we really don't. We're together."

"Wow. That was fast. So very fast. Carrie, are you sure?"

"Very, and yes, it's fast but I've never felt this way before. He's not an asshole—well, okay he can be, but I'm working on that."

She studies me a moment. "He makes you happy?"

"How do I seem today after my apartment burned down?"

"Happy," she says, surprise in her voice.

"Yes. Happy. I'm alive and so is this company. And Reid—he matters to me."

The sound of her phone ringing on her desk has her grabbing my phone to answer it. "Eric," she says. "One moment." She glances at me and I nod. "Let me patch you through to Ms. West." She hands me the phone and rushes away.

"Eric," I greet. "I'm excited we're working with you."

"I'm looking forward to seeing what you can do, and if this is what you do while your apartment's being burned down, I'm quite certain I won't be disappointed. I'm about to email you and Reid the agreement. I'm sure I'll be hashing out the legalities with him, but I wanted to welcome you on board."

"Thank you. We'll do an amazing job for you."

"I know you will. More soon, Carrie." We disconnect, and I call Reid.

"Eric just emailed us contracts for the rest of the work. I'm about to pull them up and review them."

"I'll go through them at the office."

"I'll email you my notes."

His phone beeps. "That's Eric calling me," he says. "I'll let you know if he adds anything new to the conversation."

We disconnect and the phone on my desk rings. I smile. I love this day. I love Reid. I grab my phone and dive into the craziness. This is where I belong. This is where I want to be.

Reid shows up back at the office mid-afternoon and he and Eric have hashed out our contract. An hour later, we ink a letter of intent to sign a contract with the owners of the Japan event center. We have one month to come to terms or the bids can reopen. We finally leave the office at seven and order from our favorite sandwich place on the way home.

Home.

With Reid.

It's really surreal.

It's on the walk through Battery Park that it hits me we haven't talked about his father's retirement. "Your father?"

"No response, which means Gabe and I will close out our current projects, take on no new clients, and leave officially in six months. An announcement will go to the staff after the board meeting next week."

"How do you feel about it?" I ask as we enter the building.

"It's surreal," he says. "That place has been my life, but it feels right. Gabe said the same thing."

Surreal, I think, as we enter the apartment. There's a lot of that going around today.

Half an hour later we're both in sweats, on the couch, with wine in our glasses and work spread out on the table, when our sandwiches arrive. Reid sets them out on the table and surprises me by asking, "Is there anything you want to change in the apartment?"

"Change? It's beautiful. I don't want to change your place, Reid."

"It's *our* place, Carrie. I want it to feel that way. We can redecorate if you want. Hell, we can sell it and buy something new. I want this to feel like home."

"We love Battery Park." I scoot close to him and settle my hand on his leg. "Thank you, but *you* are what feels like home. I don't need to make changes. And really, this place is stunning."

He lays me down on the couch. "You're stunning." He leans in to kiss me.

"Oh no," I say, feeling the press of his erection against my belly. "Feed me first. I didn't eat all day. Then take me to bed and do all the naughty things you can think of, please."

"I do believe I can live with that deal." He pulls me back to a sitting position and we both reach for our sandwiches.

"If we buy a place, Gabe and I could open the office in that building. Of course, we'd have to tolerate him because he'd probably move into the building, too."

"You really want to sell and buy something new?"

"It's something to think about," he says.

We talk about that and I tell him about Cat's call. "Mom *would* approve, Carrie," he assures me. "I hate that you can't meet her."

The doorbell rings. "Who can get past security?" I ask.

"Only my family, which means it's Gabe." He glances at his watch. "Technically my father has two hours to get us the papers. Gabe must want to ride this out here."

"Or he's having second thoughts?"

"Not Gabe. He doesn't have second thoughts. You'll learn that about him."

He walks to the door, and I hear it open, followed by the sound of a deep male voice. I stand up. That's his father. I hold my breath and wait. About sixty seconds later, Reid walks back into the room and indicates an envelope in his hand. "He shoved the retirement agreement at me, and then said, 'you win.'"

"And?"

"And then he left."

"So we're not buying a new place so that your office can be in the same building? Because if we're staying, that lamp," I point to this tall steel thing that looks like a street light, "is actually ugly."

He laughs and closes the space between us. "The lamp goes as long as you stay."

CHAPTER SIXTY-SEVEN

Carrie

Three weeks after I move in with Reid, I've replaced most of my wardrobe and we've settled into a routine as if we've been together forever. We run in the mornings, lift weights several times a week, shower together, sit in that extra room off the bedroom and drink wine before bed, and generally do a lot of naughty things before we sleep, between, and after, all of the above. And every morning, I wake up with him wrapped around me.

I haven't talked to my father, and the few conversations I've had with my brother were all business. Instead, Reid's family is becoming mine. Gabe comes by the apartment at least twice a week and Cat and I have lunched and shopped, while I've become even more obsessed with the inner workings of her column as I get to know her. I still believe she's pregnant, but she doesn't mention it and you don't ask someone if they're pregnant without them thinking you're telling them they're getting fat. And it's not my business. If she is, she'll tell Reid when she's ready.

All in all, every day I fall more in love with Reid. He listens to me and yes, he talks to me. Beneath the stone is a man who isn't unaffected by the fact that his father is now out of his life. They haven't spoken at all, and like me, we both battle that these two men are family that are growing older, and will one day be gone. But we battle these feelings together.

We also battle to get the Japan deal done and with one day to spare to hit the one-month mark, the deal is done. Reid sets a board meeting to announce it with me present, and on that Friday night we meet Gabe, Reese, and Cat for dinner. "To banking in Japan," Gabe says, holding up a glass filled with expensive champagne. "And to Carrie, who made this happen. Love ya, babe, and I don't care if Reid knows. Welcome to the family."

Family.

Welcome to the family.

It infers long-term, marriage even, maybe? Is the where we're headed? Reid reaches down, squeezes my leg and leans in and whispers. "Yes to everything you're thinking. I told you. I'm not letting you go."

I reach up and cup his cheek and look at him. "Good. I don't want you to."

He kisses me and when I glance up, I find Cat staring at us, a smile on her lips. I smile, too, but there is a ping in my belly. These people are my new family and my father hates them, while their father hates me. And neither of them are men to remain silent, and yet, they are.

Gabe tells a joke that has something to do with a mama tomato screaming "catch up" to her kids that has everyone rolling their eyes, and I forget my worries. I love these people and Reid. I'm going to enjoy them.

Reid

Six weeks after Carrie moved in with me, the special order I placed four weeks before arrives at the office. "Cat is here," Connie says. "She has it." She smiles ear to ear. "I can't believe this is really happening. Maybe I'm next."

"Send her in," I say, more than a little eager myself to see what Cat has in hand.

"I'm already in," Cat says, walking in my door, and shutting it. "I so love that you had me help you pick this out."

"I needed you," I dare say. "This is a big deal." I stand up. "Let me see."

She holds up a brown bag and hurries toward me, setting it on the desk. "The brown bag special and yes, I peeked. I had to see the finished product. It's gorgeous. She's going to love it."

I inhale and open the bag, pulling out the ring box she's hidden inside. I lift the lid and the emerald and diamond ring I had a well-known jeweler design and create for Carrie stares back at me. "The color of her eyes," I say, glancing at Cat, "but what if she prefers a traditional ring?"

Cat leans on my desk. "Reid, there are three carats of the best diamonds in the world surrounding the band and the emerald. No woman could be unhappy with that ring. You designed it for her. That's special. When are you going to do it?"

"In Paris, for Christmas, right after we leave Japan to coordinate the Bennett takeover of the event center. She doesn't know about the trip. It's a surprise and as much as I want us to all be together, I think it will keep her mind off her father's silence."

"That's a good idea. And for a proposal, that's perfect. I'm so happy for you."

I shut the box and stick it in the bag and then in my desk in case Carrie comes in. "Cat."

"Yes?"

"There are reasons I was like I was to you."

She holds up a hand. "You don't have to do this."

"I just want you to know that I regret a lot with you."

"Don't do anything to regret anymore. That's all that matters. Okay?"

"Deal."

She walks around the desk and kisses my cheek. "Later, big brother."

"Later, little sis."

I watch her leave and I know that this new bond with Cat might have begun before Carrie, but Carrie is why it took root. My family is closer because of her, but I still battle with the secret between us. And yet, there is nothing I can do about it. If I tell her, we both lose everything, including each other.

Carrie

Two days before Reid and I leave for Japan, I'm planning details for the Bennett takeover of the facility with Sallie when my father calls. "I need to take this alone," I say.

She nods and leaves, shutting my door. "Hello," I say.

"How are you?"

"I'm well, very well."

"And still with Reid, I hear."

"That's not going to change. What's happening in Montana?"

"I proposed to Stella. We're getting married in January. I'm taking over the ranch management and I've convinced her to drill on limited portions of the property. You should have your money back and increased thirty percent by summer."

"That's all great," I say, trying to sound sincere, when it's hard to be sincere with someone who doesn't offer that in return.

"I want you at the wedding, but not him. He doesn't get to come."

"He's a part of me now."

"No. You just don't see him for what he is and—"

"Stop," I bite out. "Stop talking. I need to go. I'm leaving for Japan in two days."

"What about Christmas?"

"I'm spending it with Reid and you're spending it with Stella. I love you, dad. I really hope we can get by this. I hope we can find each other again, but that's going to mean you get over the hate for the man I love. He's not his father."

"He's worse."

"Goodbye, father."

I hang up and I'm shaking. I don't know why this got to me so badly but when my door opens and Reid stands there, he knows immediately. "What's wrong?"

"My father called."

His expression hardens and he steps inside and shuts the door. "What happened?"

"He's worse than your father. He's getting married, but you can't come to the wedding. He owns the ranch now and they're drilling oil. I get my money back and more by summer. That about sums it up."

He rounds the desk, pulls me to my feet and kisses my forehead. "Carrie—"

"Oh and what about Christmas? He asked. I told him I'm with you, the end."

He presses his forehead to mine. "I'm here. I'm not ever leaving." He leans back to look at me. "You know that, right?"

"You know I'm having abandonment issues right now, don't you?"

"Yes. I do. And I'm not ever leaving. That's *a promise.*"

But we both know that's not a promise anyone can make. People die. People fall out of love. People separate. Relationships end. I just don't want ours to end.

Ever.

CHAPTER SIXTY-EIGHT

Carrie

With one day until we leave for Japan, it's early evening and Reid and I are both in the bedroom, packing our suitcases that are on the bed for a solid ten days away, and I glance over at him. "We really can't have a cat and a dog, can we? What about when we're gone?"

"A cat *and* a dog?"

"That's perfect, right? We get what we both want, and they have each other as friends."

"Or enemies. And we aren't gone that often. Cat and Gabe, and even Connie, would help out."

"So that's a yes to a cat *and* a dog?"

"If it makes you happy, baby, yes. Let's do it."

I smile. "I love that we're going to do this."

He laughs. "I love that you love it."

My cellphone rings and I glance at the number. "My brother. Is it bad that I dread seeing him in Japan?"

"Not from what I know of your brother." The doorbell rings. "That's our lunch," Reid says. "I'll grab it." He takes off out of the room and I answer the line.

"Hey," I say.

"Hey, little sis. I got my payday today. You rocked this deal."

"Thanks. Reid and I are a good team."

"Reid. That part of this grates on me, but the man owed us this deal. I can't believe you're living with him. I can't

457

believe dad hasn't told you why you shouldn't be living with him."

Anger starts to churn in my belly. "What does that even mean?"

"The man forced a takeover. He took dad out. That should be enough for you."

"That's not what happened."

"You're kidding, right? He forced the takeover. Look. You made me big money so I'm going to save you and our family before he has a chance to somehow turn it around on us, and he's going to. There's a plan there. I promise you. I'm sending you proof. Watch for it." He hangs up.

"Come down and eat!" Reid calls out.

"I'll be right there!"

My phone beeps with a text and I walk into the extra room and sit on the sofa. I swallow hard and enlarge the document. I start reading and it's all executed by Reid. "*To satisfy the debt, and prevent the release of all negative documents, you will allow Maxwell to buy out your stock in the format of a hostile takeover.*"

"Carrie."

At the sound of Reid's voice, I stand up and whirl around. "Did you force my father to give up his stock, or buy it out before someone else did, because the board was going to unseat him?"

He goes so very, *very* still. "I did not force your father to do anything. You know that. Where is this coming from? What did your brother say to you to make you question me again?"

I round the sofa and hand him my phone with the document on the screen. He barely looks at it and then hands my phone back to me. "That is not what it seems."

"To satisfy a debt. Did you write this document?"

"Yes. It's not what it seems."

"I love you, Reid. I trust you. Please make me understand. I don't want to jump to conclusions."

His hands come down on my shoulders. "I am not able to do anything but own up to that document and the contents. I can't explain it beyond telling you that it's not what it looks like."

"Why? Why can't you explain?"

"Because not only will my family lose everything, my father will come at you, and he won't stop. He'll destroy you and us. We both will have nothing, including each other."

"I won't say anything. I won't let anyone know I know."

"Carrie, you will. It will upset you too badly. You will and, baby, I'm protecting you, too."

"Does Royce know what you can't tell me?" I ask.

"He's trying to find out, but it's buried deep," he says. "He hasn't found anything."

"I just realized that he hasn't given me anything on my father."

"Because he was trying to find this first."

"You wanted him to?"

"Yes. It's *killed me* not to tell you this."

"My father can tell me?"

"He won't, Carrie. He won't. I tried to get him to. That's why I went to Montana."

"He's *going* to tell me."

"Or finally convince you I'm the devil."

"Have more faith in me and us than that."

He tangles fingers in my hair. "Go to Montana. I'll be on the plane to Japan tomorrow. If you're there, I'll know you see me, not the lies. If you're not, we'll end this."

"End this? That easily?"

"I've given you parts of me I swore I'd give no one. I need to know you trust me, Carrie, or we have nothing. Go to Montana. I'll make your reservations." He turns away and walks into the bedroom as I press my hands to my face. What does he think I'll find out in Montana that he dreads? Because he is too certain I won't be on that plane with him to Japan, and that terrifies me.

I force myself to walk into the bedroom, only to find Reid gone. I then force myself to finish packing. "I got you a private jet," Reid says re-entering the room. "It'll take you wherever you want, whenever you want."

A few minutes later, he walks me downstairs to a hired car with directions to my father's ranch in hand but before I climb inside, he pulls me to him. "I love you. Don't forget that I love you." He kisses me, a deep passionate, goodbye kiss that brings tears to my eyes, because it ends with him walking away.

I arrive in Montana at midnight on a snowy night, but I don't care what time it is. I dial my father as I pick up my rental car, and he doesn't answer. I leave a message. "I'm here. I need to see you."

I drive to the ranch with snow tires in place, and the directions Reid wrote down for me, but the gates are locked. I'm stuck going to my hotel room, which turns out to be really crappy because it's a small-town kind of place. I lay down on the hard bed and I want to call Reid, but I don't think he wants to hear from me. Not until I talk to my father and that guts me. I lay awake replaying our last kiss, and I don't read the document my brother sent me. I can't.

Morning comes with my alarm and I'm up and dressed in the appropriate attire of jeans and boots with a coat to beat the December cold by seven. I grab coffee and a donut at the gas station and drive to my father's place. The gates are open, and I travel a snow-covered dirt path to the mansion of a house where it ends. I park and a ranch hand informs me that my father is out on some sort of morning horse run but he's happy to let me inside the house.

A few minutes later, I'm in an elegant kitchen with a massive wooden island with my coat on a chair and coffee in hand. Two hours later, I'm getting worried about making my flight when my father walks in, wearing jeans and boots, instead of a fancy suit, with a pretty brunette beside him, dressed the same. "I assume you're Stella," I say. "And I don't mean to be rude, but I have an hour and then I need to be on a plane. I need to speak to my father alone."

"Of course," she says, graciously backing out of the room.

"Tell me what really happened with the company and Reid."

"I've told you what happened."

"I know you were behind Anthony sending me that takeover document. I know you know what it would do to me and Reid. Dad, I love Reid with all of my heart. If you love me, you will tell me what he can't. Tell me what really happened."

Stella steps back into the doorway. "She doesn't know?"

"It's complicated."

"Tell her or I will."

"Leave me with my daughter."

"He made bad deals and he was going to get caught," Stella says. "As in dirty deals that could have put him in jail, so he made it look like he'd lost his touch. He had dirt on Reid's father, things that could put him in jail and Maxwell Senior had tied Reid's name to those things, but Reid didn't know."

"I'll tell her the rest, Stella," my father says. "I'll tell her." He looks at me. "I didn't want you to know I wasn't your hero as you thought I was. I told Reid that if he made it look like a hostile takeover and buried the dirty deals, I'd bury the trouble his father could have gotten him into. My condition for handing him all the data was that you never knew. If he told you, I would get his stock. The dirt I had on his father that was attached to him was bad enough that he agreed. He wanted it over. He wanted the war to end and he didn't know you. He had no reason to ever feel the temptation to tell you."

"And then I went to him and changed that."

"You went to him?" my father asks.

I ignore the question. "What did Reid's father do?"

"Someone died," he says. "That's all I'll say. I don't want you to know the details. It was enough to make even Reid Maxwell feel really damn trapped. And I didn't tell your brother to send that document to you. He knows about Reid's father and your mother. He hates the Maxwells."

"Why did you tell him, and not me, about all of this?"

"I wanted you to have something perfect in your world. I wanted you to think I was your hero."

"And yet, you have treated me horribly over Reid."

"Because he was too close to you and knew too much."

"Would you have told me now if not for Stella?"

"I don't know."

That cuts, but at least it's not a lie. I grab my coat and purse and walk past him. Stella backs out of the kitchen to let me exit and I stop in front of her. "Thank you. You don't know me, and you saved me."

"Be happy," she says. "Then I'll be glad I did this."

I start walking and I don't look back. I need to get back home to Reid. I need to see him and let him look into my eyes and know I trust him. I never stopped trusting him.

CHAPTER SIXTY-NINE

Carrie

We're in the air when a storm delays our landing. For forty-five minutes, we circle the airport. By the time we land, I have just enough time to get home, get my bags and leave. I want to call Reid, but I think he needs to see me, to know I'm there at the airport. That plan seems wonderful until I'm at the airport and security is out the door thanks to some threat that apparently occurred this morning. Everyone is being wanded.

I try to call Reid, but I get a busy signal.

"My cell never works in this part of the airport," a man behind me says.

"Oh. Thanks."

No. No. No. This can't be happening.

It takes another twenty minutes and I run like a madwoman to my gate. I watch as the doors shut. "No!" I scream. "I'm on this flight."

"Sorry, ma'am. FFA regulations. Once the doors shut, they're shut. We can get you to a customer service agent to rebook you."

He's going to think I didn't want to be on that flight.

Reid

She didn't show up. I'm destroyed in a way I didn't know I could be destroyed. Two whiskeys and an empty seat beside me, and I can't seem to calm the damn ache in my heart. I'm two hours into the sixteen-hour flight and I decide I need to work. I need to do something to occupy my damn mind. I pull out my MacBook and log onto the internet.

An instant message pops up from Carrie: *Please tell me you're online.*

I stare at it, not sure I want to answer. Not sure of any fucking thing right now. When I don't reply she types: I made it to the gate as they shut the doors. My flight from Montana circled for an hour and then security was out the door. My father was out on the ranch until an hour before I had to leave and please talk to me. Are you there? I love you, Reid. I never doubted you. I'm in the air. I got on another flight. I'm landing first. It's a non-stop. I'll be at the gate waiting for you when you land. I know everything. I don't even know if you will see this message, but I'll be there.

Suddenly, I can breathe again. I type: *I read it all.*

She replies instantly: Please tell me you believe me. There was not one moment that I wasn't trying to be on that plane with you. I went to Montana so this can just be behind us.

I need you on this plane with me, I reply.

I want to be there with you, she answers.

What does "you know everything" mean? I ask.

The debt, she types. The way he held you hostage. But I only know because his new woman knew and she told me most of it. She forced him to tell me the rest. Even when I told him how much you mean to me, he wasn't going to tell me.

I meant it when I said that it's killed me to keep this from you, I reply.

You were right to hold back, she says. I want to say I wouldn't have confronted him, but I might have thought I could have made him back off on the deal. I think after today, I would have been wrong. You were protecting all of us.

Relief washes over me and for the rest of the trip, we talk to each other about everything from what we are doing at the time, to what to name our cat and dog. Right up until her plane lands before mine. I shut my computer and I decide I can't wait. I open my bag under my seat and pull out the velvet box.

Carrie

I stand at the waiting area, watching for Reid and when he appears, looking all kinds of masculine perfection in faded jeans and a black long-sleeved sweater, I swear my heart races a hundred miles an hour. "Reid!"

The minute his gaze lands on me, my heart sings. It's then in that moment when our eyes connect, that I can finally breathe. We're okay. We're better than okay. He steps up his pace, rounds the posts dividing us, and then I'm in his arms and he's kissing me, deeply, passionately kissing me. "I missed you."

"I missed you, too. Let's not do that again, okay?"

He takes my hand. "Come with me." He starts walking and leads me around a corner, into a rather empty walkway, where he pulls me behind another wide concrete post. "We're going to Paris for Christmas. That was going to be a surprise."

"I love that. It's a perfect Christmas destination and surprise."

"I was going to wait to do this there, but I need to do it now."

My brow furrows. "Do what?"

He goes down on his knee and pulls out a velvet box. "Will you marry me, Carrie?" He pops the lid on a stunning emerald and diamond ring that has so much sentimental value between us.

"Yes. Yes. And that ring is so, so very special." I start to tear up as he slips it onto my finger. "I had it custom-made." He stands up. "I wanted it to be as special as you are to me." He cups my face. "I want you to be my wife."

"I want you to be my husband."

"And then we can live happily ever after," he says.

"Just us and a cat and dog."

He laughs. "Yes. Just us and a cat and a dog." He slides his arm around me and we start walking.

"How about Jig and Saw for names?" I ask. "You know like a jigsaw?"

"No," he says. "We are not calling them jig and saw."

"Peanut and butter? Like Peanut Butter."

He laughs again, and I decide it will be my life's mission to ensure this man laughs forever.

The End... for now

466

Dear readers:

Dirty Rich Obsession: All Mine is coming! Carrie and Reid must manage the Japan deal, problems with her brother, both their fathers, Elijah, and Reid's growing need to protect Carrie at all costs; all while planning a wedding. I can't wait to share the rest of their story!

You can pre-order Dirty Rich Obsession: All Mine today on all platforms!

AND GUESS WHAT'S COMING NEXT MONTH!! Don't miss the next release in my Dirty Rich series, Dirty Rich Betrayal coming next month on September 26th! This is Grayson's story, and he has been so much fun to write! You can pre-order and learn more by visiting: https://dirtyrich.lisareneejones.com

For now, please make sure you're subscribed to my newsletter for all upcoming news about the Dirty Rich series and new books. And be sure to turn the page for two steamy excerpts from the first book in the Dirty Rich series Dirty Rich One Night Stand, and one of my books in the bestselling Walker Security series: Falling Under!

xoxo,

Lisa

There are a TON of Dirty Rich books forthcoming this year, and into 2019! Be sure you're up to date on all things Dirty Rich by visiting:
https://dirtyrich.lisareneejones.com

CAT & REESE	COLE & LORI	REID & CARRIE	GRAYSON & MIA
AVAILABLE NOW	AVAILABLE NOW	AUG. 22ND	SEPT. 26TH

COLE & LORI #2	ERIC'S STORY	CAT & REESE #2	REID & CARRIE #2
OCT. 10TH	NOV. 14TH	DEC. 5TH	JAN. 2ND

EXCERPT FROM DIRTY RICH ONE NIGHT STAND

"You're as perfect as I knew you would be," he says, his voice managing to be both sandpaper and silk on my nerve endings, as he adds, "and almost as naked as I want you to be."

The idea that he has wanted me as much as I have wanted him does funny things to my stomach, but more so, delivers an unexpected wave of illogical vulnerability. This is sex. The end. I don't want or need to feel anything more. I want and need him naked and fucking me now, fast, hard. That's safe. Desperate to find that safe place, to shift the control from him to me, I push to my toes, my breasts molding to his chest, and press my lips to his lips. They are warm, and he is hard everywhere I am soft.

And his response to my kiss, the answering moan I am rewarded with, is white-hot fire in my blood that he ignites further with a deep, sizzling stroke of his tongue. He slants his mouth over mine, deepening the connection, kissing me with a fierceness no other man ever has, but then some part of me has known from moment one that he is like no man I have ever known. Which explains why he is everything I want. And nothing about this night is what I expected, any more than this man is anything I can control.

But there is something intensely arousing about the idea of trying.

As if claiming I am reaching for the impossible, he molds me closer, his hand between my shoulder blades, his tongue playing wickedly with mine, but I meet him stroke for stroke, arching into him. He cups my ass and pulls me solidly against his erection. He wins this one. Now I am the one moaning, arching into him, and I welcome the intimate connection. I burn for the moment he will be inside me.

But I also want him to burn for this just as much as I do, and I need to touch this man. Really, really, need to touch him. My hand presses between us, and I stroke the hard line of his shaft. Reese tears his mouth from mine, pressing me hard against the pillar supporting the window again, and when his hands leave my body, when his palms press to the concrete above me again, I sense his withdrawal is about control. I was winning. I confirm that as reality when our eyes lock, and the dash of fire in his eyes is lit by one part passion and one part challenge.

"If I slide my fingers between your legs right now," he says, "are you wet for me? Are you ready for me?"

"Why don't you find out for yourself?" I dare him, testing him, pushing him.

Dirty Rich One Night Stand is the first standalone book in the Dirty Rich series. To read Reese and Cat's full story, please visit: https://dirtyrich.lisareneejones.com

EXCERPT FROM FALLING UNDER

"Just to be clear," he says, his voice low and rough. "I'm breaking every rule I own with you. I don't fuck women I'm protecting."

"You could hand me over to someone else," I suggest, "and it won't matter."

"Not a chance in hell," he says, his hand sliding under my hair to cup my neck. "We'll break the rules together."

"I'm not sure I like how you do 'together'."

"I'll make sure you do," he promises, his lips slanting over mine, and this time he kisses me like he owns me, like he wants to control me, and like I really am his, like I belong to him, and in this very moment, I can honestly say

I am. I want him, and I can't get enough of him.

And how can it ever be enough when he's this damn impossibly hot, and he's such a damn good kisser. The way he makes me want his mouth on every part of me and the way he makes me want my mouth on every part of him. And so, there it is. I'm his, but I'm going to make damn sure he's mine, too. I kiss him back as passionately as he's kissing me. I meet him stroke for stroke, arching into him, telling him I am here and present, and I'm not even close to afraid of him or of this. He doesn't get to control me. He isn't making me do this. I control me, and I choose him and this.

Arching into him, his shoulder holster and mine are in the way, and I want them gone. I want him naked. Just to be certain that he knows that's where I want this to go, my hand presses between us and I stroke the hard line of his shaft. He groans low in his throat, a sexy rough sound that tells me he gets the point. This isn't his show. It's ours. It's us together, or there is no show, with or without our clothes on.

His reaction is to tear his mouth from mine, his lips lingering there though, as if he wants to kiss me again, and just when I would kiss him again, he leans away just enough to shrug out of his jacket. I take one step backward, and do the same with my blazer. I reach down and pull off my boots and he does the same. Next, we disconnect our shoulder holsters, and the truth is, it's the first time I've ever been with a man who is probably more armed than me. That feels significant when it perhaps is not. He's not a cop. He's not that kind of career complication. He's a Green-fucking-Beret, and one hell of a hot one, for that matter.

He sets his weapon on the couch and snags my hand, walking me toward him and taking my holster and weapon as he does. "Just making sure you don't end up shooting me before this is over," he says, setting it with his before shackling my hip.

"I told you I'll wait until after the orgasms."

"Careful," he says, a hint of a smile on his lips again. "I might hold that orgasm and you captive."

"You can try," I say, but my head isn't in the game in this moment, and somehow my hand is on his face, right by the almost smile, that seems to have complicated what should be sex, an escape, a way to pull back the emotions that umbrella stirred in me. That smile reminds me that Mr. Robot is his wall, his way to cope with death, with whatever makes him protect Jesse Marks.

He captures my hand. "What are you thinking?"

"That you have on too many clothes," I say, before I let this go someplace emotional, somewhere that two people like us never want to go.

My hands press under his shirt, but he doesn't immediately give me what I want. He studies me for several beats and then kisses me hard and fast. Too fast, but I get over it when he pulls his shirt off. He cups my face and kisses me, his hand sliding up my shirt, his touch fire that has me helping him pull my shirt over my head. Letting him drag me to him where he now sits on the couch. I straddle him, my bra somehow gone by the time I'm there. But my hands press to his shoulders, and I hold him at bay. "I will still arrest you if I need to," I promise. "This doesn't change that."

"You aren't going to arrest me any more than you hate me." He glances down at my chest, his gaze a hot caress as it rakes over my breasts, my nipples, before his eyes meet mine. "Because you know I'm protecting you."

I ignore the ache between my thighs. Or I try. "From what? The slayer or the Jesse Marks damage patrol?"

His hand slides between my shoulder blades and he molds my chest to his. "Do you really want to talk about Jesse Marks right now? Because if you ask me questions, I'm going to ask you questions when I'd much rather be inside you, giving you as many reasons as I can not to arrest me. But you pick. Conversation or fucking."

"Both," I say, because it's the truth. I want answers and I want the conversation my emotions are having in my head to shut up. "Fucking first." I push away from him and stand up, unbuttoning my pants, sliding them down my hips, and he watches me with that unreadable, robot expression that is admittedly sexy as hell. I press my lips to his and that's all it takes.

We are crazy, hot, kissing, his hands on my breasts, my nipples, my neck. I can't touch him enough. I can't feel him enough, can't get close enough, and that's new to me. I don't need anyone the way I feel I need this man. I don't want to need anyone this much, but it's too late. At least, right here, right now, I do. He rolls us to our sides, facing one another, the wide cushion of the couch more than holding us and the next kiss isn't fast and frenzied. It's long, drugging, and somewhere in the midst of his tongue stroking my tongue, I end up on my back with the heavy weight of him on top of me...

Falling Under is the third standalone book in my Walker Security series. To learn more about the series visit:
http://lisareneejones.com/walker

ALSO BY LISA RENEE JONES

THE INSIDE OUT SERIES

If I Were You
Being Me
Revealing Us
*His Secrets**
Rebecca's Lost Journals
*The Master Undone**
*My Hunger**
No In Between
*My Control**
I Belong to You
*All of Me**

THE SECRET LIFE OF AMY BENSEN

Escaping Reality
Infinite Possibilities
Forsaken
*Unbroken**

CARELESS WHISPERS

Denial
Demand
Surrender

WHITE LIES

Provocative
Shameless

TALL, DARK & DEADLY

Hot Secrets
Dangerous Secrets
Beneath the Secrets

WALKER SECURITY

Deep Under
Pulled Under
Falling Under

LILAH LOVE

Murder Notes
Murder Girl

DIRTY RICH

Dirty Rich One Night Stand
Dirty Rich Cinderella Story
Dirty Rich Obsession
Dirty Rich Betrayal (Sept. 2018)
Dirty Rich Cinderella Story: Ever After (Oct. 2018)
Dirty Rich Bastard (Nov. 2018)
Dirty Rich One Night Stand: Two Years Later (Dec. 2018)
Dirty Rich Obsession: All Mine (Jan. 2019)

*eBook only

ABOUT THE AUTHOR

New York Times and USA Today bestselling author Lisa Renee Jones is the author of the highly acclaimed INSIDE OUT series.

In addition to the success of Lisa's INSIDE OUT series, she has published many successful titles. The TALL, DARK AND DEADLY series and THE SECRET LIFE OF AMY BENSEN series, both spent several months on a combination of the New York Times and USA Today bestselling lists. Lisa is also the author of the bestselling the bestselling DIRTY MONEY and WHITE LIES series. And will be publishing the first book in her Lilah Love suspense series with Amazon Publishing in March 2018.

Prior to publishing Lisa owned multi-state staffing agency that was recognized many times by The Austin Business Journal and also praised by the Dallas Women's Magazine. In 1998 Lisa was listed as the #7 growing women owned business in Entrepreneur Magazine.

Lisa loves to hear from her readers. You can reach her at www.lisareneejones.com and she is active on Twitter and Facebook daily.

CPSIA information can be obtained
at www.ICGtesting.com
Printed in the USA
LVHW09s2347230918
591144LV00001B/104/P

9 781725 703520